Ready or Not, Grave Intentions, Book 2

Aedyn Brooks

Aedyn Brooks Creative Works, LLC

Copyright

Ready or Not, Grave Intentions, Book 2

3 ...2...1...

Dr. Tesla Brynn is beginning her psychiatry practice in a new state and city, closer to family. When she calls her niece to plan their Fourth of July weekend, her world shatters. Her terrified niece tells her a masked stranger is texting her photos labeled Ready or Not from inside the house. Tes can do nothing but listen to her niece's screams as the line dies.

Ready or Not...

Asher Hickok lost his will to live the day his daughter was kidnapped. Seven weeks of hell and counting. With dead-end leads and no ransom demands, the only hope Asher has in finding his daughter is if the kidnapper chooses another victim. What he's not prepared for is that the next victim to be his daughter's best friend.

Here I Come...

Tes and Asher's worlds collide, forging allies as they desperately search for their loved ones. Together, they'll use every resource available, including a supernatural gift Tes' kept secret her whole life. Asher has his own secrets he'd like to keep hidden. Can this unlikely pair learn to trust each other, accept their differences, and find their family before it's too late?

Dedication

May you be blessed to find your tribe. To find the people who get you and don't judge. And may these loved ones encourage you to grow into who you want to be.

Acknowledgments

To each and every one of you, my genuine, sincere thanks. Every writer wants to share their stories and I'm sincerely honored that you selected mine.

A special thanks to my dear friends Cara Crescent, Samantha Quinn, and Cath Hickey your continued support and encouragement mean the world to me. Thank you for your input in making this book the best it could be.

A special mention must be given to my dear friend Julie M., who was the inspiration for Dr. Tesla Hickok's little quirks. It's the little things that make people real—and Julie always keeps it real.

Thank you to my kids: Kaitlin, David, and Josh. I love you more than life. You are the reason I dared to dream and believe.

Readers:

If as you read this book you find typos or missing words, I'd greatly appreciate you letting me know so I can make corrections for future updates. These errors are solely mine and not a reflection of my great editor and proofreader. Please send me an email to aedyn@aedynbrooks.com.

Contents

Friday, July 3rd

Bellevue, Washington

Simple, stressless life straight ahead.

One decade and thousands of hours later, Dr. Tesla Brynn was a full-blown psychiatrist with one interview at Overlake Hospital under her belt. She could finally start living a "normal" life. Sure, she still needed to work on obtaining her specialty license in child psychiatry, but for now that was on the back burner until she was gainfully employed. Giddy didn't begin to explain the overwhelming joy surging through her veins.

She opened the back door of her Honda Civic and instructed her trained emotional therapy dog and partner, Ruthie, "Up." Her rescued golden retriever-lab mix jumped onto the backseat and waited for Tes to buckle her in. Ruthie was instrumental in helping children talk about their issues and grief.

She'd moved to Washington last weekend to be closer to her sister and niece. Maybe this time her sister would let her be a part of her life, bury the hatchet, and forget the incident that severed their relationship. No one needed to know about Tes's past. She'd do anything to have a chance with her family again.

It was also her first weekend without schoolwork. Free time? Tes couldn't remember the last time she'd kicked back and relaxed. Once she programmed her GPS to return to her sister's house and cleared the hospital's parking garage, she dialed her niece using the car's hands-free option. Her sister Nikki was out of town and had entrusted Tes to watch her only child. Well, at fifteen, Morgan was hardly a child anymore. "Hey, Peanut, how do you want to start our motherless binge? Ice cream for dinner? Pizza? Friends over? Name it. We are going to party like it's 1999." She cringed. "Was that too dorky?"

"Aunt Tes?" Morgan sucked in a slobbery phlegm-coated breath that blasted through the car's speakers.

"What's wrong, honey?" Tes's muscles tensed.

She didn't think Morgan had a boyfriend to cause her distress. Maybe they'd found the remains of Morgan's best friend who'd gone missing on Mother's Day weekend. Everyone believed she was dead after vanishing without a trace on a sunny Friday afternoon. Like today.

"Someone's in the house."

"Come again?" She had to have heard her wrong.

"A guy's sending me selfies taken from inside the house. They're tagged 'Ready or Not'."

"Where are you?"

"In my room."

"Did you lock the front door? Set the alarm?"

"The front door's locked, but I didn't set the alarm. I was waiting for you to come—" She drew in a shaky breath. "Home."

Tes signaled, glancing over her shoulder before pressing the gas pedal to merge onto I-405 and promptly came to a stop. On a non rush hour day, she was thirty minutes away. *Shit.* Today it'd take longer. "You did the right thing, Morgan. It's okay. I'm trying to figure out how they could have gotten into the house. Can you forward me the text messages?"

"I tried. I can't. My phone's frozen. I couldn't call out, but I could accept your call."

Someone was messing with *her* niece? "Lock your bedroom door. Put your desk chair under the door handle. It'll buy you time to get out your bedroom window."

"I already locked my bedroom door. Aunt Tes?" Her voice inched higher with each syllable. "I'm scared."

"I know, honey. You're going to be fine." Tes glanced in her rearview mirror. Hopefully, it was just some sick bastard trying to scare the bejesus out of her. It was working. "Come on, Morgan, you can do this."

"Okay."

Tes heard shuffling on the phone. "Now get to the window—open it." She swallowed, bracing her heart for what she needed to say next. "You're going to have to jump." In her mind, she pictured Morgan lowering her petite frame over the window's ledge and falling into the mulberry bushes below. Did mulberry bushes have thorns? Thorns were the least of her worries. A broken leg would be much worse. Morgan couldn't outrun an intruder with a broken leg. Tes's shoulders inched up closer to her ears as she gripped the steering wheel tighter.

"It won't open."

"What do you mean it won't open?"

"I don't know. It won't slide open." Morgan grunted. "Let me try the other one." The pause stretched for eons.

Tes slammed on her turn signal and cut off a driver in the next lane, jockeying closer to the commuter lane.

"It's like they're glued shut."

"Don't panic." Ironic, since she was failing to keep calm. "Unlock the window first."

Teary sobs filled the car's speakers. "I did," she whined.

Not believing in Morgan wasn't helping. She was a smart kid. "I'm sorry, honey. I'm trying to cover our bases here." *Think. How much time did she have?* "Break the window."

"My hands feel funny." No doubt adrenaline had flooded Morgan's system.

"Take slow deep breaths in, and slowly blow out." Damn bumper-to-bumper traffic. *How hard was it to push on the pedal to the right?* "I'm on my way. I know you're scared, but I'm with you. I'm going to conference in 911. No matter what, don't hang up. Okay? If we're disconnected, I'll call back. You're not alone, Morgan."

Through blurred tears, Tes pressed the buttons.

"911, what is your emergency?"

"My niece is home alone..." Tes relayed Morgan's information and the address where her sister lived, then clicked the "conference" button. "Morgan? Are you still there?"

"Yes, I'm here." Morgan's phone chimed, indicating she'd received a new text message. She gasped. "He's outside my bedroom door!"

"Morgan, I'm sending officers now." The operator clicked keys in the background. "Stay on the line."

White, gray, and black vehicles blurred by Tes's peripheral vision as she pulled into the HOV lane and gunned the engine, whizzing past the crawling cars to her right. She didn't care if she got a ticket. She'd welcome a police officer. Hell, bring on the cavalry.

"Aunt Tes. I love you," Morgan whispered.

Resignation. "I love you too, Peanut. You're strong. You're smart."

Morgan gasped. "The closet door's opening." A high-pitched scream blared across the line.

"*What?*" Tes's breath stalled.

Morgan shouted, "He's got a gun!"

The dispatcher broke in. "Describe him."

"Tall." Shuffling. "Get away from me!" Morgan's blood-curdling scream filled the interior of Tes's car. Ruthie whined from the backseat. "Blue. Goggles."

What was happening?

"Hang up the phone...or die," a deep digital vibrato synthesizer voice said.

Gooseflesh broke out over Tes's entire body. She leaned forward as if she could teleport herself through her wireless connection into Morgan's bedroom. "I'll find you, Morgan. I love you." Tears streaked Tes's face. "Hang up. Help is on its way. And girl—you fight. Fight for your life."

Pop. Pop.

The line went dead.

***

Not one moment had passed that Asher Hickok didn't think about his kidnapped daughter, Hailey. Months later with no ransom demand and no new leads on the kidnapper, Asher started working again, though he didn't feel like it. Working for his father at Hickok Construction afforded him leniency when his life went to shit. Every day he fought the urge to withdraw from society, curl into a ball, and shut out the world. He hated being strong in the face of adversity. It was a bunch of bullshit and psychobabble from professionals who'd never walked through his hell.

Losing Hailey not only wounded his soul, but it'd also demolished his will to live. Morgan McKinley was the one person on earth who gave him enough will to carry on. She was not only Hailey's best friend, but his greatest secret. His second daughter who, thankfully, had woven seamlessly into his family's fabric since his two daughters had met in kindergarten. A court order forbade him from telling her he was her father. Few people knew but him and her birth mother—a woman who had more power and money backing her than he could ever hope for. Staying silent wasn't easy. In a few years, when Morgan turned eighteen, there wouldn't be anything stopping him from telling her the truth.

"Have a happy Fourth." Asher waved to the last few workers who'd helped him lock up the construction site. They'd wrapped up things early for the holiday weekend. His dad had already dropped by and passed out steaks for their team. It was a Hickok family tradition to give their workers food before holidays.

He pulled out his dead cell phone from his pocket before getting behind the truck's wheel. After the diesel engine roared to life, he plugged his phone into the charger and waited for there to be enough power to see if he'd missed any important messages.

Morgan was bringing her aunt Tes to the family barbecue tomorrow to celebrate the Fourth of July with the Hickok clan. Tes had given Morgan advice to pass along to him following Hailey's disappearance. He was looking forward to meeting and thanking her for trying to give him comfort while she finished school. He thought about taking her out to dinner as a thank-you, but that might seem like a date.

God, he hadn't dated in forever. How could he enjoy life when Hailey was out there alone, afraid, and held captive? Or worse, lying cold and dead in an unmarked grave?

Tears stung the back of his eyes. How he missed his baby girl. He'd won custody of Hailey when she was two years old. His ex-girlfriend had visitation one weekend a month and ninety percent of the time she'd failed to follow through in keeping Hailey for an entire weekend.

He'd dropped Hailey off on Friday before Mother's Day to spend some "quality" time with her mother, Linda. It had come as no surprise that she'd decided to head out of town with the boyfriend du jour, leaving Hailey home alone.

That was when it happened.

Asher had immediately called Hailey after he'd gotten the text message from Linda. "Hey, honey, I'm coming to get you. Your mom decided to go out of town this weekend."

"Dad? There's someone in the house."

His hackles had risen and Dad mode shifted into high gear. He'd pulled a U-turn in the middle of traffic and gunned the engine, narrowly missing a delivery truck.

Hailey's cries still haunted his dreams. She'd said she felt strange and couldn't move. He remembered her saying she was getting text messages of a man in a blue hoodie from inside the house and him saying, "Ready or not."

She'd opened the closet door to hide inside.

The digitized voice said, "Hello, Hailey. Are you ready?" The digitized laughter that followed, still jolted him awake from his nightmares.

Then Hailey screamed. The last memory etched on Asher's brain for eternity. He wasn't there to protect her or rip her kidnapper limb from limb. If he ever got his hands on the bastard, he was going to kill him. He knew exactly where he'd bury the body parts so no one could find them.

Numbness filled the days that followed. With each new dead-end lead, he became more and more protective of Morgan. He'd cloned her phone and made sure she wasn't harassed by anyone sending her text messages tagged, "Ready or not."

His gut told him Hailey wasn't the kidnapper's first victim, and he vowed Morgan would *never* be one of his victims. Not as long as he drew breath.

2

Tes turned onto Beacon Drive, slowing as she approached her sister Nikki's house. Two squad cars' flashing blue and red lights alerted the neighborhood something wasn't right at the McKinley home. The American flag waved in a gentle breeze and fuchsias spilled over the porch planter boxes, setting the scene of the idyllic two-story house Tes temporarily called home.

She'd lowered the windows for Ruthie before slamming the gear into park and cutting the engine.

A diesel engine's roar approached at breakneck speed, narrowly missing her car as it screeched to a halt behind the squad cars. A man jumped from the behemoth vehicle and ran toward the porch.

One female officer exited the house, cutting him off with her palms out, forcing him to slow his advance.

"*Morgan,*" the man shouted.

Tes shoved her door open and joined the fray. "I'm Morgan's aunt." She tried to sidestep around the officer.

"Ma'am." The officer blocked her advancement. "You can't go in there." She jockeyed to the right, keeping the man at bay too.

"Asher, you know I can't let you in there."

"Bonnie, it's Morgan." Asher moved closer to the officer. "The same guy who took Hailey has Morgan."

"Is she..." Tes stepped closer to Officer Bonnie. She couldn't say the words. As a doctor, Tes knew what two gunshots could do to the human body. Still, she didn't want to hear it.

Bonnie lowered her hand. "We've searched the house. She's not here."

Tes nodded to the man. "How did you know Morgan's missing?"

"I'm Asher Hickok. My daughter Hailey is Morgan's best friend. She was kidnapped on Mother's Day weekend."

That's Asher Hickok? Tes's breath hitched. *Oh God, this can't be good.* Morgan called Hailey's dad "Uncle Asher." She glanced over her shoulder at his big-ass truck. What if Morgan was unconscious, wrapped in a tarp, concealed in the truck's bed?

Officer Bonnie turned her attention to Tes. "And you're Morgan's aunt?"

She swallowed the lump lodged in her throat. "Yes. I'm Dr. Tesla Brynn. My sister Nikki is out of town and Morgan was home alone."

Another officer came out the front door—older, gray-haired, same blue uniform. "All clear."

"She's not..." A sob caught in Tes's throat. "She's not here?" Her knees wobbled. She heaved the air from her lungs, doubling over.

Asher's strong hand gripped her elbow to keep her from collapsing. She looked at his face. He hadn't shaved in days and his brown eyes were rimmed in red.

The older officer stepped down the three steps to the sidewalk and stood next to the other officer. "No, ma'am. No one's in the house."

Tes jolted around the officer. "I need to see for myself."

The older officer hooked an arm across her waist and hauled her back into her initial spot with ease. "Any evidence in there needs to be processed by our forensics team, and the FBI will be here shortly. We're going to need you to answer some questions."

Asher held up his phone. "I've already called Special Agent Krysinski. He's the lead investigator on Hailey's case."

Tes stared at Asher. His eyes reflected a haunted grief that broke her heart.

"When Hailey was taken, I cloned Morgan's phone. Every message she's received was also sent to me."

Tes's mouth flopped open. "A bit intrusive, don't you think?"

"I'd say I'm overprotective." He clamped his mouth shut and stared at the sky. "My gut told me something was going to happen to Morgan too." He cocked his stubble-riddled square jaw. "I'm glad I did." He handed his phone to Officer Bonnie. "We've finally got evidence."

Hm. Rather convenient.

The officers looked at Asher's phone, scrolling from screen to screen.

"Please?" Tes held out her hand. She had to see the last images Morgan saw. She had to face the monster who'd taken such a beautiful girl full of hope and promise.

Officer Bonnie handed her the phone. The first picture showed a person standing on the McKinley's porch. He wore a dark blue hoodie covering his head, and he concealed his face by wearing one of those all-white Halloween masks. Except for the streetlight's faint glow, there wasn't much detail. The man held the phone above his head, putting it about the same height as the doorframe. She stared at Nikki's porch. "He's maybe five-ten." She glanced at Asher—he was several inches taller. "He had to unscrew the lightbulb. He didn't take this picture today. He took it at another time. He's been in the house before." She scrolled to the next picture. He stood inside the house. This time the porchlight was on, showing the faint light as he stood on the stairs. She tapped the picture and made the background bigger. Gasped.

Asher leaned closer. "What is it?"

"These pictures were taken before Mother's Day."

Asher's dark brows furrowed as he cocked his head.

"Morgan removed this picture from the frame—the one of her and Hailey in Disneyland—and kept it by her bedside." She pointed to the picture for Asher. "Nikki and Morgan got in a huge fight over it." She looked at the officers. "My sister's a bit of a control freak."

Asher huffed and mumbled under his breath, "Understatement."

Tes scrolled to the last picture. "Outside her bedroom door." Fresh tears blurred her vision. "He'd been planning this for months." She handed Asher his phone. "I thought I heard gunshots—"

"There wasn't any blood in her room," the gray-haired officer said. "I saw a bench in the backyard. I'd like to have you wait there while we're waiting on the FBI."

Tes hadn't noticed the additional police units arriving. They weren't going to let her inside. If only she could check for herself, she could believe the officers. The logical side of her brain said to trust them, but the emotional part wanted to make sure Morgan wasn't curled into a ball wounded somewhere in a closet or other hiding place.

"I need to get Ruthie." Tes went to her car as the forensic team made their way up the driveway. She unbuckled her dog and snagged her purse. Asher was already sitting on the bench under the pergola draped in white fabric. She peered into the kitchen through the sliding glass door framed by lace curtains before taking the empty space beside Asher. Ruthie snuggled close to her legs, laying her head in Tes's lap.

A million thoughts jumbled through her mind. "Did you come straight from work?"

He motioned a hand at his dirty jeans and work boots. "Yeah. North Bend."

"Is that far from here?"

"About thirty minutes on a good day."

They'd been about the same distance away when Morgan got the texts...if he wasn't lying.

"I'm sorry about Hailey." She looked him in the eye.

He leaned forward, bracing his elbows on his legs and buried his face in his hands, shaking his head. "I can't go through this again."

"Yes, you can." She wanted to touch his shoulder. To offer some sort of comfort, but she wouldn't do that as a psychiatrist and right now she was psychoanalyzing the man who cloned Morgan's phone. "You're strong, Asher. Morgan always said so."

He shifted his gaze to meet hers. "I don't feel strong. I feel helpless. I wasn't here."

"I shouldn't have gone on that interview. If only *I'd* been here." She blinked back fresh tears.

"If only, huh?" He leaned back. "I've said that a million times."

She noticed his tanned skin speckled with white paint. "I'll regret this day forever."

"Me too."

The K-9 unit arrived. Ruthie's tail thumped a hollow tattoo against the wooden deck at the German shepard's arrival. Tes rubbed her ears. "Good girl," she soothed, rewarding her for staying at her side and not running off to play.

Out of the corner of her eye, she could see Asher staring at her. Did he blame her for not being here? Hell, she blamed herself, so he might as well too.

They could see forensic scientists wearing booties over their shoes, hairnets, and safety glasses as they searched the kitchen. They looked as though they were in a meth lab instead of her sister's country-chic home.

An older man impeccably dressed in a blue suit stepped onto the deck carrying a couple of bottles of water.

"Tom." Asher jumped from the bench.

Tom handed Asher one bottle and shook his hand before handing him the other bottle.

She waited until Asher returned to his seat and the suited man pulled over the Adirondack chair to sit closer. "I'm Special Agent Thomas Krysinski. Call me Tom." He shook Tes's hand.

"Dr. Tesla Brynn. Morgan's aunt. Please call me Tes."

Asher cracked the bottle's screw-top lid before handing it to her and opening his own. His thoughtfulness caught her off guard. "Thank you." Their gazes met for a moment before he turned back to Tom.

Cold water refreshed her dry throat. She chugged half the bottle then slowly poured some in her cupped hand for Ruthie.

Now for the interrogation. She'd never been questioned by the FBI and given her fragile emotional state, she wasn't sure she was up for the barrage of necessary questions.

Asher's knuckles brushed against hers. She glanced his way before pulling her hand onto her lap. She wanted his comfort, but not until she knew he hadn't taken Morgan. As far as she was concerned, he was suspect number one, but the FBI agent seemed to like him well enough. Maybe she had it all wrong. She'd jumped to conclusions because he'd cloned Morgan's phone. Whatever that meant. Why would he openly share information with her and the police if he was guilty?

Asher shared the photos with Tom, relaying the events from his point of view.

How in the world was she going to explain this to her sister? Part of her was thankful she didn't have to make that call. Nikki and her new boyfriend, Ben Winslow, were on an Alaska back-country fishing and hunting trip. Far away from phones, televisions, and AMBER alerts.

Tes had until Sunday to find Morgan before Nikki came home. Morgan was Nikki's world. Had been since the day she pushed her scrawny, red-faced bundle into existence: Morgan Nikola Brynn McKinley. A strong name to go with their Welsh bloodline.

"Are you okay?" Agent Krysinski interrupted her reverie.

"No." Tes petted Ruthie. Her smooth fur helped calm Tes's nerves.

"Are you able to answer some questions?"

Tes shared the chain of events, followed by rapid-fire questions. "Why hadn't the officers arrived sooner? If they'd arrived within moments of her phone call, Morgan would still be here."

"You'd mentioned Morgan's mother is out of town with her boyfriend. Where's her father?"

"Stanley McKinley gave up all rights to Morgan when she was five and he went to prison for grand larceny. He got out a few years later. Lives in Montana now with his new wife and family."

"Has he made any attempt to contact Morgan?"

Tes shrugged.

"No," Asher answered. "He calls on her birthday and that's about it."

Tom's gaze shifted between them. "Would Morgan want to visit her dad?"

"I don't know," Tes answered. Would Nikki let Stan anywhere near Morgan now? As a former criminal, Stan could have the connections to abduct his oldest child. Would he have cooked up an elaborate scheme and kidnapped Hailey to draw off suspicion? Tes's stomach churned.

"The next twenty-four hours are the most important, right?" Her gaze shifted to the FBI agent. He had to be a seasoned officer. Old enough to be her dad—he even looked like him too. Kind blue eyes and lines etched deep in his forehead like he'd spent hours deep in thought. At least he wasn't a rookie.

"What about your parents?"

"My parents divorced a long time ago. My mother moved back to Wales with her new husband. My father passed away five years ago." Old family arguments bubbled in her mind. Betrayal. Pain. Death. Those days weren't reflected in the photographs on the mantel.

"Does your family have any money that would lead someone to hold Morgan for ransom?"

Tes sniffed, stroking the top of Ruthie's head. "When my dad died, Nikki and I split everything 50/50. With her share, she built this house." She waved her hand at their surroundings. "I paid for my college education. Nikki put some money in a trust fund for Morgan's college."

"How much?"

"I don't know."

"Enough to entice someone to kidnap her?"

She hadn't paid attention at the time. It wasn't any of her business. "I'm sure there's a bank statement around here somewhere. Maybe in the safe in Nikki's bedroom?"

"Do you know the combination?"

"Yes." Nikki always used her birthday—reversed. "But I can't get my hands on the money to help Morgan. I'm not listed on the account and my sister won't be back until Sunday night."

"Could Morgan withdraw the money?"

"I don't think my sister would let a fifteen-year-old kid have access to her trust fund."

Asher shook his head. "Morgan can't have access until she's twenty-one." He looked Tes. "Hailey told me about it when Morgan found a statement that came in the mail."

If Asher were guilty, he wasn't in it for the money. Her theory of imagining the worst of him was fleeting. Still, she was leery.

The FBI agent flipped his notebook paper to a new page. "What do you know about your sister's boyfriend?"

"I met him for the first time when I dropped them off at the airport on Monday. You see, I moved here to be closer to my sister and Morgan a week ago. He was quiet."

Tom's bushy brows rose, then bobbed his head at Asher. "Have you met him?"

"No, but I didn't typically meet any of her boyfriends," Asher answered. "He's the latest new guy in a long line of new guys. Nikki's great at scoring a date or two, but hanging onto them is another story."

Tes added, "Nikki lives for first dates. She loves being romanced."

"How long have they been dating?" Tom jotted notes.

Asher and Tes exchanged a glance and shrugged.

"Do you know what the new boyfriend does for a living?"

There was a flash from inside the family room as a forensic specialist snapped pictures, catching Tes off guard and interrupting her thoughts. She knew they were cataloguing Morgan's last moments like a high-fashioned photo shoot.

Where are you, kiddo? If only she'd return, saying she'd pulled one over on her—naïve Aunt Tes, gullible Aunt Tes. Not Morgan. She was a high school counselor's daughter, and no way in hell would she do something that might bring shame to Nikki. Shaming the family was simply not permitted.

"You were saying?" Tom prompted.

Tes took a deep breath. "He's a consultant of some type."

"How did they meet?" Tom jotted more notes.

Tes answered, "Online."

"Which website?"

Tes huffed. "No idea. My sister belonged to all of them at one time or another. If she could transport herself back to the Victorian era and be courted by some English gent, she'd be in heaven." She snapped her fingers. "Now I remember. Ben Winslow is from England. He's here to sort out a merger of some kind. Morgan's trust fund wouldn't be anything to go after."

Krysinski flipped the page in his little notebook. His expression hid his thoughts.

Tes answered questions for what seemed like an eternity. "Was Morgan's phone upstairs?"

"I'm not sure. I didn't go upstairs." At least the agent didn't make false statements.

"Who are they going to call for a ransom?" Tes asked.

Tom glanced at Asher before answering. "There was no ransom request when Hailey was kidnapped."

"What?" Tes's mouth opened, staring at Asher. "Why?"

"We don't know why. No one called. No mail or email. Nothing. Just...gone." Asher's voice cracked.

Oh, this was worse than Tes could imagine. Was it for revenge? Her stomach clenched. "They're not going to give her back, are they?" Her breath hitched as fresh tears cascaded down her cheeks. Why else would someone want to take a kid who loved playing the drums and dreamed of the day she could get a rad tattoo?

Officer Bonnie approached. "The forensics team isn't finished yet, but we'd like to move you inside."

Krysinski closed his notepad and tucked it in his inside suit jacket pocket.

Asher's phone blared an alarm: AMBER alert.

It was official. Morgan McKinley of 436 Beacon Drive, Whitman, Washington, was missing.

3

T he security lights flickered on, signaling dusk had arrived. Tom stood and resituated the Adirondack chair. "After you, Tes."

Finally. Tes grabbed her purse and Ruthie's harness.

Asher stood, brushing the dust from his pants. "Nikki wouldn't want me in her clean house."

She paused. "Please. It isn't like you have the bubonic plague. You're a bit dusty from work. Come inside."

The corners of his mouth tipped briefly. "Would you like me to feed Ruthie?"

She bet he had a nice family who had instilled strong values and good manners. "Sure. Thank you." She was used to being self-reliant. It was a rare moment to have someone offer help, and even more rare for her to accept it. "Her food's in the big bin in the pantry. You can't miss it. If you do, Ruthie's happy to point it out for you."

He waited for her to enter first. "Nikki's particular about her floors."

"I think right now her floors will be the least of her worries."

Tom held up his hand. "Wait here. I'll grab some booties for you." He returned and Asher slipped them over his work boots.

Tes set her purse on the kitchen counter as Asher went straight to the pantry, Ruthie sidling up to him like he was her new best friend.

Tom shut the door and motioned her toward the living room. "Let's head upstairs to see if you notice anything out of place."

One blue flip-flop lay on the fifth stair. A yellow placard labeled number six marked it as possible evidence. *Morgan only had one flip-flop?* How could she outrun her captor without shoes? She sucked in a deep breath, fighting back her tears. Now wasn't the time to fall apart—there would be plenty of time for that later. She continued up the stairs and down the hall toward her niece's bedroom.

Tes lowered her voice. "Could you have an officer look in the back of Asher's truck?"

Tom stared at her a long while. "Asher didn't take Morgan."

"How can you be sure?"

"The man in the pictures doesn't have half the build he does."

She hadn't thought of that. True, the picture didn't appear to be someone who did physical labor for a living. Asher's arms were tree trunks. "Maybe someone else took the pictures."

"Look, Tes." Tom stepped closer. "We've investigated the Hickok family at length. Disgruntled former employees, lost contracts, small-claims court filings, and we've found nothing. We've looked into Hailey's mom Linda's former boyfriends. She and Asher never married. In fact, he's had custody since Hailey was two. Some of Linda's exes had outstanding warrants, but none of them took Hailey."

"Asher's been to hell and back. Losing Hailey was unbearable. With Morgan being taken as well, I'm not so sure he's going to have a reason to live. Right now, he needs you to need him."

"I don't need anyone." Tes lifted her chin and instantly regretted her knee-jerk reaction. "Sorry." She glanced down. "It's our way. Brynns are strong. We don't show our emotions publicly, nor do we lean on strangers." *There's no disappointment if trust is never given.*

"Tes, when we investigated Hailey's kidnapping, we looked at everyone remotely close to her. I learned your family is well connected."

A chill crashed over the back of her neck. "*My* family? What would my family have to do with the Hickoks?"

"Nikki and Morgan were investigated." Tom paused. "You."

She stepped back. "Me? I'd never—"

Tom's eyes narrowed. "Your family has enemies."

"My mother's husband may have enemies. You would too if you were a politician."

"Perhaps, but now that we know Morgan was part of the kidnapper's plan, prior to taking Hailey, we can safely remove Asher and you from our suspect list, but that doesn't omit your stepfather's affiliations."

"Please don't say that." Tes's chest ached.

Tom tilted his head. "The fastest way to get to someone in power would be through family."

"Do you think there will be a ransom demand this time?"

He glanced away. "All we can do is wait and see."

"How are we going to find them?" She braced a hand against Morgan's door frame, turning away from Tom. There was no way her mother's husband had anything to do with this. That wasn't a nightmare she wanted to face. She swiped her hands across her cheeks, wiping tears away. The agent had to be speculating. Nothing more. He was trying to bait her to reveal anything about her family. Well, her family had secrets. *She* had secrets that better never come to light. "I told Morgan to put her chair underneath the door handle."

"This is how the officers found her room. The door was open."

Of course, it was. Otherwise, how did the kidnapper get out of the house? Tes turned to look along the stairway. The pictures weren't askew. Was Morgan able to fight back? She could have sworn she heard gunshots, but there wasn't any blood.

Tes stepped into Morgan's room. The chair was tucked into its spot at the desk. No new divots from the chair's legs on the carpet. He'd put it back exactly in the right spot. Black smudges lined the chair's back. She'd need to clean the house before Nikki returned. If Nikki found fingerprint powder everywhere, she'd reach a whole new level of OCD. At least her sister let her niece keep her room the way she wanted.

Latest heartthrob posters and boy bands covered the walls. Clothes littered the floor and half-hung out of dresser drawers. Morgan's backpack had been tossed in the corner after the last day of school a couple of weeks before. If she'd fought, it wasn't evident in the chaotic aftermath of Morgan's normal teenageryness.

Tes crossed the room. Krysinski followed, jotting more notes. What must he think of her? She wasn't a blithering mess—did that make her look guilty? No one liked an unstable emotional mess. Her mother said tears made women look weak. Snorting while laughing? That would get you grounded. Decorum at all costs.

Being a psychiatrist didn't mean those old tapes turned off inside one's head.

"Morgan said he was in the closet." The light inside was turned on. Tes looked for shoe imprints on the carpet. "How'd he get in here? He had to have been here before she got home."

"Where did she go?" Krysinski tapped his pen against the notepad.

"She had a gabfest with girlfriends at Braewood Manor Coffee and Tea House this morning." Had the kidnapper watched her leave and then broken into the house? He must have stayed in the closet for hours, waiting for that pivotal moment to send her demented text messages.

"Did someone pick her up?"

Tes shook her head. "She rode her bike or ran." Morgan had a zillion bolts of energy. "She was on the track team." She eyed the walls, looking for holes. "I thought I heard gunshots."

The agent watched her. "The items collected will be checked for residue."

"The windows?"

Krysinski pulled back the curtain, and opened the window with ease. He closed it and moved to the other side of the bed and demonstrated the same. "Would she have jumped? Unless she had an emergency ladder, she'd have to jump. Was she prepared to do that?"

"She was so scared." She moved over to Morgan's queen-sized, never-made bed. "Did the forensics team take her laptop?"

"Let me check." Krysinski stepped into the hall and shouted his question. A few moments later he came back into the room. "There wasn't a laptop among the items in her room."

"Then the bastard took it." Tes stared at the bed. "Where's her bedspread?"

"Forensics bagged it. That's standard protocol."

Was it? Tes didn't want to know why.

Her shoe nudged something hard underneath the bed. She got on all fours and lifted the bed skirt's corner. Under a track sweatshirt, she found a cell phone. She stood. "Tom? This isn't Morgan's cell phone." She held it up. The black cell looked newer and a cheaper model than the latest tech gadget.

"Put it on the bed. I'll let the forensics team know."

"They didn't even look under her bed? What kind of forensics team is this?" She didn't want to be angry, but dammit, she needed the best to show up to do their job today, not the "B" team on a holiday weekend. He'd taken her cell phone and computer. Did he know Morgan and Hailey? A school friend, perhaps? Maybe a guy they'd made fun of?

As Tes tossed the phone on the bed, the screen lit. "Tom," she called. When he re-entered the room, she pointed to the cell's screen. The clock ticked the seconds, adding time to the 429 minutes glowing on the screen. The kidnapper must have been listening to everything going on in Morgan's bedroom for over seven hours? That meant he had to have placed it under the bed shortly before Morgan returned from Braewood Manor.

Tom put a finger to his lips.

Tes leaned over. "Whoever you are. I'm going to find my niece, and you're going to prison for the rest of your life."

Static filled the line. A low synthesized, digital voice replied, "You're next...*Aunt Tes*." *Click.*

Her heart lodged in her throat as she backed away from the bed. Whoever had taken Hailey, and now Morgan, was out of her league. In order to find Morgan, she was going to have to go places in her mind she didn't want to go. A place her soul had gone once before.

A place she called the Shadowlands.

***

Asher washed his hands and forearms after feeding Ruthie. She was about the most adorable lab-retriever mix he'd ever seen. The first of the news crews arrived as he dried his hands. Probably digging for a juicy storyline for the eleven o'clock newscast. He closed the living room blinds. Would Tes know what to say to them? Would she be as terrified as he was the first time he was in front of the cameras? He was a shy guy—desperate for community help—and when he saw himself on the six o'clock news, he was mortified. He should have hired a professional spokesperson. He learned to hold his head up when answering media questions, and he'd worked hard not to melt down when they asked questions that ripped his heart out. *Anything for ratings.* Krysinski had warned him about that. Still, he hadn't been prepared.

What were the odds that whoever had abducted Hailey kept her well fed, warm, and safe? He supposed that was asking too much. At first, his thoughts of what the kidnapper may or may not be doing to her consumed him. It would have driven him insane with worry had his family not stood by his side, forcing him to eat, sleep, and recently, try to get back to a regular routine.

When Hailey's mother took off to Sturgis, North Dakota, on the back of some guy's motorcycle, explaining there wasn't any reason for her to stay in Washington, Asher knew he had to face the fact that his daughter might never return. He wouldn't give up hope, but he was at a weird place of in-between and he barely hung onto reality on a good day.

Ruthie's tail wagged after she gobbled her meal. He slid his fingers deep into her thick fur. "Need to go outside?"

She barked, lifting her front paws off the floor. He opened the back door. A camera crew slid along the backyard fence. He lifted Ruthie's harness and escorted her outside.

"Mister, a word?" A field reporter held a microphone over the fence.

Asher wanted to give them plenty of words. Bleepable words. "Why don't you leave the family alone and let the authorities handle this?" The only thing the media helped with when Hailey was kidnapped was bringing out all sorts of crazies from the woodwork. From "psychics" to people with dowsing rods. He wanted his daughter back without every whacko stirring a pot of nonsense—false hope that never panned out.

He turned at the sound of Tes's high heels on the kitchen's wooden floors. Asher let go of Ruthie's harness so she could run back to Tes, who bent, waiting for Ruthie to run into her open arms. She closed her eyes, pressing her lips together once the dog put her head on Tes's shoulder. Yeah, he knew what she was going through. She didn't have anyone. No way would Nikki hold Tes blameless. The Hickoks banded together in times of trouble—and he might as well welcome Tes to the fold. His family would take her in like a wounded pup.

"Thank you for coming by." Tes stood while Ruthie continued inside the house.

She was dismissing him. "I know you're probably not hungry, but you need to keep your blood sugar up," Asher said. She entered the kitchen when he neared the door. "Maybe a glass of orange juice?"

"Sure."

She moved to grab a glass from the cupboard, but he put a hand on her shoulder. "Go sit. I'll bring it to you."

Krysinski nodded. Man code that he was glad he was there. The old man had that fatherly look down pat.

"Tes, please." Krysinski motioned for her to take a seat in the family room.

Tes sat on the brown leather couch and hugged a floral pillow to her chest. She kicked off her shoes and put her feet on the sofa, tucking them to the side. Ruthie brought Tes her ball, plopping it onto her lap. Tes chucked it into the kitchen. *Nice arm.* She'd make a great third baseman at the Hickok family barbecue.

Asher opened the fridge and grabbed the orange juice. Morgan loved orange juice, preferring it over water or soda. A moment of nostalgia swept over him. He forced himself to get a grip. He needed to be the strong one now. His hand tightened on the glass as he took a deep breath. *Morgan was gone.* Who was taking the most valuable people in his life?

He prayed that on some plane of existence she was with Hailey and that both were alive, clinging to each other right at this moment. Even if it was in heaven.

He poured the juice and swiped at his tears. He needed to be strong for Tes. If he gave over to bawling like the big baby he was, she'd cave too. Krysinski didn't have enough handkerchiefs for the two of them.

Asher liked the seasoned agent. He'd been the pillar his family leaned on when Hailey went missing. He was logical, succinct, and never gave false hope.

Asher shoved the orange juice container back into the fridge and brought Tes the glass.

"Thank you." She patted the blanket she'd placed beside her on the sofa. The corner of his mouth tweaked. She was thoughtful. Booties and a blanket. Damn, if the guys from work could see him, they'd tease him unmercifully for the rest of his life.

"What do we do now?" She looked first at him, then to Krysinski. She licked her lips, lifted the glass, and drank.

"We wait." Krysinski pulled out his notebook. "How many of Morgan's friends have you met?"

Tes stared at the floor. Ruthie brought her ball over again and Tes tossed it against the wall, which ricocheted down the hallway. The dog scrambled after her toy. "Don't tell Nikki I hit the wall, okay?"

Asher wasn't able to keep the smile from his lips. How in the world was she related to Nikki? "Do you want me to take her for a walk?"

Tes shook her head. "I can't bear to have her out of my sight."

"I understand." Asher leaned forward, bracing his elbows on his knees.

Her gaze drifted to his sleeve. She lifted the material. "You have Morgan's name tattooed on your arm?"

"Hailey's on my left arm, along with my family's crest." He twisted so she could see. "Morgan's like my second daughter." He swallowed. An easy lie he'd told often enough. "She's spent a lot of her time at my house since she and Hailey became friends in kindergarten. My family and I love her like she's family."

Tes stared at him for a while before taking another swig. "Morgan's lucky to have you and your family in her life. She spoke of you often." Tes shifted her attention to Tom. "I haven't met any of Morgan's friends. I was hoping to this weekend." Her voice softened. "I follow Morgan on Instagram and I'm a friend on her Facebook account." She turned to Asher. "Could you please get my purse?" She motioned toward the counter.

He retrieved her purse and tossed the ball for Ruthie when he returned. She fished out her phone, unlocking the screen, then drinking most of the glass's contents.

"Would you like some more?"

She scrunched up her nose. "I think I need to eat something first." She lifted the glass. "This is going to my head."

"I didn't put any vodka in it." Asher frowned. "I could if you want me to—after you've had some food."

"It feels like you slipped something in there." Her dark blue eyes blinked. She lifted her eyebrows as she blinked again, trying to focus on her phone's screen. She held it at arm's length, moving her head forward, then back.

Krysinski grabbed the glass out of her hand. He dialed someone on his phone as he stepped into the kitchen.

Tes's phone slipped through her fingers, dropping to the floor. She tried to reach over to get it. Asher stopped her fall by grabbing her shoulder. He rolled her back onto the couch. Her eyes were closed and her head lolled to the side. He felt for a pulse. "We need an ambulance."

Krysinski jiggled his phone in his hand. "Way ahead of you, kid."

Kid. Krysinski was the only person who'd called him that. He brushed Tes's hair from her face. Damn, she was beautiful. He perused her soft, relaxed features. Though she and Nikki were the same height and build, they looked similar, yet nothing alike. Maybe from a distance, they'd be mistaken one for the other. Tes was kind, gentle, accepting, and it showed in the softness around her mouth and eyes.

Ruthie's tail wagged as she came to Asher's side. She dropped the ball next to his foot and panted in Tes's face. She pawed at Tes's arm. Asher petted Ruthie's head. "It's all right, girl. I'll take care of you until your mom can." She leaned into him. Damn, he was falling in love with her dog.

"The ambulance is on the way. I'll have the forensics team go through everything in the kitchen. Seems whoever took Morgan didn't clean up after himself as well as he should have." Krysinski's mouth thinned as held Tes's wrist. "Her pulse is strong."

Guilt settled in. "I didn't know the juice was drugged."

Krysinski placed Tes's hand on her abdomen and gave Asher's shoulder a squeeze. "I know."

Asher moved Tes's legs to lay flat and pulled her other arm out from behind her back, resting her hand over the other one. He held his hand over hers. God, what had he done? What if she died? Hell, what about the camera crews circling like vultures outside?

4

E arly the next morning, Tes slipped into her day-old clothes in the small hospital bathroom. A quick shower and brushing her teeth helped her feel normal after spending the night puking her guts into a bowl.

Do you still have the rock I gave you? Brick, a spirit child Tes had met a few days ago, appeared on her left. He was dressed in a black tux and white shirt with a "Hello, My Name is Brick" tag on his lapel. How she wished all ghosts appeared with a nametag.

"Yes." She bent to his level. "It's in my purse. Um, well, my purse isn't with me, but I can get it."

Brick smiled. *You're going to meet my parents today.* He clutched his hands around her arm, squealing with excitement. *They're meeting with that psychic I told you about.*

Tes knelt in front of Brick, shaking her head. "I'm so sorry, buddy. I can't today. My niece was kidnapped and I need to find her."

He frowned. *But you promised.*

"I will meet your parents one day, I promise. But it can't be today."

You have to do it today. Brick's pleading tone and tears brimming in his near-invisible eyes broke her heart.

"What will happen if I don't meet them today? Will the world end?"

He looked away, bottom lip quivering. *It's Chester.*

"Your younger brother?"

Yeah. Brick looked devastated. *He's not doing well. He's not eating or sleeping, and hasn't said a word since...*

"Since you drowned."

Please, Dr. Tes. It won't take long.

How could she explain to a dead child that the living came first?

My mom and dad are meeting with a great psychic. I bet she could find your niece.

Oh, to have the faith of a child. "I wish I could but I need to stay focused."

Brick looked around the small room. *You're sick?*

"Yeah."

But you're better now?

She nodded.

I bet you're hungry.

"Not really." Her stomach growled.

I bet hot coffee and some banana bread sounds good. Brick tilted his head. *My mom makes the best banana bread.*

He was being nice, letting her off the hook.

Hope you find your niece.

"I've got to. Anything you can do from the other side would be greatly appreciated."

Brick shrugged as he faded. *I don't know how.*

***

Asher pulled his truck into a parking stall inside Overlake Hospital's parking garage. Krysinski had called and given him the green light.

He glanced at Tes's purse on the front seat beside him and sucked up his manliness as he clutched the long strap in his hand. Men carried purses for their wives all the time, right? At least she didn't have a tiny yappy dog that fit inside the purse. Then he'd be carrying it in a paper sack. Hell, if only he'd thought of *that* sooner.

Holding Ruthie's harness and puffing out his chest, he exaggerated his manly walk across the garage and into the elevator. John Wayne would have been proud. Good. No news media mulling about snapping photos either.

Krysinski had texted him with Tes's room number, so hopefully he'd navigate the long halls without too much emasculation. He smiled to a nurse. She didn't point and laugh. Maybe it wasn't so weird he was carrying a purse. A group of teenagers rounded the corner.

"Nice murse, dude." A snarky teen's head jerked as he burst out laughing. His friends joined in.

It was high school all over again.

One elevator ride and a short distance later, Asher knocked on a half-opened door. "Tes? You decent?"

The bathroom door opened. "Hi, Asher. Tom let me know you'd be dropping by to take me home." She knelt. "Ruthie." She wrapped her dog in her arms. "I've missed you."

"Did you find out what was in the orange juice?"

"I was roofied." Tes kissed Ruthie's head. "Yesterday when Morgan said on the phone that her hands felt funny, I wasn't thinking she was drugged. I thought she was hyperventilating."

"I'm sorry, Tes. If I'd have known—"

"I don't blame you." She stood. "You wouldn't have drugged me." She eyed her purse. "May I?"

"Oh, of course. Sorry." He handed over the bag. "I put your cellphone in there, too."

"Thank you." She set the purse on the bed and rifled through the contents, smiling at something she'd found. "I've got my discharge papers." She folded and stuffed the papers into her purse. "Let's go before the nurse returns with a wheelchair. I need a fresh change of clothes before we start looking for Morgan."

"Sure, but Tom said the forensics team wasn't finished yet. He'll call when the coast is clear. We could grab some coffee first." He motioned for her to walk ahead of him into the hallway. "They're still dusting for fingerprints and taking samples of different foods in the fridge and pantry."

"Great." Tes's shoulders sagged. "I know they're doing their job, but how am I going to have time to clean Nikki's house *and* find Morgan?"

Asher pulled his phone out of his pocket. "I can get someone over there to clean Nikki's house."

"On a holiday?" Tes's expression was dubious.

He'd forgotten today was July 4th. "I've got this."

She eyed him with trepidation. "How long did it take the police to get there? I mean, the kidnapper had time to put back Morgan's chair, grab her laptop, cell phone, and her."

"Hey." Asher put a hand on her shoulder. "Quit beating yourself up over this." Rich words, considering he'd been doing the same thing to himself for months. "You called the police right away—got someone there faster than I did with Hailey."

"Like it did any good." She crossed her arms. "I don't even know where to begin."

"Once my family saw the AMBER alert, they huddled and made a plan. Flyers have been posted in business windows first thing this morning. News stations are flashing her picture everywhere. We're bound to get something."

"Do flyers work?"

"They help bring in tips to the FBI hotline. Someone had to have seen something. It's hard to have faith." Asher pushed the elevator button. "I'm hoping Morgan's with Hailey now—and at least they're together."

"I sure hope so." She sighed, running her fingers through Ruthie's fur. "To think of any alternative would be too much."

***

Tes climbed into Asher's truck while Ruthie slipped onto the micro backseat. Tes never understood the point of a backseat that had zero leg room. They should call it a pet bench. It made her nervous that Ruthie didn't have her seatbelt harness.

Ruthie placed her front paws on the between-seat console, staring out the front window. Tes smirked. "You let her ride in the front seat, didn't you?"

Asher glanced out the side window. "Guilty as charged. I lowered the window and let her ears flap in the breeze until we reached the highway."

"She's never ridden up front before."

"Why doesn't that surprise me?" Asher narrowed his eyes, then shifted the truck as they sped up, entering the freeway. Something about a stick shift made a man hotter. It proved he could multi-task.

She popped open his glove compartment. It was kind of like opening a woman's medicine cabinet. This was where men kept their secrets. The contents of a man's hiding place told a lot about him. How many, if any, condoms let her know he took safe sex seriously. Receipts implied how unorganized he was and/or where he hid receipts from his wife or girlfriend. Asher's was chock-full. An owner's manual, a flashlight, the vehicle's registration, travel-sized bottles of hand sanitizer, lotion, and lots of small tissue packets. So, he enjoyed masturbating. Why else have a glovebox full of tissues and no condoms? Hopefully, he didn't do that in his truck, but no judgment. She slid him a side glance.

"You looking for something in particular?"

"No. Just nosey."

He laughed quietly, smiling.

What would she look like two months from now? When something this catastrophic happened to a family, it changed life forever. She'd never be the same. She'd been cautious before, but now? Now she'd wonder if every face she encountered had known Morgan and if they knew who'd want to take her?

Tes petted Ruthie's soft head. "Last night was the first night I slept without her."

Asher's mouth twitched in a shame-filled glance. "She slept with me."

"Oh, so that's how it is, huh?" She smiled, scratching the dog's ears. "You meet a cute guy, and you're in his bed before the day's through?"

"You think I'm cute?"

Oh, yeah. "Come on. You know you're cute."

He shook his head like he'd never been told that before.

"Please. Don't act so shy."

One corner of his mouth tweaked.

"You don't have a girlfriend?"

"After going through this? No."

"Did you have a girlfriend when Hailey was kidnapped?"

"I haven't had a lot of time to date. I've had a girlfriend here or there, but nothing so serious that I wanted to pop the big question."

"Why not?"

His hands gripped the steering wheel tighter. He scrunched his lips. She bet he didn't believe he could be happy, settle down, and enjoy being loved—even before Hailey was kidnapped. *Interesting.*

Asher took a deep breath. "I'm sure you've heard about my past."

"What? That you never married Hailey's mother?"

"Oh, hell no. I was sixteen when I got her pregnant."

Tes's eyebrows shot up. How did that affect his relationships? "Did you want to marry her, after you turned eighteen?"

"Never. I mean, it was a spur-of-the-moment decision. Backseat of my dad's '67 Mustang. Horny teenager kind of thing. Rushed."

She tried hard not to laugh. "Spontaneous?"

"If that's what you want to call your first time a girl says yes." He paused. "She was sixteen and was the first girl who let me touch her boobs. I didn't know I'd react so— immediate."

"Kind of like a '67 Mustang, huh? Zero to, oh yeah baby, let's do this?"

He smiled. "Yep." Seriousness returned in a flash. "When I told my parents, I thought for sure they were going to rip my head off and I'd be living on the streets."

"Do you still feel guilty?"

"Sometimes. My mom pulled me into her arms and said words I'll never forget. 'Sometimes mistakes are heaven sent'." He blinked a few times. "I grew to respect my mom a thousand percent that day."

"She sounds like a great mom." The polar opposite of hers.

"My dad said if I got a girl pregnant, I best start making a living. I've been working for him ever since."

She bet he worked harder and longer than anyone else.

"I never missed a child support payment—well, until Hailey came to live with me when she was two."

Wow. Impressive for a teenage kid. "Hailey's fortunate to have you for a dad."

"If only I knew where she was."

"We're going to find them, Asher. We have to." Preferably before six o'clock tomorrow evening, when Nikki's flight landed. It seemed unrealistic, but for now, it was all Tes could hold onto. Nikki would never forgive her—even if Morgan was found in time.

Tes had put all her hopes into building a relationship with what few family members she had left, only to have it dashed in one week. Clearly, the Universe had other designs for her life.

Asher's breathing shuddered loud enough for her to hear. He'd been living this burden every moment of every day since Hailey's kidnapping but pretended to keep up a strong front. Losing someone close to you was devastating, but two? She couldn't imagine how much he must be dying inside.

5

B raewood Manor Coffee and Tea House was an old converted Victorian mansion. Tes climbed out of her seat as Asher came around to lift Ruthie, placing her on the ground. They made their way across the parking lot, up the wide veranda, and stopped at the door.

Her gaze moved to the poster taped inside the window at eye level. Asher stiffened, gently took her hand, and gave it a squeeze before letting go. A picture of Hailey and Morgan, in full color, framed by the word MISSING. Their biological stats and the FBI's phone number were provided.

The impact of the situation, in full technicolor, hit her square in the chest.

Asher opened the door.

"Please extend my gratitude to your family for getting word out into the community so quickly." Would the kidnapper see the flyers?

Delicious smells seduced her senses. Cinnamon, coffee, and freshly baked yeast dough encompassed her like a warm hug. Though she didn't feel like eating, her stomach rumbled.

"What would you like?"

Tes tilted her head. "You take Ruthie and find a seat. Buying you a cup of coffee and breakfast is the least I can do after all you've done for me."

He stared at her, narrowing his eyes. He dipped his head and lowered his voice. "Are you not used to a guy taking care of you? This isn't a feminist thing, is it?" He waved between them.

"No. I feel guilty taking advantage of your kindness."

"This isn't a date. This is coffee and a snack. Trust me, if I took you on a date, you'd know the difference." His scrutiny made her fidget. "Tell me what you want and go find a table for us, okay?"

"Tall mocha and a piece of banana bread or a bran muffin, whichever they have." That shouldn't send her stomach into spasms. A slight headache pulsed in her temples from caffeine withdrawal.

The neighborhood coffee shop's busyness overwhelmed her frayed senses. Machines hissing as they made steamed milk, underlying chattering voices, and the clink of spoons tossed in the sink melded together. A burst of laughter broke the monotony.

A baby in a highchair seemed to be the only one to notice her standing by the front door, and he wasn't looking at her or Asher, but fixated on Ruthie. He screeched in short bursts, his eyes wide, his little hands clutching air. No doubt he wanted to get his sticky hands on her dog.

"Shh, Sammy," his mother cooed. "You have puppies at home."

Tes gave a polite smile to the rueful mother.

"Sorry," the mother said. "He's never seen a dog in here before."

Brick appeared at the woman's side. He moved the chair next to the woman away from the table. *Over here, Tes.*

The woman's eyes darted to the moved chair, and immediately went to Brick. *Could she see him?*

"Please." The woman motioned to the vacant seat as Brick disappeared.

Tes slipped into the chair, eyeing the cute couple enjoying a lazy Saturday morning coffee while their son ate Cheerios.

Sammy screeched again, adding a whine at the end.

"Would you like to pet him?" Tes asked the little boy.

His blond eyebrows rose, and his big, blue-green eyes widened as he stared at her in disbelief. Tes glanced first at his mother, then the father—yep, the little boy had the mom's unique eyes. She slid her purse over the back of the chair.

"Is it okay?" she asked his parents.

"Just a warning." The dad's smile slid up half his face. "He may fall in love with you for life."

"It's a risk I'm willing to take."

His mother pulled him out of his highchair and held him in her lap.

"Ruthie, sit." Tes's command coincided with a hand signal. Her dog sat at attention as if she knew she was working now. She dipped her head and sniffed the little boy's hands before licking them.

Sammy squealed, pulling back his hands. Then promptly offered them to Ruthie again.

"We have two lab retriever mixes at home." The woman showed her son how to pet the new dog. "Pet nice, like Mav and Missy."

The woman's fingers brushed Tes's as they both petted Ruthie. It was one of those moments that passed in an instant and yet stretched for an eternity.

Something about this woman was different. A good kind of different. Tes stared at her for the longest time, taking in her chestnut hair and kind face.

Sammy wrapped his hand around her index finger. The sticky cereal residue sent willies up Tes's spine. She wasn't into kid spit. He cocked his little head to the side and looked at his mother.

"I'm Joni Gregson." She shook Tes's hand.

The full connection of her hand brought a calming effect over Tes. "I'm Dr. Tesla Brynn. Call me Tes. I'm a psychiatrist and this here is Ruthie. I specialize in helping children struggling with change and grief."

They stared at each other. The strangest sensation left Tes feeling that somehow she knew Joni, not from this lifetime, but another one perhaps. She didn't have any logical explanation for the strong and instant connection.

Maybe she reminded her of someone, though no one came to mind. It was what her father called a quantum correlation, limitless between time and space. He'd been a mystic scientist who pushed the boundaries of physics.

Sadness filled Joni's eyes. "You're terrified."

Tes took a steady breath, fighting her emotions. "My niece was kidnapped yesterday." Saying it out loud didn't ease her discomfort.

"The AMBER alert?"

Tes fought back tears. That door to her pent-up emotions tried to open, and she firmly shut it in her mind. "Yes." She hated crying in public. Her mother's voice rang in mind. *You're ugly when you cry. Go to your room. No one deserves to see your horrid face. You can come out once you've regained your composure.*

"I know you're going to think I'm crazy, but I'm a psychic medium." She gripped Tes's hand. "Your niece is alive. If she were dead, I'd know."

"We don't know how to find them."

Joni gave her hand a gentle squeeze before letting go. "Them?"

"Yes. Her best friend was also kidnapped. I'm here with the girl's father."

Joni's jaw firmed. "We're going to find them and my team's going to help."

"You have a team?"

Joni stood, balancing Sammy on a hip. "This is my husband, Zeke."

Tes shook his hand. "Nice to meet you."

"Honey, her niece is the one the AMBER alert was for yesterday."

"I'm sorry." Zeke's tone relayed sincerity. "I can't imagine what you're going through. It's every parent's worst nightmare." He had kind brown eyes, and a don't-mess-with-me air all at the same time.

Joni slipped Sammy back in his seat while Ruthie panted at his side, her tail wagging a mile a minute. The dog would love to have a boy of her own.

Tes leaned back in her chair as Asher arrived at the table, sitting opposite her. He held a coffee in each hand and a little brown bag clutched between two fingers. "This is a grande."

He took the lid off his coffee. "If Eric's working when I come in, he always bumps me up another size. He went to school with Hailey and Morgan. He graduated last year."

"How nice." Tes glanced over her shoulder to see a lanky young man making another espresso. His gaze connected with hers. He mouthed the words "I'm sorry." She nodded and turned back around to face Asher.

She motioned to the couple at the table next to them. "This is Zeke and Joni Gregson. That's their adorable little boy Sammy. This is Asher Hickok. His daughter Hailey was taken on Mother's Day weekend."

"Hi." Asher avoided eye contact.

"Joni's a psychic medium."

Asher's frame stiffened, his jaw tightening as he glared at Tes.

"Her team is going to help us find Morgan and Hailey."

"Tes." His tone was full of warning with an edge of anger. He turned his attention to the couple. "Listen, I know you mean well, but I've been down this road a little more than I care to admit. I'm not letting Tes be jerked along a false chain of useless hope."

Wow. She never imagined he'd be so opinionated or protective. "It's okay, Asher."

"No, it's not. People like them are going to come out of the woodwork."

"Asher." It was her turn to have an edge of anger to her tone.

He stopped and clamped his mouth shut, flattening his lips into a tight thin line.

Tes gave his hand a quick squeeze. "She's not like the ones you've met."

"How would you know?" He lifted his chin in a short jerk.

"I know." She wasn't going to tell him how, because he'd never believe her. Few ever did.

***

Asher stared at her dark blue eyes and wanted to reach across the table and force some common sense into Tes's head.

"What will it cost us to listen?" She shrugged. "We don't have any other leads."

"The evidence isn't back yet. Once Krysinski—"

"Special Agent Tom Krysinski?" Zeke interrupted.

Asher asked, "You know him?"

"We've worked on cases with him before. He'll vouch for Joni and our team. We're not in it for the money, if that's what you're worried about."

So, they had a new angle. They'd eventually ask for money. They always did. *A donation.*

Joni and Zeke shared a long look, then Zeke nodded. Joni turned her attention to them. "Can you come to our house around eleven?"

Zeke glanced at his watch. "Don't you have a client meeting at ten-thirty?"

"I do, but I have a feeling Tes can help them more than I can."

The women exchanged a glance before Tes answered, "I'd be happy to help."

Joni smiled. "We look forward to seeing you later."

Asher shook his head at Tes. "Just don't go getting your hopes up."

"Thank you." Tes sipped her coffee.

There was no way he was going to let her do this alone. He knew what to look for when scam artists manipulated people. No way in hell was anyone going to take advantage of Tes. He'd make damn sure of that, and they'd be having a little chat before they got to the Gregsons' home about not feeding said "psychic" any information.

Zeke put a business card on the table. "Here's our address. And trust me, we don't give that out often." He paused. "I'm sorry you've had bad experiences with psychics in the past. Trust me, I was the world's biggest skeptic until I met Joni. And look where it got me. I married her."

Who said a sucker was born every second? Asher shook Zeke's hand as he stood to leave. Ruthie returned to Tes's side.

Zeke plucked his son from the highchair. "It's going to be okay, Asher. Joni's not a precognitive psychic." Like he knew what the hell that meant. "She sees and talks to the dead. If she's not seeing your daughter, or Tes's niece, then it weighs in your favor that they're still alive."

Asher swallowed. He'd spent countless hours thinking of what could be happening to Hailey. Wouldn't death be a better alternative to what she endured? He didn't want her to suffer, starve, or, worse, be repeatedly raped.

His gut twisted. She'd been gone for months. The latter was more than likely true.

"Asher," Joni said, gaining his attention. "We can ask the dead for help."

A chill raced up his spine. Tes straightened in her chair, turning to Joni. "We can?" Joy lit her face.

Asher knew that Tes's father had passed away when Hailey and Morgan were in middle school. Good Lord, invoking the dead as partners? *Shit.* Maybe he could convince her to cancel.

The psychic gave Tes hope she had no business dishing out. "I have some powerful people on the other side that I trust."

Here we go. And how much was that going to cost? How much did the dead charge? Were they paid in U.S. dollars or did they take credit? Or did it help build another wall in the mansions one built in heaven, hoping for a glorious afterlife? Seriously, did these people ever listen to themselves?

If cases could be solved by dialing a psychic, more murders would be solved, fewer houses robbed, and more kids home tucked in their beds safe at night. Psychics were supposedly celestial messengers—the best guesstimaters on the planet. That was all they were. Read someone's body language and bam—your message delivered from heaven. Telling you what you already knew but never voiced out loud. Damn, he didn't want Tes going through anything like that.

Tes held Joni's hand before they walked away. "Thank you." Tears filled her eyes, making them bluer than the sky. If anyone needed a good long cry, it was Tes. She was acting like a pressure cooker, tapping off the pent-up steam with a burst here or there. Asher didn't understand why she hadn't dissolved into wailing. Then again, his family didn't keep things bottled in—they let it out there for the world to see.

Joni let go of Tes's hand, leaned over, and hugged her. "It's going to be okay. Trust me."

Tes's lips curved in a hope-filled smile. He wished he could count on Joni the way Tes seemed to. Sure, he'd been an easy mark for con artists in the beginning too.

After they walked away, Tes turned to him. "I know you're angry. I get it."

"No, you don't. I've seen vultures like them." He twitched a thumb toward the door they'd walked through.

"Not her."

Asher shook his head. "Tes, they're a dime a dozen out there."

"I know this isn't easy for you. Do you believe in serendipitous moments?"

"It's up there with love at first sight and the cow jumping over the moon." Now he sounded like a damn cynic.

"You don't believe in love at first sight?"

"I believe you choose to love people because you've learned they are worthy of it."

The corners of her mouth dipped as she rolled her eyes. "How romantic." She took a bite of her banana bread.

"Romance has nothing to do with love."

"Oh, tell me, sage one, tell me the difference between love and romance." She snickered.

He drank his coffee. Damn, he'd walked right into that one. He'd rather not talk about his love life, or lack thereof. "How do you like to be romanced?"

She choked on her coffee, sputtering droplets onto her chin. She dabbed her face with a napkin.

"Do you need me to pat you on the back?"

"No." She coughed again. "I've never been romanced, so I wouldn't know. But every girl dreams of the guy that brings her flowers and treats her like she's something special."

"You mean you've never had a date bring you flowers and take you on candlelit dinners?"

She picked at an edge of the banana bread. "Once."

The hollowness of that one word caught his breath. Flowers should never break someone's heart. "What are your favorite flowers?"

"I don't have one."

"Look at me." He waited for her to stop pulling crumbs off her bread and look him in the eye. "Roses?"

She shook her head and focused back on the small pile of crumbs she was harvesting. Since she wasn't going to give up the answer, he crossed his arms and leaned back. "What kind of flower would a *Tesla* like? A psychiatrist? Daisies are too plain. Too simple." His attempt to lighten the mood failed. "No. You're a complicated woman. Anything in the mum family would be too chaotic, too random and bursting at all angles. No. You want a controlled flower that bloomed the same every single time." *Didn't they all?*

"Are you trying to analyze *me*?"

"Tulips. You're a tulip kind of gal. Maybe irises if you're in a frivolous mood." The corner of her mouth twitched. He tore a corner off the banana bread and held it in front of her lips. "Choo-choo-choo—*brah-brah*-chugga-chugga-chugga-choooo-choooo."

She covered her mouth as she burst out laughing. Why did she hide her beautiful smile?

"Come on, Tes. You need to eat."

She opened her mouth and let him plop the bread inside. He brushed his thumb against her bottom lip as she closed her mouth before he pulled his hand back. He watched her chew, swallow, and take a swig of coffee. "I like fallen maple leaves. Acorns. Pinecones."

Asher forced a smile. Dead leaves and seeds. The promise of life, but not a real life. *Interesting.* "Where did you grow up?"

"Did you grow up around here?" She waved a hand.

Now she didn't want to talk about her own life. How bad could it be? With a sister like Nikki? Was Tes the sister that lived in the shadow of an older sibling? Nikki was a school counselor and Tes a psychiatrist. Was she the one trying to live up to someone else's perfect world? Whose? Her father's? Her mother's? "Yeah, I grew up here. You didn't answer my question."

"Caught onto that, did you?" She looked at that damn piece of bread. He was about to throw it out, just so she'd look at him. "I grew up between San Jose, California, Versoix, Switzerland, and Cardiff, Wales."

"There's a good story in there somewhere."

"None worth telling." She took another bite, probably to keep from saying more.

Her shoulders were tense. She looked tired. He lowered his voice. "Tes, you're worried. I get it. Boy, don't I get it. But I didn't do it alone. You have your dog. A dog's great, but it's not the same as someone who will stand beside you. Hold you while you cry."

"Who held you?"

"My mom, dad, brothers, sisters, aunts, uncles, friends. I bawled like a baby for a week straight when Hailey went missing. You've teared up but keep shoving all your worry and pain deep down inside. You're the psychiatrist—you know that's not—" He wanted to say "normal" but thought better of it. "Helping the situation."

"You ever watch British TV?"

He loved Monty Python. Did that count? "Like *Top Gear*?"

She rolled her eyes. "I was raised to have a public face, and a private face at my mother's house. When I was with my dad, I could be myself. I don't like crying in public or around strangers. Trust me, I cried plenty last night."

"You don't have an accent."

"Only when I'm in Wales or extremely nervous." Her gaze focused on him. "It feels nice to not be alone."

"Let's make a pact right now." He motioned a finger between them. "Until the girls are home, we're in this together."

She scrunched her mouth. "I'd like that."

"Great. Finish up so we can get you home and give you a chance to change before Krysinski arrives."

6

As Asher pulled his truck in front of the McKinley home, Tes sucked in a deep breath and held it in as if it could turn back time and make the last twenty-four hours vanish. It'd taken decades for Nikki to grant Tes a chance to come back into her life. After all, Tes was to blame for everything that went wrong in their family, whether she was present or not. She was cursed and they'd treated her as an outcast since she was eight. A year none of them would ever forget. At seven years her senior, Nikki was the golden child in their mother's eyes. Tes was quite the opposite.

Even if they found Morgan, Nikki could still ostracize her again. Tes needed to be prepared for that. She highly doubted Nikki would lean on her and make a unified front. No, she'd be blamed for misfortune coming to her door. After all, Nikki had lived in Whitman for twenty years and the week Tes had arrived, Morgan was kidnapped. Yeah, all the blame would land squarely on Tes's shoulders. It would be easier to blame Tes than to admit demented people existed. Especially in Nikki's hyper-controlled world.

Thank God Tes didn't have much to move. She'd sold everything she had. Not that her college furnishings and kitchen ware were anything of value. Her life's belongings fit in three large suitcases—two of which fit in the trunk of her Camry with one in the backseat. She'd mailed some textbooks via third-class mail. They'd arrive eventually. Maybe Nikki would let her come get them. Otherwise, she might have to stalk her porch.

A police car and forensics van were still on the street outside Nikki's home.

Tes exhaled, leaning over her legs, resting her forehead in her palms.

"What's wrong?" Asher asked.

"I've got to clean the fingerprint dusting powder off everything before Nikki gets home."

"It's Nikki's house. Let her clean it up."

"You don't understand. If Nikki so much as sees a coaster out of place, she comes unglued. Fingerprint dust everywhere?" Tes shook her head. "I'm fucked."

"No, you're not. Don't go borrowing trouble." He paused. "I told you, I got this."

"Now you're Mr. Clean and the Tasmanian Devil combined into one?" Right now, she needed a fairy godmother, mice, bluebirds, and a lizard or two wouldn't hurt.

"No, but I've got a magic wand." He held up his phone. He scrolled through his contacts and dialed. "Hey, Sue. It's Asher. I have an urgent need to have a house cleaned by sundown today. Can you get a team together?"

Of course, he was connected to Ms. Clean and a team of super maids. She wanted to hug him. "How much?"

He held up his index finger while he gave Nikki's address to Sue. He ended the call and leaned over the console. "It's not going to cost you anything." He stared at her for the longest time. "I don't know how to say this, but your sister isn't exactly kind, thoughtful, or forgiving."

"She's a bit a much?" Tes let out a half-hearted laugh. "I feel like I'm always walking on eggshells, hoping she's going to accept me for who I am."

Asher laid a hand on her shoulder. "Would you live here if you didn't have to?"

"Do you know of a cheap apartment I can rent?"

"I can do you one better." He removed his hand and pushed a button to roll down the windows. "I have a guest room that you're more than welcome to—free of charge."

She shook her head. "I couldn't take advantage of you. I'd have to pay you something."

"Sure—whatever you believe is a fair price." He shrugged. "But I don't need the money."

"It'd sure help with my guilt, though."

"Okay. We'll call it grocery money or the vacation fund." Movement from her peripheral vision caught her notice as an officer approached the truck.

"Can I help you?" The officer held a clipboard and flipped back to the front page.

Asher put his hands on the steering wheel. "I'm Asher Hickok. This is Tesla Brynn. She lives here."

The officer looked over the piece of paper on his clipboard. "The forensics team is packing up now."

"Can I go inside and get some fresh clothes?" Tes grabbed her purse.

"Sure, ma'am."

"I'll be quick." Tes put her hand on the door. "Ruthie, stay." She left the truck and headed toward the porch.

She froze. Her stomach flipped as her foot hit the bottom step. Did the kidnapper take Morgan out the front or back door? Did the forensics team find any evidence of a tampered lock? She crested the threshold, finding black smudges of fingerprint dust all over the doorjamb. Whose prints were there? Hers, Morgan's, Nikki's, maybe Ben Winslow's. The mailman? Nikki's friends? Morgan's friends? Good Lord, the process of elimination was going to take longer than the twenty-four hours. They needed a frickin' miracle.

She crossed through the quaint foyer and saw a few hazmat-suited people mulling around the kitchen before starting up the stairs to her room. Her pulse stuttered as her breath caught in her throat. Every corner was darker than before. Every shadow shifted. What if there was a secret way inside the house and the kidnapper was coming back? What if he left cameras in the bedrooms, bathrooms, or even here somewhere on the stairs? She glanced to the dark corners. What if he was watching her every move? She struggled to breathe.

"Tes?" Asher called from the doorway.

How could him saying her name leave her feeling less lonely? She wouldn't have guessed she needed a rock to lean on, and he was a handsome rock at that.

"You okay?"

She wanted to be brave. The previous day's memories rushed in full tilt. Morgan crying, screaming, then...gone. Her hand gripped the railing like a lifeline.

Asher came up behind her, resting his warm hand over hers on the bannister. "Come on. I'll go with you."

Leaning back against his solid chest melted the frantic surge that consumed her thoughts. "I— I—"

"I know." He pried her grip loose. "It all comes rushing back. Reliving it all."

She covered her mouth with her hand.

He wrapped his arm around her shoulders and walked with her up the rest of the stairs. At the end of the hall was the small guest room she and Ruthie occupied. "I need to grab Ruthie's food and dishes."

"I'll get them."

Where should she start? Should she change first or throw everything in her suitcases and put them in her car?

"Tes?"

"I know."

"Please look at me."

She wiped her eyes, took a deep breath, and looked into his compassionate eyes.

"I know you don't know me and moving in with a stranger seems odd, but you and I both know Nikki. Moving in with me will spare you from a constant barrage of one endless guilt trip. You don't deserve that."

Part of her knew he was right. Part of her thought running from her problems never solved anything—but then, Asher had spent more time with Nikki than she ever had and if he knew that...

"It's just for now. Maybe after Nikki comes home, she won't blame you." His expression didn't hide his lie. "I have a guest room that's never been used." He paused, glancing away for a moment. "The house is empty without Hailey and Morgan."

Tes bit her lip, fighting her tears.

"Do you want me to help pack your things?"

Shaking her head, she slowly let out her breath. "I can do this."

"Do you want me to stay?"

"No." Her lips trembled as fresh tears heated her cheeks.

He stepped over to her sliding closet door, pulled it aside and then checked the other half. He bent to the floor and lifted the bed skirt and looked under the bed. "No one's in here. Shut the door and lock it if you want. Get changed. I'll grab Ruthie's stuff and we'll head to my house and get you settled in before heading to the Gregsons. Okay?"

"Okay." She hiccupped back a sob.

He squeezed her shoulder. "I'll be back in a few minutes."

As soon as the door was shut, she tossed off her heels and unzipped her skirt. She opened her suitcase and pulled out a clean pair of jeans and knock-off designer T-shirt. She rolled up the sleeves and made quick work of grabbing what few items she'd unpacked and tossed them in the only suitcase she'd opened since arriving.

Everything in the bathroom fit in a small satchel. In a few minutes, she'd slipped on her canvas tennis shoes and was ready to go. She lined up the suitcases on the landing, tossed her satchel and purse over one shoulder, and lifted a suitcase. She was halfway down the stairs when Asher came back through the front door.

He took his time looking all the way up her legs, a smile framing his mouth. "I like this look a lot better. Not so formal."

That British girl was still tucked inside, the prim and proper one her mother insisted she be. How else did she prevent herself from wearing her heart on her sleeve? "We can put my suitcases in my car." She pulled her keys out of her purse.

Asher took her suitcase. "Unlock your car. I'll grab the rest."

She'd unlocked her trunk by the time he carried all three of her suitcases to the car, one tucked under his arm. His muscles flexed as he maneuvered the cases into the trunk. He managed to get all three to fit, stacking them on their sides. Why hadn't she thought of that?

"You ready?" He picked up the satchel at her feet and nestled it to one side.

"I'll follow you then?"

He closed the trunk. "You want Ruthie to ride with you?"

"No." Tes couldn't believe she was saying this. "She likes riding in your truck."

He held up his hands. "I promise to keep her in the backseat."

"Fair enough." Who would have known she could trust a stranger?

***

They slowly proceeded through the busy neighborhood where families gathered for block parties, some already shooting off fireworks. Tes never had that kind of holiday. Maybe that was what she'd been searching for when she moved to Washington. Americana. A slice of normalcy and calmness surrounded by family.

Asher pulled into the circular driveway in front of a large log cabin. The front yard was beautifully landscaped with a small fountain where bluebirds bathed. Now, if this wasn't an idyllic scene, she didn't know what was. The intricately carved front doors had etched glass windows on each side, depicting one continuous forest scene with deer, butterflies, and a bear against a mountain backdrop. She wouldn't have ever pegged Asher as an artisan, but man did he have a gorgeous home.

Asher helped Ruthie out of his truck and she tore off running after the bluebirds.

Tes jumped from the car. "Ruthie, come." She snapped her fingers and Ruthie came to her side. "I'm sorry. She's never done that before."

"What? Chased after birds? She's a dog. A retriever. That's what she was bred to do."

"Still. We don't hurt living things."

Asher walked to the rear of her car. She popped the trunk. It felt weird moving in with him, but there was no way she could sleep in Nikki's house alone. Not after a kidnapper had broken in and threatened that she'd be next. He must have bluffed, but still, it was unsettling.

She grabbed her purse and satchel, shut the trunk, and followed Asher up the wide front porch. "Did you ever date Nikki?"

"No." He frowned. "Why would I?"

"You seem her type. Hailey and Morgan are best friends. Seems natural."

He unlocked the door and set her bags inside the entry way. "Nikki thinks about Nikki. Did you know the day Morgan had her tonsils out, they were thirty minutes late checking in because Nikki had to stop for coffee? Then go to the store because *she* needed to be comfortable while she waited. That's the kind of shit she could have done ahead of time or waited until Morgan was under anesthesia. And that's one example in a long line of examples I could provide."

Tes knew Nikki could be selfish, if not self-centered, but not to that level. "Were you there?" Tes stepped inside the air-conditioned house. It was a nice reprieve from the hot July sun.

"Yes." Asher closed the door.

"Why?"

"Because Morgan asked me to be there. She was scared." He blinked and looked away. "I've been the only dad in her life. I was there for her first dance recital. Her first band practice. Her first—" He sucked in a deep breath. "Everything. She and Hailey were inseparable." Tears hung on his dark lashes. "Did you know she spent every weekend with us?"

Tes's mouth opened. "*Every* weekend?"

"Yeah. So Nikki could go out with the girls, or out with whomever she was dating. I didn't want Morgan around some guy who wanted to get in your sister's pants and didn't care if a kid was there to watch. I didn't want her waking up Saturday mornings with a different guy in the house than the weekend before. And I sure as hell didn't want her being at risk."

She knew what he meant. "So, yesterday, when you got those text messages, it was like losing Hailey all over again."

7

A sher walked into the main room, shoulders sagging. "Yeah," he whispered.
Tes followed, stopping him by putting a hand on his arm. "I'm so sorry. I didn't realize. I mean, Morgan always called you 'Uncle Asher,' but I had no idea she was that close to you. I thought you were a close family friend...not actual family. I mean, the tattoo makes more sense now. Who gets someone else's kid's name tattooed on their arm?"

"She means the world to me—and her being kidnapped..." He pulled out a chair from the round kitchen table and crumbled, burying his face in his hands as he openly cried.

This strong, burly man wept. Sobbed. How Tes admired his ability to cry so easily. She pulled out a chair next to him and wasn't sure if she should touch him or not. Her own tears blurred her vision as she pulled a napkin out from the holder off the lazy susan and handed it to him, then grabbed one for herself.

Ruthie placed a paw on his lap.

He wiped his face with the napkin and looked at her dog. "Thank you, girl." He petted her. "She held me while I cried last night. We definitely had a bonding moment."

Tes understood he was trying to make light of the moment, but she couldn't laugh or smile. "She has that effect on people."

"So do you." Asher wiped his nose.

"Me?"

"Through Morgan. You gave her a lot of advice after Hailey went missing. Morgan forced me to keep going because you said that was the best thing for me. Other people don't know what to say after a while. They avoid you like the plague. Not Morgan. She came over many days after school, and on the weekends. She did laundry, dishes, and kept the house straightened up—even pointed out which bills needed to be paid because I was too full of grief to do that myself. She helped take care of my parents and Tango. Lots of people from the church dropped off meals. Morgan wrote the thank-you notes and returned the dishes to each family. She's a thoughtful person." He looked her in the eye. "She's a lot like you."

Tes blushed, remembering conversations with Morgan on ways she could show up and make a difference in the Hickoks' lives when Hailey went missing—and Morgan clearly hid her own anxiety and pain from Asher. "Thanks. Who's Tango?"

"My mom and dad's German shepherd."

"Well, thank you for coming to my rescue." She grabbed his hand. "I'm glad I'm not going through this alone."

He squeezed her hand. "Me too."

She shifted her focus. "Did you build this house?"

"With my bare hands."

"It's beautiful." A master-chef dream kitchen occupied the back wall with a breakfast bar that ran the full length of the marble countertop. The stone fireplace had a big-screen TV over the mantel. Large ceiling-to-floor windows flanked the fireplace. Sectional leather furniture anchored the room. Overall, the place was tastefully decorated.

"When I built this house, I pictured needing all this space someday, but the older I get, the more I realize I could have built a much smaller home."

"How big is it?"

"Four bedrooms, four and a half baths, three thousand square feet."

"Holy cow. I mean, I've lived in a postage stamp-size apartment for the last five years. Before that, Dad and I had a small house. The garage—his workshop—was bigger than the house."

"A man after my own heart." He stared at her hand holding his. "Let's get you settled in."

"Thank you for offering, but I'll find my own place in a few days. I can't intrude on your hospitality. You know, guests and fish smell bad after three days."

He lifted a suitcase. "I get it, but know you don't have to if you don't want to."

"Thanks."

"I'll show you to your room."

He carried her suitcases and headed up the stairs. Pictures of Hailey and Morgan dotted the wall. Tes stopped to admire each fun-filled picture. Two girls fishing, skiing, even helping Asher build a doghouse. Lots of other people were in those pictures. A close family who spent hours enjoying life and each other.

"You coming?" he called.

"Yeah. I've never seen Morgan like this."

"Like what?"

"Smiling and enjoying family."

He frowned as he opened a door at the end of the hall. "She smiles all the time."

Not around Nikki. That troubled Tes. "Nikki mostly has formal pictures at her house —and the only informal picture was Morgan and Hailey at Disneyland."

The guest bedroom had a high four-poster bed that had stairs to help the sleeper reach their destination. The whole room looked like it could fit in a Colonial revival home. "This is beautiful."

"Bathroom's through here." He opened a door. "If you need more towels, you'll find them in the hall closet." He crossed the room and opened another door. "Closet's in here, along with a dresser. I can snag some hangers from the girls' room next door."

"Oh no, I won't need any. I'll live out of my suitcase for the next couple of days."

He hung his head. "Let me know if you need anything. Please, make yourself at home."

"Thank you."

"Would you like some coffee?"

"Tea sounds great, if you have some."

"My mom's the tea connoisseur. I'll have her drop some by." He closed the door as he left.

She could hear him talking to Ruthie. Asher Hickok was a good and kind man. Morgan and Hailey were two lucky young ladies.

Once she was freshened up, adding a bit of makeup so she looked less than bedraggled to meet the Gregson's, she headed downstairs.

An older couple sat at the kitchen table with Asher.

"Tes, meet my parents, Isabella and Grant Hickok."

She shook their hands. "Pleased to meet you."

Asher's mother was busty with salt-and-pepper, chin-length hair. She had a bright, wide smile and Asher's deep-set, dark brown eyes. His dad had a dark tan and thick black hair that grayed at the temples. He was a handsome, fit man for his age. He scruffed Ruthie's ears. "Who's a good dog?" Ruthie licked his face.

Isabella poured her a cup of tea from the pot. "It's nice to meet someone who loves tea as much as I do."

"Thank you." She took an empty seat to Asher's right, sitting across from his parents.

"You sure look a lot like Nikki." Isabella settled the pot on the trivet. "We're praying for Morgan."

"We're Catholic," Asher whispered.

Tes was sheepish and ignorant about most religions. "In my family, we only went to Mass on Easter and Christmas, whether we needed it or not."

"See? You're half Catholic already," Asher teased.

Isabella pinched his shoulder.

Tes liked the camaraderie between mother and son. "I bet Asher was the son that tried your patience."

"Tried? Oh, honey, he was the son that gave me every gray hair on my head. I blame them all on him."

Asher leaned forward, a boyish smile framing his lips. "She looks great with gray hair, doesn't she?"

"She does." She couldn't help but return his smile. He was different around his family. They were close. Loving. Everything she'd ever wanted.

Tes had discussed science breakthroughs and theories with her dad. Her mom's house was filled with formal dinners, teas, and social events where she had to keep her white gloves clean. She could be seen, but never heard, no matter if she was nine or twenty-nine. It was easy to watch everyone from the outside looking in. She was fascinated by body language and facial expressions. That was what got her interested in being a psychiatrist. Asher was an open book. He owned every moment of his life. What would living that kind of life look like?

Grant took a sip of his coffee. "We've canvassed the area with posters this morning."

"We saw the one at Braewood Manor. Thank you." Tes fought back fresh tears. "I don't even know where to begin to look for Morgan."

"We're meeting a psychic at eleven." Asher rolled his eyes.

Isabella stiffened. "Oh, honey." Sympathy framed her eyes. "I know you need to do this. We did too after Hailey was taken."

"I think the Gregsons will be different."

Asher exchanged a look with his parents. "I don't want you getting your hopes up," he said to Tes.

"Hope is all I have right now." Her voice cracked.

"Tes." Isabella pulled her attention. "We're worried sick over Morgan, but I can't imagine how hard this is hitting you, especially with Nikki out of town."

"There's out of town, and then there's a hundred miles from civilization. She didn't take her cell phone, so there's no way I could leave her a message." Tears pricked her eyes as her voice strained. "I should have waited to go on that job interview until Nikki returned."

Isabella grabbed her other hand. "Honey, you don't blame yourself, do you?"

"Who else is there to blame? I was the adult in charge."

"Oh, honey." Isabella shook her head. "You didn't arrange for a kidnapper to take Morgan, any more than Asher arranged for someone to take Hailey. There's a sick, demented asshole out there taking teenage girls. He's to blame. Not you."

"But—"

"No." Isabella squeezed her hand. "It's easy to take on blame, but it's harder to come to grips with the reality that there's someone in this small community targeting best friends."

Tes frowned. "I hadn't thought of that. Could that mean Hailey's still alive?"

"I can't give up hope." Isabella gave one short nod. "I'd know if something happened to either of those girls, like I knew Asher had gotten a young lady pregnant. A mama can read the signs long before the words are spoken."

"You're an optimist," Tes huffed.

"And you're not?"

Tes swallowed. "I'm a realist. Pragmatic to the core. Facts form truth, not speculation and feelings."

Isabella patted her hand. "Well, you'll have to trust me for now. I have enough faith for both of us."

Tes tucked her hair behind her ear. "Thank you. It's hard not to blame myself, but you're right. I didn't ask for this."

"No, you didn't. Neither did Asher." Isabella leaned over, kissed his cheek, and rubbed his back. "I keep telling him not to worry, but he does anyway."

Tes snagged a napkin from the holder and dabbed her eyes before drinking her tea. She needed more caffeine.

"You hungry?" Asher asked.

"No. The tea's lovely. Thank you, Isabella."

Asher glanced at his watch. "We should be heading out. Could you watch Ruthie for us?"

The way he said "us" warmed her heart. It wasn't like Ruthie had paid Isabella any attention. She'd glommed onto Grant like he was the alpha dog.

"We'd love to. We'll even give her a bath later if she goes rolling in the mud."

Tes swallowed. "She's never rolled in the mud."

Grant's brow furrowed, a boyish grin framed his lips. "We're definitely going mud rolling today."

She liked his teasing manner. "Thank you, but we can take her with..."

Asher pinned her with a stare.

"What? She's a service dog. Legally, she can go anywhere I go."

"You've never left her with anyone, have you?"

"Not until last night, when I passed out from being drugged."

Asher held her hand and squeezed. "Trust me, my parents will take great care of her while we're gone."

"But—"

"She'll have fun playing with Tango while you and I talk to this psychic." He cringed. "You'll be less distracted."

"True." She looked to Isabella. "You'll watch over her? Not let her wander near the road?"

"We have an invisible fence," Grant said. "We could put a shock collar on her, but you don't look like the kind of person who would handle that well."

Asher laughed. "He's kidding."

Tes didn't see any humor in Grant's comment.

Asher let go of her hand and stood. "We won't be long." He looked her straight in the eye. "The baby's in good hands. They've raised five kids and tons of dogs along the way. Ruthie'll be fine."

Tes stood, taking her cup to the sink.

Grant came into the kitchen. "Come here." He flicked his fingers. "You look in sore need of a hug." He wrapped an arm around her shoulders.

Comfort eased over her as she leaned against him.

"It's going to be all right, Tes. You're not alone." He wrapped the other arm around her and patted her back.

How she missed her dad's hugs and remembered his dying words. *Hug more. Love more.*

Isabella rubbed her back and Grant wrapped her in the group hug. "We're here for you, Tes." The older woman kissed her cheek.

"Thank you." She hugged them back.

Asher pulled on her hand. "We gotta go."

Tes pulled away from the hug, knelt, and petted Ruthie. "You be good for the Hickoks and no wandering into the road."

Grant squeezed her shoulder. "We'll take great care of her. Promise."

Still, there was that whole mud-rolling thing Tes wasn't sure about.

"Tes..." Asher opened the front door.

"Stay with the Hickoks." She placed one last kiss on Ruthie's head before she picked up her purse and followed Asher out the door.

***

Tes was an emotional mess. She'd never left Ruthie with strangers. She hated to admit Ruthie was her safety blanket and not a guise to help her young patients talk about their deep-seated issues. Stepping outside without Ruthie at her side was like being in public wearing only a skimpy nightgown.

The quiet, shaded, tree-lined streets made it hard to stay awake. Asher turned on the air conditioning and before she knew it, she'd drifted off.

Images flashed through her mind. Strobe light-like flashes in black-and-white similar to slides flipping from an old projector on a timer. Two women. A man. A dagger. Long brown tunics. Black hair under veils. Hot, sandy air. A breeze twitched the flap of their tent.

"He loves me, not you," one woman said.

The man intervened. "I never loved you, Nephriti. Delilah and I are to wed. Your father has promised her to me."

Nephriti thrust a dagger into Delilah's stomach.

On a conscious level, Tes gasped at the sharp pain. Damn, that was intense. Rusty-tasting fluid filled her mouth while bile gathered at the back of her throat.

"If I am deprived of him, so you shall be. For this lifetime. For every lifetime." Nephriti's lips twisted in hate. "I curse you both. May you always be born together and never together as husband and wife. The first to profess love will die."

The man shoved Nephriti away. Delilah fell to the ground. Dark blood spread over her tunic.

The man hovered over her, his hand on the blade. Out of the corner of Delilah's eye, Nephriti lowered a spear and the red-hot, metal tip ripped through his back. Blood spurted across his chest. Nephriti yanked it out. He slumped against Delilah, plunging the blade farther.

"Atticus," Delilah whispered. "I will always love you."

"And I you. Eternity is ours, my love."

Nephriti poised a dagger over her heart. "By my blood oath, I swear for eternity, profess your love before you marry and one of you will die. The other doomed to live a lonely life." She thrust the blade. Blood gushed from her lips. She staggered and fell near Delilah and Atticus. The three pools of blood coagulated together, sealing the bond.

Sealing the curse.

Tes jolted awake. *Where the hell did that come from?*

8

"You okay?" Asher asked.

"Yeah." Tes straightened in her seat. "Just a bad dream."

The haunted yet sympathetic look in his eyes showed he'd had plenty of nightmares since Hailey's kidnapping. If only Tes could mention that wasn't the kind of dream she'd had, but some weird-ass dream that felt so real. Creepy real.

After a left-hand turn, a guard shack came into view. Two armed men stood in front of a gate and one inside the shack. There were blockades and tire spikes that disappeared into the road when they were given the okay and the steel bar raised.

They continued until the road cleared into a large cul-de-sac with mini mansions forming around a large circle. Tom Krysinski stood out front next to his car.

After exiting the vehicle, Asher shook Tom's hand. "Who are the Gregsons?"

"Joni Gregson is a psychic with exclusive clientele." Tom glanced at Tes. "She's the real deal. When none of our leads panned out on Hailey, I contacted her and asked for help. I never told you, Asher, because Joni won't tell you what you want to hear. She's honest. One thing I've learned is that when she says someone's alive, they're alive. She hasn't been able to connect to Hailey, which means she's alive."

"I'd like to believe that." Asher tucked his hands in his jeans pockets.

"LeBron Jacobs is the team's tech support." Tom led them toward the house. "Whoever manipulated Morgan's phone from preventing her to call out, indicates he has coding skills with illegal hacker capabilities. But I'll let LeBron explain. He's the computer genius, not me."

Anticipation warred in Tes's gut. If they got details they could act upon, it was worth the trip. She didn't have time to discuss theories and speculations. That would only suck time and energy, both of which were in short supply.

"Tech support." Asher huffed. "So, Joni's psychic abilities are backed up by whatever the tech guy finds." He pinned his glare on Tes. "You sure you want to do this?"

"What have we got to lose?"

"Then let's do this." Asher shook his head. "You're not psychic, are you, Krysinski?"

Tom's eyes darkened as he gave Asher a fatherly glare. "I don't know how to explain this. When you're around Joni, your life changes. She's connected me with messages from my wife and son who've passed. You may not believe a word she says, but you know, it helped heal a gaping hole in my heart. I'm not asking you to believe in everything she says. I'm asking you to keep your mind open." Tom continued along the sidewalk to the large oak front door. "And listen. Just listen."

Zeke opened the door before they could knock. "Hey, Tom." Zeke shook his hand, wrapping his free hand around his shoulder and giving him a hug.

Tes tried to smile, but her heart wasn't in it. Asher placed his hand on her shoulder blade and ushered her forward. Zeke shook her hand first, then Asher's. "Welcome to our home."

Zeke stared at her for a moment, backing up, and letting them in the house. He waited until they'd all entered the foyer before closing the door.

"Come on, guys, let's wait out back." He tilted his head for the men to follow him. "LeBron will be here in a few minutes." They entered the hardwood foyer. There was an office area to her right and a huge living room to her left. The place had a true decorator's touch. A grand piano received the full light of the bay window in the living room. A man, woman, and young boy sat on the white sofa opposite Joni. A dark cherry wood coffee table added the perfect touch.

"Hey, Tes." Joni smiled and waved her over.

Asher gave her hand a quick squeeze before following Zeke and Tom through the kitchen.

As Tes approached, unsure if she should intrude or not, she recognized the pop star. Her songs jingled in her head, mostly repetitive choruses that had been ear worms at one time or another. Her husband was a famous actor, a comedian with a witty sense of humor who performed on the big screen. Their little boy wore glasses. He slipped his bum off and on the seat cushion, trying his best to behave. *This must be Brick's family.*

Joni made quick introductions. "Tes, you may recognize Samantha and Jason."

Tes shook their hands. "Pleased to meet you." She glanced at the kitchen. Good. Asher was outside.

"I asked Tes to meet with us today because I believe she has a message for your family." Joni motioned to the fidgeter. "This is their little boy, Chester." Joni paused for a moment, lowering her voice. "Samantha and Jason lost their older son about a month ago."

Sensations washed over Tes as Brick appeared at her side dressed in his usual tux. His last memories came into focus.

Brick had tried to save Chester, gulping for air, breathing in water. The water was dark. Cold. Forceful. One more push and he could get Chester to the surface. "Brick. That was your son's name, correct?"

Tes didn't mind ghost children. It was the adult ones that scared the bejesus out of her.

Samantha nodded.

Tes bent on one knee in front of Chester. "It must be hard losing an older brother."

Chester stilled. His tiny hands clutched the edge of the seat cushion, knuckles turning white.

He's not sleeping, Brick said, standing next to her.

"You're not sleeping very well, are you?"

The little boy shook his head.

"Why?"

He glanced at his parents before casting his eyes down.

Tes put a finger under his chin and lifted his head until he looked her in the eye. *Tell him I love him. I don't want him to forget me. I don't want him to forget all the fun we had.* "He loves you, Chester. He'll always be your big brother. You wouldn't be here if it weren't for him, huh?"

His bottom lip quivered.

Images of their happy childhood rolled in her mind like an old eight-millimeter movie. Backyard barbecues and playing in the family pool. Disneyland and dancing with Mickey and Minnie Mouse. Red carpet events for movie premieres. Playing on the backlot of a famous movie set. Singing with their mom at the top of their lungs. Brick and Chester huddled under the blanket reading comic books by flashlight. They were inseparable. Until death intervened.

Tes swallowed back the lump in her throat, enjoying their poignant memories. "Remember when you'd be in the backyard pool and you'd both tread water for as long as you could?"

Chester stared. Nodded.

"Neither of you had ever swum in a large lake before that day. Right?" She waited for Chester to shake his head. "You both didn't think the water would be any different than your backyard pool. You didn't know about rip currents. It happened so fast." She caressed his arm. More images came. "It wasn't your fault, Chester. He loved you so much. Brick fought to swim as hard as he could to push you to the surface. Do you remember him holding your foot and pushing you up?"

He leaned against his mother's leg. Samantha wrapped her arm around his shoulder.

"Brick wants you to remember the happy times you had together, and not the day he died. He showed you what a big brother's job was. When you become a big brother, he wants you to remember the things he taught you."

"I'm not a big brother. I'm younger."

Samantha burst into tears.

Jason gasped. "He hasn't spoken since Brick died."

Tes's heart sank. "You're not a big brother yet, but you will be." She glanced at his parents.

Samantha placed a protective hand over her abdomen. "We haven't told anyone."

"Brick knows," she explained.

Did you bring the rock? Brick asked.

Tes opened her purse. "Remember the rocks you painted that weekend?"

"We threw them in the lake." Chester's eyes appeared larger than they were, framed by his glasses.

"Do you remember what Brick wrote on his rock?"

"I can't read yet."

Tes smiled, palming the rock in her hand. "I was running on one of the mountain trails around here about a week ago and this rock appeared out of nowhere on my path." She opened her palm.

Samantha sucked in a sharp breath.

"Brick made this rock for you. It says, 'Big Brother'. He's always with you, Chester. Brick will keep watching over you, and if you ever want to talk to him..." She put the rock in Chester's hand. "Hold this and talk to him like he was sitting in front of you."

Tes watched Chester show the rock to his parents. "He's always with you. He loves you all very much."

Chester stared at her for a long time. "How did you get his rock?"

"He gave it to me, so I could give it to you." She waited. "Chester, it was Brick's time to go."

"No." His little lip pouted and tears fell.

"Yes. We all have a time when we can exit this world. He sacrificed his life so you could live. So your parents would only bury one boy that day and not two."

Samantha and Jason broke into sobs.

Joni passed them a box of tissues, grabbing one for herself.

"Brick knew all of this before he passed away. He'd had dreams for a long time before it happened." She gently took Chester's hand. "Death isn't for forever. It's just for now. You'll miss him, but he wants you to go on and be the best son in the world for your parents. He wants you to know he'll never be far from your side."

Sobs wracked his little body as he wrapped his arms tight around Tes's neck. She hugged him and patted his back. He pulled off his glasses as he swiped away his tears.

Samantha tugged his shirt so he would turn around and come back to his parents. Chester's dad was a blubbering mess as they held onto each other.

Tes got to her feet and wasn't sure if she should leave or stay. Joni patted the couch cushion next to her.

Opportunities like these didn't happen every day for Tes, but when she could use her gift to help others, it made her heart soar like this was what she should be doing. As she sat, she pulled her business card and a small bell from her purse. "You know, when I had these made a month ago, I didn't know about your situation." She slid three of her cards across the table. "On the back is a poem I tell my patients to say before they go to sleep." She held up her hand. "Sometimes saying the words out loud helps quiet your thoughts."

Samantha read the poem out loud. "I am safe. All is well. My heart is quiet as I ring the bell."

Tes handed Chester a bell. Chester rang it, as his mom continued to read. "Today is done. Today has passed. My body rests. Dreams come at last. My eyes are tired. I turn out the light. I will sleep soundly through the night."

"Mama, can we go home now? I'm tired."

Samantha stood. Jason lifted Chester into his arms. Tes was shocked when the pop star wrapped her in her arms. "Thank you," she whispered in her ear. "If I need to talk to you again, can I call you?"

"Of course. It's hard moving on after someone we love dies. It takes time and seasons to adapt. Time doesn't heal wounds. It gives us the space we need to adjust to coping with them. Call me any time."

Chester and Jason hugged her next. Chester rang the bell again, his eyelids growing heavy. "Tell Brick I love him and miss him."

"Sweetie, he already knows."

Brick smiled, leaned over, and placed a kiss on her cheek. *Thank you, Tes. I hope you can find your niece now.*

Tes dabbed at her own tears as Joni showed her guests to the door. She turned around. Asher stood in the kitchen. His lips were a thin line, his jaw taut. "Why didn't you tell me you were one of them?"

9

A sher wanted answers. Why didn't she tell him she was psychic? He'd made the biggest fool of himself at breakfast, insulting Joni, and, now he realized, Tes.

"It isn't like I walk around telling people sometimes I see the dead. I usually see little kids, Asher. Ones whose families are struggling because they've passed. Those are the spirits that come to me. I'm not like Joni. I can't see anyone I want to see."

He shook his head, not trusting his tongue.

"Are you mad at me?"

"You could have given me a little insight before I threw psychics under the bus." He waved a hand at the living room.

"I'm sorry. It isn't something I talk about."

He wanted to get this whole ghost business out in the air. He hated secrets. He hated when others kept secrets from him—secrets that he needed to know so he didn't make a fool of himself.

"What is it you have a hard time believing? That the dead walk among us, or that people can communicate with them?"

"I don't know. How long have you been speaking to ghosts?"

"Since I was struck by lightning and died when I was eight years old." Tes dropped her gaze to the floor.

Holy shit. Questions riddled his thoughts.

"My mother would humiliate me if I ever talked about seeing spirits, especially in front of her friends."

She looked ashamed for something she couldn't help. Damn, her family messed with her head and he wasn't helping matters.

"Please don't make fun of me," she whispered.

Now she was breaking his heart. He'd never make fun of her—not like that. He may tease her, prick at her controlled, orderly life, but he'd never criticize her for something she couldn't help. "I'd never do that. I'll work on my disbelief." He turned around to see Zeke standing behind him, arms crossed and a lopsided grin sliding up one side of his face.

"I knew she was psychic when I met her. My wife knew. How didn't you know?"

"Maybe because we met yesterday." Every paranormal movie with haunting, ghoulish children flashed through Asher's memory. Damn. Nope. *Don't want to see child ghosts.*

Asher turned so he didn't have his back to Zeke. Something about the look in his eyes made him a man not to mess with. It was the kind of look that made Asher want Zeke on his side in a bar fight.

"Yesterday?" Joni joined the group, wrapping her arm around Tes's shoulders. "I thought you two had been married for years. You have that aura about you. Like you were meant to be together."

Joni was feeding him a line of crap. Wasn't she? He couldn't deny he was attracted to Tes. Why would a doctor fall for someone who built houses for a living? Someone who liked getting into muck up to his elbows and fixing things that broke? She deserved someone who was as intellectual as she was. Someone who could discuss Chaucer, high tea, and which fork went with which serving. Not a plastic-fork, paper-plate kind of guy like him. No. He'd rather be her friend because relationships that start with intense situations didn't always have staying power—even if she was beautiful, talked to ghosts, and for the first time since May he didn't wallow in his own misery.

Joni motioned toward the living room. "LeBron will be here any moment. Please, come sit. Can I get you anything? Some fresh-squeezed lemonade or iced tea?"

"Iced tea, please," Tes answered.

"Lemonade for me. Thank you." Asher gently took her elbow and led her to the couch.

Tom came down the stairs. "Sammy's asleep."

"Thank you, Tom." Joni kissed his cheek.

"I'm sorry to disappoint you, Asher." Tes's voice was weak, barely above a whisper.

"You're not a disappointment. Dammit, Tes, don't ever say that." Asher grabbed her hand, engulfing it in his. "I don't—I mean didn't—believe in psychics because I've been burned. I wish you would have said something."

"Sure, that would have gone over well. Hi, I'm Tes and I see little ghost children."

Asher almost laughed. "Yeah. I see what you mean."

"I tried to tell you at breakfast that Joni was different, but you were so hellbent on protecting me from the posers." She squeezed his hand. "And I appreciate that."

That almost made him feel better. "Any more secrets you want to tell me?"

"Yes, but not today."

He smiled. "Yeah, I suppose we all have secrets."

"And it's okay not to share them."

"Agreed."

One day Tes would learn he was Morgan's father, but he had a few years. By then, their friendship would be on solid ground and she'd still like him afterward. Maybe. If he was lucky.

Tom entered the room carrying glasses for each of them. "Tes, can you grab the coasters from the top drawer?"

She opened the coffee table's top drawer and placed several around the table. "Thank you, Tom."

Tom sat next to Tes and took a drink. "I'm glad you two came to Joni and Zeke. Their team is top notch and can tackle a case from every angle possible. When I retire, I'm joining their team."

"When are you retiring?" Tes asked.

"As soon as we find Hailey and Morgan."

Asher swallowed some lemonade to loosen the lump that tightened his throat. "I appreciate it, Tom. My family is indebted to you for helping coach us through this nightmare."

"It's my job—I'd like to do more of this kind of work." Tom paused, hearing a door open off the hallway.

A tall, Black man entered the living room, a tablet secured with a strap to his hand like a TV news anchor. "Hey. You must be Asher Hickok and Dr. Tesla Brynn. Tom."

Asher shook the man's hand. "Yes."

"I'm LeBron Jacobs—tech support." He shook Tes's hand before sitting across from them. Joni and Zeke settled on the couch on either side of him. "I've reviewed the text messages sent to Morgan yesterday before her abduction. Tom forwarded the 911 call as well. I've cleaned up some of the background noise." He lifted his left hand with the tablet.

Tom braced his elbows on his knees, his pen and notebook ready.

***

Tes took a deep breath and tried to center her jumbled nerves. Emotions ricocheted in her stomach. Asher wrapped his arm around her shoulders, pulling her close to his side as if he could shield her from the news they were about to hear.

"Your niece, Morgan," LeBron started, "was taken at 3:05 yesterday afternoon. Having the exact time is helpful. Calling 911 to timestamp the event was smart."

She rubbed her sweaty palms against her jeans.

"The pictures sent to Morgan were sent from a burner phone." LeBron tapped on the tablet's screen, showing the progression of pictures. "He didn't take these all at the same time. The blue sweatshirt is different in the last picture. According to the crime scene photos, the stairway would have ample light this time of year, but natural lighting is somewhat minimal in the last picture." His long fingers flicked across the screen. "From what I can tell from the lighting, these pictures were taken around late January this year."

Tes snapped her gaze to Asher. "Well before Hailey was taken."

"You'll notice that the sweatshirt shows the hoodie ties as flat and straight, like it was brand-new in the first picture, but in subsequent pictures the ties are kinked and frayed a little." LeBron magnified the pictures. "Sorry they're grainy, but it's hard to zoom in on details of someone else's poor pictures."

"How many times had he been inside Nikki's house?" Tes shook her head. "He has to be a friend of Morgan's."

"Maybe." LeBron drew their attention. "Since I do contractual work for the government, I was able to gain access to satellite photos from yesterday."

Tes leaned closer.

"A new picture is taken every minute, but from the progression of pictures, we happened to catch the kidnapper hauling Morgan over his shoulder through the backyard."

Tes gasped. "To where? The lake?"

"Yes." LeBron widened the picture. "There's a small rowboat with an outboard motor on it tied to the dock. Of course, as soon as I saw this, I notified Tom."

Tom said, "Agents are going door-to-door asking if anyone has a security camera facing the lake. If we're lucky, we might get a picture of the kidnapper's face."

Tes covered her mouth with her hand. "The roadblocks they put up may not have helped."

"That's the interesting part." LeBron glanced at Krysinski. "It took me a while to find where the public boat launch was from the satellite." He tapped on the map. "You can see here. He left her in the boat covered by a tarp while he drove away. Before the roadblocks were put in place."

Tom leaned over Tes to see the photo. "Did you check traffic cameras?"

"I did, after calculating the time he'd need to get to each light." He shook his head. "The black pickup pulling the small boat wasn't at any traffic light. Remember, traffic lights take a still picture about every five minutes or longer, so he had a big-enough window to drive through the area unseen."

"He had to have gone somewhere." Tes hated how whiny her voice sounded. "Maybe he pulled into a garage?"

"I ran an algorithm on which houses would have a large-enough space to park a boat of this size." His mouth quirked. "Too many, unfortunately."

"How many have black pickups parked out front?" Asher asked.

Tom sighed. "We're making a list of anyone who owns black pickups in Whitman and the surrounding area. It's going to take a while."

The small glimmer of hope LeBron had offered yielded nothing. "Thank you for trying." Tes felt for Asher's hand. "We appreciate it."

"Tom asked me to look into Hailey's disappearance about a month ago." LeBron changed files. "We can tie the same kidnapper to both incidents." He enlarged a picture of a man hauling Hailey over the kidnapper's shoulder to a back alley. "He prefers to use a backdoor exit—less chance of being seen. In Hailey's case, I was able to look at traffic light cameras and found one that matched the truck's description. The license plate isn't readable, but the person driving is a white male." He cleared his throat. "*If* this is the same vehicle. It looks similar, but black pickups are a dime a dozen. But this one—" He showed a new picture "—also shows a blue tarp covering the pickup bed. I compared this to the tarp covering the boat and they have one distinctive feature."

LeBron smiled. "Duct tape in the corner. Here." He showed a circle on one picture, then scrolled to another picture. "And here, covering the boat from yesterday. I believe we can use this to identify the kidnapper."

"How are we going to find that duct-taped tarp, though?" Tes's heart sank. It was like having an assembled thousand-piece puzzle with one missing key piece. In the end, it wasn't complete. They weren't closer to finding Morgan or Hailey.

"That's not all I have."

Asher squeezed her shoulder.

"Remember the sounds you heard during the 911 call?"

"The gunshots?"

"They weren't gunshots." LeBron minimized the images on the screen and brought up new charts. "I compared the sounds on the call against gunshots and the closest I came up with was a pellet or dart gun."

"Not enough to wound Morgan?" Tes clutched to the brief victory. "What kind of dart gun would he have used? Those have to be regulated, right?"

"No." LeBron glanced at Tom. "They're pretty easy to buy. They're not like a regular firearm. However, I scanned anyone who'd purchased one in the last two years, and I narrowed the list to a little over seventy-five people locally."

"Why would anyone need a dart gun?" Tes looked to Tom for an answer. "Morgan was already drugged. Mixing in an additional drug could have killed her."

"He might have missed the first shot." Tom furrowed his brow. "He more than likely couldn't guarantee Morgan had enough of the oral drug to make her completely incapacitated. He needed her unconscious or paralyzed to move her quickly without resistance."

Tes didn't want to think of how the diabolical kidnapper executed his plan.

"The white lettering at the bottom of Morgan's pictures," LeBron said, drawing their attention back to the picture, "says—"

"Ready or not," Tes finished. "Morgan told me that on the phone. What kind of sick bastard sends someone these types of pictures with that kind of warning?"

Tom explained, "It implies, 'Here I come'. Coupled with the photos, it served its intent —to scare them."

True, Morgan had been terrified.

"At first glance, it looks like it's a common font." LeBron's finger hesitated a moment before he advanced the screen. "It's a font called Bonafide, modified to 8.5 height. Very specific. I like that this guy is specific."

Tes didn't like it at all, nor did she understand why that would matter.

"It'll help us narrow our suspect pool," Tom said. "LeBron can run a cross-check between people who've downloaded that font, with dart-gun purchases, and those who own black pickups." He patted her arm. "We're going to find them, Tes."

LeBron showed a composite of all the pictures layered on top of another. "He's in his early twenties. Slight frame, but strong enough to carry a hundred pounds." His deft fingers clicked on more folders. "I've come up with a list of people who Hailey and Morgan know through social media. I've eliminated immediate family, like your dad and brothers, Asher. It's clearly not a woman, so I've removed all of those as well." He handed the tablet to Tes and she shared the screen with Asher.

"I had no idea they knew so many young, white men." Tes's heart sank. They weren't ever going to find them.

LeBron took back the tablet. "Some of the men on the lists are brothers of the girls they knew from high school. If it's a younger man, my guess is that he knows where they live, he knows their routine, and he knows them well enough to know where they may possibly hide a key outside the house. Did your sister keep a key outside the house?"

A dull headache formed in Tes's temples. "I don't know. She never told me about one, but that doesn't mean there isn't one."

"Hailey's mom did." Asher ran his hand through his hair. "Every guy she ever dated knew where it was. She didn't have a lot of discretion about who slept on her couch. If you needed a place to crash, she'd let them in."

"I'm glad Hailey lived with you." Tes leaned into Asher.

Asher caressed her shoulder. "How are we going to find them?"

"I'm still cross-referencing dart-gun purchasers with black pickup owners, by residence. Since our alleged kidnapper is young, the vehicle or dart-gun may not be his but belong to someone in the household. For now, I'm staying within the high school boundary lines. Then the FBI will do the door-to-door check from there—after they have warrants. Usually in kidnapping cases, warrants can be obtained quickly." LeBron sat back for a moment. "Now it's Joni's turn to explain how she helps in our investigations."

Asher blew out his breath.

Tes squeezed his hand. "You can do this."

"Listening." He rolled his eyes.

"I have helpers on the other side." Joni leaned forward.

"Spirit guides," Tes offered.

"Really?" Asher raised a dubious brow. "Who are your spirit guides?"

"Children." She avoided looking at Asher. "Sometimes I've met them before. Not always."

"How do you know what they're saying is from them and not from some demonic force?"

She patted his leg. "That's your church upbringing and Hollywood talking, not reality. At least not my reality." She tilted her head. "You just know. It's a gut thing."

Asher cocked a corner of his mouth. "I'm so glad I don't have that gift."

"You will." LeBron glanced at his tablet again. "You hang with them long enough, their world spills over into yours. It's inevitable."

"You see dead people?" Asher pinned LeBron with a disbelieving stare.

"I see them. Hear them. Sometimes, they touch me—that's when I scream like a little girl. Joni always knows when I've been touched." He smiled. "Zeke loves ribbing me about it. He was the biggest skeptic when we met him. He didn't believe ghosts were real, either—and he'd been up to his eyeballs surrounded by dead people while working on a case."

Asher's Adam's apple bobbed. "Why were you surrounded by ghosts?"

"I was a detective," Zeke answered. "I think that's why Tom and I bonded so fast."

A thought popped into Tes's head. "Speak easy." She looked at Joni. "That's the message from your spirit guides."

"How did you know that?" Joni asked.

"I heard it. In my mind."

"If Christian starts talking to you, let me know." Joni took a sip of her iced tea. "Mambo Janetta also sends messages. She has a thick southern accent. I'm going to ask her to work with you, so you can hone your gift. Right now, it seems to be more random than purposeful."

"Who's Christian?" Asher asked.

"Christian was my twin brother," Joni answered.

Tes could see a man standing in the kitchen dressed in a black suit with a matching thin black tie and white shirt. His blond hair dipped across his forehead. He was a handsome guy who looked nothing like Joni. "Was Christian in the CIA?"

Zeke glanced at Joni. "Why do you ask?"

"He dresses like he was."

"He liked us all to believe he was a G-man, but in the end, we never found out who he was." LeBron's hand went back to moving across the screen.

"You can see him?" Asher whispered in her ear. "Right now?"

Tes nodded.

"Where?"

"Over there." She pointed.

"I don't see anything."

"That's why I'm psychic and you're not." A smile tugged at the corners of her mouth.

Christian didn't seem threatening. Tes pleaded with the ghost. *Find them. Tell them we want them home. Show them a way to escape.* He tilted his head and faded. It gave her comfort to know she could enlist trusted spirits into their ranks. She hadn't heard from her dad since he passed. He'd help if he could.

Asher stood and helped Tes to her feet. "Thank you, LeBron. With your help, we're going to be able to find them. We want them home sooner than later."

"I understand." He stood and held out his hand.

Tom shook LeBron's hand next. "With this new evidence, we'll see if we can narrow our list of suspects further. You're always a great help, LeBron. Greatly appreciated."

"If it brings them home, that's all that matters."

Joni and Zeke stood, moving toward the front door. "I know you're new to the area, Tes, but when you get settled and are looking for a job, I'm hoping you will consider working for our foundation. It's a business Zeke and I started to help people like yourself. People who need psychic help—the Paranormal Intelligence Foundation."

"What could I possibly do for you? I'm a psychiatrist."

Joni smiled. "Oh, I can think of a million reasons to have you on our team. If anything, to do what you did for Chester. I fall apart when children are involved. Please, Tes, say you'll consider it?"

"I've already downloaded the foundation's app on both of your phones." LeBron's fingers flicked across his tablet. "I put Joni's app on your phone—so you two can chat ghosty stuff."

Tes chuckled. "How can you do that without my permission?"

He smiled. "Magic."

"Either way." Joni squeezed her arm. "I'm so glad I met you. I hope we can grow to be good friends."

"I'd like that." Tes was making friends. That was a first too.

10

Tes's eyelids grew heavy on the ride back to Asher's house. Anxiety skittered along her nerves. She hoped that ghosts worked faster than algorithms and detectives. She might as well relax and sleep the twenty or so minutes it'd take to cross town.

Someone turned the lever on the old Victrola, giving the Charleston a tinny whine in her ear. The red, black, and gold décor was obscured in hazy, thick cigar smoke. She wore a glittering black headband to match her black coiffed hair and danced along with a couple of other girls, flipping their legs in time with the music. Her beaded dress bounced and swayed with each step, and she was fully cognizant of Aston leaning against the bar. He stared back. She knew him—in the Biblical way. He was her lover but not her husband. Her husband sat at a gambling table along with other staunch men chewing cigars that dangled from their lips and tossing coins in the middle of the table. The dealer dealt cards for another round. She watched her husband's eyes shift from her to Aston. She swallowed hard. He knew. Damn, she wished she could hide the look on her face. She should have run away with Aston when he'd offered. He was her bodyguard. Her protector. Her only friend in a crowd of false faces. The pretenders. The moochers. The ones controlling her life.

"Hey, La-La," her husband shouted above the din. "Get me another scotch—and be quick about it."

Tes moved to the bar. Don't look at Aston—it'll give you away. Yet, she couldn't fight the urge to gaze at his smoldering strong features. His five-o'clock shadow framed his strong jaw, and all she wanted was to be in his bed, consumed in his love. Aston didn't give her away, but she did when she smiled at him from across the room as she placed the scotch in front of her husband.

Other lifetimes where they'd met and failed at happiness rushed through her mind like microfiche scrolling through old newspaper headlines. A medieval monk and a nun.

They were lovers. She died in childbirth, disgraced. As pilgrims, they were children, friends, and dead before the first winter in the harsh new land. He was a soldier fighting for the North, she was a southern belle. His troop invaded her family's plantation. He seduced her. She loved him, but it was only a day before he died.

In another lifetime, she sat by an old woman's hearth. The fire soothed her skin, but not her heart. She was desperate for answers, or else she wouldn't have come. The fortune-teller held her hand.

"How can I be rid of this curse?"

"Love professed foretells love failed."

A ringtone jolted Tes awake. *What was up with the strange dreams?* She wished she could dream of where Morgan was being held.

Asher connected the call, glancing at the caller ID displayed on the center console. He clicked a button on his steering column. "Hey, Dad."

"Hey, Ash," Grant greeted through the truck's speakers. "Could you drop by Mrs. Wallen's house? She's saying she has a pipe leaking underneath the kitchen sink. Again. I swear that woman loosens her own pipes just so she'll have company once a week."

"Sure, we're not far from her place." He glanced at Tes. "You don't mind, do you? It'll be a quick in and out. It being the Fourth of July, she'll probably have baked us a pie."

"Sure." She waved a hand.

"See you soon." Asher ended the call.

The three-story, blue, gray, and white Victorian with the wraparound porch filled the clearing. A sign long in need of a new coat of paint read "Wallen Bed and Breakfast." A "Closed" sign hung on rusted hooks.

"The place was too much for Mrs. Wallen to keep up after her husband died. Her son's considering reviving it now that he's getting closer to retirement." Asher lowered the windows before turning off the engine. "You okay?"

She waved a hand. "I'm fine. Sorry for falling asleep."

"No problem. Did you get any sleep last night?"

"None. Thank you for understanding."

Asher cracked the door. "It won't take but a minute to tighten the valve."

"I can wait here."

"Nice breeze today."

Her phone buzzed. "It's Joni."

"Be right back." Asher jumped from the truck, plucked his toolbox from the compartment under the backseat bench, and headed up the graceful porch steps.

"Hi." Tes opened the truck door, held onto the handle, and eased to the ground. She needed to stretch her legs.

"I'm loving that we have an app to connect through."

"It's convenient, for sure," Tes answered. "I'm hoping LeBron can find Hailey and Morgan."

"If you and Asher don't have plans for tonight, you're more than welcome to join us to shoot off fireworks. You can meet the rest of the team."

Tes wasn't ready to belong to a team. "That's so sweet of you, but we're having a barbecue with Asher's family." She didn't know if it was true but celebrating seemed wrong. Since first impressions couldn't be redone, she'd rather not meet strangers in her frazzled state of mind.

"I know. Too soon. I get it. I'm being overly enthusiastic to have met someone who has gifts as strong as my own."

"It feels great to meet a kindred spirit. I can't tell you how natural it felt to chat with you today. I appreciate it." Tes took a few paces and stopped under a maple tree's shade. It must be at least four hundred years old. She rubbed her hand against the rough bark. "I've worked hard to become a psychiatrist. I don't want to waste my education."

"I understand." Joni sounded disappointed. "Maybe you can be a consultant for the team. You know, when we need help with kids."

"That would be lovely." Tes glanced at the porch. The hairs on the back of her neck rose. An old woman stood in front of the screen door staring at her.

Something was off. The tilt of her head. The way her hands dangled at the ends of her wrists. She turned her head back inside the house. Her shoulders listed, followed by her hips.

Chills raised the little hairs over Tes's body.

Oh God. Not again. Not now. "Ah, Joni. I gotta go."

***

Asher knocked on Mrs. Wallen's screen door before opening it and letting himself in. She was somewhere in her nineties and he knew getting out of a chair wasn't easy for her. "Mrs. Wallen," he called. "It's Asher. I'm here to fix the pipe in your kitchen."

He saw her hand raise from the den where a game show blared over the TV.

Even though Asher's dad had remodeled the kitchen twenty years ago, its light-yellow paint and blue plaid curtains still looked nice. The white-tiled counter had three apple pies cooling on racks, and a plate of chocolate-chip cookies. "I'm eating your cookies," he shouted, hoping his voice droned above the gameshow host and track laughter. She made the best cookies. Asher paused while the chocolaty gooey sweetness melted across his tongue.

His family had been dropping by to check on Mrs. Wallen most of his life. And no one left Mrs. Wallen's house without eating. It didn't matter if you'd just finished a Thanksgiving-sized foodie binge, you still shoved something in your mouth, or she'd be deeply offended.

Asher laid on his back, head deep under Mrs. Wallen's kitchen sink. He wrapped the wrench around the pipe and tightened.

"Roses are red, violets are blue. Don't say I love you, until you say I do."

Asher paused. "Mrs. Wallen?" He scooted out from under the sink, sitting up.

Mrs. Wallen's feet didn't touch the floor. Her arms were at a ninety-degree angle from her elbows, hands dangling at the end of her wrists. Her knees lifted her blue dress with tiny daisies, like a marionette's, not quite touching the ground as she glided closer. Her arms bobbed, her hands jiggled, and her head tilted from side to side. "Roses are red—"

Asher tossed his wrench in his toolbox. *Holy fucking shit.* "What's wrong, Mrs. Wallen?" He got to his feet. "Do you need some medication?"

"Violets are blue. Don't say I love you, until you say I do."

The back door slammed open. A blond man in a black suit and thin black tie propped open the screen door with a hand. "Run!"

He glanced back at Mrs. Wallen. Her skin was pale, maybe a little gray. Her bottom jaw moved, but her lips didn't form the words. "Roses are red—"

Asher grabbed his toolbox and ran out the back door. He jumped, thudding hard against the sidewalk. He came around the side of the house, beelining for his truck. He glanced to the dining room window as he ran by. Mrs. Wallen skated along the windows like she was on a conveyor belt at the airport, staring at him. *Shit.* "Tes! Get in the truck!"

Tes was near the front door.

"Hurry!" he yelled.

She glanced at the screen door and jumped off the porch, running full tilt.

He tossed his tools into the truck's bed and was in the seat, door closed and keys in hand as Tes pulled her door shut.

He locked the doors.

His fingers jumbled over his keys, searching for the right one. *Shit. Work faster.* He slipped it into the ignition and pulled up on the window levers, willing them to roll up faster. "Come on, come on, come on."

The battery's energy drained. "No. No. No. *Not now.*"

The windows had an inch to go and wouldn't budge. *Click. Click. Click.* "Dammit!" He hit the dashboard. "The battery's dead."

Mrs. Wallen appeared outside the passenger side window, staring at Tes. Her aged, bony, liver-spotted fingers curled over the edge of the passenger side door glass. "Don't say I love you, until you say I do."

Tes trembled, tears lacing her eyelashes. She stared at him instead of Mrs. Wallen clutching at her window.

Asher tried the engine again. *Nothing.*

"I'm sorry," Tes whispered. "I have to do this."

"I'll do it." Asher didn't want to unlock the door and pry Mrs. Wallen away from his truck, but whatever had come over her, it wasn't Tes's responsibility.

"Asher."

Something in her tone made him stop and look at her.

She began rubbing her hands back and forth vigorously. "Whatever you do, don't touch me." Her stare intensified. "It'll kill you."

He frowned. *What the hell was she talking about?*

Sparks arced between her hands as she pulled them apart like threads of contained lightning.

Mrs. Wallen frantically slammed her hands against the window, shaking the truck.

"What are you doing?" He'd watched his favorite old person become the creepiest thing he'd ever seen and now Tes was stretching bands of lightning in her hands? What the hell? Was he dreaming? Was he caught in someone else's nightmare?

She placed her hands on the dashboard, and the white bands of energy skittered along the surface. "Try the engine now."

"Roses are red, violets are blue," Mrs. Wallen continued. Her nails scraped against the glass, sending willies the size of Texas up Asher's back.

He swallowed back his fear, his questions, his doubt about what Tes did, what Mrs. Wallen was doing. It was all freaky as hell. He stomped a foot on the clutch, the other on the brake. The engine turned. Asher shoved the gear into reverse and pinned the ghoul with a firm stare. "Get off my truck, Mrs. Wallen."

The bright summer sky vanished in the blink of an eye, casting them in darkness. He leaned forward and saw dark, threatening storm clouds rolling overhead. The stench of rotten eggs filled the air, like someone had cut the worst fart ever. "Whoa." Asher waved a hand. "Get off my truck, Mrs. Wallen."

"Don't say—"

A thick, black arm snaked around Mrs. Wallen's waist, yanking her from the running board and tossing her to the ground.

What stood there now was something Asher's mind couldn't comprehend. Solid black. Deep charcoal-gray eyes. Spiky head. Jagged teeth. It stared at Tes. *Growled.* Black goo dripped from its lips.

"What the hell is that?"

Tes shook harder. "I'm going to guess it's a demon."

The demon made a fist and broke the glass, grabbing Tes's arm.

She turned her head away as glass shards flew in the air and she screamed.

The scent of foul, burning flesh filled the cabin. Sparks flew around the demon's hand. Lightning threaded up his arm. It smiled, absorbing the energy.

A sound emitted from Tes, like a transformer amping juice. Every hair on Asher's body stood on end. He took his hands off the steering wheel. Would his rubber soles ground him? She reeled back her free hand, a bright light splintering inside the cab. A loud crashing sound came as she hit the demon square in the chest. The demon screeched, letting go of Tes's arm, falling away. Or disappearing. It didn't matter. No demon meant it was time to leave.

Asher stomped on the gas and looked over his shoulder, backing up. He shifted into first, popped the clutch, and was ready to shift into second as they came to the road. He didn't see any cars and punched it. They were a mile away before he could swallow his stomach back into place. The sun reappeared. "What the hell happened?"

Tes wrapped her arms around her legs, sobbing. She rocked back and forth. "Hurry."

She held her hands away from her legs. Her fingers were blue with dark blue streaks spreading from her hands, over her wrists, and up her arms.

"Are you in pain?"

Nodding, she pressed her lips together, but she wouldn't look at him.

"You've seen this before, haven't you?"

Again, she nodded.

"What the hell happened to Mrs. Wallen? Was she a ghost?"

"No." She sucked in a breath between clenched teeth. "She was worse than a ghost."

"What's worse than a ghost?" Asher knew he was yelling, but the circumstance called for it.

"A living corpse."

Holy Mother, what the fuck? Did she say corpse? "Is she dead?"

"Obviously."

It may be obvious to Tes, but to him? Mrs. Wallen looked tired, her skin a bit loose but, hell, the woman was ancient. Mrs. Wallen grew up in that house. She'd raised a big family there and grew a thriving business. She'd never pranced around soulless and spouting poetry. No one would believe him if he told them the truth. If Mrs. Wallen was dead, he needed to tell the authorities. *Shit.* That was a phone call he sure as hell didn't want to make. Would it appear like he'd killed her?

"Zombies aren't real," he muttered under his breath. Yet, Mrs. Wallen wasn't alive. Did a demon break his window? *Oh, hell no.* No one would believe that.

Tes's fingers curled. Her hands shook. Was she trying to contain the electricity she'd started the truck with?

The tires screeched to a halt in front of his house. He got out and around to Tes's door as fast as he could.

"Don't touch me." She unraveled her body and carefully lowered herself without touching her hands to any surface. She looked around and walked over to the landscaped circular island that formed his driveway. She dropped to her knees and placed her hands on the ground.

The marigolds, pansies, and phlox doubled in size. The bushes grew too. The grass beyond the driveway started to grow, turning a lush green during a normally dead-grass season. The wave of greenery continued far across the lawn, reaching his brother August's house. The ivy he'd planted last spring wound around the trellis as it grew.

Bippity-boppity-boo. What the hell?

Tes's back heaved as she drew each deep breath. Finally, she sat up, leaning back on her heels. She wiped the back of her hand across her forehead. The dark blue streaks were gone from her hands, but she wasn't flesh-toned either. He started to help her up, but she jerked away.

"I said, don't touch me," she snapped.

He yanked his hand back. What could he say to comfort her? Did her family know she could do this? How often had it happened?

She got to her feet. Her lips were blue, her face ash gray.

"Tes, who should I call? You need medical attention."

She shook her head, tightening her lips. "May I please use your bathroom?" She still wouldn't look at him, dammit. She examined her wrist where the demon had touched her. The red burn had faded to a light scar. Was she healing that fast?

"Of course." He led the way to his front door and unlocked it. He stepped out of the way so she could enter and not risk brushing up against him, then opened the bathroom door.

"Wow, even your bathroom's beautiful. You're incredibly gifted." She shut the door with her foot.

Asher paced back and forth in front of the door. The toilet flushed. The water turned on. Good, she was almost done. Another five minutes ticked by. *Come on, Tes, come out so I know you're okay.* "Do you need me to open the door for you?"

"No. I can do it."

Another minute clicked by. The grandmother clock on the wall in the hall echoed in the foyer. What is she waiting for? Was she scared to face him? Was she embarrassed?

The knob turned. She held a towel over the handle and once the door was open, she folded it and put it back on the counter. Her lips and eyes were swollen.

"Thank you for offering to let me stay here. I truly appreciate it."

No way in hell was she walking away without talking about what had happened. "You're not going anywhere."

"I'll grab Ruthie and be out of your way." She hesitated before she grabbed Ruthie's harness and her working-dog vest from the counter, avoiding contact with any metal.

"Why don't we talk about the big fucking elephant in the room?" Asher shoved his fingers through his hair out of frustration. He wanted to grab her, make her look at him, and sure as hell get answers to the nine million questions bouncing around in his head.

She winced, closing her eyes.

He dropped his hands and tried a different approached. He calmed his tone as much as he could. Through tight lips, he said, "Please, Tes. Sit. Let's talk this through."

Tes stepped to the back door. *Oh, she better not be going for the dog. She wouldn't dare.*

Asher turned his gaze to see what Tes was looking at. Mom soaped Ruthie in their backyard dog washing station. Tango was sopping wet and gnawing a bone at his dad's feet by the backyard brick fire pit. His brothers sipped beer and chewed the fat with Dad.

Tes wrapped her hand in Ruthie's working vest and opened the back door.

"Tes, please. Talk to me."

She rested her forehead against the doorframe. "All of my life, I've wanted to meet someone like you. Someone who made me feel safe. Someone—" her voice cracked. "I'm so sorry."

"You have nothing to be sorry about. What the hell happened?"

Her lips whitened as she bit them hard. Tears plopped onto her cheeks.

"Honey, you're breaking my heart." He put his hand on the doorjamb above her head. "Tes, don't shut me out."

"How could you ever trust someone like me?" She swiped the backs of her hands across her eyes, making her way over to his family.

Asher pulled the door closed behind him. The July heat smacked him in the face along with a mosquito. He swatted it away. For a damned psychiatrist, she sure as hell couldn't sit and talk about her feelings. Why was she being so damned stubborn? It pissed him off that she wouldn't sit and explain what the hell had happened to Mrs. Wallen.

"Thank you for giving Ruthie a bath, Mrs. Hickok."

"You okay, Tessie?" Dad asked.

"Yeah," she whispered.

"You look a little pale. Why don't you take a seat and rest a moment, okay?" His dad tapped the armrest of the chair next to him.

"I should be going." Her shoulders slumped.

"Where to? We're about to fire up the grill for dinner." Dad looked at him and then back to Tes. "What happened?"

Fireworks blasted at the neighbor's house, reminding him this should be a day people celebrated. Instead, it would be forever etched in his mind as Hell Day. "You wouldn't believe me if I told you." Asher's phone buzzed in his pocket. He pulled it out and saw Zeke's face fill his screen. When did his number get added to his phone? He hit the screen and accepted the call. "Hey, Zeke."

"Christian told us what happened. Krysinski's en route to the Wallen residence."

He turned his back and walked out of earshot of his family. "Joni's dead brother?"

"The guy in the suit."

The guy that opened the back door and told him to run? "Oh. Him." He barely registered what he'd looked like.

"You saw him?" Zeke paused followed by a muffled "Asher saw Christian."

Joni replied to her husband, "Great. He's coming out of his shell."

What the fuck? He didn't have a damn shell to come out of. "Tes isn't doing so well. She's insisting on leaving. Something went wrong."

"We'll send Dr. Whitefeather to you. He's a medicine man. He'll be able to help."

Last thing Asher wanted to count on was more mumbo-jumbo and weird shit. "I can take her to the emergency room."

Joni said something he couldn't make out. Zeke said, "The last thing you can do is take her where there may be more dead people. Keep her there. Help's on the way."

Asher ended the call. What did they know that he didn't? Had Mrs. Wallen become the walking dead because of Tes?

"Come on, Ruthie. We have to go."

Asher turned around to see Tes hand Ruthie's harness to his brother August. Asher shook his head, signaling his brother that he wasn't to put it on the dog.

"She needs to dry off first." August tucked the harness behind him.

"Please." Tes's voice cracked.

Mom stood, wiping her hands off on a towel. "Tes, honey, you don't look so good. Why don't you come inside and lie down?" She jerked her head toward their house.

"Thank you, Mrs. Hickok, but I need to get going." Her shoulders lifted as she took a deep breath.

Was it his imagination or had she lost weight? Her jeans looked baggy and her shirt draped across her back. Oh my God, what was happening to her? Did using lightning take that much out of her?

Tes almost tripped over her own feet, turning around. "Come on, Ruthie. We need to go." She staggered forward, staring at the ground, doing her best to take another step. One wavering step left caused her to put her arms out to balance before trying to step right. Shit, she was about to faint, and he wasn't allowed to touch her.

"Tes!" He ran to her side.

She dropped to her knees.

Asher put his arm out to catch her. Ruthie hit him square in the chest, knocking him out of the way as Tes face-planted into the grass, butt sticking up in the air. Ruthie barked in his face, keeping him away.

His family gathered to Tes's side.

"Don't touch her. Not yet." Asher held onto Ruthie.

The grass grew tall and lush around Tes. Dandelions sprouted around her fingers.

"What the hell?" Dad took a step back.

Mom stepped closer, kneeling beside Tes. Ruthie barked. "It's all right, girl. I'm not going to touch her. What's happening?" She slid one of those mom looks at Asher like he better spill his guts and tell the truth. She'd know if he was lying.

Tango crouched low, saddling to Mom's side. He sniffed at Tes, startled, and jumped back. His ears went straight back and he lowered his head. The deep growl he emitted was a sound of warning, out of fear. If Tes moved, Asher was sure Tango would lurch and bite her.

Asher looked at his family's concerned faces as they stared at Tes. "Yeah, it's been quite the day."

Mom crossed herself. "Is she dead?"

Ruthie smelled Tes, her head lowered, ready to bark if anyone came near her. They waited until the grass stopped growing and the dandelions changed from petals to seed, blowing on the summer breeze.

"Never seen that before." Dad swore under his breath.

"I'll call 911." Aaron pulled his phone out of his back pocket.

"No." Asher waved a hand. "A doctor's on the way. One that can help her." He hoped the medicine man could help Tes. He was scared to think what might cure whatever she had. He knelt beside her. "Can I touch her, girl?" He smoothed a hand along Ruthie's damp back.

She touched Tes's back and barked.

11

Asher carried Tes inside and laid her on his bed. Her gray-hued face looked pale against his navy-blue sheets. Was she breathing? Her chest wasn't moving. He felt her wrist for a pulse. None. He put two fingers on her neck. Thump. *You can't die on me, Tes.*

Mom sat on the other side of the bed and held Tes's hand. "Poor thing. What happened?"

They'd think he was a lunatic if he told the truth. He shook his head, clamping his lips tight. He needed time to process what the hell happened before he said a word.

Dad and his brothers, August and Aaron, came in the room. Ruthie jumped on the bed, and Tango crowded in too. Ruthie licked Tes's face. She didn't react. Dog breath would have jarred him awake.

The doorbell rang.

Asher looked at August. "That should be the doctor Joni and Zeke mentioned. Do you mind getting the door?"

August was out the room before any of them could respond.

"He must have been in the neighborhood." Mom grabbed the edge of his blanket. Asher removed Tes's shoes. Her toes were blue. Long blue lines spread up her feet, disappearing under her jeans. Mom pulled back the covers while he put his arm underneath Tes's legs and lifted her butt so they could get her under the covers. He pulled the blanket over her chest. Maybe she was in shock.

The medicine man carried a small carry-on suitcase and a bottle of oxygen. He placed the items in the hall, put his hands together, and bowed. "Aho." He picked up his items and entered the room. "I'm Dr. Whitefeather."

His black hair was woven into a long braid that hung to his waist. Asher could only imagine his dad's opinion and prayed he wouldn't say anything. Grown men didn't wear braids in their family. The doctor wore a simple white shirt and jeans with a pair of brown moccasins.

Asher moved out of the way. "I'm Asher Hickok. Are you also a regular doctor?"

Whitefeather pulled a stethoscope and blood pressure cuff out of his suitcase. "Yes. I'm a medical doctor and a medicine man." He frowned at the dial showing Tes's stats. Without hesitation, he removed the cuff and slipped a tourniquet around her arm, patting the back of her hand. "She's dehydrated. I'm going to give her some fluids and electrolytes."

"Is she going to be okay?" Asher and his mom asked at the same time.

Dr. Whitefeather paused before answering. "She's in the Shadowlands. It's up to her to decide if she wants to return."

She has to return. "Shadowlands?" Asher swallowed, his throat tightening.

Dr. Whitefeather concentrated on her IV line. Once he was done, he turned to them. "She's in between life and death."

"Like in a coma?" Asher stared at Tes's lifeless form.

"Kind of. Were you with her when this happened?"

Asher swallowed. "Yes."

"Do you want to tell me what happened in front of your family or alone?"

Aw, shit. This was serious. Asher glanced at his family's faces. "You might as well hear what happened, but if you believe me, it'll be a miracle."

"You're not a liar, Son." Dad clamped a hand on his shoulder. He could always count on Dad's support.

"We went to Mrs. Wallen's house, like you asked." He glanced at the medicine man. "Except she wasn't Mrs. Wallen anymore. Not the woman we've known over the years."

Dr. Whitefeather interrupted. "Was she already dead when you arrived?"

"I don't know. I don't know if she was dead or..." Asher shoved a hand through his hair and took a step back from the bed. "Possessed. She wasn't herself. That's for damn sure."

"Did she say anything?" Whitefeather probed. He set up a tripod and hung the bag of fluids dripping into Tes's vein.

Asher relayed the tacky poem Mrs. Wallen repeated like a broken record. He'd never be able to erase that horrific message from his memory.

In his mind, he relived the whole scene. His heartrate ratcheted up a notch as he relayed the information. Tears pricked at his eyes. He took a deep breath, doing his best to keep his composure and turned back around. "Special Agent Krysinski is going to Mrs.

Wallen's house to check on her." Asher heaved a sigh of relief. So far, no one was laughing. "Have you heard of anything like this before?"

Dr. Whitefeather scanned each face before answering. "We call them dead walkers. Only someone with incredible energy has the power to give the dead life. It's also referred to as the Frankenstein complex, which Mary Shelley wrote about in her book."

Mom crossed herself.

Dad lowered his brow and twerked his mouth in a dubious expression. "Listen, Doc, we're Catholic, and we don't believe the dead get up and walk around."

The Native American shrugged. "Your religion refers to people like Tes as 'resurrection angels.' Many scholars believed Jesus was a resurrection angel." He lifted his hand. "This has nothing to do with doctrine or religion. Pray to your saints and god, and I'll pray to mine. She'll need all the hope and prayers she can get."

Dad stepped toward Asher, anger twisting his mouth. No one messed with dad. "What do you mean, Mrs. Wallen was acting possessed? You sure you weren't mistaken?"

"I saw what I saw. Mrs. Wallen moved around like she was being pulled on strings. Like a damn puppet. It scared the shit out of me."

Whitefeather motioned toward Tes. "What did she do?"

"The closer Mrs. Wallen got to us, the more my truck battery slowed, then died." This was the part Asher didn't want to say. He wanted his family to like Tes. If he told them the truth, would they want anything to do with her? How could he tell them what she did without them having an altered opinion of her for the rest of her life?

Whitefeather held Tes's hand. "She started the truck."

"How did you know?" Asher frowned.

Whitefeather's guarded expression let him know he knew without having to tell his family the gory details. He breathed a sigh of relief. "Did Mrs. Wallen touch either of you?"

"No." Asher hesitated. "I don't think so. The window wouldn't roll up all the way before the battery died. Mrs. Wallen hung onto Tes's window."

"I'm not surprised. Touching Tes would have been her goal."

"*Why?*" Asher's jaw dropped.

"To take her energy. The kind of energy the dead seek for...resurrection." He paused long enough to look at his parents. "Enough to bring Mrs. Wallen back from the dead. Reunite her body with her soul." The doctor listened to Tes's heart and lungs.

Dad cussed a blue streak.

"Nothing touched her?"

Asher didn't want to mention the demon. Father McClarey would be called. God knows who else.

Whitefeather lifted Tes's arm. "How'd she get this mark? Did she have this before the incident with Mrs. Wallen?"

"No." Asher rolled his eyes, puffed out a breath. The doc wouldn't let go of every detail, would he? "The demon touched her."

Whitefeather snapped to attention. "What demon?"

"The black, rotten egg-smelling demon."

"Spikes on his head?"

Asher jerked his head back. "You've seen him?"

"No, but I know someone who has. She has the same scar."

"Who?"

Whitefeather cocked his head. "Joni."

Asher glanced at his parents. "She's the psychic we met with today."

"That's concerning." Whitefeather frowned. "Did he let go willingly?"

"No." Asher shifted his stance, lowered his voice. "Tes blasted him with um...energy."

Whitefeather smiled. "I'm sorry this is uncomfortable for you."

"It's unbelievable. I've seen things today I could have gone my whole life without seeing." Asher let out a defeated sigh.

Whitefeather said, "There have been people like Tes since the beginning of time. Her energy, even now as she hangs between life and death, is strong. However, I would be remiss if I didn't tell you that she can easily choose not to come back." He pulled out a bunch of wires with sensors on the ends from the suitcase. He pulled his phone out of his pocket and plugged it into the bottom. He began placing the first probe down Tes's shirt and stopped. He pulled her cell phone out of her bra. "Weird place to put a phone." He placed it on the nightstand and attached one white pad to her chest, the other to her side. Whitefeather turned on his phone. It showed Tes's slow heartbeat.

"That's cool." August stepped closer.

"Modern technology has come a long way. It saves me from having to haul around a heavy heart monitor."

"How do you know so much about Tes's condition?" Mom asked. "Or do they teach this in medical school now?"

The doctor's face fell into sadness. "My sister was like Tes. She was struck by lightning when she was a kid. When the paramedics brought her back to life, she was...different."

Asher wanted to ask if Whitefeather's sister made the grass grow, bushes flourish, and vines creep along their path. "She's learned to cope with this?"

The doctor shook his head, looked at the ceiling, blinking as if he held back tears. "She died a long time ago."

Whitefeather's dark eyes foreshadowed a possibility Asher didn't want to acknowledge. "Tes was struck by lightning when she was a kid."

"She came back with one foot in each land, like now. We're going to have to call her back to our world." Whitefeather stared at each face. "Are you willing to help?"

Asher held onto the life preserver of hope. "We can do that?"

"Of course, we'll help." Dad elbowed each of his brothers who flanked his sides. "She's Morgan's aunt. She's family."

"Yeah, we're all in." August's eyes widened. "How do we do that?"

"We need to form a drum circle."

Asher's parents looked at each other with one of their knowing expressions. "As my husband explained, we're Catholic," Mom argued.

"Think of it as holy water for the soul."

"I have some holy water." Mom moved toward the door.

"It won't help her where she's at." The doctor brushed Tes's hair away from her face. "You see, she needs to know there's people here who want her, because there are plenty of souls there that want to keep her." His gaze shifted to Asher. "Not all of them are good."

12

T es walked a narrow path. Where was she? Dense fog surrounded the lush forest. She couldn't see but twenty feet at a time. Each bend in the narrow path only revealed more of the same. No pinecones or branches littered the way. The sound of soft rain fell, yet she didn't feel wet. Odd.

She kept glancing over her shoulder. She couldn't shake a creepy vibe that someone was watching her. Eyes beyond the obscured foggy wall. The air swirled to her right. She stepped onto the moss-covered ground. Her foot sunk deep into the mushy soil. She stepped back.

Shadows shifted ahead. "Hello?" her voice echoed. Weird. She wasn't in a cave.

A branch snapped behind her. The fog swirled. She squinted into the mist. Black figures appeared on the edge. No faces. No limbs. All rhythmically marching forward, the dense air keeping them hidden from plain view.

The hair at the nape of her neck tingled. She'd seen this before. Her heart pounded. She'd *been* here before.

She took off running. Those shadows weren't ghosts. They were the dead. The dead who wanted to touch her. She glanced back to see if they followed. She turned back around, gasped, and skidded to a halt.

Her dad stood a few feet in front of her, hands in his pants pockets, wearing his usual blue sweater that matched his eyes with his alma mater's patch over the upper-left breast pocket. She'd gotten her quizzical mind from him.

He's dead. He's not real.

"Hello, Tesla."

"Hi, Dad." What would she give to have one more hour by his side. To argue about complicated math equations and his latest discovery. She'd never had a chance to discuss her thesis paper with him, nor share her results.

He held out his hand. What would happen if she touched him? It was her dad. The one person in all the world she could trust. He'd never hurt her.

Her hand shook as she grasped hold of his.

He was warm. Solid. *Alive.*

The sun broke through the fog and rain dissipated. An iridescent rainbow filled a vibrant blue sky above the grass field. The air was crisp, fresh, and free of pollution. A strong breeze caressed and soothed the tension from her muscles. Unconditional love seeped deep into her pores, her soul. She walked with her dad, hand in hand.

"I graduated," she told him.

"I was there." Sadness dipped the corner of his eyes. "I'm sorry your mother and sister didn't attend."

"It's okay. I mean, I was in school for a long time. I'm sure they were glad I was done and available for regular family events." It was the lie she told herself. To face the truth that her family didn't care would be too much to bear.

"They should have been there, Tesla." He wiped away the tear that slithered down her cheek. Yeah, it hurt that no one in her family was there for her big defining moment. Bleachers filled with spectators and not one butt was on a bench to represent someone was there for her, cheering her grand accomplishment. She'd sacrificed holidays, copious hours staring in a microscope, not to mention what seemed like years of sleep deprivation. None of it mattered to her family. Not even a phone call or card. Nothing.

Ruthie was there. She'd walked across the stage with Tes—and she told herself it was enough.

"Tell me about Asher."

He knew about him? "He's Hailey's dad."

"He's more than Hailey's dad, isn't he?"

"Well, I guess God knew I needed a friend, so He sent Asher."

"You never were good at keeping friends. Why is he different?"

She tweaked the corner of her mouth. "No one wants to be around someone like me. You know that. I'm a freak of nature. I'm better off staying here with you. I've missed you." She wrapped her arm around his waist, and he looped his strong arm around her shoulders. He wasn't always present when he was in the room, often engrossed in his thoughts. The one thing he did without fail was pick her up from boarding school. He'd fly halfway around the world when it was time for his visitation. Chauffeurs or nannies came for the other girls, but rarely an actual parent. Dad would always be waiting in his rental car in front of the large stone mansion. Often, she believed he was her only friend in the whole wide world. At the end of every visit, she'd begin the countdown to when she'd see him again. Until she turned sixteen and went to live with him permanently in San Jose, California.

Here he was. Once again proving he was the one person she could always count on, even in death. She was dead, wasn't she? Was it a choice? She shoved the thought aside. She'd make the most of this second chance.

"Do you ever wonder what it would be like to be truly in love?" Her dad usually didn't ask philosophical questions regarding emotions.

"Not really." Not after her first serious boyfriend showed her that love could be misplaced. That she could never know another human being. A twinge pricked her hand, sailing up her arm, straight to her heart. She stared at her hand in confusion. *Weird. What caused that?*

If the dreams held a thread of truth, Asher had been in her life many times. A true love kind of thing. Doubts could plague her heart otherwise, but not here. Not where time stood still. "Do you believe in curses?"

Dad stopped walking. "Tesla, you've always had enough strength to break any curse. Every experience you've had has prepared you for this."

"How?"

"Love professed foretells love failed. Don't say 'I love you' before you say 'I do'." *How did he know?* Did he know everything? Hm, wouldn't that be convenient? They continued walking. "It's three simple words. Keep them to yourself."

"That's easy. I'm British."

He narrowed his eyes. "You're nothing like your mother."

She swallowed. "I'm more like her than I care to admit. It's like I'm afraid she's going to pop out around every corner and admonish me if I do something that's on her long list of forbidden behaviors."

"Don't live your life in fear. It's not you. You're stronger than that."

She leaned into him. "I don't feel strong, Dad." She'd failed. "Now that Morgan's missing, Nikki will hate me forever."

"Nikki blames others. It's what she does." He waved a dismissive hand. "She looks for reasons to dislike people, where you look for ways to help them. That's why you became a doctor. Yeah, she's going to hate you since Morgan was kidnapped." He stopped and put his hand under her chin. "My sweet angel, you are full of love. People know it without you saying a word."

It was nice to hear that someone had faith in her—even if it was from her dead dad. "Wait. You know Morgan was kidnapped?"

"Of course." He shrugged like it was no big deal.

"Can you take me to her?"

"Where do you think we've been going?" His smiled widened, showing his aged, crooked teeth. He didn't have a Hollywood, thousand-watt smile, but he had her favorite smile.

"Go on." Her dad motioned toward the mansion. "I'll wait here. Stand guard."

Guard against what? She didn't want to know.

***

Asher held Tes's cold hand, hoping that touching her would show that he cared.

"We need more people." Dr. Whitefeather slipped a plastic tube under Tes's nose and turned on the oxygen.

"I'll call Alyssa," Dad said, offering to call Asher's younger sister. He held up his phone and stepped into the hall. The frown furrowing his brow hadn't eased.

"I'll ask if Joni and Zeke can come." Not that they got him into this mess, but Asher had an inkling they'd be good people to have around in a situation like this.

Whitefeather ruffled Ruthie's ears. "Can you boys bring in some chairs?"

"Sure," Aaron answered. August followed.

"Best get a bathroom break in while I can." His mom left the room, leaving him and the doctor alone, while he finished the text message to Zeke.

Asher paused, making sure no one was going to walk back in. "If Tes never came in direct contact with Mrs. Wallen, how is it that Tes made her get up and walk around?"

"Was Tes sleeping when you arrived at the Wallens' home?"

"She'd nodded off in the truck just before."

"That's when she expends energy without knowing it. In sleep, she's between worlds. Always."

"So, Tes is resting."

"No." Whitefeather bit his lips together. At least he didn't give false hope. "Look at her hands. Her face."

"She looks pale."

"She looks dead."

"No, she doesn't." Asher refused to believe that nonsense. "She has a pulse. She's breathing."

"Asher, she's cold. Her eyes do not move under her lids."

He couldn't allow Tes to slip under the veil and pass that easily from this life to the next. "She can't die." He choked back a sob. "You've got to promise me she won't die."

"I can't. It would be irresponsible of me to say otherwise." Whitefeather clasped a hand on his shoulder. "It's her life. Her choice." He pulled something from the case. "I'd like to do a quick blood test. It'll tell me if she's truly a resurrection angel or not."

"Okay." Asher took a deep breath and steeled his nerves.

Whitefeather used a lancet, like diabetics use, to prick the end of her finger. A drop of blood formed, and he slid it onto a glass slide.

Asher grabbed a tissue from the bedside table and held it over Tes's finger. He pulled the paper away, revealing her healed finger. He turned his gaze to the droplet on the slide. It'd turned to dust. "Is that what's in her veins? Dust?"

Whitefeather shook his head. "How do you think the legends of vampires were created?"

"Don't tell me Tes is a vampire. She doesn't get burned in sunlight. I've seen it."

Whitefeather laughed. "The root of the vampire story is about the blood. That they need human blood to survive. In truth, her blood can heal anyone." He paused. "Or any living thing."

Asher frowned. "Like plants?"

"Animals too." The doctor smiled. "She's a true resurrection angel. Healer of life." He swallowed. "I wish my sister had lived long enough to have met her. Let her know that she wasn't the only one."

"How rare is this condition?"

"Tes is the second resurrection angel I've met, so I'd say rare enough."

Asher thought of vampire legends and wondered what else Tes had in common. "If she uses her blood to heal people, plants, or animals, do they become resurrection angels?"

"We'll have to ask Tes if she returns."

"What if she donated blood?"

Whitefeather's eyebrows rose. "Theoretically, if the blood doesn't touch air, she could donate it. More than likely, the person would be healed forever—of all ailments."

Which only formed more questions in Asher's mind. "Can she die?"

"Of course." Whitefeather put the blood pressure cuff around Tes's arm and began pumping the balloon. "All living creatures die...eventually."

His brothers shuffled in and out, bringing in the dining room chairs and the one from his office.

Afraid to ask anything that could be overheard, Asher waited in the hall until reinforcements arrived.

"Hi, Asher." Joni and Zeke ascended the stairs. "You have a beautiful home."

"Thank you."

A knock sounded below, and Mom answered. "Hi, Tom. We're about to begin."

Tom grabbed the last lawn chair from Asher's sister, Alyssa, before filing into the now-overcrowded bedroom. Mom and Dad followed.

"Thank you for coming." Asher shook Tom's hand. "How's Mrs. Wallen?"

Tom glanced at his parents before answering. "I called the local authorities. It looks like she had a heart attack after retrieving the mail."

Whitefeather lifted Tes's arm. "Joni," he whispered. "She encountered the same demon as you."

Joni looked at Tes's arm and held up her own arm with a faded scar. "How's that possible?" Fear slanted her brows. "He can't be gaining strength." She shook her head in disbelief. "He can't." She swallowed, slicing her hand through the air. "I don't have enough in me to fight him again."

Zeke placed his hands on her shoulders. "You have plenty of strength, but no one wants to see his ugly ass again."

"Especially me." Joni turned in his arms and held onto Zeke. "He's coming after my friends." Tears welled in her eyes. "He's still trying to get to me."

Zeke smoothed his thumb along her cheek. "He's still watching."

Asher didn't understand what they were talking about, but from the worried look on their faces, it wasn't good. "Dr. Whitefeather thinks he attacked Tes because she—"

"She's a resurrection angel," Whitefeather finished.

Joni turned around. "What does that mean?" She stepped closer to the bed. "Does she have special powers?"

Whitefeather was eager to answer. "She has her own special powers. She can raise the dead."

Zeke stepped back. "Are you kidding me?" He rubbed a hand down his face. "Can she bring the demon back to life?"

Whitefeather raised one brow. "It would explain why he grabbed her arm."

Zeke let out a deep breath. "We can't let that happen."

"Agreed." Whitefeather put Tes's arm under the blanket. "Thing is, I don't know how to keep the demon away from her." He stared at Tes's face. "When she's sleeping, she's between worlds. He could easily reach her from the other side."

"We've got to protect her," Joni said.

Whitefeather shook his head. "We can't do it for her. She's got to learn to protect herself."

Asher went to his closet and dug out a little-used rosary from a drawer. "This was my grandmother's. For now, it'll have to do."

Whitefeather took the rosary and placed it beside Tes on the pillow.

It should also appease his parents.

Everyone gathered around Asher's bed, sitting in a tight semi-circle. Tango lay at Dad's feet while Ruthie snuggled close to Tes on the bed. Ten people in all, not including Tes. No one said a word.

Whitefeather passed out drums to some, rattles to others. He held a wooden flute with long white feathers tied to the end with a piece of white leather.

"We need to sound like one voice. All the drums and rattles must be on the same rhythm." Whitefeather took the drum from Asher to demonstrate. "One, TWO, three, FOUR." Emphasizing to hit the drum harder on the second and fourth beats.

Asher groaned, watching his musically challenged family. He could tell his mom and dad were uncomfortable, hardly moving their instruments. Alyssa kept smiling at Whitefeather like she'd met her favorite teen idol. In true goof-off-brother-mode, Aaron and August acted like they were rock stars, overemphasizing everything. The only ones taking this seriously were Tom, Joni, and Zeke. When Joni rolled her eyes, Asher knew they were in trouble.

"No. Together." Whitefeather's frustration grew. "Stop, stop," he shouted. "You're killing Native American music." He pointed at Asher. "You start. Then we'll add one more drum and so on, until you're beating as one voice." He groaned and shook his head.

Asher did his best to keep the rhythm going like Whitefeather instructed. Alyssa started with her rattles to a cha-cha beat more in time with "La Cucaracha."

Whitefeather buried his face in his hands and shook his head. "Hopeless."

Asher put his drum down. "Lyss. You've got to keep in time with the drum, not do your own thing."

Alyssa flipped her dark hair over her shoulder. "I *am* keeping time."

"No, you're not." Whitefeather rose and took the rattles from her hands and gave them to August and took his drum and gave it to Alyssa. "Maybe you could beat a drum better than you can shake a rattle."

"I can shake a lot of things well." Her eyes, rimmed in dark lashes, blinked.

All Asher needed was his sister to develop a crush instead of focusing on the fact Tes's life hung between worlds.

"I bet you can." Whitefeather ignored her flirtatious glance and returned to his seat. "For the love of God, people, get this right. She doesn't have all day. The longer she stays in the Shadowlands, the more tempted she'll be to stay, or the souls will keep her there." He picked up his flute again.

"You mean, you're serious?" Alyssa's eyebrows rose. "I thought you guys were teasing, that this was some big joke and that a camera crew would jump out of the closet and say this was some TV show."

Where the hell his sister got her ideas, Asher would never know. "Tes needs us, Lyss. Now get your head out of your ass and pay attention."

Her eyes widened. "Okay. Geez, you'd think she were an angel sent from heaven."

Whitefeather didn't skip a beat. "She's a resurrection angel."

"Not again with the angel stuff," Dad growled.

How in the world would his family look at Tes and not remember this moment? "Guys." Asher grabbed their attention. "We're all she has. There's no family worried if she's okay. No one rallied to her side when Morgan was kidnapped. She moved here a week ago with three suitcases full of her worldly belongings packed in her car, and Ruthie. That's it. After Morgan..." He closed his eyes, clenching his jaw, fighting to keep his shit together. "We've prayed for total strangers for years. Tes is a stranger, but she's right here in front of us needing our help." His voice strained. "We don't have any trouble being loud in this family—put that energy into the damn drum or rattle."

13

Tes traversed the wide art-deco stone steps to the mansion's veranda. The light-pink marble façade must have cost a fortune, even if it was built a century ago. She walked through the door into the foyer and onto checkerboard marble tile that glinted with flecks of gold throughout the luxurious décor. A marble table in the center featured a nude female Grecian statuette. An angered laugh came from the hall.

Tes entered a dark walnut wood-paneled room with built-in bookshelves. Classic novels and rare books lined the dusty shelves.

A man sat behind the broad, cherry desk, a cigar dangling from his lips, the end chewed and drenched with spit. Tes swallowed back the distaste on her tongue.

A younger man sat in a high-backed chair in front of the older man. He bowed his head forward, leaning over his knees. She could see his short, blond hair, styled like a lot of kids his age, shorter on the sides and longer on top.

The older man gestured, throwing his hand in the air. "Now get out of my sight before I throw you out of my home."

"You wouldn't have this home if it wasn't for my mother's life insurance money."

"Which meant she didn't die in vain. So, be happy, kid." The old man grunted, clearing his throat. "You're lucky I let you live under my roof. I promised your mother I'd watch after you until you turned eighteen. You're nineteen, for God's sake. Be a fucking man, grow some balls, and get a real job."

The teen's shoulders slumped forward. "I'm reminded of that every day," he muttered under his breath.

Tes knew what it was like to be lucky to have a place to live and be at the discretion and mercy of others. One event could change everything.

The man opened a top desk drawer. "Don't get comfy. One more wrong move and you're gone. I don't give a shit if you live on the streets peddling your skinny ass for rent.

Next time, you better be ten minutes early to pick up my son from football practice, or don't bother coming home at all. You hear me?"

"I heard you the first time." The young man hitched his purple and gold University of Washington hoodie over his head and left the room.

Tes stared at the older man, who pulled out his cell phone and dialed. "Hey, baby. Whatchu wearin'? Up for some company?" He snuffed his stogie out in the ashtray. "Mm."

As horrible as the old man was, she didn't get the sense he knew about Morgan and Hailey. Otherwise, he'd be moving to assault one of them. Unless they were already dead. She clenched her hands and tabled her fear.

A light shone around the bookcase behind the old man. She waited for him to leave before looking for the lever. Her hand sailed through the book she tried to move. She smacked her forehead. *I'm a ghost. I don't need a lever.* She walked through the wall and down a steep flight of stairs that ended in a room that was lit by a single incandescent bulb casting deep shadows across the bleak, gray cinderblock walls.

Morgan and Hailey clung to each other on a twin-size bed on the other side of a chain-link fence secured with a chain and padlock.

They're alive!

A door opened behind Tes. She turned and saw a man in a skin-tight blue unitard that covered every inch of skin, including his head. A white mask covered his face with slits for eyes and nose. "Tell me, Morgan." A deep voice synthesizer disguised the man's voice. "Are you proud of Mommy now?"

"I'll never talk to her again," Morgan whispered. "She's *disgusting*."

A man and woman's moaning drew Tes's attention toward the TV that the girls watched. She walked around the bed to see what they were looking at. The video showed Nikki doing a foursome with three guys.

Oh, Morgan. I'm so sorry. I had no idea.

The video changed. Another woman with bleached-blonde straggly hair shoved money into her bra as she closed a hotel room door. Her bright blue eye shadow was offset with black eyeliner.

"This is what he's been showing me." Hailey glanced at Morgan. "My mom turning tricks for drug money."

Why would he show them these images? Tes stared at Morgan and Hailey. They showed shame on their faces. No daughter should ever see their mother like this.

The small room had an apartment-size refrigerator, a sink, and a makeshift screen made from weathered doors where a toilet was hidden. At least the kidnapper gave them privacy. Interesting.

There was no hope of escaping through the chain-link fence. There was a small slot cut out in the fence. That must be where he passed them food.

From the shadows came a deep, mechanical voice. "Your mothers are whores. They'd rather fuck anyone than spend time with you."

Morgan shook her head. "I can't believe this. My mom gives speeches on abstinence every year. This isn't real." She motioned toward the TV.

The screen changed to Nikki on her bed with two men.

Shock registered on Morgan and Hailey's faces.

Morgan choked back tears. "High school football players? *Minors*. If anyone ever knew about this, she'd be fired. Go to jail."

The screen changed again. The same guys stood in a circle, several wearing letterman's jackets.

"Holy shit, man. Mrs. McKinley is hot in bed. She let us tag-team her." The football player nudged the guy next to him. "You guys have to understand fucking a cheerleader is nothing compared to a grown woman. A woman who knows how to do things to you." The boy stopped, blowing out a deep breath. "All I can say is my balls ached after coming, man."

This is so sick. Tes focused on Morgan and Hailey, her heart sinking, her mind reeling, her emotions bounced from rage to sympathy. If they ever escaped, Tes couldn't let Morgan return to Nikki's house. Every instinct inside Tes told her Morgan wasn't safe in her own home, and it soured her stomach. *How could you do this, Nikki?*

Morgan bit her swollen lips as fresh tears cascaded down her cheeks. "I had no idea my mother was having sex with the football team."

Tes couldn't believe it either. Overcontrolling Nikki risking her career and reputation with minors? Who would have guessed Miss Uptight prim and proper was a pedophile? Tes always pictured Nikki being an in-the-dark-under-the-covers-missionary-style kind of gal. She couldn't say the word "sex." When Nikki thought Morgan was old enough for the sex talk, she'd asked Tes to tell her about the birds and bees. Why did she go to such lengths to act like a damn prude, when in reality she was entirely different?

The modulated voice said, "Now you know. What are you going to do about it?"

"What can I do?" Morgan wiped a sweatshirt sleeve across her eyes. "I'm a kid. I have no rights."

"Do you want to be whores like your mothers?"

Hailey snapped, "Of course not. My dad has custody of me. He rarely lets me visit my mom. He knew. He kept her away from me."

"Your dad is the exception. Most men will fuck anything that spreads their legs."

Morgan's shuddered breath wracked in her chest. "Why are you showing us these videos?"

Blue stepped closer to the fence. *Ready or not.* "When I took you, it was to make your mothers suffer. I hoped they would see your absence as a way of seeing your value, but no. What did your mother do, Hailey?"

"You said she moved away." Her voice was faint, distant, unbelieving.

"Yeah, so she could be a whore in a derelict town in the middle of fucking nowhere."

"My mom's away for the week." Morgan's hands twisted in the blanket. "Once she knows I'm gone, she'll be remorseful. You'll see."

"Do you want to see how much your mommy's thinking about you, Morgan?" Blue clicked on his cell phone, linking it to the TV screen. A large room came into view with beautiful snow-capped mountains outside the window. The king-size bed engulfed the four nude adults. Two men and a woman with Nikki. The camera zoomed in on Nikki's face, her eyes closed in pleasure, moaning like a porn star. Tes knew her sister enjoyed being the center of attention, but this? This wasn't the sister she knew.

Tes closed her eyes. She couldn't unsee this. How long would it be until she'd try and engage Morgan into their orgies? What would happen if Morgan walked in on Nikki with three guys in her bedroom? Would Nikki be ashamed? Would she apologize to her daughter?

"Please, stop." Morgan sobbed. "I get it. I hate her. *I hate her.*"

"Not enough. You will never hate her enough, Morgan." Blue clicked, changing the images again. "You're the perfect daughter, and it's still not enough. You're smart. You're talented. And still she'd prefer to take it up the ass than be with you. Do you want to see her first date with Ben Winslow?"

The screen's images changed. "She made good ol' Benny dinner and sucked his dick before dessert. Thank God the Hickoks took you in on the weekends."

There are cameras inside the house? A cold chill raced over Tes.

"I get it. My mother's a whore." Morgan hid her face in her sleeve-covered hands.

"Look at it, Morgan!" Blue rattled the fence.

A black shadow shifted beside Blue. A spikey head leaned over, whispering something in his ear. What did the demon have to do with Hailey and Morgan being kidnapped? An uneasiness settled in Tes's stomach. She stepped back into the corner, hiding in the shadows. Was this the same demon that touched her? She stared at her arm. In this realm, she didn't have a scar.

"Don't you take your eyes off that screen." Blue's anger verged on rage. "You keep looking. You ingrain every fucking motion to your memory. Because when I let you go, I want you to kick your mother's ass out of your life. You need a new mother. And I think I've found the right the solution."

Tes's gaze moved from Blue to the screen.

"She's intelligent. She's kind. She likes dogs. And from all my research, I can't find one selfie of her tits. I can't find that she's ever lived above her means or ever had a one-night stand. She's responsible. Her only fault is already moving in with Hailey's dad." The TV screen changed. "I know I'd like to fuck her."

Tes gulped. Her gaze dipped to Blue's crotch. His hard-on strained against his unitard. "You already know her as Aunt Tes."

Morgan's glare and tightened lips challenged Blue. "She didn't move in with Uncle Asher."

Hailey tsked. "My dad's never met her."

"Yeah, well, he's ready to fuck her—and we all know men want to be with a great piece of ass." The screen changed to Asher packing her suitcases into her car. Then him removing them from her trunk, carrying them into his house. *There are cameras outside both homes?*

Hailey's lips trembled as she looked at Morgan. "He looks happy."

"Wow." Morgan's response lacked luster. "Aunt Tes and Uncle Asher. Who knew those two would hit it off?"

A cold breeze swept passed Tes's legs. She turned and saw a panel rattle by the toilet seat. She pressed against it, but it didn't move. Instead, she passed through the wall and into another dark, damp pathway. The bricks dripped condensation. Mold and mildew tickled her nose as she made her way along the narrow passage. At the end, she crossed into the forest. She turned and looked around. The house wasn't anywhere in sight. The moss-covered ground was overgrown with blackberry bushes, ferns, and other vegetation. No one had used that entrance in a long time.

"Tesla?" Her dad appeared from the mist. "Let's prop that door open so they can see which way to turn when they find the door."

"How are they going to find the door?"

"I'll take care of that." He pointed to a bent sapling. "Grab that."

Tes half-expected her hand to go through the branch. Instead, she felt its weight in her hand. She brought it to her dad, and he slipped it in the small opening. "Come on. We need to jump on it together to get it to move."

They gripped forearms, silently counted to three, then jumped on the branch. It nudged the cavern door open. "Excellent. Just wide enough to show light, but not far enough to let in the wild things." Her dad wrapped her in his arms. "I sure love you, kiddo."

"I love you too, Dad."

He held her at arm's length. "Now, you need to get back to that handsome man and make grandbabies for me."

She laughed—her dad hadn't ever pushed her into a relationship, let alone asked for grandchildren. "But you won't be there to watch them grow up. Walk me down the aisle."

"Aw, Tesla, when have I ever missed an important milestone in your life?"

She lay her head against his chest. "Never," she whispered. "I want to stay with you."

"You can't stay here, Tesla. You need to go home to Asher now. He needs you far more than I do."

"But—" She leaned back and he was gone. In an instant, she was back where she started. The shadows shifted beyond the fog.

Drum music called.

14

A sher glanced at his watch. They'd been beating as one loud circle for over fifteen minutes. What if it took hours?

Whitefeather played his flute. The higher notes caused Ruthie to sit up and howl. Tango joined in.

"Quiet," Dad bellowed. Both dogs curbed their howls into high-pitched whines. Ruthie rested her snout on Tes's stomach.

Tes's eyelids twitched. Whitefeather continued playing but moved by the bed. He stared at the heart monitor. He motioned for them to drum louder.

Her mouth gaped open. She took a deep breath.

"That's it, Tes." Asher dropped his drum on his chair and sat on the side of the bed. He squeezed her hand. "Come on, Tes."

She squeezed his hand.

"Yes!"

Ruthie barked.

Tes gulped air like she'd run a marathon. Whitefeather put down his flute and held her other hand. "That's it, Tes. Come on. Open your eyes."

Her eyelids fluttered. She shivered, teeth clattering.

Asher placed a hand on her shoulder. "Is she having a seizure?"

"No." Whitefeather motioned for everyone to stop playing their instruments. "Her soul's adjusting to entering her body again."

Asher cringed, hoping his parents didn't hear that.

Her eyes were a lighter blue than before. "Hey," she whispered.

"Hey, yourself." Asher kissed the back of her hand. "Welcome back, sunshine."

"Tessie?" Dad stepped to the end of the bed. Everyone else followed suit.

She blinked, taking in the surroundings. "Why is everyone staring at me like Dorothy returning from Oz?"

Dad squeezed her foot. "I'm glad you're back."

Tes looked at Whitefeather. "Thank you."

His smile beamed from ear to ear. "Aho."

"Aho," Tes whispered.

"Thank you, Dr. Whitefeather." Asher put his hand out there for him to shake. Anything to get him from staring at Tes like they were long-lost lovers.

"You're welcome." The doctor shook his hand. He immediately turned his attention back to Tes. "I haven't seen someone like you in a long time."

"Like me?"

"He says you're a resurrection angel." Dad's sarcasm wasn't missed.

"Well, if anyone would know, it'd be the good doctor," Zeke said.

"I didn't know there was a word for what I am." Tes's face held a poignant smile and stared at each face, then frowned. "Who are all these people?"

Asher forgot Tes hadn't met his brothers or younger sister and made quick introductions.

Tes turned to Asher. "I saw them. Hailey and Morgan are alive. They're being held in a basement."

What did she say? "How?" Asher frowned.

She looked away, as a pained expression stole over her face.

"Are they injured? Are they shackled?"

"No." She bit her lips together. "They're going to come home. The kidnapper promised he'd let them go—once Nikki returns and shows remorse."

Asher stiffened. "Nikki? What does *she* have to do with this?"

Tes sniffed. "Everything. It was all about Linda and Nikki."

Asher shook his head. "This guy has a mother complex?"

"He hates women who don't put children first."

Asher scooched off the bed and stared at his parents.

Dad stared at Tes like she spoke a foreign language. "Where are they?"

"It isn't like I got an address." Tes covered her face with her hands and started to cry. "I'm so sorry. It's not enough."

Tom pushed Asher aside and sat beside Tes, taking her hand. "Close your eyes. Take a few deep breaths. I want you to walk through what you saw. No matter how small the detail—tell me what you saw, heard, smelled."

Tes stared at Tom and glanced at the others.

Tom looked over his shoulder. "Can everyone give us a few moments?"

"No." Asher moved closer. "I need to know what she knows."

Tom cocked a fatherly brow, a cold glare in his eye. "I think Tes is still processing what she saw and doesn't need an audience."

Whitefeather cleared his voice. "I'll be right outside the door in case you need me." He held his hands at his side, effectively sweeping everyone from the room.

Asher dug in his heels. "I need to hear this, Tes. There's nothing you can say that I haven't already imagined."

She huffed. "Let me talk to Tom, please. Alone."

"What do you think I'm going to do? Drive over there and rip that asshole a new one?"

Tom stood so fast he almost knocked Asher back. "Go." He waved a hand at the door. "Now."

"This is the thanks I get?"

"It's not about you." Tom's lips firmed into a thin line.

"Fine." Asher cussed under his breath and slammed the door as he left the room.

***

Tes couldn't hold back her tears. "It's so much worse than I thought it'd be."

Tom sank to the mattress and pulled Tes into his arms.

"He said he'd let them go once Nikki got back—as long as she showed remorse."

"It's okay. You're safe. I got you." Tom rubbed her back, rocking her in his arms. "What else did he say?"

"He wants them to hate their mothers." She gulped air, sobbing. "He knows everything that Nikki and Linda have done. He's videotaping everything. For all I know there's a camera in this room." She glanced around the room, looking for a computer, a photo frame, or a stuffed animal—like a nanny cam. "He showed videos outside and inside Nikki's house, and outside Asher's house. How can he do that?"

Tom gently pushed her away to look at her face. "They both have video doorbells. He must know their wi-fi passwords. One thing we didn't tell you and Asher is that the kidnapper turned off the alarm system from the time Morgan left to be with her friends until shortly before she got home. I'm presuming the kidnapper had a way of tracking Morgan through being friends on a social media app."

"He can do that?"

"Easy. I could do that—and I'm not tech savvy like LeBron."

"It doesn't look like he's mistreated them, other than mentally. He's using brainwashing techniques to make them hate their mothers."

"What aren't you telling me?"

She rested her forehead against his chest. "I can't. What if what I saw wasn't real?"

"What if it was?"

"My sister." Tes sucked in a deep breath, grabbed a tissue off the nightstand and wiped her nose. She kept her voice low in case Asher's ear was pressed to the door. "It appears Nikki's engaging students in sexual activity."

His mouth gaped. "Holy shit. That's what this is about?"

"The kidnapper showed the girls videos of Nikki in bed with football players. There was an additional clip that appeared that she could have done this before they graduated. I don't want to destroy Nikki's life, if this was a manipulated film. Some people can create real-life looking videos that aren't real."

"That's not for you to worry about." Tom wiped a tear from her chin. "Exploitation of children is a felony."

"I know." Fresh tears soaked her cheeks. "What if the kidnapper was Nikki's victim? I mean, why else would he go to this extreme? Nikki risked everything. Her career. Her reputation. Jail. Why would she do that?"

He clamped his mouth shut and shook his head. "We're going to need to find proof. Someone will come forward and corroborate the information."

"We have to find him to find the evidence."

"I'll ask our tech team to search Nikki's house. They'll know what to look for." He hugged her. "What are you going to tell Asher?"

She waved a hand between them. "Not this. No father wants to hear what they've been subjected to. I can't, Tom."

"Tell me more about where they're being held."

Tes described what little she could remember. "I wish there'd been a house number, but I didn't notice one. I'm sorry."

"Don't be sorry. This is the first real lead I've had since this nightmare began months ago. Don't beat yourself up over this." He kissed her forehead. "You get some rest. You think of anything else, call me."

"I will." She stared at the bedroom door. "I don't know what to tell them. How to face them."

He winked. "I'll take care of it." He stood and opened the door. "She's ready now."

***

Asher paced between the kitchen and dining room. His parents sat at the table talking in whispers. Why couldn't Tes include him in what she'd seen? He'd thought of every possible scenario his daughters could have been subjected to—truly there wasn't anything he wasn't prepared to hear. Why exclude him?

The second Tom opened the bedroom door, Ruthie bolted up the stairs.

Tom joined his parents at the table, sitting across from Mom and Dad. He pinned Asher with one of his mastered fatherly looks. "Sit."

"Why are you pissed at me?"

"I'm not." Tom smiled. "Pacing isn't helping."

Asher yanked out a chair and sat. "Well?" He crossed his arms.

"Unfortunately, Tes doesn't know where they're located. She provided details of the house and its interior and we'll do everything in our power to search for the location." Tom's expression softened. "If what Tes saw is real, the girls are distraught, but they're not physically injured. They're in a caged room and the kidnapper stays outside of that room. They have adequate access to a bathroom and water, and neither of them looked like they hadn't eaten. It could be far worse."

Sure, Tom shared a lot of shit, but he was skipping over nitty-gritty details. "What else did she say?"

"The last thing Tes needs is for you to march up there and demand she relive what she went through. She doesn't need you hounding her, nor does she need your anger." He placed a hand on his arm. "She told me, and only me, as a way to protect you."

"Sure, she did." Asher rolled his eyes.

"If I were in your shoes, I'd want to kill the bastard who took my daughters."

Asher cocked his head. Did Tom know? Not being able to question him in front of his parents took restraint. Did Tes learn that from her walkabout in the Shadowlands? Is that possible? *Shit.*

"You wouldn't have Morgan's tattoo on your arm if you didn't think of her as a daughter."

Saved that one, agent.

Tom looked at Dad. "Keep him down here until his temper's under control."

Dad nodded. "We all have questions for Tes."

"Let her rest." Tom stood. "I need to get to the office and follow up on what Tes shared. I'll let myself out."

Tom didn't have his trusty notebook in hand—so whatever she told him, he'd committed to memory.

Asher braced his elbows on the table. "I just want them home."

"Tes said once Nikki gets home. That's tomorrow, right?" Mom's optimism didn't wane.

"God, I hope so. I can't keep doing this."

15

O nce Tom cleared the threshold, a man with a stethoscope draped around his neck entered. "Thank you." Tes lifted her IV-ladened hand.

"I'm Dr. Shiloh Whitefeather. It's a great honor to meet you."

"Are you going to explain to me what a resurrection angel is?"

He laughed. "You already know. You have the power to make the dead come to life. Only resurrection angels can do that."

"I'm no angel." She had plenty of memories that weren't angelic.

"But you are. You're rare. My sister was like you." He looked away. "I never thought I'd meet someone like her."

Ruthie jumped on the bed, licking her face. "Aw, I missed you too." Tes petted Ruthie's head. "I've always thought what I did to the dead was a curse."

Shiloh smiled. "May I remove your heart monitor?"

She lowered the blanket. "I'm a psychiatrist."

"You are a great healer." His hands were cold.

She giggled when he removed the patch on her side. "I'm sorry. I'm ticklish."

"Don't ever apologize. Not to me." His smile was infectious. "We are going to be great friends."

"I'd like that." She glanced up at the IV bag and noticed it was almost empty. She grabbed the tubing, closed the valve, and pulled out the IV. Shiloh followed with a Band-Aid for her hand, but she waved him off. "I've been ashamed of who I've been for so long. I don't know how to be anything else."

"You can choose a new beginning." Shiloh tucked everything inside a suitcase. "Other than rest, the only thing I can prescribe for you is to not say 'I love you' before you say 'I do'."

"What do you think that means?"

"If the dead give you a message—you better wake up and take notice." He took a deep breath. "Get some rest. We can talk more tomorrow. It has been my greatest honor to meet you." He bowed. "Aho."

"Aho." Tes smiled and waved as he left the room. Fighting fatigue, she turned her attention to Ruthie.

"Hey." Grant Hickok stood in the doorway. "Got a minute?"

"I have a busy schedule, but I think I can squeeze you in." She waved him forward.

He entered the room and sat on the side of the bed. "How are you feeling?"

"Pretty craptacular."

"I can imagine." He shook his head. "That's a lie. I'm not so sure I believe what the doc said about you being in the—" He crooked his index fingers in the air. "Shadowlands. Have you ever had these episodes before?"

Tes focused on the hair around Ruthie's ears, smoothing it back. "Once," she whispered.

"What do you see when you're there?"

"Today, I saw my dad." She paused.

"It was all a dream, right?" Isabella stood in the doorway.

Tes shook her head. "I don't know. I've only been there once before—and it was a long time ago."

"Asher said you started his truck." Grant focused on the one moment Tes wanted to forget.

"It's all a blur. All I know is that whoever was coming after us was also draining the power from the engine. So, I did something that I thought would help." It was a passive, cop-out answer. Why couldn't they drop it? It was over. She couldn't undo what had already been done.

Isabella's expression wasn't as rigid as Grant's. "You made the grass grow when you fainted."

Tes glanced at them before focusing back on Ruthie. "Yeah. I can do that too. Energy is energy."

Grant huffed.

Maybe if she told them how it all started, they'd understand. "When I was eight years old, I was swimming in a lake. My mom kept telling me to get out of the water because a storm was rolling in, but I wouldn't listen. I was still angry at her for divorcing my dad. Lightning struck the water." She swallowed. "I died."

Isabella sat beside her and brushed a hand through Tes's hair, something her own mother had never done. Her throat tightened. What would it like to be loved by this family? To be accepted by them? She was crazy. They were grilling her to make sure she wasn't certifiable before letting Asher near her again.

"When I came back to life, I couldn't walk. The lightning kind of short-circuited the nerve endings in my lower spine." She let out a heavy breath. "My first experience at affecting the dead was a couple weeks later when my grandmother died." Tes closed her eyes, forcing back the memory. She'd only spoken about what happened in the creepazoid part of her past to one other person besides family. What did she have to lose? They already thought she was weird. What would it hurt to tell them the rest?

"My grandmother had a stroke and wasn't expected to live. Being in a wheelchair, I couldn't—" Tes tilted her head. *Go for broke.* "I couldn't maneuver very well. I was working on my homework alone at the dining room table, since I wasn't able to go to school. Grandmother came down the stairs like a marionette, each leg lifting at a ninety-degree angle." *Like Mrs. Wallen.* "My grandmother hadn't walked in years. I don't know how or why I did it, but I clapped my hands together. Rubbed them until the energy arced between them. Then I balled it all up and threw it at her. I hoped it would stop her. Instead, her body twitched like she was having a seizure. I started screaming until our butler came running into the room."

"Butler?" Grant interrupted.

Tes averted her gaze, embarrassed by her privileged upbringing. "We had a cook, maids, and a butler." She glanced at Isabella, who patiently waited for her to finish. "My grandmother opened her eyes and sat up. She looked right at me. 'Let me go,' she said." Tes shook her head. "I didn't know what she meant. I wasn't holding her there—or so I thought. My mother chose that moment to walk through the door. My grandmother's head about twisted off as she turned to look at my mom. My mother freaked out. Understandable, of course. Hell, I was freaked out. A lot." Tes tried to tell the facts and not feel the memories. She didn't want to remember the cracking of bone, her mother's screams, or the butler's cursing. "My grandmother permanently died a few hours later. I was sent away to boarding school after that. The next time the dead woke up was when I was in the cadaver lab at medical school."

There were other incidents, minor ones, she thought best to keep to herself. "I have to be honest. I don't understand why being hit with lightning has anything to do with my ability to put energy back into the dead or make things that are growing grow more. I wish I did, but I don't. It just...happens."

Isabella leaned over and kissed her forehead. "You must have been so scared."

"Terrified. I'm still scared thinking about Mrs. Wallen." Tes focused on Isabella's caring eyes. Grant was too intimidating.

"She passed away today." Isabella kissed her again.

All Tes had ever wanted was to be loved like this from her mom. To receive such kindness from a stranger threatened her senses to the breaking point.

"I know." Tes didn't want to say anything else. Yet, here they were, sitting on the bed like she was an honorary Hickok. The only person that had come to her sick bed before was a nurse or nanny—never her mother. Asher was a lucky man. "I made Mrs. Wallen move around the yard, but I didn't mean to harm her."

"You didn't." Asher looked at his parents. How long had he been standing there?

"We're trying to understand." Isabella brushed back Tes's hair from her face. "We're Catholic. Things like this don't happen to us."

"You mean, being a resurrection angel?" Tes gave a weak laugh. "Yeah, I'm not so sure I believe it myself."

"Good." Grant squeezed her ankle. "Let's leave it that way."

"I wouldn't do anything to harm any of you. Please believe that." *Not on purpose. Ever.*

"Of course you wouldn't." Isabella squeezed her hand. "We'll get out of your way so you can get some rest."

Isabella waited for Grant to come to her side before they left the room.

Tes motioned for Ruthie to get off the bed before pulling back the covers and sitting up.

"Whoa, where are you going?" Asher stepped forward.

"To the bathroom." Her bladder was feeling the IV fluids.

"You're not still set on leaving, are you?"

Tes swallowed. "I'm too tired."

"Good."

She glanced into his caring eyes.

"I'm sorry I lost my temper." He offered his arm. "Tom told us you didn't know details."

"They're alive, Asher." Fresh tears stung her eyes as she took his arm to steady her balance. "That's what matters. The kidnapper said he'd let them go after Nikki returns tomorrow." Tes had to hold onto that promise. Even if the girls found the escape door, it didn't mean they'd have the courage to walk barefoot down a dark tunnel. "If I could rest here tonight, I'd greatly appreciate it."

"You have a room here for as long as you like."

"That's kind of you." She wanted to protest but didn't have the energy. "Thank you." She put a hand on the doorjamb. "I appreciate your hospitality, given what happened today."

"Next time this happens—"

"Oh, there won't be a next time." She vehemently shook her head and sliced a hand through the air.

He stared at her, his brows inching closer together. "How can you stop it?"

If she only knew. "I'll do better. I promise."

"Sure you will." He laughed. "It's who you are, I guess."

"If I weren't so tired, I'd go somewhere else. I'm sure if I called Joni..."

"Stop that nonsense." He pulled her into the hall. "You get ready for bed and I'll tuck you in, okay?"

"You don't have to do that."

"I want to."

"Keep your enemies close and all that?" Her stomach twisted.

"I'd never hurt you." He looked offended. "And you're not my enemy." He sucked in a deep breath. "I hope I can consider you a friend, at the very least."

That was the third time that day someone said they wanted to be her friend. An odd sensation flitted over her fried nerves. People never wanted to be her friend before. Or did they, and she never noticed? It was easier keeping people at arm's length. Today, people saw her at her worst and they didn't run. They didn't point their fingers and yell she was a freak like they had when she was a child. Even her own mother called her horrible things. Yet, Asher's family asked questions to understand, not to judge or blame.

If that wasn't a miracle, she didn't know what was.

She pulled away from Asher as she approached the guest room door. "Thank you. I'd like that. If—"

"No ifs. You scared the shit out of me today. Whitefeather understood what was going on. He tried to explain it to us." He blew out a long breath. "I may never understand what happened. The thing is...I don't have to explain it. It happened. What's done is done. You didn't die." He motioned to himself. "I didn't die. We're good, right?"

"Yeah." She gave him a faint smile. "We're good."

Such a guy thing to chuck everything in the past. They made it out alive. No further discussion needed.

16

T es woke the following morning with one thought on her mind.

Sunday. All they needed was for Nikki to be remorseful—then Hailey and Morgan would be let go.

Tes got ready for the day, praying good news would come, and headed downstairs to the living room.

Asher sat in the corner sectional, ankles crossed, feet resting on a large ottoman. He had a coffee cup in one hand and petted Ruthie with the other.

A commercial touting the benefits of feminine products aired. *Lovely.*

"Good morning." Tes moved toward the kitchen. "Mind if I grab some coffee?"

"Help yourself."

She joined him on the couch, sitting on the opposite side of Ruthie. "She likes you."

"I'm kind of in love with your dog. Is Ruth a family name?"

"No. I named her after Dr. Ruth, the sex therapist."

He smiled. "Huh. Would have never guessed."

She took a sip, enjoying the warmth and comfort caffeine would bring. "I may have hang-ups about intimacy, but not about sex."

"You must be feeling better if you're back to being Dr. Tes."

She gave him a weak smile. "And a little hungry."

"I'll make you breakfast."

"No. I can grab something."

He stiffened. "You're planning to leave already?" He leaned closer. "You're not used to people offering to help you, are you?" He squinted, shaking his head. "For being a psychiatrist that's kind of like an oxymoron, isn't it?"

"Evaluating and assessing patients is different from personal interactions."

"Hm." He tilted his head. "You're a compartmental thinker."

She lifted her brows and stared at the TV. "I guess I am. What kind of thinker are you?"

"Not that."

She couldn't help but smile. Why was he trying to analyze her?

"Breaking news," the TV interrupted. The news anchor sat with her perky smile behind a fake Seattle skyline backdrop. "Mother of kidnapping victim Morgan McKinley arrived moments ago at SeaTac Airport. She learned of her daughter's situation after arriving from a remote fishermen's village where she and boyfriend, millionaire Ben Winslow, of Winslow Industries, had gone for the holiday weekend. Jim?"

"What the hell?" Tes jumped to her feet, putting her coffee cup on a coaster on the table. She glanced at her phone and unlocked the screen. She'd received two messages from Nikki. One read, *Call me.* The second, *How could you let them take Morgan?* There it was in plain black-and-white. The blame she'd been bracing for had arrived. All wrapped up in less than ten words.

"Thanks, Angie." The image cut to the field reporter, who showed great concern to the audience. "Moments ago, I talked with Nickola McKinley, counselor at Whitman High School. Mid-Friday afternoon, Morgan McKinley was allegedly kidnapped." The camera's image split, showing Nikki's house. "Nikola learned of her daughter's kidnapping from the AMBER alert once they arrived in Anchorage late last night. Attempts to reach Nikola's sister, Dr. Tesla Brynn, have gone unanswered. Police are unsure if she was part of the kidnapping or fell to foul play herself."

Asher came to her side, wrapping his arm around her shoulders. Ruthie jumped off the couch and flanked her other side.

Tes showed Asher the messages from Nikki.

He tossed her phone on the ottoman. "The news twists things for ratings. I'd like to say you'll get used to it, but you won't."

The TV showed Nikki at a podium. Six microphones crowded in front of her, all labeled with their stations' logos.

Great. International news.

Tears streaked her sister's face. "Hi." A heavy breath reverberated across the microphones. "I'm Nikola McKinley. My only child, Morgan, was taken from my home while she was under my sister's care." Nikki turned away from the camera's harsh light shining across her pale features. Ben Winslow stood at her side and handed her a tissue. He draped his arm around her shoulders, showing solidarity.

Nikki took her time and several breaths before speaking again. "I've never left my daughter before. *Ever.* This was the first time."

Asher swore under his breath. "Liar. What about Vegas, Nikki?" He glanced at Tes. "She wasn't there for Hailey and Morgan's twelfth birthday because of it."

Tes frowned. "They have the same birthday?"

"Yeah. You didn't know that?"

"I guess I didn't."

Asher's jaw flexed.

Tes braced her heart for the next blow.

Nikki tucked her hair behind her ear. "Ben and I went away because he wanted us to be together in the most beautiful place on earth where he proposed to me." She flashed the evidence in front of the cameras.

Was that before or after the orgy?

"We were coming home to tell Morgan our good news. When—" Nikki covered her mouth.

Tears actually flowed from Nikki's eyes. Maybe she was sorry. Would it be enough for the kidnapper to let Hailey and Morgan go? Then again, Nikki was always a pretty crier and used tears to get her way as often as she could.

"My sister, Tesla Brynn, hasn't returned my calls."

"*She didn't call.*" Tes was pissed. "Texting is not calling."

Nikki continued, "I don't know if she was involved with taking Morgan."

"That bitch." Tes grabbed her phone and dialed.

Nikki's phone buzzed on camera. *Didn't leave that in the safe after all, huh?* She made a desperate gesture to take the call. Nikki glanced at the cameras, shock and surprise filled her face. "It's her. It's my sister." The cameras stopped flashing. The room paused, holding its breath. Silence surrounded Nikki as she pressed the button. "I'll put it on speaker."

"Tesla?" Nikki choked back a sob.

"I didn't take Morgan. If you would have talked to Special Agent Krysinski, the person in charge of Morgan's case, you would have known that. The same person that kidnapped Hailey Hickok took Morgan. Just once, Nikki, why don't you tell the truth? You're not the mother you're trying to portray. I know the truth. The kidnapper knows the truth—or he wouldn't have taken Hailey and Morgan in the first place."

Asher yanked her phone from her hand and ended the call. "*You can't say that to the public.*"

Before Tes could rebut, a knock interrupted.

Asher went to the door. "Tom. Did you hear?"

"Yeah." He grabbed Asher and pushed him inside before shutting the door. "They're okay. The girls were found by a park ranger about an hour ago. They've been taken to

Children's Hospital."

Asher stumbled backward and collapsed on the stairs. "They're alive?"

Tes joined them in the foyer.

"Yes. Both are a little battered and bruised from navigating the forest in the dark, but none the worse for wear."

Tom crouched in front of Asher. "The news is going to be all over this. I'd like to take Asher separately from you, Tes. Your sister's going to be there. Winslow's already coordinating a news conference with the hospital staff within the hour."

Tes glanced back at the TV. "Then why did Nikki go on TV to act like she'd just found out about Morgan's kidnapping if she also knew she was at the hospital?"

Tom raised a brow. "Winslow coordinated the news conference yesterday. There will be a follow-up segment in time for the five o'clock news. Winslow's negotiating exclusive interviews with major networks as we speak."

"Anything to make a buck." Tes sat beside Asher and hugged him tight. "I told you they would come home."

He kissed her cheek, cupping her face in his hands. "You did."

"I'm so happy for you, Asher." She pulled away. "Go. You've been waiting too long for this moment. I'll be right behind you."

"I need to tell my parents. My family."

She motioned toward his phone. "Call them on the way. Get going."

**

The car ride seemed to take an eternity, even with blazing lights and blaring sirens. Hospital officials ushered Asher directly to Hailey's bedside.

"Daddy?"

Asher hung in the doorway for a split second, taking in the sight of his baby girl and the sound of her voice. A lifetime of memories cascaded over him, from her first step to that last phone call. It was true. She was here and alive. He stepped into the room and pulled her into his arms as he sank beside her on the bed. "Hey, my sweet Hailey. I love you."

"I love you, Dad." She felt thin. She'd lost weight. There wouldn't be any talk about the horrors that'd happened. There would be plenty of time for that later. For now, all he wanted was to hold her, rock her, and let her know she wasn't alone anymore. There was a good chance she'd have a babysitter for the rest of her life, but that was a protective dad's prerogative.

"Let me look at you." He pulled away and looked her over. She looked relatively clean. There were a few smudges of dirt on her face. He licked his thumb and wiped the one on her jawline away.

"Da-a-ad." She pulled away. Yeah, she still didn't like that.

He laughed. "Not a moment passed that I didn't think of you." An IV poured fluids into her vein. She must have been dehydrated.

"All I thought about was you."

He kissed her cheek and held her close.

"Daddy." Hailey's sobs broke his heart.

He rubbed her back the same way he did when she was a baby. "It's all right now. You're home. You're safe."

"We escaped. He's still out there."

He smoothed her hair, rocking her in his arms. "No one's ever going to hurt you again." He'd kill the motherfucker first.

She pulled away, tilting her head. "Is it true?"

"Is what true?" He furrowed his brow.

"Is Morgan my sister?"

Asher's breath seized. No one knew. The court records were sealed.

Here was one of those big moments of truth. If he lied, he'd never recover any ounce of validity as a parent worth believing in. "No one knows. How did you find out?"

"The kidnapper told us everything."

A hacker.

Shit. The original court documents were on his computer. Maybe on Nikki's computer too. *Shit.* He'd never wanted to explain how Morgan was his daughter—sure as hell not at a moment like this.

"Where's Mom?" Hailey's eyes drifted to the doorway.

"She moved to North or South Dakota. I can't remember which. It isn't like we kept in touch."

"He'd told me that too. I, you know, hoped."

The kidnapper had kept tabs on everyone? Hairs rose along his arms. "What else did he tell you?"

"He has a lot of respect for you."

It must be someone he knew well enough to know secret details. Was it the lawyer who drew up the parenting agreement between him and Nikki? His family didn't even know Morgan was his daughter. His one big lie. His one big secret. His one Achilles heel.

"Nonna! Poppop!" Hailey threw her arms open as his parents arrived.

Asher moved back to give his parents access to Hailey. He needed to see Morgan. He glanced at Hailey and hitched his thumb toward the door.

"It's okay, Dad."

He stepped into the hall and Krysinski tilted his head toward the next room. Morgan sat alone on the bed.

"Dad?" she whispered. Her chin dipped low, eyes full of worry.

Asher stepped into the room. Tears streaked her face. Her hands twisted a blanket into a crumpled mess. "Hi, Morgan." Like he did with Hailey, he sat on the mattress and hugged her hard, as if for the first time ever. "I'm your dad." He dragged in a shaky breath between his lips. On one hand, he never thought he'd say those words and, on another, he was glad his secret was out.

He pulled back, cupping her face in his hands. "I love you and I'm so proud of you."

She cried harder. "Why didn't you ever tell me?"

He wrapped her tight in his arms. "Because your mother made me promise—had a court order that said I wasn't allowed to. I'd planned to tell you after you turned eighteen. Your mother said if I ever told you, I'd never see you again. I never wanted to put you through that. Not after having you in my life—even if it only was on the weekends." He pulled back to see her face. He wiped away her tears with his thumbs.

Morgan sucked in a deep, slobbery breath. "All this time, she made me believe my dad was a criminal. A loser. I always thought I was half a loser. It takes a demented stranger to tell me that you're my dad. I always wanted you to be my dad." She pulled away. "You were just a kid."

"Shh. Don't think about it." He cradled her head against his chest. He sure as hell didn't want to relive the details. How in the hell was he going to explain everything to his family? Tes? That was why secrets shouldn't be locked up tight. Scandals had a way of eking to the surface like a submarine breaching the ocean.

Nikki burst into the room. "Morgan," she blubbered through her sobs, stretching out her name as if it were a paragraph.

Asher pulled away, taking in Nikki from the doorway. He was so pissed at how she'd thrown Tes under the bus in front of the media that he didn't trust his tongue.

"Get the hell away from me." Morgan sneered at Nikki.

"Morgan." Asher tried to calm her down with his fatherly tone.

"She's a whore. I'm never going to live with you ever again. You kept me from my real dad and I *hate* you."

Nikki gasped short breaths. Her mouth dropped open. She tightened her jaw and chiseled her glare on Asher. "You told her. *You bastard.*"

"No, I didn't." Asher stood, blocking Nikki from getting to Morgan.

"He didn't," Morgan snapped. "My kidnapper told me everything about you. About you and Ben and God knows who else you've been with. *You're a whore.*"

What. The. Hell? Asher stared at Morgan, then Nikki.

The shock on Nikki's face showed the truth. "What? Those are your first words to me after being kidnapped?"

"Yeah, did you know good ol' Ben records everything and saves it on his computer? I got a front row seat." Morgan curled her upper lip. "*You disgust me.*" She threw back the thin blanket and dangled her legs over the edge. Asher grabbed the IV stand so Morgan wouldn't rip it out of her hand if she went after Nikki.

Ben entered the room and stood behind Nikki.

Morgan glared and pointed. "Get that asshole out of my room. I never want to see him ever again."

"That's a little hard, since we're getting married." Nikki flashed Morgan her engagement ring with a motherly raised brow. "You're a kid. I'm the mom." She pointed to herself, then Morgan. "You'll do as I damn well say. That will be the end of the discussion."

"No, it won't. I'm going to live with my dad. My *real* dad. The one you raped when he was a kid."

"I never raped him." Nikki glanced at Asher.

Of course she didn't see it that way.

Ben Winslow stormed away.

Nikki glanced over her shoulder. "Ben. Wait. It's a lie."

Tes stood there, Ruthie by her side. Her bewildered look explained she'd overheard enough.

Nikki clenched her hands and unloaded her wrath. "You did all of this. You couldn't even watch Morgan. I should have known better than to ever leave you in charge."

"That's enough." Asher let go of the IV stand and intervened. "Your dirty little secret is out. You don't get to take it out on Tes."

Nikki narrowed her eyes. "You'll never see Morgan again. I'm getting her out of here—and we'll be out of your life before sunset today."

Krysinski stepped forward. "You're not taking Morgan anywhere."

Asher felt an inkling of relief.

"You two will have your day in court to settle your parenting disagreement. In light of what we've heard today..." Krysinski glanced at Tes. "We have a court order that relinquishes Morgan to her biological father until the investigation is completed."

"And what information is that?" Nikki glared at Tes.

Krysinski lowered his voice. "Allegations of you having sex with minors. Students."

Nikki's mouth twisted in anger and she stepped closer to Asher. "You know the consequences of your behavior."

"I don't have anything to be worried about." Asher raised a brow. He wouldn't have guessed he'd ever have custody of Morgan and he couldn't be happier.

***

Nikki hissed out a frustrated breath and turned to Krysinski. "I want to see this proof you have. The age for consensual sex is sixteen in Washington."

Tes slid her jaw to the side. "You think that's going to hold up in a court? I can't wait to see how justifying your life choices works to your benefit. Nikki, your job clearly states you can't have sex with students. You act like you're a doting mother, but I know differently. How you conduct yourself in private is your own business. I don't care who you have sex with, as long as they are a consenting *adult* and not a student. My main concern is that Morgan is raised in a good, loving home, and I know she'll have that with Asher and his family."

Nikki stepped closer to Tes. "I've been the only parent in her life since Stan—"

"Seriously?" Tes cut her off. "Stan wasn't her father." Her words were hollow, as if his secret finally registered. "Asher's been her father and he has proof that she's been staying with him every weekend for the last ten years. He has witnesses, and you have plenty of online pictures I'm sure Mum wouldn't want flashed across social media."

"You're blackmailing me?"

"Blackmailing is when someone holds a secret over your head for some kind of gain. I gain nothing in this. You threw me under the bus on a live newscast." Tes turned her focus to Morgan. "I'm glad you're home safe, Peanut." Her gaze shifted to Asher. "I'm glad you have a dad that loves you." She lifted her chin and swallowed. "Nikki, you need to watch your back. That kidnapper's still out there. You're the reason he took Morgan in the first place. He'll be coming for you next."

"I bet you know who it is." Nikki waved her hand in the air. "Another one of your little ghosts tell you he's coming for me? Another imaginary friend?"

Tes pulled on Ruthie's leash and the two of them walked away.

Mom came out of Hailey's room and into Morgan's. "You know, I always knew Morgan was our granddaughter."

Asher grabbed her arm. "Can you stay with Morgan? I need to talk to Tes."

"Of course."

He had to find Tes and explain this shit storm.

17

Tes waited as the last couple exited the elevator. Only when the doors closed again did she lean back against the wall and let the wave of pent-up emotion heave out of her chest.

Asher was Morgan's father? How in the hell did that happen?

It didn't matter if she and Asher had some cosmic connection in shared past lives. She was the sister of his childhood hookup. Fling? Rape?

If Morgan and Hailey were the same age—then Asher was sixteen when he had sex with Nikki. Anyone could do the math and realize Nikki was in her early twenties at the time. Tes had turned fifteen when Morgan was born. *He'd slept with a married woman.* Had he known she was married?

Ruthie leaned against her, giving her love. "What are we going to do?"

Tes knew what she was going to do. She had her earthly belongings in the car—and she was tempted to drive back to California. She was going to get away from all this family drama like Speedy Gonzales. *Arriba, arriba. Andale, andale.*

The elevator dinged and the doors opened. She'd stepped out into the cool parking garage when the door to the staircase flew open.

Asher grabbed her arm. "Tes, wait. Let me explain."

"You don't owe me an explanation. Go back to your daughters." *Go back to your life.*

"Tes, please listen." He dropped to a knee and grabbed her hips. He rested his forehead against her stomach for a moment before turning those beagle-brown eyes on her. Ruthie bumped his arm with her nose, and he let go long enough to pet her and scruff her ears.

Tes looked around. No one was in the area. "You don't need to tell me anything."

"Yes, I do. I owe it to you. My family. To Morgan."

"Nikki—"

"I want to tell you the truth."

She didn't want to hear it. She tried to wrestle out of his grip.

"I was sixteen. The week before, I'd had my first sexual experience in the backseat of my dad's Mustang. The next weekend, I was at a friend's house for a party. His parents were upstairs with their friends." He stood, taking hold of her shoulders so she wouldn't move. "I was coming out of the bathroom as Nikki was coming in."

"I don't want to hear this—what two consenting people do isn't any of my business."

"I was a kid, Tes. She pushed me back into the bathroom."

She thumped her forefinger against his chest. "When I asked if you ever dated my sister, you didn't think to tell me about this?"

"No one knew about it. Not my family. Not Morgan. If anyone deserved to know, it was Morgan. She deserved to know first. Trust me, when she turned eighteen, I'd planned on telling her. Once she was out of your sister's clutches." His grip tightened.

"She asked me to unzip her dress. I was confused, thinking what the hell? I could be nice and do that. She was completely naked underneath. She dropped the dress and turned around. Hell, I hadn't seen a grown woman naked in person before. She had my fly unzipped and her lips around my cock so fast, I didn't know what the hell was going on—and yeah, it felt good. I hadn't ever experienced that either. She sat me back on the toilet, turned around and—" He ran his hand through his hair. "You know the rest. She didn't even kiss me. It isn't like I lasted that long. She got up, put on her dress, asked me to zip her up, and left the bathroom like it was something she did every damn day." He swiped at his tears. "If it'd been a guy doing that to a girl in a bathroom—it'd be statutory rape. Being sixteen, I was confused. I didn't tell anyone. A few weeks later, I found out my girlfriend was pregnant. The only decision I made was to never have sex without a condom again." He took a deep breath and let his other hand drop.

Tes grabbed his hand. She needed to touch him. Wanted to comfort him.

"Fast-forward five years. First day of kindergarten. I'm walking Hailey up the sidewalk and guess who I run in to?" Asher pulled her into his arms and cried against her neck. "Morgan looked like my mom when she was that age, but with blue eyes." He pushed her to arm's length. "I filed a petition to verify Morgan was mine. When the test results came back as positive, Stan went off the rails."

Tes's mind whirled trying to process everything. "Nikki never said a word."

"I promised to keep my mouth shut. I pay child support and we have an agreement I get custody of Morgan if Nikki ever died. I also got the right to see her as often as I wanted. Morgan doesn't—sorry, didn't know—until now."

"You pay her child support?" Now that was rich.

"Of course."

"Did she ever disclose her financials?"

Asher shook his head, confused. "Why?"

"She has a trust fund that pays her thousands of dollars a month. How do you think she can afford new BMW's, cashmere sweaters, and vacations to Disneyland two times a year?"

He was stunned. "All I wanted was to have Morgan in my life. I didn't give a damn how much it cost."

"Then Stan was prosecuted and went to prison." Tes knew that part.

Asher lifted her hand and placed it over his heart. "It wasn't until years later that I realized what Nikki did to me was wrong. I'd do anything to keep Morgan in my life. Even keep my mouth shut."

Tes squared her shoulders. "I understand, Asher. Thank you for telling me." She plastered a smile on her lips. "You know, we didn't get off on the right footing. I appreciate you letting me stay with you. You have your daughters back. This is your time to heal. I don't want to be a third wheel while you guys figure out where to go from here."

"You don't have to go." He shook his head. "There's something between us, Tes. I don't know what it is, but I'd like to find out."

"Maybe. Just not right now. Give it some time, Asher. Re-adapt to your family life. Settle into a normal routine again. Then maybe someday..."

He kept shaking his head. "After all we've been through in the last few days—you'd throw away our friendship that easily?"

"I'm not throwing away anything. I'm stepping back. Letting you enjoy your children."

"I'm never going to see you again, am I?"

No. He wouldn't. He'd seen her dirty, dark secret, and she'd seen his. Souls filleted and bared to the bone. An uncomfortable silence welled between them. "It isn't like we had some clandestine love affair. We've been supportive to each other. I'm only a phone call away." Or text. Preferably never face-to-face again. She could only imagine what garbage Nikki would dish out. It was going to get ugly. God, she wanted to hide under a blanket and never come out again.

"I can't let you go." His mouth twisted. "I can't."

"Asher. It's going to be okay." She squeezed his hand. "You have two beautiful daughters that are *home*." One last hug and she'd be able to walk away. They'd done this before in other lifetimes. Except in all of those, one of them slipped from life to death.

This was a much better karmic ending. Parting as friends. Put the curse behind them and go their separate ways. It was shit like that she'd told herself all her life. *For the greater good.* "You know I'm right."

"This isn't about being right. This is about possibilities. Us."

Us. As beautiful as that word sounded to her ears, it wasn't meant to be. Maybe someday, but not today.

He slipped his hand into his jeans pocket and pulled out his keyring, removing a key. "Please, Tes. Wait for me until I get home."

She grabbed the key from his hand, knowing full well she'd never keep it. She'd place it under the welcome mat and text him later where she'd put it.

One last look at his incredibly handsome face. She cupped his face in her hands, committing to memory his gorgeous eyes, sexy smile, and strong arms. She'd cherish him forever. She went up on tiptoe, wrapped her arms around his neck, and kissed him. He held onto her like she was his only lifeline, crushing his lips against hers, and holding her tight.

Nothing had ever felt so perfect. Their soul connection was undeniable. He was home. Her true north star. Her logical brain put up the wall that kept her from committing anything further.

She pulled away and instantly regretted it. How could one kiss tear a hole in her heart? "Go," she whispered against his lips. "Those girls need their father."

He stared into her eyes, his gaze brushing over her face, and kissed her again. One more soft, sweet kiss that made her want to hold onto him and never let go. He stepped away, then turned back. "Their father needs you."

Why did he have to say things like that?

***

Tes unpacked her groceries, careful not to upset the lone chocolate-with-chocolate-frosting cupcake. Her pinky finger snagged the faucet, toppling the cupcake onto its side. "Dammit." It slammed onto the counter next to the tiny fridge. The cupcake jostled, smearing more frosting inside its clear plastic casing.

It was an omen. Nothing would ever be right again.

The motel with a kitchenette met the creature comforts in life but lacked the ambience of a real home. She'd selected the roadside dive because it rented for a decent price per month. The dog park and grocery store were within walking distance. For now, it was home sweet, tacky home.

Meditation and a normal routine with Ruthie helped Tes focus on her goals. She'd been successful at ignoring Asher's phone calls, but how many lame excuses was she going to have to come up with before he went away forever? Deep down, she didn't want that. Every time she listened to his voice mail messages, an emptiness settled heavy in her chest. He'd invited her over every day, and she'd found excuse after excuse why she couldn't drop by or join in on the Hickok family fun. Giving him space was the right thing to do. In all honesty, she wasn't sure if the time and space was for him or for herself. In reality, the distance was making her heart ache more every day she didn't see him.

One big obstacle kept her at bay. If she accepted Asher, it meant she accepted Morgan as his daughter. With Morgan came interactions with Nikki. Could she do that? How could Asher look at her and not think about Nikki taking advantage of that innocent teenager? Maybe if she didn't look so much like her sister, it'd be easier. One thing was for certain, her every thought had been consumed with Asher. She hardly knew him yet her resistance was dwindling.

Thank God, Nikki had carried through with her original plans of speaking at a teachers' conference out of state, so Morgan didn't have to have daily battles between her parents. Then Nikki and Ben went to Mexico. She hadn't learned this from Nikki herself. No, it was from the daily texts from her niece that kept her in the loop.

Texts from Morgan were the lifeline to the only family she had left. Morgan shared that, overall, she was happy. She had a dad, aunts, uncles, and grandparents for real now. Most of all, she loved being a sister to her best friend. The online posts of them reconnecting on a deeper level warmed Tes's heart.

At least her niece got a happy ending.

One question lingered in the back of Tes's mind. Who was the kidnapper? Was he still watching, biding time for his next move?

That lone semi-smooshed cupcake reminded her that tomorrow was the anniversary of the worst day of her life. Other people celebrated their birthdays like rites of passage from one stage of life to the next. Tes's birthday reminded her of the day she had died. Boy, if she could go back in time and hit the reset button, what kind of life would she have had then? She spent this momentous anniversary crying in her pillow every year. She allowed herself one day a year to indulge in self-pity. She also openly acknowledged she'd be alone the rest of her life. No one in their right mind would want to be near someone like her. She was dangerous to mankind. Hell, she was dangerous to herself. All it would take was one more burst of electricity and she'd fade from this life to the next.

"Damn, what a defeatist," she said aloud, more to herself than Ruthie.

Ruthie's ears perked. "Not you, baby." She petted her for reassurance.

Tes needed to make permanent plans. Either she stayed here in Washington or moved back to California. She stared at the pros and cons list she'd been crafting the last week, hardly making any progress.

Tes didn't have a job yet. Either way, she would have to hang her shingle somewhere, buckle down, and pay bills like everyone else. She also needed to find a permanent place to live. Washington was expensive. California, more so.

The empty "pro" columns stared back at her like an LCD flashlight on high beams. She tapped the end of her pen against her cheek. Were there any pros?

A knock interrupted her thoughts.

Asher better not have traced her cell phone. Ruthie jumped off the bed and stood at the door wagging her tail. She pawed at the floor, anxious for Tes to open it.

Tes tiptoed to the door, leaned over, and looked through the peep hole. She smiled and opened the door. "Hi, Joni."

"Hey, Tes. I thought you could use a friend right about now."

She had no idea. "Come on in."

Joni wrapped her in a warm hug and held her long enough for it not to be weird, but comforting, caring, and thoughtful. "Great place. Love your decorator." Sarcasm dripped in her tone.

"Yes, it's early millennium with a dash of hungover '90s. A rare find, really."

Joni laughed. "I brought some junk food." She set the cloth grocery bag on the dinette table.

"I have snacks." Tes waved a hand over her fare on the nightstand.

Joni looked at the food and narrowed her eyes. "What a rebel you are with grapes and apple slices." She pulled items from the bag. "Girl, junk food enjoyment is binging on ice cream, Cheetos, and Snickers. In that order."

"Well, I never was good at partying." Tes opened the top drawer in the small kitchenette and pulled out two spoons. "Did I ever mention that once I start eating ice cream, I can't stop?"

Joni smiled. "Me either. That's why I buy the extra-small size."

Okay, so there was a pro. The Gregsons were an amazing family. Joni was the only person on earth Tes had ever met who didn't freak out over her talking to ghosts. A kindred spirit was a good reason to stay—if she could avoid running into Nikki and Asher. She was bound to see him eventually. Morgan was going to graduate from high school in two years. By then, Asher would have forgotten all about her and they could shake hands and smile nice for the camera. Two years from now had a nice ring to it.

Joni held up the two containers of ice cream. "Rocky road or mint chocolate chip?"

"Whichever one my friend doesn't want. I love them both."

"Aw. I knew I liked you for a reason." She slid the mint chocolate chip her way.

Tes twitched her head toward the bed. "Let's get comfy."

Joni sank to the mattress opposite Tes, both sitting crossed-legged, knees almost touching. Ruthie jumped on the bed and panted in Joni's face until she petted her before settling down, her tail beating a tattoo against the mattress. She read Tes's list. "What's this?"

"I'm making a pros and cons list for staying here or moving back to California."

"You don't have any pros."

"Cons come easier."

Joni scribbled words on the pad, paused a moment, and wrote a few more. She turned the page around so Tes could see.

Under Washington pros she wrote "new best friend, new job, new life." Under California cons she wrote "smog, expensive, crime rate, all alone."

"I think settling in a place where I have a new best friend is the best reason to stay."

"You bet it is." Joni held up a scoop of ice cream. Tes lifted a spoon as well. They clicked the utensils to their futures and filled their mouths with sweet yumminess.

Small talk ensued where Joni shared about Sammy's latest developments. Before long, she asked the million-dollar question. "So, how's Asher and the girls?"

Tes took a deep breath. "They seem to be doing well."

"Why haven't you called him?" Joni's dark lashes peered over the edge of her spoon. She blinked a few times.

"Asher's been in contact with you and Zeke?"

"He's called Zeke. They're going fishing at the crack of who gets up at that gawdawful hour tomorrow. Once I hear the words 'tie a fly,' I tune out." She waved a hand and rolled her eyes.

Tes laughed. "I hear you on that. I don't understand fishing. I think I'd rather watch paint dry."

"You do know I have a house built with no one ready to move in it, right?"

"I'm more of a fifty-square-meters kinda gal." She waved around at her abysmal environment. "A whole house to myself would make me feel like I was wasting space on nothing. You should save it for when a family needs to move in."

Joni pulled up a corner of her mouth. "I was hoping you'd move into the neighborhood. Then I could drop by and have ice cream any old time. Besides, when you're working for the foundation, it'll be nice to have you close by."

"I can do work for the foundation, but I see myself as a stand-alone psychiatrist. I've been scoping space in Bellevue, but man, is it expensive."

"You don't want to join a clinic?"

Tes shook her head. "I've considered it, but let's be honest. No one's going to put up with me talking to ghosts." She swallowed another bite. "I love working with children and I want that to be my specialty. I know I'm going to have to take on adult clients while I get established."

"That creeps you out, doesn't it?"

She let out a pent-up breath. "Like you wouldn't believe."

"You wouldn't have that issue with the foundation. You can work strictly with kids." Joni leaned forward. "When I woke from my coma, Sammy came to me."

"Your Sammy?"

"He was my first spirit guide. We specialized in finding missing children." Joni grew pensive. "Since I had my Sammy, I get the willies when I see child ghosts." She paused. "And besides, I'm pregnant."

Tes gasped. "Congratulations."

"Thanks. I can't have child ghosts around my baby." Joni rubbed her belly. "This time when I take time off after the baby's born, I need someone who can run things for me while I adapt to a toddler and newborn. Please, Tes. Please say you'll join us."

With no solid job prospects in place, how could she turn her down? "It would mean I have to come out of the medium closet."

Joni laughed. "You already have. You already have a new client."

"I do?"

"Samantha and Jason would love to have you help Chester with the adjustment to their new baby and being a big brother. They'll be back in town next week. If you're up for it."

"Okay."

Joni squealed and wrapped Tes in a hug. "I'm going to love working with you."

"I sure hope so." Worst-case scenario, she'd give it a try and look for something else while getting paid. It was a solid business plan.

"Oh, Tom Krysinski's retirement party is Friday. He asked me to invite you because you don't have a permanent address yet."

"He said he's going to work for you."

"Yep and he's moving into the neighborhood. I surround myself with family." Joni lowered her voice. "You're going to be part of our family."

That sounded wonderful. Since Tes was currently between families, it was a promise laced with hope. Her empty heart filled a little more. It was an odd sensation to have hope. She glanced at her cupcake. What would it be like to not have to buy only one cupcake next year? She petted Ruthie's belly. "You hear that, Ruthie? We're part of a family now."

"So, in the meantime, while you're between homes, why don't you come live with Zeke and me?"

"Oh, hell no." Tes rolled her eyes. "You have a baby. Babies wake up in the middle of the night. They make messes."

"Oh my God. You love kids but don't want to live with any, is that it?"

"You got it. I value my sleep. My me time. No toys to step on. No dirty diapers." Tes cringed. "I want a kid that's beyond all that when I adopt in a few years."

The smile fell from Joni's face. "What are you talking about? You're marrying Asher and having a houseful of kids."

Joni's words reverberated in her heart. In an instant, hope welled up from the bottom of her soul to the top of her dreams. *Children with Asher.* No, no. She tamped the elation back in place. There wouldn't be any dreaming of a glorious life filled with love. She couldn't. It was leaping too far in the field of faith—and her faith in love had been shaken her entire life. *How could Asher love her when her own mother didn't?* "Asher needs to concentrate on the girls. We're friends."

"You're more than friends."

"He's cute."

"Cute?" Joni mumbled something under her breath. "You'd jump his bones in a heartbeat."

If the right circumstances revealed themselves, yes, she would. Then again, why would he when she looked like Nikki? How could he look at her and not think of that moment? "I don't think he thinks of me that way."

"He's a guy. Trust me, he thinks of you that way."

Their father needs you. "I wouldn't ever want to get my hopes up."

Joni took their empty ice cream containers, dropped them in the trash, put the spoons in the sink, and snagged the Cheetos on her way back to the bed. "What are you afraid of?"

"Love. Being loved. To count on it being true. Forever. Free of curses." Here she was baring her soul again. This whole opening-up crap had to end.

18

"Curses?" Joni popped the Cheetos bag open, folded back the edges, and placed it between them.

"I've been having the strangest dreams since meeting Asher." Tes explained each snippet she'd experienced. "Then Mrs. Wallen pranced around in her after-death state saying 'Roses are red, violets are blue. Don't say I love you, until you say I do'."

"Damn, that's some deep stuff. Let me consult with Mambo Janetta. She's a wise woman from the other side. She'll know what it means and, if there's a curse, how to get rid of it."

"I think it's pretty obvious, don't you? I can't say those three little words to Asher." Tes closed her eyes for a moment. "How can I miss a guy I hardly know?"

"He's your soulmate."

"I don't believe in soulmates."

Joni crunched a Cheeto. "You have more contradictions in one person than I've ever met."

"I suppose that's true."

Joni licked her Cheetos-covered fingertips. "I can help you learn to control the energy bursts."

"How?"

"It sounds like you go all-in instead of increasing it in increments."

Tes thought a moment. "I think I've only used it when shit hits the fan. You know, when dead people walk around when they shouldn't."

"Yeah, I totally get what you mean." Joni laughed. "I had to practice a lot with my telekinetic abilities."

"Your what?"

"Moving things with my mind. At first, I'd cause full-scale earthquakes even when I wanted to move something like a spoon. It took time to understand how much energy to expend. It was hard to focus at first, but it became easier the more I did it. Next time—"

"Oh, there won't be a next time." Tes waved off the thought.

"There's going to be a next time. Think about it. You could save someone's life. What if someone had a heart attack and there weren't any defibrillator paddles nearby? You could restart their heart."

"They'd have to be totally flat-lined first. It's dangerous to restart a heart that doesn't need it."

Joni rolled her eyes. "Yeah, whatever. You're a doctor. You'd know when. Trust your training." She paused. "Trust your gut."

A knock sounded at the door. "That's probably Zeke. He dropped me off. Did I mention I don't drive?"

"Really?" Tes rose from the bed and opened the door. "Asher," she choked, shocked he stood there in person. Her hand clutched the doorknob like a lifeline.

He hung back by the rickety wrought iron railing. He looked like hell. His cheeks were sunken and dark smudges surrounded his eyes. "Hi, Tes."

She tried to swallow the sudden tightness in her throat and coughed. "Do you want to come in? Joni's here."

Ruthie shoved past her and jumped on Asher, licking his face, tail wagging a million miles per hour. He petted her and hugged her close. Tes wanted those arms around her.

"Ruthie, down." She gazed into Asher's sad eyes. "She's not supposed to jump on people."

He continued stroking Ruthie's back, digging his fingers through her hair. "You haven't returned my calls, so I thought I'd take a more direct approach."

Nothing like twisting the knife. "Asher—"

Ruthie licked Asher's face one last time before meandering back inside the room, jumping onto the bed next to Joni.

He held up his hand. "I won't keep you. My sister Ava and her family arrived from Vancouver yesterday. We're having a family picnic tomorrow. I'd like you to meet them."

Her heartstrings bowed close to a snapping point. If it were any other day than tomorrow, she'd say yes in a heartbeat. It was easy to lie in a text message, but how could she look him in the eye and lie to his face? "I'd love to, but I'm busy tomorrow."

"You would?" He lifted his chin and smiled. "You'd love to come?"

"Tomorrow's not a good day for me."

"What are you doing? How late will you be? You could join us when you're done with whatever you're doing."

He wasn't going to let it go. She glanced over her shoulder at that cupcake. It screamed, "Don't forget me." *Remember our annual commiseration party?* "Tomorrow's a hard day for me."

He furrowed his brows. "Is it the anniversary of being hit by lightning?"

"It's not a day that I spend around people. I'm sure you understand."

"No, not really." He shoved his hands in his pockets. "You'd prefer to spend the day alone than be surrounded by family? People who want to support you and have you in their lives?"

"I don't have a family." She dropped her gaze to his feet. She whispered, "Not anymore." Tears pricked her eyes.

"What about Morgan?"

Damn, he knew how to go for the jugular. "I suppose she's my niece, but more important, she's your daughter." *Nikki's daughter.*

"She misses you."

Tes lifted her gaze to his chest. "I miss her too."

"Then why don't you come to the family picnic, so we can celebrate the girls coming home?"

She scrunched her nose and shook her head. "It's not a day I've ever spent being happy. I don't want to be the Debby Downer at your party."

Silence welled between them. She returned to staring at his feet. *Nice tennis shoes.*

Joni came to her side. "Zeke, Sammy, and I will be there. We don't know Asher's family, and we're going."

This visit was feeling less like a girl-bonding time and more like an intervention.

Joni rubbed her arm. "You know what it feels like to be alone in a crowd. To feel like you don't belong." She paused. "I'd feel less alone if you were there. Do it for me?"

"I'd do it for Morgan, if anyone. She's a kid struggling with a lot right now."

Asher stepped forward. "Then do it for Morgan."

She glanced at his face. He was sad. Was it because she wouldn't do it to see him? What was she talking about? She wasn't going. Then again, Asher wasn't going to leave unless she agreed to go. She'd text him in the morning saying she'd changed her mind. She never knew she was such a chicken shit before. Now, she knew *that* too. "What time would you like me to be there?"

"Noon." He smiled.

She liked his smile. "Can I bring anything? And by bring anything, I mean, what can I pick up at the store?"

He shook his head. "Just bring you." His gaze drifted inside the room. "And Ruthie. You know my mom will make more than enough food for everyone, plus a hundred more."

"Great." Joni stepped back inside giving them some privacy.

Tes imagined Isabella preparing today for tomorrow's festivities. Asher's sisters were probably helping like they'd done a million times before. It was a memory she'd always wanted for herself, but her family never cooked meals together.

He stared at her Cheetos-crusted fingers, making her feel more conscientious than before. The second his hand touched hers, energy pulsed through her. She fought the urge to pounce. Slowly, he licked the salty goodness from her forefinger, scraping his teeth against her flesh. Goosebumps soared up her arm, tightening her nipples. Heat pooled between her thighs. He did the same to her thumb. She was practically coming. She heaved deep breaths, hitching when he nipped her thumb. "Can I hug you?"

He crushed her against his chest. Her equilibrium spun. The worries and tension that'd stored in her muscles faded. He kissed her hard, licking Cheetos crumbs from her lips, suckling each one as she panted, digging her nails into his back. He tried to pull away, but her death grip stopped him. She didn't want him to go. "The girls are in the truck." He kissed her one more time, softer, lighter. "I'll see you tomorrow."

She loosened her grip and waved as he walked away. Her gaze drifted over the parking lot and she saw the girls in Asher's truck high-fiving each other. Maybe it wouldn't be so bad having two loving daughters.

Once Tes closed the door, she took a moment to let the air conditioning return her to a normal temperature. She sank onto the bed, leaning against the headboard, a pillow tucked tight against her chest. "God, what that man does to me."

"It's a good kind of crazy, isn't it?"

"Yes, it is."

They talked for another hour before Zeke and Sammy showed up to take Joni home. Tes got to give Sammy some goodnight kisses and cuddles. Babies weren't so bad.

The gaping hole in her heart threatened to mend. She'd have to trust in this new life. Trust that someone could genuinely care for her. Maybe even love her. Trust wasn't easy. It was foreign territory, like being sent away at eight to a boarding school in Switzerland. Wheelchair-bound and all alone. Trust was exactly like that. She didn't know the language, she didn't know the customs, and she wanted to stay in her room, barricade the door, and never interact with people again.

Back then, she'd been forced to come out of her shell, pried open as though she was a sea clam. It took months for her to talk to others. She was the "special" one, all right. The word *outsider* might as well be stamped across her forehead. She'd spent a lifetime without a best friend. To trust that too? Damn, any more of this healing and she'd be in therapy herself.

19

After a morning run with Ruthie, a shower, and a bowl of oatmeal, Tes settled back against her pillows, letting sadness enter her soul.

"Happy birthday to little ol' me." She tugged Ruthie closer to her side. Dying on your birthday should be against a universal law.

She hadn't looked at her scar in years. She wouldn't look at it today either. It was there, hanging out as an ugly reminder of what happened twenty years ago.

A fist thudded against her door hard enough to wake the dead. "Housekeeping."

"I left the damn 'Do not disturb' sign out there for a reason."

The second knock was louder. "Housekeeping."

All the good intentions in the world would have to interrupt her trip down haunted memory lane. Ruthie yawned, lifting her head, exhausted from their run. *Nice guard dog.*

Tes stomped to the door, shoved the chain aside, and yanked the door open, ready to rip the maid a new one, and froze.

Joni smirked, sliding her sunglasses to the end of her nose. "Guess who's baa-aack?"

Tes hadn't even texted Asher yet to tell him she wasn't coming. "Did you forget something?"

"Yeah. You." Joni flipped her finger, motioning her to back away from the door. Tes didn't budge. "You don't look ready for the picnic."

"I'm not going."

"Yes, you are." Joni stepped forward. "You're going and you're going to like it." She kept coming.

Tes yielded, backing into her cool, dark room.

"You planned on sitting in the dark all day?" Joni flipped the light switch and shut the door with her foot.

"What difference does it make? It's my life. If I want to spend the day cast in darkness, I shall."

"Your accent is slipping." Joni moved to the closet, turned on another light, and started thumbing through the few items Tes had unpacked.

"My accent is not slipping." Tes cupped a hand over her mouth. *Dammit.* She couldn't help it when she was nervous or angry. At the moment, she was a combo platter of both.

"This is cute." Joni pulled out a jean skirt, a white T-shirt, and a plaid green and blue shirt. "Or you can go in your sweats. I don't care, but when you have a nice guy to meet, a girl's got to put in some effort."

"I refuse to go."

Joni stared at her and laughed. "Okay, I have to admit your British accent makes you sound like you're hugging ten fuzzy kittens when you're mad."

"It most certainly does not."

Joni paused, stared at her for a few seconds, then burst out laughing again. "Get dressed, Cinderella. You're going to the ball."

Tes folded her arms and lifted her chin. "You're daft. I'm not going."

Joni shoved her tongue into her cheek. "You do remember I'm telekinetic?" She demonstrated by hanging Tes's clothes in mid-air and layering them on the bed. "Don't make me get forceful with you."

"I can't go." Tes shook her head and slumped onto the bed. "You don't understand."

Joni slipped her warm hands around hers, crouching in front of her. "I know you're scared. God, I know what it feels like to open your heart to people you don't know and trust that they're going to love you back. I know what it's like to hope for happiness and be so terrified you'd rather do anything else but believe it could happen. All of your dreams can come true."

"I don't have dreams."

"Yes, you do. I can see them in your eyes when you look at Asher." Joni stood and took in the room. "Besides, today's moving day and we need to pack up all your stuff."

"Moving? I'm paid up through the end of the month."

"Zeke took one look at this place last night and about came unhinged. He put his foot down. You're moving into our penthouse apartment in Bellevue. You'll have security and sure as hell not a flimsy-assed chain to keep you from the outside world." She blew out a deep breath, fluttering her dark bangs. "Trust me, you want to deal with me and not him right now. If he has to come up here and get your ass moving, it's not going to be pretty. There are lectures." Joni moved her hand waist-high. "Then there are Zeke lectures." She moved her hand way above her head. "Trust me, you don't want a Zeke lecture. When that man gets on a tirade, you might as well give in, or you'll be there until you do."

"Why should my safety be any of his concern? I have Ruthie."

"Aw. You have a sweet, widdle, fluffy puppy." Ruthie wagged her tail at Joni's sweet tone. "She'll lick whoever comes through that door. Yeah, that's a great defense tactic." Joni tilted her head. "Zeke's a former Marine."

Tes's eyes widened. "What's that supposed to mean?"

"It means, get your ass dressed before he gets here in five minutes."

"I don't like being bossed around."

"I'm sure you don't. I sure as hell hate it, but sometimes you need a good ass-whooping to get your head on straight. Today's that day."

Tes glanced at her clothes.

"Happy birthday, by the way."

Tes snapped her glare on Joni. "LeBron told you."

"Yeah, well. So what? You're not spending another birthday alone as long as I live."

"It's more than just my birthday."

Joni's expression softened. "I know what today means to you. Mambo Janetta told me that too. Come on, sis. We have a celebration to go to. About time you give Morgan a hug and let her know she didn't lose her aunt when she kicked her mom out of her life."

Damn guilt trips, you'd think they were on sale next to the day-old chocolate cupcakes.

***

Tes lingered behind Zeke and Joni as they exited the car in front of Grant and Isabella's house. She didn't want to be here. Anywhere but here.

She let Ruthie off her leash so she could go romp around with Tango.

Grant shook Zeke's and Joni's hands, and he kissed little Sammy's head. Tes hung back, not wanting to intrude.

He opened his arms. "Hey, Tessie." His voice was soft and low, as warm as his hug.

"Hello, Mr. Hickok."

He rocked her. "We've missed you."

She pulled back. "Sure you have."

One strong, gentle finger lifted her chin. "We've missed you."

Tes clenched her jaw. "Thank you. I've missed you too."

"That's my girl." He crushed her in his arms again.

"Aunt Tes?" Morgan came to Grant's side.

"Hey, Peanut." Grant stepped back and let Morgan come closer so Tes could hug her tight. "How are you doing?"

"Horrible." Morgan's chest heaved while her body shook. "I'm struggling."

"I'm right here, kiddo." Tes smoothed her hand down her back. "Still not talking to your mom?"

Morgan pulled away. "I'll never talk to that bitch ever again. I'm going to change my last name to 'Hickok'."

"Morgan." Tes squeezed her hand. "I know you want to push your mom away right now for all the deception and lies. I get it. But she's also your only mother."

"I don't care. What she's done." Morgan clamped her lips closed, sniffing. "I hate her. She doesn't deserve to be part of my life. What she's done is going to come out on national news, and I don't want my name dragged through the mud with hers. Once the school's office is open, I'm reporting her."

How could Tes blame her when she'd come to the same resolution? "Agent Krysinski is aware and is investigating. Yet, I understand you need to do what's right for you. If you want, I'll go with you." She paused. "Thing is, how are we going to prove what she's done?"

Morgan's smile was too smug. Too content. Too set on revenge. "The kidnapper said if I told the school board what I knew, he'd know, and he'd send them all of the evidence they'll need." She glanced over her shoulder, seeing Hailey approaching. "If I don't, he said he'd hurt someone else in our family."

You're next. A chill swept through Tes. "Let's hope it doesn't come to that."

Hailey nudged Morgan out of the way. "Hi, Aunt Tes. Thank you for coming."

Tes hugged her tight. "How are you doing, Hailey?"

"Better. Way better." Her smile glowed. "I'm here with my family." She draped an arm around Morgan's shoulders. "I have a sister. And we're home. Life can't get any better than that."

"Your dad was worried sick."

"I know." Hailey tugged her hand. "Come, he'd love to see you."

Tes sucked in a nervous breath. Best get this over with. She was only staying for lunch. Then she'd be back at her two-bit dive and crying her eyes out. If only the pushy Gregsons hadn't forced her to ride with them. Joni had seen clear through her intent to ditch early.

Asher stepped away from the grill, handing the spatula to his brother. "Hey." He cupped her face in his hands and stared into her eyes for longer than she'd like, making her glance away.

"Tes," he whispered, resting his forehead against hers.

She closed her eyes and put her arms around his waist.

His arms wrapped around her, holding her close as he slanted his mouth over hers.

This was more PDA than she'd expected, yet he had a magnetism she couldn't shake. She loved his affection. Soaked it up like dry bread dunked in soup.

Whoops and hollers sounded from the crowd. For the first time in her life, she didn't care.

"I've missed you," she whispered.

He kissed her forehead. "How do I get you back?"

She swallowed past her emotion. How could she look in his eyes and tell him she wasn't ever his? *Yes, she was*. Always his. "I'm confused. I don't want to overstep my bounds."

He kissed her cheek. "Can we take it slow?" Cocked his head. "Try?"

"Not everyone goes through what your family's been through. I don't know where I fit into all of that, or if I fit at all."

"You fit." He smiled, pulling her tight into his arms. "I think you fit perfectly right here with me...and the girls."

Lord knew she'd love to get used to his hugs. What would it be like to wake up every morning knowing these strong arms waited and wanted to hold her like she mattered?

Isabella stepped closer. "Tessie?"

"Hi, Mrs. Hickok." Tes bent her head and stepped back from Asher. "Thank you for inviting me."

"Oh, no need to be formal. You're always welcome here." Isabella's warm hug made tears sting her eyes. Her mother hadn't ever hugged her, not once that she could remember. Man, this family could hug. They should give lessons to families like hers. "Come, see the birthday cake."

Tes froze. Stiffened. "What birthday cake?"

"The chocolate one I made you." She smiled. "And Sammy. His birthday's next week, but we're celebrating early." Isabella winked as if she knew it'd be easier for her to celebrate Sammy's life over her own.

Yeah, she liked the Hickoks. This whole growing into a new life wasn't going to be easy.

Where had self-pity ever gotten her?

***

Tes stared into the fire pit's flames, cuddled under a blanket with Asher in the double-seated lounger. The birthday party wasn't near as horrible as she'd built it in her mind. Well wishes and sweet teases were overwhelming, but not malicious.

When Isabella handed her a birthday present, she'd about lost her shit in front of everyone. Tes hadn't opened a birthday present on her actual birthday since she was seven—the year before she'd died. Dad always gave her a gift well over a week in advance of her "real" birthday, and he'd always left the house for the day so she could wallow in her misery.

And she'd believed that was all she was entitled to celebrate.

Then she'd stared at the Wonder Woman wrapping paper and tried to connect with that inner child she'd abandoned decades ago. The one she'd put in a box in the closet and tucked far into the recesses of her mind. That little girl didn't want to come out to play, be acknowledged, or be remembered.

Her hand shook as she carefully tried to undo the tape. Everyone told her to rip the paper, but she couldn't. They had no idea what this festive, kick-ass, amazing paper meant to her—and she wasn't about to tell anyone why.

Hug more. Love more.

Staring into the smiling faces, hearing their laughter carry across the yard, she thought her heart couldn't take much more. It'd been a great birthday. One she'd remember for the rest of her life.

Asher held her close as fatigue settled in.

"I'm going inside," Morgan announced, rising from her chair. "Thanks for coming today, Aunt Tes."

"Thank you for having me and thank you for the cute shirt."

"Good night, everyone." Hailey followed Morgan.

Asher stared as his girls crossed the yard. Tes could feel his whole body tighten. Sammy had crashed early and the Gregsons had already headed home.

She patted his leg. "I'll call an Uber. You should head inside."

"You don't want to stay the night?"

Her hand caressed the diamond heart necklace he'd given her. "We shouldn't. Not yet. Not after what Hailey and Morgan were exposed to."

Asher frowned. "What do you mean...exposed to?"

Tes swallowed. "What did they tell you about the kidnapper?"

His voice lowered. "What do you know, Tes?"

"You shouldn't hear it from me." She stood. "Ask them." She motioned toward the house.

"I have. They don't want to talk about it." He grabbed her hand. "Honey, please, tell me. You know something."

She sat her butt on the edge of the lounger. "The kidnapper's still watching. He's installed cameras inside Nikki's house. He hacked into both of your video doorbells."

"What are you talking about?"

"He may have cameras inside your house." She watched the girls go inside and flip on the lights. "He knew I'd moved into your house. He wouldn't have known that unless he was watching your house or possibly a listening device. We can't sleep together." She sucked in a deep breath. "Unless we're married." She held up her hand. "We're not ready for that, but I can't shake the feeling he's watching. We may not know him, or where he lives, but the one thing we do know is that he knows a lot about us. We're his obsession. Until he's caught, we need to play it safe."

"And what if he's never caught? What if we never know who he is?" He caressed her hand. "I'm not living my life by 'what-ifs' and neither should you."

"He respects you. He doesn't respect women. His biggest issue is when mothers don't put their children first. Women who have open, sexually active lives. He's the judge, jury, and possibly gearing up to be an executioner."

"You said that at the hospital."

"Because he views women as whores. It's not how I view them, except Nikki has demonstrated poor judgment." She glanced at Asher's house. "Morgan wants to tell the school board about Nikki having sex with students." She held up her hand at Asher's shocked expression. "I have to agree. I promised to go with her."

Asher took in a deep breath and, when he exhaled, his shoulders sagged in defeat.

"You weren't the only one, Ash." She leaned forward and kissed his cheek. "It didn't stop with you. It wasn't a one-time thing."

Muscles rippled along his jaw. "That's what you saw in the Shadowlands?"

Tes shuddered. "He showed the girls videos of their mothers having sex with several partners. In Nikki's case, some of them were students." She let that sink in before saying more. "It's so wrong on so many levels. It doesn't matter that she's my sister. It matters that kids are left thinking she's doing them a favor. What she's doing is wrong, and I can't keep silent about it." She brushed her fingers over his worried brow. "Krysinski was also going to notify the school board. I want to make sure they don't brush this under the rug because students haven't come forward directly."

"Can we talk to the girls about this before this becomes five o'clock news?"

"Of course, but I won't change my mind, and I don't think Morgan will either."

"I want to make sure the girls are prepared for the backlash. High school's hard enough without having your mother prosecuted. Kids can be cruel." Asher hung his head, wiping a hand down his face. "I want them to trust me."

"They do trust you, but they also know how their being kidnapped has affected you." Tes ran her fingers through his hair. "The girls don't know what I know. They couldn't see me when I was there. I was a ghost."

He rubbed his hand across his forehead, squeezing his eyes shut. "Why can't we be normal? Why can't we go on with our lives? Why does this bastard get to steal one more moment of my life with you?" He pulled her tight against his chest. "With us becoming a family?"

Tes edged away. There it was. He didn't see her as normal. He wanted to forget what she was and his daughters being kidnapped. She couldn't blame him. "I don't know what the future holds, but I know we need to give it space to breathe. Time to adapt. Time to accept." What if he never accepted her?

Once again Fate dealt the fatal blow. Sure, Asher and she were tossed together again in this lifetime, but this time Tes was created into an abomination Asher wouldn't ever trust and love. Not completely.

Tes stared at the flames in the fire pit. She'd never be normal. There was no "us" in this scenario. "Good night, Asher. Thank you for the beautiful necklace."

"Please, don't go. Let's go talk to the girls." He tugged on her hand.

"I'm tired. They're tired. It's been a long day, and everything will be better in the morning light." *One of her favorite lies.* Things wouldn't be any different than right now, other than perhaps not entering a touchy conversation when they were both exhausted.

Zeke pulled into the driveway.

"They must have forgot something." Asher stood but wouldn't let go of her hand, leading her to where Zeke approached them.

"Hey." Zeke paused and looked at Tes. "You ready to go home?"

"Yes." She smiled at Asher and gave him a hug.

"Let me grab Ruthie for you." He kissed her cheek and headed into Grant and Isabella's house.

"How are you holding up?" Zeke asked.

"It's been a long day."

"Joni was worried about you."

"I like your wife."

He smiled. "Me too." He rocked back and forth. "I hope you still like us when you find out where your new home is."

"Joni said something about moving me to a penthouse in Bellevue. That's not necessary."

He narrowed his eyes and stopped rocking on his feet. "You'll be in a safer place, Tes."

"No one's going to attack me." She wiggled her fingers. "I can take care of myself."

The intensity of his stare made her fidget.

"I'm paid up through the end of the month."

"Ah." Zeke dug into his pocket. "Here's the balance they owed you." He handed her an envelope. "Cash."

"What about my car?"

"Moved."

"How'd—" She clamped her mouth shut. "You know, you should ask people first."

"Nope."

"That's it? Nope."

"Yep."

Where was the Zeke lecture she was supposed to be so afraid of? She'd grab her things and head straight back to her fleabag motel.

"Don't even think about it."

"Think about what?"

"Grabbing your shit and returning to that hell hole you were calling home."

She feigned being shocked.

"Asher and I agree on this. Our penthouse, or his house. That's it. Those are your two options."

"Do I look feeble? Do I look like I can't make decisions for myself?"

"It has nothing to do with your looks." He stepped closer. "That kidnapper's already said you're next—or did you forget that part?"

She stepped back. "How did you know about that?"

"Krysinski told me."

Hm. Figures. "I need to know if everything was packed from my room." She lifted her chin.

"Nope. We got it all. Joni and I inspected everything after we left here today."

"Do you always intrude in people's lives like this?"

"No, but we made an exception for you." Zeke narrowed one eye. "My wife has a friend that gets her. Who's seen what she's seen. And I'll be damned if I'll let some drive-by shooter or rapist damage that relationship, or you."

Tes rolled her eyes. "Listen, I haven't had anyone watching out for me since I was eight years old. I know you mean well, but—"

"Tessie," Grant called. How long had he been listening? "You can stay with us if you want."

"Oh no, I couldn't intrude, Mr. Hickok."

Zeke smiled as Asher brought Ruthie out of the house with her leash on. "Well, guess a penthouse apartment with amazing views of Lake Washington will have to do."

Asher and Zeke shared one of those all-male knowing looks like "I got your back, dude."

"I'd like to take you on an official date tomorrow." Asher handed her Ruthie's leash.

"I'm all the way in Bellevue now, thanks to the Gregsons."

"I know." He pulled a card out of his back pocket. "They gave me a spare key—you know, in case you need help with Ruthie. I promise not to use it without your permission."

Oh, now that was playing dirty. A secured building where the kidnapper couldn't watch them?

That wasn't just a key.

That was temptation.

20

A sher shuffled the large vase with two dozen pink and white roses to one hand so he could knock on Tes's door.

She opened the door, wearing a flimsy robe. Sexy, bare legs. "You're early."

He handed her the vase, heat rushing to his groin. "I thought I'd come early and take Ruthie for a walk while you finish getting ready." At least that was what he'd told himself when he'd left the house. Now, the only thought in his head was skipping dinner, their official first date, and spending the evening nestled tight between her thighs.

"We've already had our two runs today." She backed away from the door, taking the vase. "These are gorgeous."

Ruthie's tail wagged like crazy as he let the door slam shut. He petted her before Tes wrapped her arm around his shoulder. "Thank you for the flowers." One hug wasn't going to be enough.

"Mm, you smell nice." His body tensed, warring between being casual, no pressure, and horny as hell.

"Come see the view." She tugged his hand, pulling him into the living room.

He adjusted his growing hard-on, hoping she wouldn't notice.

"Isn't this an amazing view of Lake Washington?"

There wasn't a view more captivating than her.

When she bent over to place the vase on the coffee table, her robe parted, showing a healthy portion of her bare breast. She pulled her robe closed as she stood.

"You don't have to cover up on account of me." He couldn't stop smiling.

She returned his smile and dropped her hand.

He untied her robe. Her pink lacy panties made his cock throb. He could see plenty of cleavage, but her nipples remained obscured by the robe. Damn, she had a body to die for. Toned. Curves that drove him wild. "This is a view I wouldn't mind seeing all day."

A blush crept up from her clavicle to her cheeks as she glanced away.

"Don't be shy, Tes. Not in front of me. Not when we're alone." He dipped and kissed her cheek, lingering, rubbing his cheek along hers.

She looked at him through her lashes. "I'm almost ready. I just need to get dressed."

"Or...we could get naked." He moved closer and when she didn't protest, he kissed her neck. "Stay in bed." He swallowed. "Make love."

She wrapped her arms around his neck and kissed his cheek. "I thought we had reservations."

He ran his tongue up her neck, kissing her under her earlobe. "We have a little time." Hell, he'd forego dinner altogether.

Ruthie settled on her dog bed near the couch and chewed her bone.

Tes lifted her legs, wrapping them around his waist. Her sweet spot rested against the top of his cock. "Hello." Her brows rose.

"One look at you and I'm ready."

She slanted her mouth over his, deepening their kiss, moaning as she undulated her hips. "I'm almost there."

"Where's the bedroom?" He cupped her ass, pressing her harder against his cock.

One quick nod.

He turned and headed down the short hall. The king-size bed filled the room.

She lowered to the floor, her fingers slipping around his belt buckle as he made quick work of his shirt's buttons. He pulled a condom from his jacket pocket. He'd brought it along, just in case. Man, he was happy that past Asher had enough insight to think of future Asher's horny needs. He tossed it onto the bed as he stripped off his upper layers, staring into her beautiful blue eyes.

Once his pants hit the floor, she palmed his cock through his boxers.

He stopped and closed his eyes, fighting to gain control or he'd be spending into his underwear.

Her robe pooled at her feet. Taut, pink nipples begged for sucking.

He bent and gave undivided attention first to one breast, then the other, cupping the weight of each in his hands.

A sucking sound filled the room as she backed away, edging onto the bed. Asher dropped his boxers and in full, hardened glory, sank one knee onto the bed. He latched his fingers under her panties and pulled them off. He stretched out on top of her, regaling in feeling her flesh against his. Her soft curves fit nicely against him. His cock pulsed, desperately wanting to be buried inside her. First, he needed to make sure she was ready. He slipped a finger between her folds and stroked her clit. Damn, she was wet.

He sat back on his knees and grabbed the condom, ripping it open, and smoothing it down his cock.

She smiled. Wanton. Spread her legs.

Yes. This is what he wanted from the moment he'd met her. He knew that this was their destiny. He leaned over, bracing his arms on each side of her, kissing her thoroughly. She wrapped her arms around him, tilting her pelvis for him to enter.

He slipped a hand between them. Her heat was intoxicating. He pressed the head of his cock at her opening.

She moaned, wrapping her long, sexy legs around his back.

He eased in an inch, pulling out a bit, inching in more. Her nails dug into his back, as he tortured her before he was buried to the hilt. Long, teasing, steady strokes caused her to make sexy high-pitched whines from the back of her throat. Her eyes closed as he increased his pace.

"Harder," she whispered.

He rolled them over. "Ride me."

She leaned forward, her back tensed, her jaw taut. Her pace increased, hard and steady.

He bucked his hips forward, causing her to moan louder. "That's it." He sucked one nipple as he pinched the other, matching her pace.

Her pussy tightened around his cock, making each thrust a delicious combination. His balls retracted. Shit, he was going to come. Reaching a hand between them, he circled her clit, pressing harder against it.

She screamed. Spent. Creamed him. Her scent was intoxicating.

He moved his hand, grabbed her hips and shoved her down hard. Stars exploded in his periphery as he came. Damn, he'd never had an orgasm like that.

***

Tes collapsed on top of Asher, trying to catch her breath. He wrapped her tight in his arms, making her feel safe, secure, and loved. Quick, passionate sex was what the doctor needed.

He rolled her to the side, pushing her hair out of her face. "Look at me, love."

Her gaze snapped to his. "Don't say that." She placed her fingers against his lips. "We can't. No matter what."

"I know." He kissed her fingers.

It was like he was made for her. If home had a feeling, this was it. A mind-blowing, post-orgasmic euphoria. She kissed him. "Thank you."

"Mm. Thank you." His hands cupped her ass, pushing his cock inside. "You're perfect. You know that?"

"Nobody's perfect."

He cupped her chin. "We are when we're together." His eyes widened. "Shit." He rolled her onto her back. "I'm about to lose the condom."

"What?"

His fingers gripped the head of his cock, the condom hanging off the end. "In my haste, I must not have made sure I'd put it on right."

"No worries. I'm on the pill."

He stared. Smiled. "So...I didn't need a condom?"

"It never hurts to use a condom. And we're not in a committed relationship."

His eyebrows lifted. "I'm committed. For life." He yanked a few tissues from the nightstand and wrapped the condom before tossing it in the trash.

She smiled and kissed him as he wrapped her tightly in his arms. "Yeah, I could definitely get used to you being in my bed."

"Agreed." He rolled onto his back, tucking her tight to his side. "I'm trying hard not to have a post-orgasmic nap, but I'm pretty damn content right now. It's like I've waited my entire life for this moment."

"Go ahead and have a quick nap. I'll finish getting ready."

He moaned when she tried to pull away. "Stay with me. I'm supposed to be the one to bring you a warm washcloth."

She grimaced. "Really? Is that a thing?" She'd never had a lover do that.

"I'm taking care of you. I—" He opened his eyes, pain registering across his face. "It feels natural to tell you..."

"I know." Her heart ached, wanting to say how much she was falling in love too. She'd never met someone as thoughtful and caring as Asher. Never did she believe for a moment anyone would ever genuinely love her—but yesterday, he'd implied she wasn't normal. Maybe she shouldn't get her hopes up. "Are you sure?"

His mouth descended on hers as he rolled her onto her back. "I'm one hundred percent sure."

"It's that." She licked her lips. "I'm not normal."

"You're all I can think about. Us. Forever."

She didn't believe in soulmates. Then again, her heart hadn't ever fluttered like it did when he was near. Her soul registered his absence when they were apart. It was like he grounded her anxious energy and she'd never craved someone's touch like his.

"We're going to make it, Tes. Let's come up with a word that replaces that other one we're not supposed to say."

"Kiss me." She leaned over him and gently kissed his neck.

"Honey, if we keep at this, we're going to miss dinner."

She let out a sigh, suckled his earlobe. "You're right. We need to date before we can—"

"Oh, we can do this again after dinner."

She giggled. "Are you officially my boyfriend now?"

He cupped her face, propped up on an elbow, and devoured her mouth. "We're definitely a couple."

Her heart soared. She wasn't alone. He was hers. Her special someone.

Wait. She was a couple now. That meant she had to discuss things with someone else when she wanted to do something.

Change. Sure, she could do this. She could compromise. It was a good change, right?

***

Asher showed Tes the webcam filming Ruthie sleeping on her dog bed, snoring away. "See, she's fine." Tes was going to be a fretter, and he couldn't be happier.

"I don't like leaving her alone."

"She's a great dog." Asher placed his cell phone screen side down on the table. The restaurant wasn't busy, so they had a nice corner booth to themselves. They sat close together and shared bites of each other's meals, stealing kisses.

The server dropped by, removing their empty plates. "Would you like to look at the dessert menu?"

"Yes," Asher answered.

"No," Tes replied, waving a hand. "I'm full."

"Bring us something chocolatey. The chocolaty-er the better." He wrapped his arm around Tes's shoulders as the server walked away.

"Fine, I'll run ten miles tomorrow." Tes leaned into him, smiling.

"How many miles do you usually run?" Asher didn't hear her answer because he noticed Nikki's lawyer making his way across the room. *How the hell did he know where I was?* His gut plummeted. Was he being followed? It didn't take a rocket scientist to know why he was coming over. He'd had his lawyer send papers to Nikki's lawyer, filing for full custody of Morgan.

"Good evening, Asher. Sorry to interrupt."

"If you were sorry, you wouldn't interrupt." Asher took a long draw on his beer. "Tes, this is Nikki's lawyer. Clyde Hofstedder."

Tes straightened. "What do you want?"

"Nikki's going to counter-sue for full custody of Morgan." For the first time ever, Clyde looked disappointed to be delivering bad news.

"She won't get it." Tes folded her arms. "Not after what Morgan and Hailey are going to report to the school board."

"We're fully aware of Nikki's exploits." Clyde glanced between them. "I've convinced her to tender her resignation." He swallowed. "She and Ben Winslow are leaving the U.S. and returning to England."

"She can still be extradited. Prosecuted for her crimes." Tes stiffened. "I'll make sure Nikki will never work with children again."

"And how would you do that?"

"I'll contact my stepfather." Tes lifted her chin.

"He's the one orchestrating Nikki out of the country." Clyde smiled, a little too happily for Asher's liking. "Quietly. She prefers to take Morgan with her."

Tes tsked. "She won't get custody of Morgan. Morgan doesn't want to see Nikki."

"Well, judges can be bought. And this has nothing to do with you." Clyde moved his beady-eyed glare from Tes to Asher. "This is strictly between Morgan's biological parents. I came to tell you as a courtesy."

Asher huffed in disgust. "Well, hope you're in for a good fight. I'm not giving up custody of Morgan. After what she's been through, she needs a stable home. Not the Winslow whorehouse."

Clyde pinched his lips in a tight pucker. "Time will tell. Expect to be served in a few days."

"Bring it on." Tes lifted her wine glass and gave him a mock toast. "My sister's going to regret this decision."

Once Clyde walked away, Tes set her glass down, hand shaking. "The kidnapper can't learn about Nikki leaving. Quitting her job? She has no idea what he might do. Do you think he'll try and take the girls again?"

"Not a chance." Asher shook his head, clenching his teeth. "And he better not touch you either."

She forced a smile to her lips as the server returned with dessert. "That's beautiful. Thank you."

It was chocolate on chocolate on chocolate cream, with chocolate sprinkles. As soon as the server walked away, Asher pulled Tes tight against his side. "I want this nightmare to be over. I want to have one normal day where you and I and the girls are happy. No interruptions. No drama. No lawyers trying to ruin our future. Is that too much to ask?"

"No, sweetheart. It's not too much to ask." She placed a soft kiss on his lips. "We're going to have to fight for what we want, that's all. I'm game if you are."

Not having to go through legal proceedings alone? To have a woman to lean on and stand beside him? Maybe after the sacrifices, the hard work and late hours, maybe he was able to reap the rewards he deserved.

"You know, I thought you wouldn't want to go out with me once I found out what Nikki did to you. We look alike."

"You look nothing alike. Besides, it was a moment in my past. You're my future. You're my everything." He kissed her cheek. "I want to fill that house I built years ago to the rafter with more kids."

Tes pulled back. "Kids? Why would you want to start over?"

"Because I never got to experience it the way I'd always imagined it should be the first time. You know, feeling my baby move in their mom's belly, seeing ultrasounds, being there when they were born, watching their first step, their first word. It was always later, but never that first one. It was the first one with me. I want all the late-night feedings and messy diapers. I want to look at our baby's face and know we created that little perfect person."

She cleared her throat. "I never thought about having kids. I mean, someone like me shouldn't have kids."

"What do you mean, like you? You're amazing."

"I'm not human."

He frowned. "Yes, you are."

"Not anymore. When the lighting hit me. It changed me. I died. I've seen things. Done things. I affect...things. Asher, what if our kids turned out to be like me?" She whispered, "What if they can raise the dead?"

He hadn't thought about that. "We'll cross that road if we face it." He smoothed a hand through her hair. "I can't imagine us not having kids. They'll be half like me too. They could be Italian to the core."

"Until I met you, I never dreamed of the possibility of kids. I'm afraid to get my hopes up. What if I can't have children?"

Fear registered in his gut. "Don't say that—if we can't, we'll adopt."

"You're disappointed."

"No." He picked up a spoon. "You're going to make a great mom to all of our kids. Even our grown ones." A lump seized his throat as he cut a bite of gooey cake. "Trust me, Tes. We're going to have a house full of love. Tons of kids at our feet."

"Maybe not a ton. A ton simply terrifies me."

He put the spoon to her lips. "Yeah? Good. Life should scare the shit out of you regularly. Otherwise, you ain't livin'."

21

Tes stared at herself in the mirror, shoving one more bobby pin into her hair to make sure the French twist wouldn't come undone. She sprayed enough hairspray on it to shellac it in place. Fifty-mile-an-hour winds wouldn't be able to move her hair.

The week flew past in a flurry of meeting new clients, having coffee with Isabella, and taking the girls to get mani-pedis at a local strip mall. Tonight was Tom Krysinski's retirement party and everyone wanted to look their best. The event was downstairs in the hotel's grand ballroom. She'd agreed to leave Ruthie upstairs and meet the Gregsons, the ones hosting the event.

Tes entered the ballroom wearing a simple black sleeveless dress that hugged her frame and ended mid-thigh. She accessorized her outfit with long black satin gloves and her great-grandmother's necklace, a gift from King George VI before he married Elizabeth Bowes-Lyon. What few times Tes had visited her grandmother, she never tired of hearing how the future king and her great-grandfather played cards to win the opportunity to court her great-grandmother. Prince Albert, Bertie to family and friends, was never a sore loser, according to her grandmother. He wished them happy and "bestowed" a necklace on her wedding day.

Three strands of pearls hung gracefully around her neck, ending in a heart-shaped ruby, surrounded by a row of diamonds. The necklace cascaded over her shoulders, with the six strands coming together at her shoulder blades by heart-shaped ruby wings outlined in diamonds. An additional six strands dangled down her back, tipped with rubies, diamonds, and fresh water pearls. The necklace was worth a small fortune. Odds were that more than a few people would be carrying guns at Krysinski's retirement party. Where else could she wear the priceless piece and be as protected?

White tablecloths formed islands around the ballroom floor. Matching votives and roses with a splash of greenery added classic elegance to the room. However, arriving at the event, taking in the crowd, she felt like heading upstairs and changing. Her mother's voice replayed in her mind. *One didn't underdress for formal occasions.*

She spotted Zeke and Joni right away. Zeke bounced Sammy in his arms. Other children dashed in and out of adult groupings. A couple of little girls danced on the floor, twirling in their lace dresses.

Joni turned around. Her mouth opened as her eyebrows rose.

"Am I overdressed?" Tes asked, placing a hand over the necklace.

Joni was the first to recover. "You do know every man here is staring at you right now."

Heat flushed Tes's chest and neck, settling onto her cheeks. "I didn't wear this for attention. I thought you said this was a formal affair."

Zeke passed Sammy to Joni. "Do you want me to get you something to drink?"

"I would love a glass of wine. Thank you."

Joni lifted her glass. "Sparkling apple juice. I love redneck champagne."

"Aunt Tes?"

She turned around to see Morgan and Hailey entering the ballroom, dressed up for the occasion.

Tes wrapped an arm around each girl and kissed their cheeks.

"Wow, the family necklace is more gorgeous in person." Morgan picked up the ruby heart. "My mother was always jealous of this piece."

"Yes, she was." She looked at Hailey. "My sister wanted to wear it on her wedding day. When I refused to let her, you'd think I'd committed the greatest sin of all. In truth, I wanted to keep it for my own wedding day." She held them close. "Maybe my daughters would want to wear it on their wedding day."

She looked past their shoulders as Asher approached. He held out his arms. She let go of the girls and fell into his arms. Every worry melted away. He lifted her chin with a gentle hand and brushed his lips across hers. Not too much affection, but enough to let every man there know she belonged to him, and likewise, every woman knew he was hers.

He held her at arm's length, twirled her around so he could get a three-sixty view of her outfit, and let out a slow wolf whistle. "You're the most beautiful woman in the world." He pulled her tight against him and kissed her again. "I've missed you."

"You should wear a suit more often. It was like you wanted us to look like a couple."

"You figured out my diabolical plan." He pulled his phone out of his pocket and handed it to Zeke as he returned with a couple of wine glasses. "Hey, can you take our picture?"

Asher pulled her to his side. She wrapped a hand around his waist. He put his arms around Hailey and Morgan as they all leaned in and smiled.

Zeke took a couple more. "What a good-looking family you have." He shook Zeke's hand as he handed back his phone.

Tom approached and congratulations were given. Asher's parents arrived and joined the photo-op with their honored guest.

Laughter and chatter resounded across the room as music filled the empty dance floor.

Asher held up the phone and took a selfie of the two of them. He slipped the phone back in his pocket, staring into her eyes. "You know, I don't think we've ever danced."

"Can you dance?"

He unbuttoned his suit jacket. "*Can I dance?*" Onlookers from nearby tables quieted and stared their way. Tes's nerves skittered. She didn't like people staring. His mocked offense made her smile.

"Dad." Hailey shook her head. "Don't embarrass us."

"I'll have you know." He led her by the hand to the dance floor. "My mom and dad taught me everything I needed to know about dancing. The question is, do *you* know how to dance?" He was never cuter than when he pulled that teasing smile of his.

Tes took a deep breath, trying to hide her inner girlish glee. "I've been formally trained."

"Formally?" He squinted. "There's nothing formal about the sprinkler." He crooked one hand behind his head and incrementally moved the other like a sprinkler head. "How about the running man?"

Tes couldn't stop laughing as he ran in place. The crowd quieted and watched, enjoying Asher's antics.

"Can you do the moon walk?"

She shook her head as he walked backward like Michael Jackson. "Not in these shoes."

"Oh wait. There's always a classic. The macarena." He glanced at his daughter and winked. "Hailey taught me that one."

She couldn't stop laughing.

Asher did his best dancing baby imitation. Who wouldn't love a man who'd be silly and didn't care who watched?

"Or did you have something else in mind?" He took her hand in his, another around her waist. "Perhaps a tango?" He bounced his eyebrows.

"I'd love to tango with you."

"Maestro." He glanced over at LeBron, who was playing DJ for the evening. "A tango for the lady, please." A familiar seductive tune rose over the speakers.

She loved the look in Asher's eye. They stepped in time to the music, crouching low, perfect tango pose, covering one end of the floor to the other. He dipped her low and pulled her back up, placing a kiss gently on her lips.

He twirled her around, pulling her back against his chest. He whispered in her ear, "The kids are spending the night at Nonna and Poppop's." He spun her out and brought her back. "Ruthie too."

They continued their way. Of course, he'd thought of everything.

As the music quieted, he lowered himself to one knee. Tes thought his shoe had come untied until he opened a box with a diamond ring and took her left hand in his.

Her breath caught in her throat. She placed her other hand over her heart. Her mouth gaped. The center square solitaire had a halo of smaller diamonds. The scroll work of the band was intricate and delicate.

"Dr. Tesla Brynn, my days will be brighter with you by my side." His gaze slid up her legs to her eyes. "My nights will be longer." Whoop whistles sounded from the crowd. He smiled. "I would be the happiest man alive if you would agree to be my Mrs. Hickok."

She scrunched her lips together and shook her head. "I cannot become your Mrs. Hickok."

***

The crowd gasped.

Asher hung his head. Tears flooded his eyes. His heart ripped in two. Could someone die from a broken heart? He didn't mind making a fool of himself in front of strangers, but having his balls ripped out and handed back to him? That he minded. Why couldn't she say "yes" in front of everyone and gracefully break up with him later?

How could he live without her?

"There's already a Mrs. Hickok—and she's the best Mrs. Hickok in the world." Tes's voice held a playful note.

He lifted his eyes to look at hers, blinking back his tears.

"I'm afraid the only name I can have is...*Dr.* Tesla Hickok."

Oh, she was good. He shook his head, thumping his hand over his heart to make sure it was still beating. "Is that a yes?"

"Yes, it's a yes."

The little minx. He bit the end of her middle finger, gripping the seam of her glove in his teeth. She squealed. Then he repeated the process with each finger before pulling her black satin glove free. Giggles erupted from the women on the edge of the dance floor. Once the satin material hit the floor, he took the ring from the box and slid it down her finger.

She held up her hand, tears in her eyes. "It's beautiful."

"I'm glad you like it. The girls helped me pick it out." He picked up her errant glove and flung it over his shoulder as he slipped the ring box back into his pocket. He wrapped her in his arms and kissed her. He didn't give a damn if he smeared her lipstick.

LeBron queued a famous waltz that everyone loved at the end of that cartoon about the girl who got her prince.

When they ended their kiss, she wiped the lipstick from his mouth. "I want to grow old with you."

He kissed her cheek, holding her close. "Me too. First, I want to make babies with you."

She bit the end of her other glove and yanked it from her hand. *Jesus Christ*, how was he going to make it through dinner when all he wanted to do was take her upstairs and make sweet love to his future wife?

He took the glove dangling between her teeth and flung it over his shoulder along with the other one. Touching foreheads, the tension in his shoulders eased. Her touch was like coming home after a long day at work. He instantly relaxed. There wasn't any other woman in the world for him.

It'd been a risk asking her to marry him so soon after they'd committed to one another, but there was no way he was going to be able to not tell her how much he loved her—the only solution was to get married. And quick.

He took her hand, held her waist with the other, and waltzed her across the floor. Those eighth-grade gym class dance lessons came in handy after all. *Thank you, Mrs. Stetson.*

They only made it halfway across the dance floor when his family swooped in, crushing Tes into the mix of congratulations and hugs. Mom cried, dabbing a tissue to her eyes, while Dad used his hand to wipe his tears. He wrapped his strong arms around Asher, crushing him in an embrace.

"There for a moment, I thought she was going to turn you down." Dad slapped his back.

"You?" Asher's stomach fell, reliving that split second. "I'm the happiest man in the world."

"That's how you should feel when you ask the right girl."

For the first time, Asher was glad he hadn't settled for a woman to be a mom for his girls. He'd found the woman who was right for him *and* his daughters. No one would be better than Tes.

The wait staff filed in, signaling time for dinner. Asher grabbed Tes's hand and pulled her over to their table. He recognized the young man placing the salads in front of his girls, as did they.

"Hey, Eric." Hailey waved. "I didn't know you worked here."

"Hi, guys," Eric replied. "Yeah, I work a few jobs and go to school. I'm trying not to incur too much college debt as I go." He was a little older than his daughters, tall, blond hair, blue eyes. The all-American boy next door.

"Hi, Eric." Asher stood and shook his hand. He always appreciated his silent support while the girls were gone, bumping up his coffee order an extra size for free. It wasn't much, but it'd meant a lot to Asher. Most people avoided making eye contact. "Honey, you remember Eric Ehome from the coffee shop."

Tes shook Eric's hand. "It's nice to see you again."

"Great proposal, Mr. Hickok." He leaned over and held Tes's left hand. "Beautiful ring." A wry smile curved one side of his face. "It's good to know some people get it right, you know?" He let go of Tes's hand. "I hope when I propose, it's that awesome."

"If you ever need a job, let me know." Asher squeezed his shoulder. "I'm always looking for extra hands to clean up construction sites."

"I'll keep it in mind. For now, I wait here on occasion, serve coffee four days a week, and deliver pizzas most evenings." He bobbed his head. "It all adds up, you know."

"I admire someone with a strong work ethic." Asher patted him on the back.

Eric looked at his daughters. "I'm glad you guys are home. You both look amazing."

The smile fell from Hailey's face. "We're doing okay. It'd be nice if we could catch the bastard."

Eric narrowed his eyes. "They didn't catch him?"

Morgan shook her head. "We escaped."

"Wow. That makes your being here all the more special, huh, Mr. Hickok?"

"Yes, it does."

Eric glanced around the room. "Well, I best be getting back to work, or it'll be my last night serving."

Asher took his seat.

"How do you girls know him?" Tes asked.

Morgan answered, "He graduated last year. His brother Tennyson is in our class."

"Stepbrother," Hailey corrected. "Eric's mom died in a horrible accident five years ago. She was decapitated when the car flipped over an embankment. Eric hasn't been the same since."

"Who can blame him, huh?" Tes smiled as Eric returned with more plates for their table.

After he walked away, Asher said, "At least he didn't turn to drugs like most kids his age would have. He's done all right for himself, despite what life handed him."

"He's okay." Hailey shrugged. "He was kind of a loner when he was in school. I felt sorry for him."

Morgan poured some dressing on her salad. "His stepbrother Tennyson is totally hot, though. Plays on the varsity football team."

Hailey took the dressing. "If he asked me out, I'd say yes."

Asher wasn't ready for his daughters to date. Not today. Not tomorrow, and sure as hell not before they were twenty-five, at the earliest. "Be smart, girls. No babies before their time, okay?"

"Asher," Tes admonished. "There will be plenty of time to educate the girls on how to properly date before that day comes."

"Properly date?" Morgan scrunched her nose. "You sound like Grandmother." She passed the dressing to Tes.

Tes stared at the dressing, pausing before putting some on her salad. "I suppose I did." She lifted her head and squared her shoulders. "We want what's best for you girls. However, if you got pregnant, we'd stand beside you no matter what. We're in this together. We're family." She lifted her glass and clinked it against his daughters' and his.

Asher participated in the glass clinking, though the subject of his daughters and teenage pregnancy wasn't something he wanted to discuss. The thought of a guy putting their grubby hands on them brought out his big, bad papa-bear side. "You're not going out with anyone until I meet them. Preferably on gun-cleaning night." He smiled.

"Are you two going to have more kids?" Hailey asked.

"Yes," he answered faster than Tes could protest.

"In due time." She opened her palms. "We're in no hurry. Raising teenage daughters will be enough for the moment. Do you want more siblings?"

"Absolutely," Hailey responded, but Asher noticed Morgan's withdrawal.

He tilted his head. "What about you, Morgan?"

Morgan placed her fork on her plate, staring at her greens. "I want you two to be happy. If that means more kids, who am I to stand in your way?"

Tes set her utensils down and rubbed Morgan's back. "What's wrong?"

She lifted a shoulder and leaned away. "Uncle Asher's been my father figure since I could remember, but finding out he was my real dad? I guess I'm feeling like I'm going to click my heels together three times and wake up at my mom's home surrounded by her and Ben. I have no control over anything. Not really. I want my dad to myself for a little while longer. Is that selfish of me?"

"Not at all." Tes pulled back her hand when Morgan looked away. "You will always have our love, you know that."

Eric returned with a fresh carafe of water and filled some half-empty glasses.

Morgan's shoulders slumped. "I can't live with her, Aunt Tes. I can't."

"Unfortunately, the law may intervene. Your mother has a legal right to see you."

"But I don't want to see her. I hate her. I hate—"

"Shh," Asher said. "Keep your voice down. I don't like your mother's actions any more than you do, but she's the only mother you'll ever have."

Eric walked away.

"Uh-uh. Tes is going to be my new mother."

Tes shook her head. "I know you hate her now, but holding onto bitterness and hate only hurts the person who holds onto it. It doesn't hurt your mother."

Hailey snorted. "No, she's too busy doing Ben six ways from Sunday along with a few friends."

Asher put his fork down. Sure, Tes had told him about what the girls were exposed to, but he hadn't broached the subject with the girls, and they hadn't mentioned anything yet. "Excuse me?"

"Nothing," Morgan was quick to answer. "Not here." She glared at Hailey.

Asher looked at Morgan. "I filed for full custody, Morgan, but your mother is counter-suing for custody. She and Ben are moving back to England and want to take you with them."

Morgan dropped her chin to her chest. "I can't, Dad. I can't live with her."

"I'm hoping the judge takes your wishes under consideration."

Tes squeezed his arm. "Unfortunately, we don't have any proof of what your mom did with Ben. What you girls saw when you were kidnapped." Tes motioned for Eric to take her salad plate away. "Thank you. If we had evidence, it might leverage a judge in our favor, but we don't. All we'll have is her word against ours and years of litigation where you hang in the balance. Which isn't fair to you." Tes tucked Morgan's hair behind her ear.

Asher didn't trust his tongue. "Maybe LeBron can hack into your mother's computer. He seems to be good at that kind of thing."

"It wouldn't be admissible in court." Tes sighed. "You know, tonight is our night. I don't want to spend it talking about Nikki and how she's plotting to ruin our lives."

Morgan glanced over her shoulder to make sure no one was near. She leaned forward and whispered, "Ben films everything. He saves it to his computer."

"You finished?" Eric asked her.

Morgan nodded.

"Thank you." Asher let Eric take his plate. "We're going to fight hard, Morgan. I promise, but I have no control over the outcome."

"I appreciate it." A tear slipped along Morgan's cheek.

Tes wiped it away.

Asher glanced at Zeke. "You guys wouldn't know how to find dirt on Nikki, would you?"

Zeke smiled. "We thought you'd never ask."

Joni exchanged a look with LeBron across the table. "Let's meet tomorrow. We'll share what we know."

22

Asher tried to focus on each speaker roasting Tom for over thirty years of service. All he wanted was to be alone with his fiancée. He stared at the ring on Tes's finger, leaned over, and kissed her.

Dad cleared his throat. Yeah, Asher couldn't stop staring at his future wife, and he liked that she stared back.

When Sammy fidgeted between speakers as the house lights rose, Joni pulled out a picture and handed it to him. He kissed the little laminated picture, held it to his chest, and sighed.

Asher leaned forward. "Can I see your picture?"

Sammy gave it to Asher. He squinted in the dim light to take in the painting. He'd seen plenty of the typical Catholic Church artistic depictions in his catechism classes. This one was different.

Across the bottom in big white, bold letters it read: Resurrection Angel. A woman, the spitting image of Tes, floated above a tomb. The angel's white, iridescent wings spread wide. The tips of her toes graced the bottom of her rose-colored robe with a white sash, Grecian-like. Asher focused on the angel's hands. Balls of lightning filled her palms. A large white stone listed on one edge near the entrance. Jesus crouched low, emerging from the grave.

His hands hung limply from his wrists. Head cocked, looking up at the angel, his mouth gaped open like a marionette.

A chill raced up his spine.

Tes put her hand on his and looked at the picture. Her eyes widened.

The radiance and confidence in the angel's face looked like Tes's when she was talking to Chester about his dead brother, Brick.

"It's you."

"It's someone who looked like me," she whispered. "Uncanny."

"You're even sexier when you let your accent slip."

She blushed. "I've studied art history. I've never seen anything like this painting." She took her phone out of her bodice as Asher did a double take.

"Interesting place to keep your cell phone."

"I never lose it." She took a picture of Sammy's postcard. She emailed it to someone.

"Who are you sending it to?"

"Professor Igmantani. He'll know who painted it."

Zeke leaned over. "LeBron's been researching. So far, no luck."

"Where did you find this?" she asked, handing back the photo to Sammy, who gnawed on the edge.

"In a used bookstore in Mount Vernon yesterday. Sammy pulled it out from the bottom of a stack of stuff by the cash register. We laminated it to keep him from destroying it." Zeke laughed, pulling the picture out of his son's mouth.

"Don't show it to my dad." Asher gulped. "He'd go ballistic."

Sammy held the picture to his chest and, with dreamy eyes, looked over at Tes.

She narrowed her eyes and asked Sammy, "Is that what you see when you look at me?"

Sammy smiled, a bit of drool curving over his lip.

"Dude, you're crushing on my girl." Asher winked at Sammy. He leaned over and whispered in Tes's ear, "Wouldn't it be nice to have one of our own?"

"All in good time, my lo—" She stopped herself. Knowing she felt that way about him made his heart soar. She patted his leg as the screen on her phone lit up. The caller ID read "Professor Igmantani."

"Excuse me."

"Do you think I'm letting you go anywhere alone with that necklace? Morgan said it was real." Asher followed her into the lobby.

"Ciao, professore."

Tes's Italian was pretty damn good, if her emphasis on syllables and how fast she spoke was any indication. She didn't skip a beat in answering questions. Asher understood two words: Mount Vernon.

Tes ended the call and faced him.

"Did your friend know anything about the painting?"

Tes took a deep breath, placing her hand on her stomach. "The painting is part of the Pope's private collection. Whoever forged it must have done it centuries ago. It hasn't been published in any known archives in the modern age. The original was created in the early 1600s." She paused. "Think about it. That's when the *first* Queen Elizabeth was on the throne. Shakespeare was writing plays performed at The Globe. The height of the Renaissance was in full bloom. Wow, to live back then." Awe framed her blue eyes. "That's not the most interesting part. The painter's name was…Teslasita—that's all they know of *her*."

Asher held her hand. "Kind of like all the similarities between Abraham Lincoln and John F. Kennedy. Weird, but it doesn't change the fact that you're standing here today. It happens to be a quinky-dink that you look like the resurrection angel in that picture."

"Do you know how rare it was for a woman to be an artist in the late 1500s or early 1600s? A painting that detailed? That perfect? The technique alone? It's phenomenal. She may have other works, but none that the Vatican is aware of or acknowledging over the phone. She may have sold under a man's name." Tes bit her bottom lip. "The professor will be in the Seattle area in a few weeks. He said he'd like to meet with me and explain more."

"Sounds fascinating." Asher offered his arm as people started leaving the ballroom. "Let's go get Ruthie so Mom and Dad can take her home."

***

Alone at last, Tes faced Asher once the "Do Not Disturb" sign was secured to the door and locked.

"Would you like a drink?" Her accent slipped again as she made her way over to the mini bar.

He shook his head. "Beautiful view."

"Mind if I have one?" *Damn it all to hell, stop with the damn accent.* Why was she so nervous? She poured a bit of whiskey in a glass and downed the contents. They'd already had sex. This time they could take their time and enjoy exploring one another.

He was going to see her scar. Her stomach flipped. Her last boyfriend had found it grotesque and deforming. The back of her gown didn't dip low enough to show the evidence of that lightning strike years ago. She could count on one hand how many people had seen it, including the doctors at the hospital. Her mother hadn't ever seen it. Neither had her sister. Not even her dad.

It was ugly. It was huge. It wasn't removable. She'd researched that too.

Her hand shook as she poured more whiskey.

"Hey," Asher whispered in her ear, coming up behind her, stopping her from pouring. "Take it easy. Why are you so nervous?"

He kissed her neck, sending heated chills over her body. The kind of chills that made her nipples harden and moisture pool between her thighs.

"Have you ever seen scars so horrid and gross that—"

He turned her and covered her mouth with his. His tongue mated with hers. God, she couldn't get enough of him. She pulled him closer, slanting her mouth a different way.

"I don't give a shit about any scars you may have. I want you."

Her hand slid between their bodies until she cupped his rigidness in her hand, caressing his length.

He grabbed her wrist. "You keep that up and I'll be coming in my pants."

She smiled. "You don't have to come in your pants. I have a better place for you." She pulled him over to the couch, undid his buckle, and unzipped his slacks. The weight of his belt sent the garment to his ankles. She shoved his suitcoat from his shoulders, caressing his chest. Her fingertips paused over his hardened nipples. She pinched his sensitive flesh through his shirt.

Asher grabbed her wrists. "Do you want to go to the bedroom?"

She shook her head, chewing her bottom lip. "Soon." Lifting the waistband of his boxers, she pulled the fabric past his hard-on as she lowered to the couch. "Mm. Mm. My favorite." She ran her tongue from the base to the tip of his cock, loving how the veins popped and his precum tasted as she swirled her tongue over the head. Salty yumminess. He smelled all male with a hint of sandalwood.

"I'm not going to last long if you keep that up. I had other things in mind."

"Do you trust me?"

He closed his eyes, letting out a moan as she sucked his tip in her mouth, running her tongue under the sensitive edge. She ran a finger between his balls. He stepped out of his trousers and boxers, spreading his legs apart to give her better access.

"Good Lord," he whispered as she increased the pressure against his prostate. He pumped his hips forward. He pulled the pins out of her hair, freeing the confines before running his fingers deep into her strands so he could press his cock farther into her mouth.

She gripped him with her hand and moved up and down his shaft, squeezing harder, sucking more, and moving in time with his thrusts. His juices filled her mouth, spilling over her lips. She licked her lips, letting him watch her swallow.

He knelt in front of her, resting his head against her knees, taking in deep breaths. "Holy shit, what a life we're going to have."

She ran her fingers through his soft, silky hair. "Turning you on turns me on."

"You definitely turn me on." He wiped some of his dew from the corner of her mouth. He kissed her. "I've never done that before."

She furrowed her brows. "Done what?"

"Tasted myself." He kissed her again. "Damn, you turn me on." He unbuttoned his shirt and pulled it off, followed by his T-shirt. He stood. Her eyes feasted on his rock-hard abs and still-ridged cock. "As you can see, that tapped the well. Now it's your turn."

Exhilaration flitted across her belly and up to her nipples. She wanted him.

He lifted her into his arms and carried her to the bedroom. He stopped short of the bed and set her on her feet before he began pulling the dress from her shoulders.

"Wait." She pulled her cell phone out of her dress and put it on the nightstand.

He tugged down her dress. The satin caressed her skin as it tugged past her nipples and over her stomach, ass, and the tops of her thighs. She placed her hands on his shoulders so she could kick her dress aside. If he didn't turn her around, he wouldn't see her scar.

"You're not wearing any underwear."

She shook her head, glad the whiskey gave her an ounce of boldness.

"Freshly waxed pussy?" He dipped a finger between her folds, rubbing her clit. She closed her eyes and licked her lips. She was so close to coming. She was swollen and ready for him to plunge deep inside.

"Fuck me."

He stopped. "No. I'm going to make love to my wife."

"Future wife," she corrected. "You don't want me to talk dirty in bed?" She pulled away from him, only wearing high heels and the famous necklace. She sat back on the bed, scooting to the middle of the mattress.

His strong hands caressed her calf as he removed each shoe, letting them drop to the floor. He took her necklace and placed it on the dresser. Damn, he had a nice ass and what a profile with his cock at full staff. Yeah, she could get used to him in her bed every day. When he came back to the bed, he held her feet and massaged the instep. She moaned as she leaned back on her elbows. He pulled her ass to the edge of the mattress. Her eyes widened in shock. He knelt, arranging her legs over his shoulders. He nipped the inside of her knees, taking his time on each side, nipping, licking, and sucking his sweet time to the junction of her thighs. She wanted his tongue against her clit.

They stared at each other as he explored her body.

His tongue licked her outer folds. She moaned, anticipating the length of his tongue pressed against that spot that ached for release. His tongue dove deeper, straight into her vagina. As his tongue retreated, he slid one finger inside, then another. She undulated her hips, wanting his tongue to touch her clit. She slid her fingers between her thighs, opening herself, caressing her clit. He nipped her finger. She squealed and pulled her hand back, laughing.

He smiled before sliding his tongue everywhere around her clit but never directly against it.

His tongue pressed hard against her clit, suckling and rolling his lips over her bud. The tension built as he spread her further with another finger.

He abruptly stopped and withdrew.

She couldn't help but want to finish what he'd started. He grabbed her hands and stretched them over her head, lying flat against her. Flesh to flesh, breast to breast. The heat of his balls soothed the aching spot between her thighs, but damn she wanted more.

Panting against his lips, he kissed her. She hadn't ever been so sexually frustrated in her life. God, she wanted to come. She needed to find release and he wasn't letting her touch herself. He sucked a nipple in his mouth, rolling his tongue over the peak. "I don't want to neglect these." He moved his tongue to the other breast while his fingers pinched the nipple he'd left.

He lay gentle kisses along her ribs, descending to her belly, kissing that sweet spot just below her navel. He waited for her to open her eyes and look at him before he dipped his tongue once more to her clit, taking his time to press it hard against her bud, almost sending her over the edge. She squeezed her thighs around his head as he shoved two fingers deep inside. He pressed against the interior wall. With every thrust, he pushed harder.

She screamed as her release came, thrusting her hips against his tongue, riding the wave of pleasure, knowing there was more to come.

He nipped at her hipbone. She giggled when he nipped at her side. "Are you ready?"

She swallowed to catch her breath. "I'm more than ready."

He dipped his head toward the pillows. "Why don't we get comfortable?"

As she began to move to the pillows, he stretched out beside her, laying on his side. "Where's this scar you're hiding from me?"

She tensed.

"Show me."

Tes closed her eyes.

"Honey, nothing will ruin tonight. Not even a fart."

She giggled.

"Not a big belch."

She bit her bottom lip.

"Sure as hell not a scar."

She looked away. "You know, I'm only nervous because other guys have been grossed out by it."

"You know those three little words I'm not supposed to say?"

It'll all change once he sees it. Once he knows how hideous veins rose to the surface when struck she was by lightning. Just like every other guy. She nodded.

"I feel that and so much more. There's not a scar in the world that will take away what I feel for you."

Sure, he said that now, but he hadn't seen it yet. Once he did, it'd be over. It'd be her and Ruthie and a lonely life.

***

Asher kissed Tes on the cheek. "Come on, honey. Show me."

Her lips pressed together. How could she doubt his heart?

He kissed her, suckling her bottom lip. "Well, it's not on the front of you—I've seen, tasted, licked, nipped, and suckled your front. So, it's got to be on your back. You know, eventually, I'm going to mount you from behind—because it's one of the Kama Sutra positions and we're going to try every one of them over the rest of our lives. I think I read somewhere that there's over 400 positions. We're going to be busy."

"We can stick to having sex facing each other if you don't like the scar, okay?"

That's where she was wrong. "You get to see all of me. I want to see all of you. I want you to be as comfortable with my body as I am, and vice versa. I'm going to know every inch of your body—that includes this allegedly ugly scar you have. I'm beginning to believe it's monumental in your head but nowhere else."

That got her moving from timid to angry. That's what he wanted. He wanted her to not be afraid of her own body.

"I already know your secret. You know mine. What's a scar between a husband and wife?"

She swallowed, pulled her hair to one side, and turned so he could see her back.

So that's what lightning did? "That's the coolest scar I've ever seen."

"No, it's not." She turned back around.

"It totally is." He put his hand on her shoulder and turned her back around. His fingers traced the white strands from the base of her spine and out along the many branches on each side of her spine. "It looks like the tree of life."

"It does?" Her voice held doubt.

He ran his tongue the length of her scar, layering kisses along the main branches. "Damn, woman. You were worried for nothing."

She turned to face him. "Do you want to make love to me now?"

He cupped her chin. "I'm going to make love to you for the rest of your life."

She smiled and kissed him. Hard. She shoved his shoulder against the mattress and climbed on top of him. He jockeyed his hips closer to the middle of the bed. Yeah, he liked a woman on top.

"You sure you can handle this?" he teased as she took his cock in her hand.

"Why do guys say shit like that? Babies are designed to come out of this opening. Rest assured, you'll fit." She rolled her eyes and lifted enough, and placed his cock into that sweet, wet, hot opening.

He laughed, and closed his eyes. "Mm. I like this."

She took her time working his length inside, swirling her hips, adjusting inch by inch.

Damn, she was tight. Skin to skin. No condom. Hell, he hadn't been this fucking horny since he was a teenager. All he had to do was last longer than her. In this position, odds were on his side.

He'd laid there, patiently waiting. She had him nice and slick and pumping in and out of her so hard his balls ached. He sucked her nipples. She tightened around him even more. The first throbs of her orgasm built. A few hard thrusts and she was coming all over him. God she smelled sweet as summer as her essence flowed around him. He hung on, sucking her nipple until she slowed.

He rolled her over on her back. Now it was his turn. She laced her legs behind his back. He put a pillow under her ass so that his cock rubbed against her clit just right. He was going to make sure she came again.

Slow and steady thrusts helped her inner muscles relax. She'd adjusted to his width, enough for him to increase his pace. Sweat beaded across his brow and down his back. He slammed into her so hard his balls smacked her ass.

"Harder," she moaned.

Yes. He obliged. Her muscles clamped on him again, bringing her close to her release.

"Harder," she yelled.

He pulled his length out to the edge of the head of his cock and slammed it into her depths. His balls retracted.

She screamed in his ear, bit his earlobe as she came, digging her nails into his back.

The first tingle of his release came from the base of his cock, straight up his shaft, and radiated around the tip. His come surged up his length and burst out the head. Hot sperm drenched her as he thrust and pumped until every drop was freed.

He panted against her lips, kissing her. "Holy shit. That was amazing." He rested on his elbows, brushing her dampened hair from her brow. "Was it good for you?"

She laughed. "It was fucktasmic." She cupped his ass. "I want more."

"I've created a monster."

Her hand massaged the space between his balls.

"Hm. Are you pushing my magic button?"

God he loved her smile and the light in her eyes when she looked at him. "Uh-huh."

"It's working." He stiffened inside her. "You know you're going to be pregnant by morning."

"At this point, I don't care." She thrust her hips forward. "Just keep making love to me."

"Your wish is my command." He ran his tongue along her neck and nipped the flesh under her earlobe. "Name your position."

"I don't know. I've only tried these two positions."

A wicked smile curved his lips. "Come here, my little acolyte. I've much to teach you."

She giggled.

He rolled her onto her stomach, situating the pillow low across her hips, bringing her ass in the air. He laid long, lingering kisses to her back. "Spread your thighs, my sweet. I'm going to mount you from behind."

23

Tes was sore in all the right places. She cuddled close to Asher's side. He snored softly, sated and pleased after hours of love making. They fit together better than puzzle pieces.

After a quick shower, she slipped on a robe and secured her necklace in the safe. She made her way to the living room, taking a moment to appreciate the cityscape lights sprinkled against the dark sky.

His clothes still littered the living room floor. Asher's cell phone fell out of his pants pocket as she picked them up. The phone rang. The screen read "Mom."

She took the call. "Hi, Isabella."

"Hey, Tessie. Is Asher awake?"

She liked how the whole Hickok clan used her new nickname. "No, he's resting. Do you want me to wake him?"

"Yes."

That didn't sound good. "What happened?" Tes made her way back to the bedroom, sitting on the edge.

Her voice strained. "I'll let Asher tell you."

Asher opened his sleepy eyes. She handed the phone to him. "It's your mom."

"What's up?" Asher sat up, horror widening his eyes.

Nope. Not good at all.

"He was in the house?" He paused, swinging his feet over the side. "How do you know it was the kidnapper?"

Not again. Tes was as frightened as Asher, judging by the look on his face.

Asher's mouth opened, then snapped closed. "Is Tango all right?" His eyes widened, staring at Tes. "We're on our way." He ended the call and pulled Tes into his arms. "I thought this was all over. I thought this was behind us."

"Are Hailey and Morgan okay?"

"They slept in my parents' bed. Something they've been doing since they were little kids. Movie and popcorn nights were always in Nonna and Popop's bed. Tango heard something and took off running. I don't know if I ever told you, but our old neighbor, Tango's first owner, was a cop. Tango's a former police dog. He took a bite out of the intruder. He had a piece of blue fabric in his teeth. Hopefully, we'll get some DNA too."

She was almost afraid to ask, but she had to. "And Ruthie?"

He kissed her cheek. "She's fine. She stayed with the girls."

He sure as hell gathered a lot of information in that short phone call.

***

Three squad cars were parked outside Mom and Dad's house as Asher and Tes pulled up front. He held Tes's hand as he led her past the officers on the front porch. They made their way to the back of the house into the kitchen and family room.

Ruthie ran to Tes while Hailey ran into his arms. "I'm sorry, Daddy. I know this was your big night away with Tes."

"Are you okay?" Tes asked Ruthie, as if she'd answer. Her tail hung low but wagged.

"Shh, don't be sorry." Asher held Hailey close, then held her at arm's length. "Are you okay?"

She nodded.

Tes entered the family room, grabbing hold of Morgan. Mom sat at the long kitchen table, the central hub of the Hickok household. A police officer sat next to her taking notes. Another officer was out on the back deck on his cell phone, and another sat in the family room across from Morgan.

Tes kissed Morgan's cheek. "Tell us what happened."

"We were watching a movie in Nonna and Poppop's bed," Hailey said, lowering herself onto the sofa next to Tes.

Asher noticed the officers stopped talking, turned, and listened. No doubt waiting to hear if she gave a different story, or if she'd provide more details than she'd already shared.

"Ruthie was between us," Morgan added. "Tango was on the floor in front of the fireplace chewing on his bone." She swallowed, not making eye contact with anyone. "Their ears perked up at the same time. I grabbed Ruthie's collar so she couldn't run if Tango did. I didn't want her to get hurt, Aunt Tes. I know you never let her out of your sight."

"Thank you, Morgan. That was thoughtful of you." Tes's worried gaze met Asher's.

Hailey continued, "Tango took off running. He growled." She sucked in a sob. "Then yelped." She sagged against him, bawling. "He hurt him, Daddy. He hurt Tango."

"Poppop took him to the vet." Hailey's sobs increased, breaking his heart. He kissed her head and pulled Morgan in close with his other arm.

Morgan leaned against him. "Tango bit him. He wouldn't let go. No matter what he did to Tango, he wouldn't let go."

"That's his training, honey." Asher's heart sank. "He's a good dog. I'm sure he's going to be fine."

Mom left the officer at the table and made her way over to the couch. "He's in surgery. He's cut. Bad. The first officer that arrived rushed him to the vet. Your dad went with him." She shook her head, biting her lips together to fight back tears.

Asher looked around the room. "Where's the blood?"

Mom whispered, "Upstairs. In the guest room."

"He came in through the window?"

She paled, nodding. Asher rose from the couch and wrapped Mom in a hug. "It's going to be okay." Mom was the matriarch of their family and could whip the brood into place. It was strange to see her scared.

Mom wiped her hands across her cheeks. "There aren't any alarm sensors on the second floor. Only people who know us well know that."

Asher understood her meaning. "We're getting alarm sensors on every window tomorrow."

Tes nudged his leg. "I need to go to the vet's office."

Asher weighed his words carefully. One of them needed to stay with the girls, and one of them needed to be with Dad. "Why don't you stay here with Mom and the girls?"

"I can help." Tes stared at Asher, raising her eyebrows.

Resurrection angel. Maybe she could help Tango. "Okay. We'll go."

As soon as Tes stood, Mom wrapped her in a hug. "Bring him home. I don't know what Grant will do if anything happens to him."

Tes kissed her cheek. "That's not going to happen. Not on my watch."

Asher looked at his frightened daughters. "You girls want to come with or stay with Nonna?"

Morgan grabbed Mom's hand. "I'll stay." She pet Ruthie with her other hand. "I'll watch over Ruthie."

"Me too," Hailey added. "Poppop doesn't know how to text, Dad. Please text us how Tango is as soon as you can."

***

Grant looked like hell sitting in the waiting room alone. He'd run his fingers through his thick hair so much that it stood askew. His eyes were red and swollen from crying. Tes and Asher wrapped him in hugs.

"I'm going to check on Tango." Tes extracted herself from Grant's strong arms.

Asher held her back. "You sure you're up for this?"

She nodded. *Hell no*, she wasn't up for this. She wasn't sure if they'd let her back in the surgical suite, so she was going to slink her way along the wall, hoping no one noticed. *Stupid plan.*

The electronic doors opened when she tapped her hip against the big stainless steel button on the wall. A nurse left an office and took one look at Tes and stopped her with a firm hand. "Who are you?"

"I'm Dr. Tesla Brynn. I'm here to check on Tango, the German shepard in surgery."

"The waiting room's behind you." The nurse motioned for Tes to march right back through the door she'd entered.

She closed her eyes, panic flitting along her nerves. "I'm not leaving until I see him." Her fingers began to tingle. *Don't blow your wad. Use short bursts.*

The woman pursed her lips and put a hand on her ample hip. "Uh-uh. I don't know who you think you are, but here in this hospital, *I'm* in charge."

Tes pulsed energy at the woman. The overhead fluorescent lights flickered. The woman backed up.

"Which room is he in?"

"Lady, you need to get your ass back in that waiting room." She jerked her head toward the door. Her tone and gestures no doubt intimidated most people into following her commands.

Tes stepped closer, pulsing her energy again. This time all the lights in the hallway dimmed, darkened, then flickered back on.

"I'm going to have to call the police."

Tes pulsed energy toward the phone as she walked past.

The nurse headed there and lifted the receiver. She clicked on the button. "The line's dead."

Tes paused, stretching her hand toward an electrical socket, sucking the energy through the air, and dimming the lights. "Which room?"

The woman's eyes widened. "Last door on the left."

"Thank you." The lights flickered as Tes continued down the long hall. Bright red, orange, blue, and white energy fields crisscrossed in front of her. She imagined they were the electrical and cable wiring throughout the building. She spread her fingers wide, absorbing the energy source. Her ears buzzed like high-wire electrical lines. The hairs on her arms and the nape of her neck stood on end.

Pace yourself. I don't have time for the Shadowlands today.

Tes paused outside the surgical door. *No going back now. I can do this.*

Wrapping her hand inside her hoodie jacket, she palmed the handle. She snagged a surgical mask from the container by the door, slipping it over her ears, and nudged the door closed with her foot.

"Excuse me?" a man asked.

Tes assumed he was the veterinarian since he wore high-powered magnifying surgical glasses.

"I'm Dr. Tesla Brynn. I'm here to help."

Blood-soaked gauze littered the floor. Dark blood. That wasn't a good sign.

"We're in a bit of an emergency here."

"I know." Tes made her way to the table.

There was a gash along Tango's back and under a rib, possibly a punctured lung, and maybe his liver too. An assistant and an anesthesiologist hovered, efficiently doing their jobs.

Rhythmic sighs and hisses emitted from the regulator. The heart monitor beeped, slow and erratic.

Tango wasn't going to make it.

Child, your blood is the life source. Your blood. Your breath. Your being. They are the life source of the universe.

Tes glanced to the corners of the room. *Who the hell said that?*

Channel your resurrection spirit. The angel that God placed inside you.

God did *what?*

The Almighty didn't strike you dead. He pulled your spirit to heaven and gave you an amazing gift. He gave you the gift to save others. Child, you have a purpose on earth now. Time to get busy doing God's work saving, and doing less doubting your angelic spirit.

An alarm sounded. "Blood pressure's dropping."

"Two more cc's of epinephrine," the veterinarian commanded, cool and calm. He glanced at Tes. "His liver was stabbed more than once. I don't think we're going to be able to save him."

You know what to do, child. Use your blood. Go on now, you heard me.

When did she gain a southern spirit guide? An image formed in her mind. An elderly black woman dressed in a blue dress splashed with yellow and black sunflowers stood by the assistant. *Could this be Mambo Janetta? Joni's spirit guide?*

Tes stared at one of the scalpels on the surgical tray. Could she save him? She'd gathered energy. Could it be that simple? Her hand shook as she grabbed the scalpel, careful not to touch the metal tip.

Good Lord, they were going to think she was crazy.

"You shouldn't be in here." The assistant pinned her with a nasty glare.

"Here goes nothing." Tes pressed the scalpel into her palm. The metal arced a stream of lightning, hitting the assistant in the chest. He dropped to his knees. She sliced through her skin. "Damn, that hurts."

The vet stepped back.

She held her hand over Tango's opened chest and let her blood drip inside his gaping cavity.

The anesthesiologist tried to grab her hand, but he was a little out of reach.

She poured more blood along both of Tango's open incisions.

The machine's beeping came back to a steady rhythm. The anesthesiologist focused on the instruments. "He's stabilizing."

The vet looked at Tango's liver. "I'll be damned."

"Is it working?" Tes asked.

"How the hell did you do that?"

"I don't know. A voice told me it would work." *Oh sure, that didn't sound crazy at all.*

The assistant wheezed, like he was having an asthma attack, and clutched his chest. Tes crouched in front of him, pulled down her surgical mask, then lowered his. His eyes widened. She took a deep breath and exhaled into his opened mouth.

The assistant panted at first, then relaxed and took a deep breath. *"Who are you?"*

"I'm a doctor." She helped the man to his feet.

She turned and looked at Tango. His liver had stopped bleeding. "Make sure you've pulled out all the gauze, any sponges, everything. I don't need him getting an infection."

The vet pulled out the needle he'd been using to stitch Tango's liver. The assistant bumped her out of the way and removed the clamps, tossing the used instruments in a metal bin to be cleaned later.

"Now, hold the incision closed," she instructed the vet.

This is going to hurt. She squeezed the scalpel in her hand. *Jesus, Holy Mary!*

Blood dripped from her palm, over the blade's handle, and onto Tango's shaved belly. She poured a good portion where the vet gripped the flesh closed. The bright surgical light showed the skin mending as soon as the blood touched it. *Wow. She did that?*

She glanced at the anesthesiologist. "Go ahead and increase his oxygen." She squeezed the last bit over Tango's other wounds. She tossed the scalpel into the bin. Carefully, she pulled out the intubation tube, held his mouth closed, and exhaled into his nose. "Warm blanket, please."

The assistant retrieved a blanket and laid it over Tango.

"There, there, boy. How are you?" Tes went to the sink and washed her hands. Dried blood soaked her new engagement ring. She'd have to make sure she removed it next time. *Next time?* The gouge she expected to be in her palm had healed shut. *No cut?*

Holy shit. She *was* a resurrection angel.

24

"Thank you, gentlemen. Tango and I will be going now." She looked at the assistant. "Could you carry him to the waiting room, please?"

Tes entered the waiting room with her hands in her hoodie pockets. Her hands shook from spending energy or the adrenaline rush, she wasn't sure which.

The assistant gently lowered Tango into Grant's arms. "I don't believe what I witnessed." He walked away, dazed.

"Tango's as good as new." Tes couldn't keep the smile off her lips. *She'd done it.* She'd healed him and hadn't thrown herself into the Shadowlands in the process. *How freaking awesome.*

Grant narrowed his eyes. "Did you put your whammy on him?"

She laughed. "If that's what you want to call it. Yeah, I spread a little whammy his way." She couldn't wait to tell Joni.

"Is he okay to come home so soon?"

"He's all healed now." Tes gave him a reassuring squeeze. "A bit groggy from the anesthesia. He'll be okay to eat and drink when he's fully awake."

Asher hugged her, kissing the top of her head.

They all turned to leave when the veterinarian entered the waiting room, a gun pointed at Tes. "You're coming with me." He flicked his fingers.

Asher shoved her behind him. "You're not taking her anywhere."

Zeke and another man burst through the front door, assault rifles in hand, dressed in full tactical gear, helmets, and protective eye wear—the whole nine yards.

"Put the gun down, mate, and no one will get hurt." The stranger with Zeke had a strong English accent and intense dark blue eyes.

Zeke stepped in front of Asher, pointing two fingers at them and motioned toward the exit. "Someone called the cops. They're on their way."

Tes glanced behind the counter and noticed the nurse was gone. She must have stepped outside and used her cell phone to call the cops.

LeBron came in next, holding a computer tablet in his hand. He walked the long way around the group, heading straight to the front desk computer.

Grant carried Tango outside.

Tes grabbed onto the back of Asher's sweatshirt, hiding.

The vet stepped closer. "Please. I'm dying."

Tes stopped in her tracks and let go of Asher. "Go," she whispered to Asher. "Help your dad."

"I'm not leaving you."

"Trust me." She kissed his cheek. "I've got this. No one's getting hurt."

"*Tes.*"

The stranger jerked his head toward the door for Asher to go. "SUV's outside."

"I have my truck."

"Give me your keys." Zeke put out his hand. Asher handed them over without hesitation and followed his dad outside. He paused at the door, staring at her.

"It's going to be okay." Tes put her hands up, stepping closer to the vet. "You're a greedy man. You want my blood for yourself."

"I won't need much. Please. I have—"

"Small cell lung cancer," Tes cut him off. "I don't know where that came from. I'm sorry, Doc, but some people are meant to die." *How was she getting this information? She opened her mouth and out it spilled. Was this the spirit Mambo Janetta mentioned?*

"We all have a final hour. We can't outrun it."

The vet lurched forward, shoving the end of the pistol against her chest. "If I die, you die."

Tes heard a gun cock behind her. "I got a clean shot," English barked.

Zeke commanded, "Take the shot."

"*No.*" Tes stepped in front of English's rifle.

English cussed, yanking his gun upward.

"I can take his life force," Tes said.

"What? I need you to cure me." The vet hit her arm with the pistol.

"Ouch. That hurt." She rubbed her arm. "You don't do as much good in this world as you think you do. When you get to the other side, you'll know what I mean. Unfortunately, you're destined to repeat this lifetime."

The vet fell to his knees, grabbing her legs. "Please, please, spare me."

"I can't." Tes leaned over and put her hand on the man's chest, pulling his energy from his body. His arms weakened, dropping the gun. She kicked it away.

Zeke grabbed the gun, popping out the cartridge and checking the chamber. He put them on the counter where LeBron was busy typing.

She stretched the man's energy from his being, then gripped both edges and ripped it apart. It crackled and popped as it burst, like pulling apart a plastic bag. The vet collapsed. "Why? Why?" Tears dripped from his eyes onto the green and white linoleum.

"It was your destiny. The only mercy I can give you is to end this life quicker, so that you can start a new one." She licked her lips. "Well, whenever your soul determines you need to return." She sat beside him, taking his hand in hers, trying to comfort him. "Don't worry. You'll get a chance to say goodbye to those you love most. I didn't take away your whole life—just enough so you couldn't hurt me, or anyone else, for as long as you live."

Zeke grabbed her arm, hauling her to her feet. "We need to go."

Tes jerked her gaze to the door. English was already gone. LeBron made his way toward the operating room. Zeke whistled and tossed Asher's keys to LeBron. "You got this?"

"I'm right behind you."

"See you back at rendezvous one."

That sounded so covertish. Tes giggled.

"Got it."

Zeke pulled her along to the SUV. "I bet Joni likes you in your tactical gear." Asher held the back door open. He grabbed her by the waist and put her inside, next to Grant, before climbing in and shutting the door. Zeke hadn't closed his door before English pulled away.

They hadn't gone far before Zeke turned around and pinned her with a glare. "Don't you *ever* step in front of a gun again. You hear me?"

"Sir, yes, sir," she mumbled, dropping her gaze to her lap. She couldn't keep the smile off her face. "How cool was that? I don't know how I knew that shit. It was like a download from God." She looked at Grant. "Tango's alive."

"Congratulations. You almost got yourself killed." English slammed the lid on her joy bucket. Heaven forbid she spend a moment basking in her personal happiness.

She frowned. "Who are *you*, by the way?"

"I'm Dobbs. Moniker Dobbs. From now on, I'm in charge. What I say, you do. You don't ask questions. You sure as *hell* do *not* step in front of my gun ever again."

"What?" She blinked at his glare in the rearview mirror. "Moniker—"

"Dobbs. No one calls me Moniker. Not even my mother."

Tes frowned. "You didn't know your mother." *How'd she know that?*

"*Shit.*" Dobbs glared at Zeke. "Joni's a handful as it is. Are you sure we want to take on another one? I have enough gray hairs."

"According to my wife, yes. Tes is family now. It's up to us to teach her not to get her head blown off, or her ass whooped. Though right now, I'd sanction Asher to take her over his knee and teach her a lesson or two."

"Oh, he'd like that." She smiled at Asher.

He didn't smile back.

***

Asher glanced between Zeke and Dobbs. "Would someone like to explain what the hell happened in there?"

"I saved Tango." Tes nudged him with her elbow. She couldn't stop smiling. He was happy for her, on some small level. Tonight, the world changed. Whether he liked it or not, he was caught in the middle of it.

He wrapped his arm around her. Cop cars whirled by them as they turned onto the main road.

Asher's heart skipped a beat. "What about LeBron?"

"He'll take your truck back to your mom and dad's." Zeke paused. "That's where we're headed."

"Rendezvous one." Tes giggled. Nervous energy bubbled out of her like someone had popped a champagne cork.

Asher glanced over the backseat, watching the squad cars swerve into the veterinarian clinic driveway. "Will he get out in time?"

Dobbs said, "He stayed to grab any paperwork that had Tango's and your dad's name on it."

"You guys think of everything."

"That's our job." Dobbs glanced at him in the rearview mirror. "I'm former MI-5. LeBron, Zeke, and I make a great team. We'll keep Tes safe. Congratulations, by the way, on your new engagement. LeBron showed me the big proposal tonight."

Was that only hours ago? It seemed like days had passed. What the hell had he gotten himself into? He couldn't protect her. She needed to learn to listen in intense moments like these. Brushing him aside and taking control of the situation herself? What was she thinking?

All this craziness was his new life. *Shit.* For better or for worse—this was what he signed up for. He didn't know where to begin to process what Tes had done.

"Thanks," he muttered to Dobbs.

Once Tes had disappeared down the hall, Dad explained that the person who'd broken into the house had stabbed Tango. Asher had never seen his dad so broken up before. Well, when Grandma or Grandpa died, of course. Dad loved that dog.

"Are you mad at me?" Tes bowed her head. The smile had disappeared from her sweet face.

"No." He kissed the top of her head. "You scared me back there. A man pointed a gun at you."

"He wasn't going to shoot me."

"You don't know that."

"Yeah, I do. He's a veterinarian. They're not killers by nature. They're pushovers. He was desperate."

Zeke said, "Desperate people do unpredictable things. You need to remember that."

Asher squeezed her shoulder. "What did you do to him?"

She swallowed. "I weakened his energy, so he couldn't hurt me or anyone else."

He tried to understand what she meant. "Why did you step in front of Dobbs' gun?"

She picked at a nonexistent piece of lint on her sweatshirt. "I wasn't going to let him hurt the vet either. I didn't want anyone to die."

"They were there to protect you."

"I know that now." She looked through her lashes, softening his heart. "I'm sorry."

"Honey, I think we need to have a little training with Dobbs and Zeke. You can't go putting yourself in danger like that. Okay?"

She shuddered, leaned over, and whispered in his ear, "I don't like him."

He smiled. "You don't like being yelled at."

"Figured that out already, did you?"

"Yeah, day one." Asher squeezed Dad's shoulder. "How are you doing?"

Dad held Tes's hand. "You need to make me a promise."

Tes turned her attention toward Dad.

"You aren't to ever put yourself, Asher, or the kids in harm's way. It sounds like you almost got yourself killed tonight."

She waved a hand at Dobbs. "They're exaggerating."

Zeke turned and glared.

Dobbs swore under his breath.

"Well, you are." She sank back into the seat. "No one was going to get hurt."

"Tessie, honey, if anything had happened to you, it'd break my heart."

She lay her head against Dad's arm. "I wouldn't ever want to do that."

"See that you don't." He kissed her head. "Thank you for saving Tango."

She smiled. "You're welcome."

Tom Krysinski stood in the driveway as they rolled to a stop.

Dobbs shoved the gear into park and turned to look at them. "We're moving you two and the kids to Wyoming. You need to stay in hiding for a bit. The kidnapper made a move on your family, Asher. Not sure why, other than to maybe try and kidnap the girls again."

"And Ruthie." Tes crossed her arms.

"Yeah." Dobbs looked at Asher. "We found surveillance cameras in your house." His gaze drifted to Dad. "And yours. So, we'll be installing our own cameras—in case the kidnapper returns. We thought it best to get you out of town for your own safety. He's still watching. His feed was untraceable. LeBron thinks he's backdooring onto a neighbor's wireless network."

Asher's gut sank. "What about Nikki—Morgan's mother?"

"Out of town for now—can't be reached." Dobbs glanced at Zeke. "Tom's dialed in. He'll let your ex know."

"She was never my ex." Asher opened the side door.

Tes glared at Dobbs. "Wyoming? Seriously? Could you not pick a more remote area?"

Dobbs didn't skip a beat. "Yes, but it'll do."

The look on Tes's face made Asher smile. Cameras? Tes had mentioned that, but he'd dismissed it as her imagination. Why was the kidnapper focused on his family?

He helped Tes out of the vehicle.

What if he'd had another kid out there with some woman he didn't remember, and this was his way to get back at the Hickok family?

25

Two weeks away in the country was the vacation they all needed. The Gregsons and their two dogs came along. They'd spent hours laughing and bonding. If this was Tes's new normal, she was all in. Her heart had never been happier.

Zeke and Joni's "quaint cabin" wasn't a rough-it one-room with an outhouse. No, it was one of those million-dollar homes that movie stars owned. The size rivaled a two-story strip mall. There was a central hub that was wider than Asher's home with two sides flanking like the wings of a stealth fighter plane. An intricately carved forest scene graced the French doors, which opened into a grand room. The expansive living room, kitchen, and dining area could fit an entire football team and not feel crowded. There were two separate U-shaped sectionals facing each other with rough-hewn coffee tables dotting the space in between. The head of a six-point buck decorated the massive two-story fireplace. Its glass eyes looked at the far wall, where a bearskin rug hung. In total there were ten bedrooms, twelve bathrooms, a media room, office, and enough room for no one to rub elbows if they didn't want to. Deep down, Tes didn't want to leave. This was a dream home with sweeping mountain views and no one around for miles.

Dobbs kept in touch with important news from home. So far, they weren't any closer to finding the kidnapper's identity.

Joni and Tes headed out for a hike in the foothills, far away from prying eyes and kids under foot.

"Here's a good spot." Joni stopped near a stream. "We need to figure out if water is a good or bad conductor for your energy."

Tes's stomach dropped. "Water's an excellent conductor of electricity." She had a scar to prove it.

"Yeah, but how much is too much?"

Each day, Tes learned a bit more about how to control her power. So far, she'd produced lightning, thunder, and torrential rains on command, and she'd also drained energy from fallen, rotting logs and given life to tree saplings. It'd knocked her off her butt a time or two too. With each trial, Tes learned to control the energy—though as jazzed as she was, it was hard work. She'd never been so exhausted in her life. It could be the fresh mountain air. As a city kid, Wyoming was more nature than she'd ever experienced.

"What would happen if you try to harness the water's energy?" Joni stepped onto a boulder, closer to the stream.

"You might want to step back."

"No worries." Joni splayed her fingers. "Shields up."

Tes gingerly stepped closer to the stream, palms sweating. She wiped them on her jeans. She held an arm over the water and focused. Water was powerful. It forged landscapes, wiped out towns and civilizations, fueled power stations. She should be able to tap into some of that.

Nothing.

She squatted, trying harder. Nothing.

"Touch the water," Joni suggested.

"Are you kidding?" Tes shook her head. "I could be electrocuted."

"You're scared."

"Maybe."

"You gotta face your fears. Otherwise, your enemies can use it against you."

"What enemies? I don't have enemies."

Joni laughed. "Not yet. But if an unearthly being finds your weakness, they're going to exploit it. Kind of how that demon came after you. He knew you had what he needed, and you played right into him."

Tes thought back. "How else was I going to pry his death-grip off my wrist?"

"I don't know." Joni frowned. "What if your energy can't pass through water? We need to know that going in."

Shivers doused Tes's backbone. "That could be bad." She stood. "Or we'll know I can't go near water."

Joni glanced skyward and bit her lip. "Sometimes demons multiply."

Tes stepped back from the water and braced her hands on her knees. "Are you freaking kidding me?" *Why hadn't she mentioned that before?*

"It's best you know." Joni stepped closer. "You have to know you can kick ass when the time comes."

"I can kick ass. I can drain energy. When I channel my inner resurrection angel, I know things." Tes faced the stream, weighing her options. "You sure? Demons aren't common, right?"

Joni gnawed her bottom lip.

"Just tell me."

"He knows about you now. He touched you." Joni pointed to the faint scar on Tes's wrist. "He touched me." Joni held up her right arm. "I can feel when he's near through this scar." She shook her head. "Before you blasted him with a million watts of your special blend of waking-the-dead energy. He's back. Pretty much full tilt before Zeke and I battled him in West Virginia." She stepped closer. "We need to draw him out and end his existence once and for all."

"Oh, hell no." Nervous laughter bubbled out of Tes. "We're not Daphne and Velma heading off with Scooby and the gang to hunt down demons."

"We won't have to." Seriousness filled Joni's eyes. "He'll find us."

When she was in the Shadowlands there was a demon whispering in the kidnapper's ear. Could it be the same one? Could he be influencing all of this to get back at Joni? And her? "I don't like water."

"Then you best figure this out." Joni nudged her toward the stream. "Go on. Channel your inner Xena, Warrior Princess."

Tes laughed and stepped back onto the boulder. *I can do this.* She put her hands over the water, trying hard to focus. Nothing. She crouched lower, focusing harder, visualizing the water's power lifting upward. Nothing. Her shoulders sagged. "It's no use."

Joni pulled her backpack off her shoulder and pulled out her water bottle. "Cup your hands."

Tes hesitated but complied.

Joni dripped a few drops into her palms. "Now evaporate it."

Steam rose from her palms, boiling the water.

"See?" Joni smiled. "You got this."

"Yeah, need a facial? I'm your gal." Tes wiped her damp palms on her jeans. "I think water's my Kryptonite."

"Could be. I suppose we all have one."

"What's yours?" Tes waited.

Joni licked her lips. "I don't know. I haven't figured that out yet."

Tes narrowed her eyes. "You don't want to tell me."

Joni groaned. "I hate surprises."

Tes laughed. "Aw. You poor thing."

"No, you don't understand. If I get surprised, it's like Armageddon. Like destroy everything around me, sinkholes, total destruction."

Tes lifted her brows. "Okay. No surprise parties," she said more to herself than Joni. "And stay away from large bodies of water."

"Wait a minute." Joni tapped her shoulder. "Put your hand in the water. What if you can electrify everything near you."

Tes stared at her like she was bat-shit crazy. "No."

"Why not?"

Tes thought of every lesson she'd learned this week. "I can't kill an innocent life. If I electrocute the water, I risk killing fish."

Joni rolled her eyes. "They're fish."

"They're living beings. When I drained the energy from the veterinarian, it was because I knew he'd been a horrible person—and still I couldn't kill him. I didn't have it in me."

"Is it because you're a doctor and took that oath not to harm anyone?"

Tes frowned. "I'd believed that long before taking an oath." She stared into the river. "I used to heal wounded animals when I was a kid. Baby birds. Cats. Dogs. Nothing big. I can't hurt animals."

The corner of Joni's mouth twitched. "So, this gift isn't newfound after all?"

Tes cocked her head. "I never thought of it as a gift. I only did it when I was alone. A few times."

"Sure." Joni's smile was teasing. "A few times."

"Would you kill someone or an animal?"

"In a heartbeat. If it meant me or them. It's always going to be them." Joni lifted her pack. "What if someone was going to hurt me? Would you kill them to protect me?"

That was a loaded question. "Anyone who had ill intent toward anyone I valued would suffer. Maybe not die—but would stop them from proceeding further."

"Well, that's comforting." Joni slipped her arms through her pack's straps.

Tes couldn't tell if she was being sarcastic or genuine. "I'd protect you. I promise."

"Why do I get the feeling you'd choose to die than hurt anyone?"

Tes squared her shoulders. "I'd gladly die to protect you."

Anger flashed in Joni's eyes. "You're not a sacrificial lamb. You need to remember that when we go into battle. We're fighting things we've never seen. We don't know what we're up against." Joni stepped closer. Cocked a brow. "You need to have a winning spirit and a kick-ass attitude. None of this wishy-washy, mamby-pamby passive shit that you'll lay down your life for me. Got it?"

Tes swallowed. "Got it."

"I'm not convinced."

She sighed. "I'll do my best. Promise."

"Oy." Joni hung her head. "We best get back. Zeke and I are flying home today. We want to give you and Asher time alone with the girls before the wedding." She led the way. "Are you ready to be a mom of two teenagers?"

Tes kept pace, following Joni. "I'm loving it more than I thought I would. Morgan's coming around. Hailey's happy for Asher and me."

"You know, you'd think Hailey would be the one tormented because she was held longer than Morgan." Joni glanced over her shoulder. "But Morgan's been more affected by what she saw. She sure as hell hates her mother."

"Yeah." For all the heart-to-hearts Tes had with Morgan, she wasn't budging. "She's not looking forward to going back to school."

"Do you think Nikki and Ben will get custody of her?"

"For Morgan's sake, I hope not. I believe when Morgan has a chance to talk to the judge, it'll change the outcome."

"Do you have a court date yet?"

"Yeah. End of next week." Back to reality. Coming to Wyoming was the break they'd all needed, but reality, angst, and legal battles peeked over the horizon. Avoidance had become a welcomed friend.

***

Asher and Zeke enjoyed beers while barbecuing some burgers. The girls were playing with Sammy and the dogs, their laughter spilling across the yard.

They'd had the best time. Asher realized he hadn't had a best friend, aside from his brothers, since high school. Zeke had become a friend he'd enjoy knowing the rest of his life. Their mutual love of fishing had yielded many trips to nearby streams, and enough fresh trout to keep his belly happy. Tes, he found out, wasn't a big fish fan.

Tires crunched gravel in the driveway out front. Asher put down his beer and made his way to the front door. He'd be shocked if Tes and Joni were back so soon.

A knock sounded as Asher reached the door. "Hey, Tom, what brings you here? I thought you were getting settled into your new home." He shook his hand and gave him a half hug with a pat on the back.

Tom didn't say a word. Whatever brought him from Washington, it wasn't good news.

"We're about to eat lunch. You want a beer?" Asher crossed the room to the kitchen and pulled open the fridge.

"Sure." Tom's eyes held a deep sadness.

"What's wrong?" Asher twisted off the cap and handed the cold brew to Tom.

"Nothing that can't wait." Tom forced a smile to his lips, patting Asher on the shoulder.

Tom stepped onto the deck and held his arms wide. "Oh, my goodness. Sammy's walking now?"

Sammy waddled, drool dripping as he smiled. He lifted his arms so Tom would pick him up.

Tom closed his eyes and hugged Sammy back. "He sure is soothing for the soul."

Zeke sat, motioning for Tom to take a seat. "How ya been?"

"Good." Tom settled in, Sammy on his lap. He took a long pull on his draft, glancing around. "Is Hailey here?"

Oh no, this had something to do with Linda. Asher's gut twisted. What if she wanted custody of Hailey?

Zeke answered, "The girls took the dogs for a quick run before lunch."

Tom looked away for a moment before looking at Asher. "Perhaps I should tell you first, and it'll be up to you how you want to break the news to Hailey."

Asher leaned forward, resting his elbows on his knees, bracing for impact.

Zeke snagged Sammy in one arm. "Let's go see if Mr. Squirrel came back for the nuts we put outside."

Tom waited for Zeke to be a fair distance away from the house. "We've received news that Hailey's mom died of a drug overdose."

Asher closed his eyes. *Shit.* He swiped a hand down his face. *When were they going to catch a break?* "Hailey's been trying to reach her. Linda never returned her calls. Never texted. We thought perhaps she'd lost her phone." He pinched the bridge of his nose. The tears that threatened weren't for Linda, they were for Hailey. How much heartbreak did she need to face in her young life? He had to tell his daughter that she'd never have a chance to speak to her mom again. "How long ago?"

"Looks like her body was left undetected for at least a week before the maid insisted on cleaning the room. The air conditioner kept the room cold, but still."

On some level, Asher knew Linda loved Hailey, even if it was through the fog of meth or crack cocaine. He'd always hoped she'd get her life together and be the mom Hailey desperately wanted. Addiction was an evil beast.

Of all the things he'd have to tell his daughter over the course of a lifetime, this wasn't one he wanted to do. He wanted to pass that baton onto anyone else. How was he going to break it to her?

Asher looked at Tom. "Thank you for coming all this way to tell us in person. That was nice of you."

"Hailey will weather this fine. She's strong."

"No one wants to hear that their mother's dead." Asher took a swig to moisten his dry mouth. "Especially when she'd hoped she'd have at least one last conversation with her. Now this? Shit." He didn't want Hailey to hurt any more. He'd best go find her and give her the bad news.

As he was about to stand, the front door opened. The bustle of dogs and daughters chattering echoed from inside the house. The entourage made their way outside to the deck.

"Dad, we saw some deer." Hailey was all smiles, slipping past Tom. "Hi, Mr. Krysinski."

"Hi, Hailey."

Hailey crowded Asher. She unlocked her cell phone screen and showed him the pictures they'd taken.

Asher's stomach plummeted to his toes. He didn't want to tell her. "Wow." He swallowed. "Tell me you didn't get that close."

"He came up to us," Morgan said, taking the seat on the opposite side of Tom. "We didn't coax it. It was like he wanted to pose for us or something."

Asher glared at Morgan.

"Hey, he seemed docile."

He was a wild animal. Small fish to fry on a beautiful sunny day, nice warm breeze on the outskirts of Yellowstone National Park. One of the most beautiful places on earth to hear the ugliest news.

"Honey." Asher wrapped an arm around Hailey's shoulders. "I need to tell you something."

26

T he next morning, out of provisions, Asher drove the girls and Ruthie to town to grab a few things for breakfast.

Tes was none too pleased with Ruthie's quick decline into begging at the table, whining for bacon every morning, nor the fact that barking and chasing squirrels had become her favorite pastime. In Asher's opinion, it was about time she was a *real* dog, casting off her Stepford dog persona.

They pulled into Whole Foods Trading Company's parking lot.

"Daddy," Hailey said. "Do you mind if Morgan and I go in alone this time?"

Asher slid the gear into park. "Why?"

Morgan released her seatbelt and pulled herself forward from the backseat. Ruthie nudged closer. "We need to buy some personal things."

"Like?"

Hailey rolled her eyes. "Feminine products."

"Oh. That." He pulled out his wallet. "Sure. Say no more." He held up a hand.

His daughters exchanged a glance and a smile.

He started to hand his card to Hailey and pulled it back. "You have ten minutes before I come in there after you."

Morgan slid her hand to his shoulder from the backseat. "We're okay, Dad. No one's ever going to take us again. Mr. Krysinski showed us some killer moves. Dobbs sent us videos on how to escape everything from handcuffs to creepy men. We're going to be fine."

"Doesn't mean it's going to be easy for me to let you two wander off into the world."

"The world?" Morgan raised an eyebrow. "It's a grocery store."

"Might as well be the moon to me." He handed over his debit card. "Ten minutes. We need a half-gallon of milk, some red potatoes, and, of course, bacon."

Morgan shook her head. "We're not getting bacon."

"You know we have bacon every morning."

"Have you noticed how Aunt Tes gets sick from the smell every morning? She said she swears she feels her arteries hardening from the smell alone."

"Ruthie likes it. Don't you, girl?" He scruffed her ears.

Asher kept an eagle eye on them as they crossed the parking lot and went inside.

True, Tes groaned every morning and went outside to enjoy her coffee. She hated the smell of bacon. She'd liked it before coming to Wyoming. Now, every time she came downstairs, she couldn't wait to get away from the smell, holding her breath while she grabbed a cup of coffee and headed outside.

Oh, hell no. She could hate the smell of blue cheese, smelly gym socks, and fish—*not bacon.* Not his favorite food group.

She'd grown more and more tired over the last two weeks. Asher assumed it was because she was training to control her energy. Zeke had even joked about putting Sammy and Tes down for a nap.

Could she be? This soon? A smile curved his lips.

Maybe he should get a pregnancy test. He turned off the truck's engine. "Come on, Ruthie."

***

Tes vaguely remembered Asher saying something about going to the store. She didn't want to move. When she moved, her stomach threatened to revolt. It had to be the red meat she'd been consuming more of lately. Hamburgers, steak, tacos, and pasta. Lots of pasta. Pasta with chicken. Pasta with beef. More pasta with cream sauce. She'd gained more than a kilogram or two, and her jeans were getting tighter with every meal. She ran every day and still the zipper on her jeans threatened to break. Very discouraging for a future bride. As much as she loved Asher and his cooking, her waistline couldn't afford it. Back to whole foods and no sauces. Sure as hell, no pasta. Carb heaven would have to be put on hold until her waistline adjusted.

She had a wedding dress to fit into.

Footsteps padded past the bedroom door. Asher always left the door cracked so Ruthie could come and go once he was up. One of the girls must have stayed home.

The TV turned on, blasting loud enough for Tes to groan. Why did teenagers only have one volume? Was she getting old?

Juice bottles clanged as the refrigerator door opened. *Staring at the empty fridge didn't make the food prepare itself.* Tes didn't understand how staring at the fridge's contents, like taking inventory, made a difference. They did the same thing with the pantry. *Kids.* This was her future.

Tes sent a text to Asher, "TV volume—seriously? We've got to talk to the girls about this."

She took her cell phone with her as she made her way to the bathroom for a shower. That would help wake her up.

Minty toothpaste would ease the bile from the back of her throat. She slid her toothbrush under the faucet when movement out of the corner of her eye caught her attention.

Brick. The pop star and actor's son. Why was he here? "Hey, buddy. It's been a while. How's your family?"

He held his finger to his lips. *Lock the door.* He pointed to Hailey and Morgan's room through the adjacent door.

***

Asher scanned the aisle directories until he found the right aisle. His heart stopped. Hailey and Morgan were standing in front of the pregnancy tests.

Tell me one of them isn't pregnant. His worst nightmare threatened to rise and slap him in the face. The hospital performed pregnancy tests on them both. They were negative. Was it too soon for the test to be positive? Why didn't they come to him? Why didn't they say anything?

He and Ruthie made their way down the aisle, listening in on their conversation, their heads huddled close together.

"This one says it can tell you a positive or negative result within ten days before your first missed period."

He cringed.

Hailey pulled a box from the top shelf, reading the package. "This one processes in fifteen minutes, but it's cheaper." She slipped it back onto the shelf.

"What about this one?" Morgan read, "It processes in five minutes, but you have to already be late for your period."

Hailey shrugged.

Asher released Ruthie's harness and put an arm around each of his girls.

They jumped. Morgan screamed, causing a woman to turn around.

"You know you girls can talk to me about anything."

Morgan slid the test back onto the shelf. "You didn't think we were getting this for us, did you?"

"Honey, I love you. I—" He swallowed his nerves. "We'll get through this together. I never want you to be afraid to tell me anything." He turned his gaze to Hailey. "Tes and I will stand by you, no matter what your decision is." *He wanted to die.* Was this what his dad felt like when he'd told him he'd knocked a girl up? Now he knew what the other side went through. No wonder Hailey's mom's family hated him so much.

"Dad," Morgan said, smiling. "The test isn't for Hailey or me. It's for Aunt Tes. We think she's pregnant."

"Thank. God." He glanced heavenward, breathing a deep sigh of relief. He put a hand over his heart, waiting for his blood pressure to calm and the ringing to stop in his ears. He looked at the shelf of blue and pink boxes. "Well, which one's the best?"

They both launched into the pros and cons of each one. The fact his daughters knew so much about pregnancy tests alarmed him. He hoped his expression didn't give his thoughts away.

"According to *Mother's Magazine*, this one's the best." Hailey pointed to a box.

"But, according to *Ladies Home Journal*," Morgan said, pointing to another, "this one's better."

"What does *Consumer Reports* say?" That's what Asher read when he needed to know the best tool or vehicle to buy. Didn't they rate everything?

The mother nearby who'd been watching, approached. She grabbed a box and tossed it into the basket the girls had put on the floor between them. "Trust me. Best one on the market. Tells you in five minutes. She won't kill you in five minutes."

Asher frowned. "What do you mean, 'Kill me'?"

The woman laughed. "Y'all think your wife and mother's pregnant, but she doesn't? No woman wants to hear that they are pregnant when they have two teenagers. Getting her to pee on the stick is going to be your hardest battle." The woman wagged a finger. "Once you've got that covered...well, she can't kill you in five minutes." The woman started to walk away, a toddler in the basket, one sitting on the seat. "She may want to, but she won't succeed."

"You sound like you're speaking from experience." Asher watched the woman's shoulders shake as she walked away.

"She's probably going to post that online," Hailey said, watching the woman walk away.

Morgan picked up the basket. "Can you go get some soda water? Maybe some oyster crackers will help."

"Why?"

Hailey rolled her eyes. "Morning sickness." Her eyes widened. "You'd think you'd never been through this before."

In a sense, he hadn't. He wasn't allowed to be around Hailey's mom during her pregnancy and he didn't know about Morgan until she was five. "My memory isn't what it used to be."

"We still need to buy some feminine things." Morgan edged a step away.

"I need some motor oil. Saw blades." Asher shook his head.

"Condoms?" Hailey snarked.

He pointed a finger at her, letting her know she was close to crossing a boundary. "Too late for those."

Morgan smiled. "Barn door and all that, huh, Dad?" She stopped and placed a hand on her hip. "I don't ever want to hear lectures about safe sex from you. You're not exactly the poster child of safe sex."

"Watch it. I'm not sixteen years old. I've been using condoms religiously for years. Until recently." *Jesus Christ.* He didn't want to explain his sex life to his daughters in the middle of a grocery store aisle.

Hailey walked backward. "You're blushing."

His girls giggled as he picked up Ruthie's harness and walked away.

They met at the cash register a few minutes later. Asher's pocket vibrated. He pulled out his phone. He frowned. What the hell was Tes talking about the TV volume?

Unless...she wasn't alone.

ithout questioning the young spirit, Tes locked the door to the girls' bedroom. She eyed the other bathroom door that led to her and Asher's bedroom. Should she lock that one too?

Quick. In here. Brick pointed to the cabinet under the sink.

"Honey, I can't—"

Shh! Brick put his little half-invisible finger to his lips, eyes wide with alarm.

She rinsed out her mouth and put her toothbrush back in the cup next to Asher's. She opened the tiny cabinet door and stared at the empty space. Of course, it was empty, because every gadget, lip gloss, mascara tube, and hair product were strewn all over the counter, compliments of two teenagers. Tes counted herself lucky to get a tiny amount of real estate for her few personal belongings.

The door handle she'd locked jostled.

Brick's eyes filled with tears. *Please.* He pointed to the cabinet.

Good lord, she wasn't Houdini. She grabbed her cell phone and silenced the ringer and vibrator. It took a few seconds, but she managed to fold herself into the tight space, tucking her knees tight to her chest. Her head hit a pipe and she bit her lip not to respond while closing the doors.

Brick scrunched inside the cabinet. His ice-cold legs wedged between hers. *Yeah, this was comfortable.*

Footsteps entered the bathroom, walked straight to the door she'd locked, and unlocked it. Tes wanted to jump out and yell boo, but something about the fear in Brick's eyes meant she was in danger and not to joke around. Enough to hide under the sink with her. He was a ghost—he didn't need to be afraid.

Whoever it was, they rummaged through the items on the counter above her head.

"Hm," a distinct male voice grunted.

Tes's pulse jumped.

"Why do girls hide their natural looks with this shit?" The voice sounded mechanical.

Ice chilled her veins. She knew that voice from visiting the girls in the Shadowlands and the only two words he'd spoken to her: *You're next.*

Panic set in. Sweat broke out across her entire body and she had one unrelenting sensation—her bladder was going to burst. Damn, she had to pee.

The footsteps walked away. "See you soon, girls."

Tes leaned against the cupboard door, peeking out.

Brick's icy cold, small hand grabbed her leg. *Shut the door.*

A blue-clad leg exited toward the bedroom. One with a distinct missing patch where Tango had taken a bite.

The kidnapper was in the house.

***

Asher put his phone on speaker and dialed his lifeline. "LeBron, someone's in the house with Tes! I don't know the address."

"Hold on—I'll dispatch police there. Where are you?"

"We went to the store." They jumped into the truck and buckled in, Hailey held his phone. He slammed the gear in reverse and maneuvered through the parking lot to the highway.

Asher could hear LeBron tell the 911 operator that there was an intruder in the house and provided the address.

Police sirens blared. Flashing lights came up fast in his rearview mirror. He pulled over to the side of the road to let them pass, then gunned the engine to fall behind the squad car. "Give me a damn ticket, I don't care."

"Hurry, Daddy." Hailey gripped the armrest.

"Let me pull up the security cameras." LeBron clicked keys. "Holy shit." There was a long pause. "Are both girls in the car with you?"

"Yes."

"I can't see Tes. She's got to be in the bathroom."

Morgan shouted, "Who can you see?"

"I don't want to say." LeBron mumbled something else to the 911 operator still on the line.

"It's him, isn't it?" Morgan crossed her arms in the backseat, staring out the window. "He found us." She buried her face in her hands.

Asher didn't want his girls to go through this. Not now. Tes could kill the bastard if she wanted to. Or at least shock him into next week.

"When you get to the house, Asher, find Tes and get the hell out of there. I'm going to mute you and tell the dispatcher where he is."

"What the fuck, LeBron?"

"Dude, you're not taking this on."

"He's still in the house, isn't he?"

"Yes, he is. The police need to get him—not you. You understand? You get Tes and you get out of the house. The girls need to stay in the car." He paused. "Promise me?"

Asher glared at each daughter in turn. "They'll stay in the car." The police blew past their road. "The police missed the turnoff."

"Shit." LeBron rattled the error to the dispatcher.

Asher slowed down, took the turn, and sped along the dirt road. In a sense, he was glad he'd be there first. "Tell me where he is."

"No."

"I have a gun in the house."

"I know you do. That's why I'm not telling you."

The truck skidded to a stop, dirt and gravel billowing in their wake. "Stay here."

"Daddy, please wait for the police. I can't lose you too." Hailey erupted into sobs as he grabbed his cell phone from her hand.

Ruthie whined and pawed at the front seat.

"Stay here—I have to go get Tes."

***

Tes leaned a little farther out to listen to the kidnapper. She heard the nightstand drawer open.

"You fucker. You didn't even use the condoms you brought."

She pulled back inside the cabinet. Should she try and escape? Could she slip into the girls' room and hide in there?

"Nice gun."

Metal slid against metal as Blue cocked Asher's gun.

"Maybe I'll blow your head off in your sleep. Ka-pow." His mechanical voice laughed, low, wicked, and demented. "They'll all be mine."

That did it. He wasn't going to hurt her family ever again.

An alarm sounded. "Shit. They're almost home." A loud clunk followed by the drawer slamming shut. *At least he put the gun back.*

Footsteps echoed as he ran from the room and down the hall. Not downstairs. Not outside. Had he been in the house with them the entire time? Did he spy on them while they slept? A chill swept through Tes as the reality of him being inside the house with them sunk into her bones. Where did he hide? Was there a crawlspace or attic in this place?

Tes opened the cabinet door as the front door opened. "Tes!" Asher yelled.

Crap. Now Blue knew she was in the house alone. It wouldn't matter. They were going home—within the hour. Then the creepy little cockroach could come out of hiding.

She'd be waiting for him back home. "Come after my family, and you're going to be sorry," she whispered.

"Tes!" Asher yelled, thudding up the stairs.

It took her a few seconds to squeeze her knees closer to her chest and wiggle herself free. She was still on the floor when Asher entered the bedroom.

His wide brown eyes said it all as he shoved open the bathroom door, smacking it against the door guard, chest heaving as he gulped air.

She motioned him over. "Can you help me get up?"

He lifted her into his arms, crushing her against his chest. "Are you okay?"

"I'm fine." She pushed against his chest, feeling lightheaded. "He's still in the house."

He eyed her with concern, looking her over from head to toe. "Did he hurt you?"

"Please." Tes shoved him aside. "I need to pee. Check the nightstand and make sure your gun's still there."

An odd expression flashed over his face before he left the room.

They needed to get out of the house and Tes couldn't stop peeing, but the relief on her bladder was welcomed. Once she was done, she quickly washed her hands and joined Asher at the bedside.

He tossed his gun in his duffle bag and shoved it under the bed. "Don't need the cops finding this." He grabbed her hand. "Let's go."

Once in the hall, Tes paused and glanced toward the direction the kidnapper had run. "He went that way." She pointed toward the other guest bedrooms.

Asher tugged her hand and they both were outside as two squad cars rolled into the driveway.

The girls jumped out of the SUV and smothered her in hugs, Ruthie nudging her way through the throng.

Asher grabbed Ruthie's harness to keep her by his side. "Inside. Upstairs," he shouted to the officers as they ran through the front door.

A sudden queasiness assaulted Tes. She walked over to the grass and sat, crossing her legs, and leaned forward.

"You okay, Aunt Tes?" Morgan sat beside her and rubbed her back.

"I'm fine. Just still a bit in shock."

"Feel like throwing up?"

Tes glanced at Morgan's smile. "As a matter of fact, yes." She closed her eyes. "He was in the house. How did he find us?"

Morgan nodded at Hailey. "Get the crackers and soda."

Something salty sounded good.

"I can't smell bacon this morning." Tes buried her face in her hands as Hailey dropped the bag in front of her.

Hailey sat on her other side while Asher crouched in front of her. Ruthie's panting hot breath nearly made Tes lose her cookies.

Her hand felt the cold soda bottle first inside the bag. She pulled it out, twisted off the cap, and took a few sips. Her nausea ebbed a smidge.

Asher said, "He hid in one of the safe rooms."

"Then he's trapped?" Morgan jumped to her feet. "I can't wait to find out who this bastard is."

Asher grabbed her hand and motioned for her to sit. "There's an escape hatch. LeBron said the sensor was triggered. He's running. Let's hope the cops catch him."

Tes put her hand into the bag again and felt a box. She pulled it out, thinking it would be crackers. Instead, it was a bright pink box labeled Pregnancy Test. Her gaze flashed to Asher's, then the girls. "No matter what you girls decide, your dad and I will respect you and honor your decision." Tears pricked her eyes. "We're a family, and we're in this together."

Hailey took the box from her. "This isn't for one of us." She waved a hand between her and Morgan. "This is for you."

"Me?" Tes snapped her head back. "I'm not pregnant. I'm on birth control pills."

Hailey smiled. "Yeah, those never worked for Grandma. I doubt they'll work for you. Nonna would have had a million kids had she not had her tubes tied."

Tes stared at Hailey. "Are you serious right now?"

Morgan bumped Tes's arm with her elbow. "Strong little swimmers is what Poppop says."

Tes closed her eyes. "No. Not happening."

Asher pulled the oyster crackers from the bag. "These might help." He popped the bag open and held it out.

Tes grabbed a few and popped them into her mouth. "I'm not pregnant." She sipped the soda. What little liquid had settled in her stomach threatened to launch up her throat.

"We also got you some applesauce." Hailey pulled a small jar from the bag. "Nonna says it's the only thing that tastes just as good going down as it does coming up."

Tes looked skyward. "I could have a stomach bug." She pointed to each person crowding her. "And I could get you sick, so best keep your distance."

Morgan frowned. "Why? You gonna hurl?"

Tes's stomach spasmed. She slammed a hand over her mouth.

"She's gonna blow!" Asher said, pulling Ruthie out of the way while the girls scrambled to their feet and gave her plenty of room.

Asshats, the lot of them. One more spasm and Tes lost her stomach's contents. "It's nerves." She took another swig to wash back the bile burning her throat. "I'm not pregnant."

Hailey slipped the box onto her lap. "Maybe we should make sure."

"I'm not ready to have a baby." Tears threatened. "I can't. I have a new job. Court next week. Getting you girls settled back into school. I don't have time for this shit."

Morgan burst into laughter. "Protesting's effective." She laughed harder.

Tes looked at the few cracker bits littering the lawn by her legs and she dry heaved. "It's a virus. I'll be fine."

Asher and Hailey joined in laughing.

"This isn't funny." Tes buried her face in her hands. "I'm not pregnant." She tossed the test back into the bag. She gagged again. "I don't feel so good."

The officers came out the front door.

Asher stood, taking Ruthie with him.

An officer said, "No one's inside. Are you sure you heard someone in the house?"

Asher explained what happened and provided LeBron's phone number.

"We'll get a team searching the forest for this guy. He couldn't have gotten far." The officer stepped to his vehicle.

The other officer looked at Tes. "Is your wife going to be okay?"

"Yeah. We're in our first trimester. You know how it goes."

First trimester, my ass. Tes dared another sip. She'd keep it down to prove her point.

A cop handed Asher a business card. "It might be best if you keep the house locked up tight, in case he comes back."

"Don't worry. We'll be packed and leaving within the hour. We're not taking any chances." Asher looked over his shoulder at them. "We were flying home tomorrow anyway."

"Can we go inside now?" Morgan got to her feet.

"Sure." An officer preceded her into the house. "I'll stay until you're ready to leave."

Asher helped Tes to her feet.

Hailey grabbed the grocery bag and looped an arm around her shoulders. "Lean on me, Mom."

Tes wrapped a hand around her waist, pulling her close. "Thank you, Hailey."

Father and daughter shared a look.

***

Thirty thousand feet in the air, Tes had peed on that stupid stick, only to prove her future family wrong. The queasiness hadn't subsided. She'd hurled three more times while packing. Applesauce soothed her raw throat and, surprisingly, helped settle her stomach. She'd already polished off half the jar.

Tomorrow was the rehearsal dinner. Isabella and her team of church ladies had everything ready. Two more days and the curse would be broken. Her stomach was jumbled nerves. Nothing more than pre-wedding jitters every bride goes through before their wedding.

The alarm on Asher's phone sounded. "You ready?"

Tes shook her head.

He pulled the test out of his pocket and turned it over.

There it was in big bold letters: PREGNANT.

"That can't be right. False positives happen." Tes shoved his hand away as if it'd lessen the impact.

He leaned in and kissed her. "We're going to have a baby."

"Let's keep this between us until it can be confirmed by a doctor."

Pain flashed in his eyes. "I want to tell the world."

"What if I have a miscarriage?"

He nuzzled her neck. "Let me tell my parents."

"Can they keep a secret?"

"Sure." His tone indicated otherwise.

"Ash." Tears flooded her eyes. "Dammit." She blinked. "I will not be an emotional mess because I'm—" She couldn't say it. "Ash, please. I'm not ready for this."

"Okay." He smiled and wiped the tear that fell. "If we were at home, I'd make love to you right now."

She cupped his face with her hand. "You're happy about this?"

"Ecstatic. I'd love to grab that flight attendant's microphone and tell everyone on the plane."

"All ten people." She'd never liked small planes.

Hailey and Morgan got out of their seats and stopped at their aisle. "Well?"

Asher held up the test. "What?" he said, noticing Tes's glare. "We can't keep it from them. They live with us."

The girls squealed and crushed Tes in hugs.

"Go, get in your seats and buckle in." Tes pushed them away.

Hailey snagged the test. "I'll throw this away."

A few minutes later Tes's phone buzzed. Then vibrated more. She took it out of her bra and stared at the group text sent from Hailey to the Hickoks, Gregsons, and God knew who else. There in plain technicolor was her positive pregnancy test. The photo tagged, "What happens in Wyoming isn't going to stay in Wyoming."

Great. Now everyone knew. How she hoped the kidnapper didn't know. That wouldn't bode well for her. *You're next.*

28

"**H**ow could he get past the deputies?" Asher was pissed. After a round of congratulatory hugs, he and Tes slid into chairs at Mom and Dad's kitchen table.

His sister, Alyssa, kept Hailey and Morgan preoccupied in the living room picking out school clothes online. It was the first time he didn't care how much money they spent.

Ruthie and Tango ran in circles around the backyard chasing each other to their hearts content. It was amazing how well Tango recovered from his injuries, like he'd never been wounded.

LeBron was already there—like he was part of the family. Mom had made him a snack and busied herself making him and Tes something to eat.

Mom poured them glasses of fresh-squeezed lemonade while LeBron queued his computer to show them the security camera footage from the lodge.

"Please tell me you know where he is." Asher pointed a finger on the aged, marred family table.

LeBron looked around at all the Hickok faces and shook his head. "You have to understand something about cops. When they enter a room, they need to know there's more than one way out. Dobbs insisted that the three safe rooms in the cabin have an external escape hatch. The kidnapper knew it too. I don't know how he knew—it's not in the floor plans filed with the county."

That piqued Asher's interest. "So, who has the floor plans with the safe rooms in it?"

"The architectural firm we used." LeBron took another gulp of lemonade, almost finishing off his glass. "I think they're on Joni and Zeke's computer as well. If he can hack into their system, backdoor something I've designed, then the motherfu—" He clamped his mouth shut and glanced at Mom. "Sorry. The idiot's better than me. And that makes tracking him near impossible."

Tes squeezed his knee under the table. "He knew Asher and the girls were returning to the house. He has an alarm on his phone that triggered him to run back to the safe room."

LeBron turned his computer around. "I'm going to fast-forward this."

The images were incredibly clear. Six cameras had simultaneously recorded everything from the back patio, the front of the house, and four different angles of the great room. None of them were in the bedrooms or bathrooms. The quality wasn't corner-store grainy where it was hard to see clear images. These were high-grade, military-clear pictures. It showed Asher, the girls, and Ruthie leaving for the store. One camera view showed them getting into the truck and driving away. A few seconds later, due to the fast-forwarding effect, a guest bedroom door opened. There he was, decked out in his blue latex suit from head to toe, with black goggles for the eyes. *Sick bastard.*

Blue passed Asher and Tes's room, where the door was left ajar, Hailey and Morgan's room, and then went down the stairs. He picked up the remote and turned on the TV.

That's why Tes texted him the comment about the volume. Blue rifled through the fridge and lifted the milk carton. He lifted the bottom part of his face mask and took a swig out of the milk carton. Too bad he didn't do that where the camera could get a look at his face.

"Tell me we got his DNA." Asher pinned LeBron with a glare.

"We're going to compare the DNA against the blue patch of his suit we got from Tango." LeBron glanced over his shoulder as the two dogs ran through the door and straight to Tango's water dish for a drink. "Besties."

"They sure do like each other." Dad smiled and patted his leg. Tango and Ruthie surrounded him, and he leaned over and pet them both.

Tes took her phone out of her bra and glanced at the screen. She placed it screen side down on the table. He could tell something was wrong by the slow way she swallowed, stared at the table, and bit her lip.

Before he could ask her about it, LeBron brought them back to the computer screen. He wrapped an arm around her shoulders and pulled her close. "He eats a handful of peanuts. Turns off the TV and heads back upstairs. He goes into Hailey and Morgan's room first."

"I'd locked the door to the bathroom," Tes said.

"He entered your room." LeBron glanced between Tes and Asher. "You can kind of see his feet near the bed through the opened door, but we can't see what his hands were doing."

Tes laid her head on his shoulder. "He pulled the gun out of the nightstand and cocked it."

Asher kissed the top of her head. "We're safe."

She shook her head. "No, we're not. We're never going to be safe with him out there."

"Then he comes running into the hall, back into one of the guest rooms, and shuts the door. From there, our sensors triggered that the safe room door was closed and then the outer hatch. He was out of the house before the first cops arrived." LeBron turned his computer back around and closed the lid. He folded his long fingers. "We can hide you and get you new phones." He paused, glancing first at Asher's parents. "Your whole family can't stay hidden forever."

"What's your plan?" Mom asked.

"You're not going to like it." LeBron tweaked the corner of his mouth. "Use someone as bait."

"Hell no!" Asher slammed his fist on the table.

"Honey." Tes covered her hand over his fist. "Let me do it. Let me get rid of him once and for all."

"No." He raised his right eyebrow, lips in a firm line.

"But—"

"I. Said. No."

"I can do this. Give me a chance."

"Not with the baby. No." He slid his hand over hers and pointed at the table.

She shook her head, took a drink of lemonade, and stood. "I'm not a delicate orchid. Give me a chance, Asher. I can do this. I want him out of our lives as much as you."

Morgan interrupted, holding her cell phone. "Dad." Her chin dipped to her chest. "Mom wants to see me."

Holy hell, why did Nikki have to get into the mix now? They had enough on their plate without her inserting herself into their lives.

Tes picked up her phone and looked at her messages. "My books have arrived. I'd like to go get them. I can take Morgan, pick up my books—"

"No." He was losing control and was pissed as a wet cat. "You're not going anywhere near Nikki without me. You'll feed her need to belittle you. I'm not going to give her that opportunity. She sure as hell isn't going to take Morgan away from me."

The last rays of the setting sun cast the kitchen further into darkness. Dad got up and turned on the dining table light.

Morgan edged closer. "I told her I could come by the house to say hi, pick up a few of my things, then I'm coming back here. She can't make me stay with her. I won't."

At least she had some of that stubborn Brynn gene in her. Asher rolled his eyes. "This is a bad idea."

"There's no way that the kidnapper could get from Wyoming to here in as short of time as we did." Tes placed her hand on his shoulder. "We took a public chartered jet. If he's headed back here—we're way ahead of him. The worst thing that will happen is I'll have to put up with Nikki's piss-poor, self-righteous attitude for a few minutes." Tes ran her hand down the length of his arm, squeezing his hand. "We'll be fine and back here within the hour. Please, Asher?"

She had some sound logic to her thinking. "How heavy are these books?"

"Not that heavy." Tes kissed his cheek.

He shook his head. "No. That's my final word. I'll take Morgan over there and get your books."

Tes rolled her eyes. "Can I go with you?"

He glanced at Mom. One nod from her meant he needed to pull back a little on his demands. "You can stay in the car."

"Let me go to the bathroom first, okay?"

Asher kissed her cheek and patted her bottom as she grabbed her phone. He sat and took a swig of lemonade. He wanted life to be normal again. He wanted to dial back time and never have his girls be kidnapped.

One thing he wouldn't change was meeting Tes...and having a baby. All they needed to do was find the damn kidnapper so they could move on with the rest of their lives.

***

Tes glanced in the rearview mirror. Her phone hadn't buzzed. She held onto hope Asher hadn't realized she and Morgan snuck out of the house. "Your dad is going to be so pissed when he finds out we left without him." A twinge of regret about being devious twisted her gut. The last thing she wanted was to be treated like a damn shrinking violet because she was pregnant.

Morgan smiled. "He likes to know when he puts his foot down, it's not going to be challenged."

"He thinks I'm helpless. I'm not."

"He loves you." Morgan squeezed her hand. "We're all excited about the baby." She leaned back. "I'm going to be a big sister. I like the sound of that."

Tes took a second to appreciate how far Morgan had come. "Thank you."

Her car's headlights highlighted the sign in front of Nikki's house: FOR SALE. Tes held Morgan's hand, slowing to a stop. "That sign means all of this is real. She's moving."

Morgan curled her upper lip, fighting back tears. "It doesn't matter. She might as well sell her soul to the devil. I'm never going to live with her again." She opened the door and slammed it shut.

Tes got out of the car and popped the trunk. Her boxes were on the front porch. Morgan stormed through the front door. Within seconds Nikki and Morgan were screaming at each other. Tes wished she could say or do something that would make their situation better, but unfortunately, it was going to take time. In some cases, time never resolved emotional pain. Tes had enough experience with that with her own mother.

One more box, and she'd close this chapter on her life. She'd never have to see Nikki except on important occasions like Morgan's court hearings, graduation, wedding, and birth of her own children someday. Maybe grandkid birthday parties. She was going to have to act like a damn grown-up and be the mature one taking the high road. Some days she hated adulting.

With the last box loaded, Tes slammed the trunk closed. She didn't want to head inside and intervene on Morgan's behalf. She wasn't the right or best person to do that, but Morgan was no match for Nikki's level of toxicity and ocean-sized guilt trips. A skill she'd inherited from their mother.

"I hate you!" Morgan screamed, running up the stairs to her room. "I'm getting my things and you'll never see me again."

Nikki turned her glare on Tes.

She put up her hand. "Don't start. You brought this on yourself."

"I'm not allowed to be happy?"

"You are, but did you have to do it at Morgan's expense?" Why couldn't Tes keep her mouth shut?

"Morgan? Morgan's going to graduate in a couple of years. Am I supposed to put Ben on hold that long?"

Tes rolled her eyes. "That's not what she's upset about." Nikki didn't have a clue that Morgan knew about her sexual preferences. "The kidnapper showed the home movies you and Ben have made with *all* of your lovers. He also showed her the ones where you had sex with underage football players—her classmates."

Nikki's mouth gaped, then slammed shut. "How did he get ahold of those files?" She ran into the family room. "Ben, you've been hacked."

Tes closed the front door and followed Nikki through the house. When she entered the family room, Ben was on the sofa looking at his cell phone while Nikki stood in front of him, demanding an answer. Maybe hoping he'd have more than a shrugging reaction?

"Nikki," Tes said to gain her attention. "Why did you film yourself having sex with minors? You're a high school counselor, why would you do that?"

"Shut up!" Her sister's eyes squinted. "You're this big-city psychiatrist and don't know jack shit about what makes teenagers tick. How they think." She pointed to her head. "How they want to explore and understand their sexuality and there's no place safe for them to do that."

Tes blinked, wide-eyed. Was her sister trying to justify her behavior? No way in hell was she going to waste arguing with a wall. "I guess that's what attracted Ben to you?" She looked at him with chagrin, sitting on the couch, scrolling through his cell phone, ignoring the fight around him.

"We like sex. We like experiencing sex to the fullest. You're nothing but a damn prude. Just like Mother."

That was rich comparing her to their mother. "Whatever you need to say to make yourself feel better, Nikki. Asher and I are getting married Saturday."

"You're marrying Morgan's father? Oh, you'd do anything to steal my child."

"I'm not stealing Morgan. You'll always be her mother."

Nikki crossed her arms. "Damn straight I will." She pointed a finger at Tes, edging closer. "I'm going to fight for custody. I'm her mother. I'll win."

Should she bluff? Should she risk Morgan's happiness? "We have the video files of you having sex with the teenagers, Nikki. If you leave Morgan alone, we won't turn them over to the King County prosecutor's office."

Nikki pursed her lips. "You're *blackmailing* me?"

"Yep." Tes chewed her bottom lip, hoping Nikki wouldn't call her bluff. "I don't want Morgan to hang her head in shame because of what you did. I don't think you'd do that to her, because we both know what you did was wrong." She had this insatiable urge to go for broke. "You raped Asher when he was sixteen and you've been raping children since."

"That's not true. That's not fair." Nikki dropped her arms and stormed closer. "He wanted sex. He's the one—"

"Don't." Tes stepped closer. Lowered her voice. "Don't. You. Dare."

"Why? Because you'll find out Asher's not the successful businessman and father you thought he was?" Nikki slapped her hard.

Tes stepped back in shock, rubbing her cheek. Nikki had never hit her before. Her pulse jumped. No. Not now. She had to control her energy. She needed to stay calm. "We're leaving."

"The hell you are." Nikki lunged forward.

The family room window's glass shattered. Mid-lurch, Nikki jolted to the left. Blood spread across the side of her head as her body bounced against the coffee table, landing hard on the floor. Eyes blank. Features bland.

Nikki was dead.

Another pane shattered. Blood splattered the family room wall. Ben slouched back against the sofa, limp, a bloody spot centered in his forehead.

"Shit!" Tes fell to the floor and scrambled to the kitchen, taking refuge behind the island.

Another shot impacted the sliding glass door, shards of glass crashing against the floor.

She held her breath as if it would keep the intruder away.

Footsteps approached. Glass crunched under heavy boots.

Tes held her knees and curled in a ball, covering her head with her forearms. If she was quiet, they wouldn't notice her.

Pain jolted through her as cold metal prongs pressed to the back of her neck. She clenched her teeth. Electricity jolted along her nerve endings. It didn't faze her, though it stung like a son of a bitch. What happened in the movies when you were tazed? She acted like she fainted, slumping to the floor, closing her eyes. Would the shooter buy it?

A hood slid over her head. Cord cinched her hands together. She had to fight her instincts to keep her body lax, squelching the need to fight back. Maybe if he took her, he'd leave Morgan alone. Once they were by themselves, she could take him out.

Save your energy. Don't blow it all at once. Be patient.

A needle pressed to her neck. A warm fluid gushed and burned under her skin.

Shit. Sorry, Asher.

29

Asher glanced at his watch. What was taking Tes so long? Maybe she was sick. He got up from the table and found the downstairs bathroom door open. He headed upstairs on the off chance she wanted privacy and used that one.

Empty.

She wouldn't. Not after he told her she was staying home. She wouldn't defy him.

A muscle ticked the side of his face.

He found Hailey and Alyssa staring at a computer screen. "Where's Morgan?" He didn't mean to bark, but dammit. If they left without him, they were going to have hell to pay.

Alyssa tucked her dark hair behind her ear. "I thought she was talking to you. She got a text from Nikki."

"Yeah, I know. I said I'd take her over there."

Hailey's brow furrowed. "Tes took her."

Rage slithered under his muscles, confirming his worst fears. "Tes? You saw Tes leave with Morgan?"

"Uh-huh. What?" Hailey glanced at Alyssa. "Maybe fifteen minutes or so ago."

He closed his eyes, clenched his jaw and fists. He about slammed his fist through the wall. "Dammit!"

Hailey flinched. "Was she not supposed to go with Tes?"

"She was supposed to wait for me." He thumped a finger against his chest. He stormed back to the kitchen. "Tes took off with Morgan. I'm going after them."

Mom tilted her head. "Ash, sit. Maybe you're making more out of this than you should."

"No, Mom. I don't trust Nikki. The kidnapper's out there somewhere. I need to keep my family safe."

Hailey came up behind him. "I'll go with you."

Asher wasn't so sure he wanted Hailey to witness a yelling match with Tes. His Italian temper was going to let her shy English one have it—and he didn't give a damn if she liked it or not. She knew better. He'd been firm in telling her no. "You stay here with Nonna and Popop. LeBron? Can you tag along?"

"Sure." He stood and picked up his laptop.

Dad stood. "Why don't I go with? There's no way Nikki has a chance against the two of us."

Asher hugged Hailey, and headed out the door. They were halfway to Nikki's house when Morgan called. He handed his phone to his dad, who hit the green button and put it on speaker. "Morgan?"

"Daddy! She's dead. Ben's dead. Blood's everywhere."

Asher's heart dropped. The air rushed out of his lungs. "Tes? Someone shot Tes? Are you okay?"

LeBron whipped out his phone. "I'll get the cops there."

Asher glanced in the rearview mirror. "Do you know the address?"

LeBron lifted a brow. "Of course. I track Morgan and Hailey's phones."

"Mom's dead."

"Not Tes." Relief whooshed through him. "Where's Tes?"

"I don't know. She's not here. She and Mom were arguing and when it got quiet, I came downstairs and—" Morgan's cries filled the truck's interior.

"We're on our way. Almost there." Asher pushed on the gas and gripped the steering wheel tighter. He registered LeBron calling Zeke. It'd be good to have Dobbs and Zeke there when the police arrived.

"Daddy, please hurry."

"Morgan," Dad shouted. "Go outside. Wait on the front porch. We're a block away." He covered the mouthpiece. "She shouldn't have to look at her dead mother's face."

They pulled up outside Nikki's house to find Morgan sitting on the bottom step, sobbing.

Asher cradled Morgan in his arms while LeBron headed inside. Dad stood by the road to flag the cops.

Two squad cars pulled up as LeBron came out of the front door. He headed straight to the back yard.

Zeke and Dobbs arrived a short time later as additional red and blue flashing lights converged on the scene. Dad held Morgan so Asher could answer initial questions to the police.

Asher stared at Tes's car, still in the front driveway. *Why didn't you listen, Tes?* His gut instinct had been right, dammit.

Dobbs pulled him aside. LeBron pulled out his phone. "This is what Morgan saw."

The screen filled with images of Nikki and Ben's dead bodies. As long as he lived, he'd never clear these images from his memory. He didn't wish Nikki or Ben Winslow dead. Not like this.

"There was a needle on the floor in the kitchen," LeBron said. "The slider door was shattered."

Dobbs pointed to the screen. "The shooter was in the tree in the backyard. Shell casings are at the base of the tree."

"It can't be the same guy," Asher protested. Tes's argument was sound. "What if it was one of the guys Nikki had sex with—a former football player?"

Zeke stared as his eyes narrowed. "It's the same guy."

"How did he get back here so fast?" Asher wanted Tes back.

Dobbs answered, "When LeBron said that the kidnapper had been in the cabin for a week, I started doing some searches on viable means of access. I scanned through police reports of stolen vehicles and airplanes. A week ago, a plane was stolen from Snohomish County Airport. It's a small airport. Small planes like a Cessna. A truck was reported stolen from Yellowstone's airport."

LeBron clicked his cell phone. "He beelined it out of there. He could come and go when he wanted, and no one would be the wiser. He had to have gotten the full floor plans and figured a way into the house that kept him undetected."

Zeke said, "Face it. Every day, that house was empty at one time or another. We went hiking. Dinner in town. He had opportunity." Disbelief filled his eyes. "He was right there—watching us while we slept."

Asher clamped a hand on Zeke's shoulder. "Guys. Don't feel guilty about this." He looked at LeBron. "Tell me you can track Tes's cell phone."

"Until it stopped pinging off the foothills." He frowned. "No cell reception."

"Let's go to the last place she showed on your radar. We know what the house looks like. Tes told us."

Dobbs grabbed his arm. "You stay here—you need to be here for Morgan. We got this."

"The hell you do. That's my fiancée." *The mother of my unborn child.*

"If Tes can text us, she will." Dobbs' face looked as worried as his own. "We might have to be patient."

He didn't do patient. "I can't lose her."

"We know." Zeke grabbed him in a hug. "We aren't going to lose her." He pushed him away and stared Asher in the eye. "He wants her alive for a reason. And remember, she's not helpless."

***

Tes opened her eyes. A muslin black cloth filtered dim light. She tried to move her hands and tugged against restraints. She moved her feet—they were free.

Where was she?

The last memories before she blacked out played through her mind. Nikki and Ben were dead. Was Morgan safe?

She closed her eyes and listened. The sick bastard had to be watching, if not in person, on camera. Well, wouldn't he be in for a surprise when she fried his ass?

At least he put her on a soft mattress and not the cold ground. The room was cold. Dim. Dank. She knew that smell.

Holy shit, Blue had kidnapped her. How in the hell did he get back to Washington so fast? She moved her roped-tied hands under her bottom and pulled her knees and feet through. She sat up against the headboard, untied the black cloth around her head, and yanked it free. Her gaze adjusted to the light, taking in the room. This was the same place Morgan and Hailey had been held. She tried not to smile, knowing about the escape hatch.

Where the hell was Blue?

Using her teeth, she undid the knots around her wrists and got off the bed. She went near the fence and peered into the darkness. Was he there? Watching? A solitary light dangled over the bed, making it impossible for her to see into the deep shadows.

She needed to get a text to Asher. She went behind the makeshift privacy screen and sat on the toilet. She pulled out her cellphone from her bra.

Zero bars meant zero reception.

First, she checked her phone was on silent before tucking it back in place. She peed because she didn't know if she'd get another chance. As she washed her hands, a metal door slid open on the other side of the fence.

Tes spied the filthy old dish towel and opted to dry her hands on her shorts. She came from behind the screen to see Blue gripping the fence.

"We meet at last." She smiled, letting him know she wasn't afraid. She stepped closer to the fence. All she had to do was reach out, touch it, send electricity through the metal— and he'd be dead.

Would it hurt her? The baby? She'd never conducted her electricity through metal before.

"You owe me," his mechanical voice said, deep and throaty.

What an odd way to start their conversation. "For what?"

"For getting rid of Nikki. Morgan's not going to have her mommy or her sick, fucked-up husband getting in your way."

"Oh, that. Thank you." Tes crossed her arms. She might as well play his game, let him think he was a hero, like his weird blue suit implied. "We appreciate you doing that. It will spare Morgan from having her mother's name slung through the mud."

"You still don't know who I am."

"How did you get back to Washington so fast? I mean, I'm impressed you got back here as quick as we did. You couldn't have driven here that fast—so my guess is you flew. That, or there are two people involved."

Blue rattled the fence. "It was always me...ready or not."

"Here I come," Tes absently added. That external voice whispered in her ear, *Eric Ehome*.

He was a kid. His mother had died in a tragic accident. "Why did you pick Hailey, then Morgan months later? Why them?"

Blue tilted his head. "Their mothers were whores."

"Like your mom?" She fished for answers.

"Yes, like my mom." His laughter started slow, building until it filled the entire room. "How did you figure that out, Tesla?"

She smiled. "Lucky guess."

"Everyone wants to believe their mother loves them. They want to believe their mother would do anything for them. Some kids though, they aren't so lucky."

"How did she hurt you, Eric?"

That snapped his head to attention. "Eric?"

"You're Eric Ehome. You can take off your mask and voice modulator. I figured it out." She smirked like she was bored.

Blue dropped his hands from the fence and turned his back.

"Eric," she whispered. "What did your mother do that made you risk everything to help keep Morgan and Hailey from experiencing the same thing? Please tell me. I'm here for you." She stepped closer to the fence but didn't touch it.

He looked over his shoulder. "She never loved me."

"I'm listening."

"You're not going to tell me she did, like all the other loser counselors out there?"

Tes shook her head. "You're the only one who knows the truth, right?"

"Exactly." He turned back around.

She'd seen several unbalanced people during her internship. They could be unpredictable. She needed to leverage Eric without him realizing what she was doing. Since he was being cooperative, she might as well get comfy. She stepped to the bed and sat. "I'm not going anywhere. Why don't you start at the beginning?"

He stepped into the shadows. She heard something but wasn't sure what it was. If he was getting a gun, she was a sitting duck under the light. She could make it go out if she needed to, but she wanted to make him think he had the upper hand.

In his regular voice, Eric spoke from the shadows. "My first memories of my mother were pleasant when my dad was still alive. She'd walk me to school every day and be there for me at the end of the day. We had a good life. A perfect life."

Tes leaned forward to show she was interested. Patient. Genuine.

"My dad died when I was nine." Tes kept quiet during the long silence that followed. "That's when my mom became a whore. She didn't do it for the money. She liked being fucked. It was like she was a perfect wife and mother one moment." He snapped his fingers. "And was a fucking whore the next. Like she had freedom and didn't give a shit about herself. She stopped walking me to school and stayed in bed with the men she'd bring home from the local bar. I was on my own."

"You wanted your mom back."

"Yeah," Eric's voice strained. "She married and divorced a few times. Finally settling on the asshole upstairs. He was the one that gave her everything she wanted. She'd walk around the house naked because he wanted her to. In front of me and my stepbrothers." He huffed. "I came home one day and found her with one of my stepbrothers. She threatened me within an inch of my life if I said anything. I kept my mouth shut. A week later, I found her with the other stepbrother out by the pool. She wasn't even trying to hide—and didn't care who watched. It seemed she kind of got off on getting caught." After a long silence, he continued. "I drew the line when she wanted me to join in."

"I'm sorry, Eric. I can't imagine how much that hurt you."

"She had no fucking boundaries!" He leaned into the light. His blond hair had prisms of blue light. Was that an aura? Tes hadn't ever seen one, but it was weird. Could his costume glow like that? Was he a demon? "I worked more. I did anything I could to never be home. I hated this fucking house."

"Asher admires that about you—a strong work ethic."

"I never hurt Hailey or Morgan. I never—"

"We know. The hospital had to do rape kits on them. I want to thank you for respecting them, Eric."

"I saved my money and arranged for my mom and me to go away together—just the two of us. I wanted so much to have the mom I knew and loved return to normal. I thought if we were together like we were before, she'd stop being a whore."

"Did she agree to go with you?"

His spasmodic breathing echoed in the sparse room. "She took the money and gave it to my stepbrothers." He sobbed louder. "She laughed at me."

"Oh, Eric. I can't imagine how much that hurt."

"I thought you and Asher were different. I thought you two would wait until you were married, but you didn't. You're a fucking whore!" He lunged at the fence, gripping the links in his fingers. For a split second his features changed. She wasn't sure if it was the bleak lighting or if what she saw was true. His fingers looked like claws and his lip curled revealing fangs.

"I'm not a whore. I'm a grown woman who makes mature decisions about my sex life. There's a difference, Eric." She stood, inching closer. Anger scored his blue eyes, spit dripping from his bottom lip, and snot from his nose. "Asher and I are monogamous. We're never going to have group sex. We're never going to cheat on each other. We're like your mom and dad were in the beginning."

"Except for one thing." He squinted his eyes and pinched his fingers together. "They were married."

"Asher and I are getting married Saturday." She looked around the room. "So, I'm going to need to get out of here for tonight's rehearsal dinner." She paused. "What time is it?"

"Time for you to die."

es burst out laughing, forcing herself to keep the mood light, keeping Eric from considering she'd be his next victim. "Seriously? You've been watching way too many corny teenage movies. You're not going to kill me."

"You're a whore."

"All women aren't whores, Eric. You've never had sex, have you?"

He growled in a feral, guttural rage. Again his features changed into something that resembled old pictures of Dracula. He rattled the fence with all his might. "I'm not a fucking man-whore!"

"Keep your voice down or your stepdad will hear you."

"That asshole's at one of his girlfriends' houses." He paused, dropping his hands from the fence.

"So, what are your plans for your life?" Tes kept the conversation going. "Keep kidnapping women you believe are whores and murder them?" She tsked. "How disappointing. You have such great potential."

"Potential, my ass." His head hung but his body frame didn't show shame. Maybe a little defeat?

"You have plenty of potential. Whoever told you that you didn't was jealous of you. Even if you went away for Nikki and Ben's murders, you'd be out of jail in less than ten years. If you could prove one of them tried to have sex with you—"

That got his attention. He stepped closer. "Who told you?"

Tes cocked her head. *Oh. My. God.* "What Nikki did to you was wrong."

Eric sucked in his bottom lip. He slumped to the floor, crossing his legs, bawling. He wrapped his arms over his head and rocked back and forth. Nikki had scarred him deep, to the point of reverting into a fetal position. *What the hell?*

"Eric, talk to me." She got on his level. "What did she do to you?"

"I had to break into her house." He hiccupped. "I had to steal the tape. That's when I found out about all the other kids."

The blood drained from her. "*Holy shit.* Eric, why didn't you tell someone?"

"Because no one would believe me."

"You had the tapes. That's proof."

"I wanted her to suffer!" He wiped his blue sleeve under his nose, leaving a trail of mucus across his cheek. Tes bit back a gag. "I wanted her to lose the most precious thing in her life."

"Morgan."

He sobbed.

"Then why did you take Hailey?"

"I had to practice on someone." He flipped her a disgusted look like she was stupid.

Tes had underestimated how calculating Eric was. "Do you still have the tapes?"

His laughter was haunting. "I have them all saved to the cloud. I've saved them on the school's servers under different teachers' accounts. I renamed the files. I can't wait until one of those teachers starts to clean out their files and finds Nikki fucking everyone. *She. Fucked. Everyone.* Guys and girls."

She gripped the fence. "Eric, what she did was wrong."

"You don't think I know that?"

"Killing her was a way of dealing with what she did to you and those other kids. There's not a jury in the world that would convict you."

He placed his fingers over hers, making her inwardly flinch. She could kill him right now, but something inside her couldn't. Eric wasn't a serial killer. He was a misunderstood, hurting little boy inside. He'd taken his pain and manifested it into bad choices, but still—if she didn't show him an ounce of compassion, no one else would either. She couldn't hurt him, not yet at least.

"You saved Hailey and Morgan." She leaned her forehead against the fence. "You were the big protective brother they never had."

Eric paused, staring at her in disbelief. "You're the only one who understands."

That's where she wanted him. Now what? "You know what you have to do."

"They're going to rape me in prison. I'm not going to prison."

"You won't. I'll make sure of that. Now we have to make it look like I came with you willingly. That you didn't kidnap me."

He lifted his head. "You'd do that for me?"

"Eric, you don't deserve to be anyone's victim ever again." She placed her fingers over his and squeezed his hand. "We have no witnesses. It'll be our secret."

"They're going to lock me away."

She let her shoulders slump. "Being in the county jail isn't like being in a prison. They aren't going to rape you there. They only rape men in prison." She'd tell him anything he wanted to hear. All she wanted was to go home and marry the man she loved. "Can I ask you something?"

He nodded.

"Do you think I'll make a good mom for Hailey and Morgan?"

His mouth slid to the side. "The best."

"Would you let me be your honorary mom?" If he'd believe she was his ally, maybe he wouldn't kill her.

Eric's face twisted, crying. "You'd do that for me?"

She squeezed his fingers. "You bet I would." Hell no, he was never coming near her family again. "I want you to have a second chance at happiness. Forget that asshole upstairs and his two idiot sons. They never loved you." She squeezed her eyes closed, forcing tears. She managed to release a few so they flowed down her face. "Let me be your mom. Let today be about you and me. How would you like to spend our day?"

A smile broke over his lips.

"Please, Eric. This is our day. Just yours and mine. What would you like to do?"

"I've always wanted to go to the county fair with my mom."

Tes forced a smile. "We're going to have the best day ever."

***

Asher was dead on his feet.

Morgan was a disaster. Hailey fretted because Morgan was upset. Ruthie hadn't stopped whining. Tes was still nowhere to be found.

His life was shit.

It was the wee hours of Saturday morning and the odds they were getting married later dimmed as each second ticked by. He had to find her.

Dobbs wouldn't let him behind the wheel of his truck anymore, taking his keys from him like he was a damn teenager not able to drive past curfew. He'd driven along every dirt and paved road trying to find the house Tes had described.

He hated the fucking media. They were all over the story of Nikki and Ben being shot and Tes being kidnapped. Another angle for them to twist their lives out of control. News at shitty eleven.

Zeke, Dobbs, and LeBron pulled his entire family and placed them in the house next to Krysinski's in their little cul-de-sac from security hell. At least the media couldn't suck another moment out of his life here. Being a prisoner was new to Asher. Zeke, Dobbs, and Krysinski took turns watching him, making sure he wasn't going to do something stupid.

If he could think straight, he'd do something, anything to find Tes. Was she still alive? The thought of her being raped by that twisted, blue, motherfucking asshole ripped him apart. If she lost the baby, he'd kill that whoreson with his bare hands.

Dobbs walked into the living room where Ruthie cuddled next to him, whining through every exhaled breath. It grated on his nerves.

He handed Asher a glass of whiskey. "Here, mate. Something to take an edge off."

Asher gladly accepted the glass and sucked it down in one gulp. He enjoyed the burn to his throat. He wanted more. Anything to numb the stabbing pains in his chest—the place that Tes filled with her kind words, gentle touch, and passion.

Dobbs sat across from him. "You look like shit."

"I feel like shit." Fresh tears formed in his eyes. "She shouldn't have gone without me."

"You gotta quit beating yourself up over that. What's done is done. Besides, you're getting married. You need to take a shower and get cleaned up for your big day."

He huffed, tears flooding his eyes. "I need my bride first."

"You want her seeing you looking like a damn yeti?"

Asher rubbed the stubble on his face. "You bring me my bride, I'll clean up. Promise." His eyes grew heavy. He narrowed them on Dobbs. "You put some-sing in my dwink?"

Dobbs smiled. "Yeah. Get some sleep, princess." He tapped his leg, grabbing the glass out of his hand. "You'll feel a helluva lot better after some sleep."

"You bashard." Asher lifted his eyelids enough to see Dobbs grab a blanket from the back of the couch and drape it over him. He'd have socked him in the jaw if he could lift his arms.

***

Tes sat in the front seat of Eric's late 1980s beat-up pickup truck. Rust and time had taken their toll on the heavy hunk of steel. Duct-tape patches covered large portions of the faded, red fabric bench seat. A long, slithering crack and rock dings scarred the windshield.

They bounced along backroads, hanging close to the Cascade foothills. She needed an opportunity to get a message to Asher. Tes prayed the fair wasn't so far out in the boonies that there wouldn't be cell reception. It would be nice if she knew where the hell she was. They'd been driving for a while—they could be in Canada and she wouldn't know the difference. Evergreens were stacked thick on each side of the two-lane road they traveled, passing few cars.

She smiled at Eric every so often. She'd told him, if she had her purse, she'd be happy to pay for everything. How she hoped in saying that he'd make the leap in believing her cell phone was also in her purse at Nikki's house, and not tucked in her bra. He was so eager to please, telling her it was no problem and today was his treat. So far, her plan was working. She didn't want to tout her success. There was still a lot of daylight ahead.

Eric slowed as they entered a small town. A sign read "Welcome to Monroe." A Kiwanis sign along with a few other blue business emblems hung underneath.

Civilization.

"Is it easier to go to the bathroom at the fair or should we make a pit stop before we get there?" She hoped they could stop at a McDonalds or Starbucks where the odds of cell reception would be better.

"Do you need to go to the bathroom?"

"Eventually. I hate those port-a-potty things. They smell so bad." She scrunched her nose to make her point.

Eric glanced her way. "We can pull into McDonald's. Do you want anything to eat?"

"Are you hungry for breakfast?"

"If you are...Mother."

That one single word sent chills down her spine. She leaned over and smiled, squeezing his arm. "Maybe we should eat something nutritious before eating junk food at the fair." She forced a laugh.

"Okay." He pulled the old truck into the parking lot. The brakes screeched as they rolled to a stop, smacking into the curb. Great, she was in a bucket of bolts with sketchy brakes.

"I'll head to the bathroom while you get us something, okay? I can't wait to get to the fair."

"I'll get it to-go."

She smiled like flipping Carol Brady. Where was her Academy Award? "You're so thoughtful."

Once inside the bathroom stall, Tes pulled out her phone.

Her phone buzzed from the messages that continued to roll in, congratulating them on their future bundle of joy. She put a protective hand over her belly. *Hang in there, kiddo. We're notifying the cavalry.*

Her thumbs made fast work, texting Asher: *I'm okay. I'm alive. Eric Ehome kidnapped me. He's taking me to a fair in Monroe.*

What if Eric wound up killing her and she never told him how much he meant to her? How much having his baby was now all she wanted? "I can't wait to kiss you." He'd know what it meant. She silenced her phone again and tucked it safely back into her bra.

She didn't want to take too long, or Eric might grow suspicious. She was washing her hands when he opened the bathroom door. He looked at the mirror and in each stall. "What?"

"I was making sure you weren't leaving a message for someone. You know, sending for help."

Tes forced a sweet laugh. "I'm not afraid of you, Eric. Why would I need to leave a message for anyone?" She dried her hands. "This is our day. I mean it. We're going to have a blast."

He handed her the coffee he'd bought her along with a yogurt. She followed him out to the truck and got back inside. She ate the yogurt as fast as she could. Who knew when she'd get another chance to eat? Besides, she was starving.

"What's your favorite thing to do at the fair?"

"I've only been to the Santa Monica Pier when I lived in California. I've never been to a real fair before. You're the expert here—what's your favorite thing to do?"

"I asked you a question."

The guttural growl of his tone set her on edge. "The Ferris wheel, I suppose." He'd grown more distrustful. *Crap.* Now she had to rebuild rapport and trust. This was going to be a long, emotionally taxing day.

"Good. It's my favorite too."

"You've been to the fair before?"

Eric shook his head. "No, but I've always wanted to go."

He never had a normal childhood of basic fun. Boy, could she relate to that.

"Where did you grow up?" He maneuvered the truck onto a large grassy field. He rolled down his window and paid for parking before following the hand signals attendants made as they directed traffic.

"I grew up in Switzerland."

"No shit?"

"I went to boarding school because my mother hated me and didn't want me living at home with her and her new husband."

He reached across the seat and held her hand. "You too?"

She bit her lip. "Yeah, me too." She poured it on thick. If she gained ground, she'd count this a success. "My dad was American. He'd come and pick me up for most holidays, so when I graduated at sixteen, I went to live with him."

"Is he still in California?"

"No." God, how she wished her dad could help her now. "He died about five years ago."

"Then you became a doctor."

"After a lot of schooling." She groaned for effect. "I mean, I'm thankful for my education, but school can be such a drag sometimes."

He laughed. When he smiled, he looked so normal. Kind, even. Tes searched Eric's eyes for that blank, hateful stare she'd seen in the pictures of other sociopaths, psychopaths, and serial killers. His smile didn't reach his eyes. This was all an act. They were still in test mode.

This wasn't a test she could afford to fail.

31

Asher's phone buzzed in his pocket, followed by the chime he'd assigned to Tes. He jolted awake, disturbing Ruthie.

Dobbs and LeBron were in the room before he had a chance to unlock his screen.

"She's alive," Dobbs announced.

Relief flooded him, but still she wasn't home. Not in his arms. Not in his bed. He read her message. "Monroe?"

"Yeah—the fair opens today," LeBron offered. "I got her signal. Ready to go?"

"Hell yes!" Asher jumped to his feet.

Mom and Dad were at the kitchen table drinking coffee. Hailey scrolled through her phone while eating a bowl of cereal.

"Where's Morgan?" Asher asked.

Hailey pouched her bite of cereal into her cheek. "Taking a shower."

"I got a message from Tes. She's in Monroe."

"All the way up there?" Dad asked.

He started to get up. Asher put a hand on his shoulder. "Dad, stay here and look after my girls, okay?"

"Asher—"

"Dad. Please. For me."

Dad cupped his hand over his. "Just because I'm old doesn't mean I'm useless."

"I know. I need someone I can trust to watch over my family."

"You got it." He stood and wrapped Asher in a bone-crushing hug.

Asher kissed Mom and Hailey's cheeks. He ran up the stairs and knocked the bathroom door. "Morgan?"

"I'm in the shower," she shouted.

He cracked the door, assaulted by a cloud of hot humidity. He shouted so she could hear. "Tes is alive. I'm going to go get her."

"What?"

Asher shut the door and headed out with Dobbs, LeBron, Zeke, and Joni. Five people to take on one maniacal asshole.

The bastard was outnumbered and going down.

***

Tes looped her hand through Eric's arm. Flesh to flesh, she could slowly drain his energy. If he was tired, he couldn't fight her or anyone else. Then again, if he was possessed by a demon, would he notice? Would he be impervious to her gift? One thing she and Joni learned was that their gifts didn't always work on each other. When Joni froze time—it didn't freeze Tes. Tes couldn't drain Joni's energy.

Would it piss Eric off if he realized what she was trying to do? What if she had that perfect opportunity to zap him, and nothing happened? Worthless thoughts. She had to keep her spirits up.

They meandered through buildings, passing every booth, and she took every opportunity to make a big deal about letting everyone know this was their "mom and son" day.

The sun burned through the early morning clouds. Humidity frizzed her hair. Did she look as haggard as she felt? The coffee, mingled with her morning breath, tasted nasty in her mouth. She'd about kill for a mint or a piece of gum. Without a shower, she must smell ripe. Maybe it'd get them through a line faster. Was her face blasted over the media? Would anyone recognize her? *Come on, people—social media didn't miss anything these days. Someone, please notice me.*

They were next in line to the Ferris wheel when she spotted Dobbs in the distance, staring at her. She breathed a huge sigh of relief. They'd gotten her message. She wasn't alone.

"Why are you tearing up?"

"Because I realized that you never got to do this with your real mom. It makes me so sad that she didn't value you enough to do something as simple as ride a Ferris wheel."

Eric caressed her cheek with the back of his hand. "You're making up for it today."

Good, he still believed her bullshit.

They stepped onto the platform and eased back into the bench. The carnie locked the bar in place, and they whirled ahead before stopping to let other passengers on.

Tes clung to her side of the seat, hoping she could unlatch the wide metal bar holding their legs in place if the ride slowed close enough to the ground to jump.

Eric put his arm around her shoulders and tucked her close to his side. He glanced at his cell phone. "No cell reception. That's odd."

Could LeBron block out cell capabilities? She wouldn't doubt it. At least Eric couldn't track anyone if he didn't have reception.

They dipped back down and halfway up again before the ride slowed to a stop. The second time they twirled around, Tes saw something odd in the carnie's eyes as they passed...fear. They whirled around to the two o'clock position and stopped.

Tes glanced behind her. They were the only ones on the ride.

Eric glanced too.

Oh no, this was it.

He gripped the back of her neck, pinching hard, nails digging into her skin. Fury twisted his mouth. He bared his teeth, revealing long, pointed fangs, and leaned closer. "What did you do..." His fangs grazed her cheek as he spoke. *"Mother?"*

Shit. "Ouch! You're hurting me." She smacked his arm. "It's not nice to hurt your mother." *It was worth a try.* Her pulse thudded in her ears, drowning out the sounds below.

Everything silenced. No hawkers, crying children, laughter, or voices from the crowd.

"I don't know how you got a message to Asher, but you did." He jerked her neck.

She winced back the pain and began rubbing her palms together, gathering energy. Would she get shocked if he held onto her? Would it be like the Taser and she wouldn't be phased by the electrical current?

One electrical shock coming up. She gripped his thigh and shocked him.

Eric screamed, but he didn't let go of her neck. "Dammit! How did you do that?"

It worked! She could shock him.

Though it wasn't easy through his tight grip, she turned her head and stared. "I could have killed you at any time, but I was doing my best to give you a redeeming chance. Take your hand off me, or I'll kill you with the next blast."

He narrowed beady eyes, jerking his head, sniffing her hair. "What the fuck are you?" He pulled a gun out of his waistband and shoved it under her chin.

Great...add an exploding device to an electric current. This ought to be fun. She couldn't shock him with his finger on the trigger. Muscles could clench when shocked.

Grabbing hold of his hand in both of hers, she drained his energy, weakening his grip on the gun.

He jerked away the gun and smacked her in the head. "Stop it!"

She flinched. This was her chance. She put her hand on his stomach and jolted him as hard as she could.

Eric's body violently convulsed. At first his grip on her neck intensified, then loosened as he lost all muscular control. The gun fell to his lap.

This was her chance. She pulled herself to the opposite side of the metal bench and undid the latch to free her legs. She couldn't jump to the seat above her. She couldn't jump to the ground—it was too far up. Her only option was to try and jump to the seat below them. Anything to put distance between her and Eric.

The seat teetered as she stood. One foot on the seat, one on the back of the chair, she jumped. For a second she flew, suspended, adrenaline giving her extra strength to brace for landing. Both feet landed on the bench. Her weight rocked the chair, pitching her forward. She gripped the chair back as her body flung over the side, smacking hard against the metal, fingers aching. She rock climbed. Holding on wouldn't be hard. She jockeyed her weight, shifting for a better grip.

The wheel lurched into motion.

A shot rang out.

Pain coursed through her chest, knocking the wind from her lungs. She couldn't let go. Not today.

The Ferris wheel paused, then spun faster. Shit, it was going to come around again and Eric would be behind her.

Another shot rang out. This one passed through the metal seat in front of her face, grazing her arm. Searing pain coursed through her right arm, causing her to let go. Dangling by one arm, she bit back pain, and tried to lift her wounded arm back to the seat but couldn't.

Could she leap to another chair? No. She didn't dare let go. She didn't have the momentum. The strength. In a moment, she'd fall to her death. It was too hard to hold on. Her fingers were slipping.

More shots fired from the ground.

She glanced to where the shots came from. Zeke and Dobbs were there, guns poised, taking careful shots.

Asher stood behind Joni.

Her eyes connected with Joni's. She'd stopped time. The rides, the people, the breeze. Everything was motionless, except their team and Eric.

As she crested the top, Eric's seat came into view behind her. Blood gushed between his fingertips as he held his wounded arm. He picked up his gun and pointed it at her, anger twisting his face in rage.

The wheel spun. Another shot rang out, piercing his forearm. Blood splattered. Bone cracked. He dropped the gun. It clattered at his feet, then cascaded over the edge. A high-pitched *ting* sounded as it first bounced off the Ferris wheel scaffolding, and then thudded against the ground.

Tes looked at the grass. She let go, falling to her knees. She got up to get out of the way.

"No," Zeke yelled. "Stay down."

The ride, continuing its trajectory, smacked her in the back of the head. Her world faded to black as she face-planted into the grass.

***

Asher hung back while Zeke and Dobbs took control. *Eric shot Tes.* How she hung on after being shot a second time was beyond him. She was strong. Resilient. She had to live.

Dobbs controlled the ride, bringing it around where they could get to Eric.

When Joni stopped their surroundings, Zeke debriefed him on what was going on. This wasn't the time to question what he'd witnessed. He needed to make sure Tes was all right.

Eric's body slumped at an awkward angle. One arm over the back of the chair, legs out in front. He could have easily slipped off the ride.

Asher rushed to Tes. As gentle as he could, he lifted her body, keeping her neck stable. He had to move her from underneath the ride to get a closer look at her wounds.

Zeke holstered his gun as he knelt on her other side. "Let's gently roll her over." He held the back of her neck, making sure to move her as little as possible.

Asher inspected her arm. "Looks like a graze." Nothing a large bandage couldn't cover.

His heart stopped as he opened her white chambray shirt. There wasn't any blood. He'd seen her shot in the chest. A hole in her tank top showed where the bullet had stopped. He pulled out her cell phone. The bullet had lodged into the phone but it hadn't gone through Tes. The plasma screen's cracked surface left bits of glass in her bra that he brushed out of the way with shaking fingers. Tes was fine. A slight flesh wound was all. Damn, she was one lucky angel.

He smiled. "You're going to be fine, honey." He caressed her face, kissed her lips. "Come on, Tes. Wake up."

Zeke stood. "What the hell?"

Asher stood so he could see what Zeke was looking at.

Eric's eyes had popped open. His head tilted in an unnatural way. He first looked left, then right. Creepy-ass crawlies slithered up Asher's spine.

Holy shit—Eric was a dead walker.

His broken arm dangled below his elbow where bone shards protruded through his skin. Blood soaked his hand, dripping from his fingers. His head lolled forward, focusing on Tes. His bottom jaw flopped open.

Oh, hell no. Not this again.

"Come here, Tes. Come to me." Eric's body snapped erect.

He exchanged looks with Zeke and Dobbs.

Eric's mouth framed a menacing smile. His brow furrowed deep above unblinking eyes. His head lolled to the right, tilting the angle of his head to the side. He braced his good arm on the back of the teetering seat, knees underneath him. His chin whacked against the metal edge. As if being lifted by the back of his shoulders, he lifted straight up, knee-walked across the bench, arms dangling at his sides. He slumped his body over the bench's side, hurling over the seat's edge toward Tes, who lay on the ground not far away.

At first, Eric appeared like he wasn't going to move at all once he hit the ground. He raised his head. "Wake up, Tes." His limbs all akimbo, his lolling head looked at one arm before it moved forward in an army crawl. When he went to move his fractured arm, he dug bone into the ground and grass, impeding his progress. He frowned at his bleeding appendage as if it were a nuisance. His head twisted to look at them as a knee launched his entire body forward, closer to Tes.

If Eric reaches Tes, he'll come back to life.

Dobbs came up behind Eric, shooting several rounds into his back.

Eric smiled wider, lifted with ease and dug his broken arm into the soil, leveraging it, as he pulled himself forward with his other arm. The fingers of his good hand inched along like that magical bodiless hand from that 1970s gothic sitcom.

Asher knelt. He'd move Tes out of Eric's path.

Eric's torso and a leg thrust him forward. "Te—e—e—s."

"He's trying to reach Tes."

Dobbs popped out his emptied clip, slid in another, put his muzzle at the back of Eric's head, and pulled the trigger.

Eric's skull shattered.

Dobbs stood back, poising to shoot him again if he moved.

Eric's back vibrated and his body shook like involuntary muscle spasms.

A blob moved under the earth, as though a bowling ball rolled under the grass. It dodged between bystanders, coming up behind Joni.

"Joni, look out—" Asher tried to warn.

It knocked her off her feet, landing her hard on her ass. Zeke ran to her side.

The grass and dirt trail continued to snake past Asher, dipping out of sight as it neared Tes.

They waited. Glanced at each other. Where would the grassy blob appear?

Tes's body lurched skyward, the grass and ground lifting her up over their heads, toppling Asher to his knees.

The blob held Tes mid-air, leaned back, and hurled her toward Eric.

"No!" Asher jumped to his feet. He tried to grab her, anything to stop her from reaching Eric. His fingers scraped along her arm, but he couldn't stop her forward momentum.

Tes landed directly on top of Eric's body.

It wouldn't matter. Eric was dead. Touching Tes wouldn't bring him back to life.

Eric's back arched. Tes's unconscious body draped over him.

What was happening? Asher closed the distance.

Eric's body convulsed. A roar split the air as his lifeless body undulated.

Tes slumped to the side as Eric stood.

Eric's next roar was more forceful, splattering blood across Asher's chest and face, making him wince. He wiped the back of his hand across his face, eyes, and spit the rusty liquid from his lips.

Black claws ripped at Eric's clothes and flesh, ripping remnants away.

Asher dodged and ducked as bits of tendon and organs were flung toward him. "Jesus!"

Eric's mutilated head snapped off his shoulders, revealing a new head. A new face. He shook his head. White pointy ears protruded from the sides of his grayish, bald head. White fangs dripped thick yellow saliva. Beady, glossy black eyes focused on him, then Tes.

Asher gripped Tes beneath her armpits and pulled her out of the way.

Vampire-Eric grabbed her leg, jerking them to a stop. He roared, bobbing his head to one side to the other. More bones cracked. More white flesh gave way to gray, waxy new skin. Eric's shoulders widened.

Zeke and Dobbs moved closer. Dobbs knelt. Fired. Hitting the newly formed vampire square in the heart.

Eric hunched, clutching at the wound. He stood, arching his back, rolling his shoulders. There wasn't any blood. Eric hissed and roared, stepping closer to Dobbs. Skin rippled under where the bullet had entered Eric's body, exiting through the wound it'd created. It landed by Dobbs' knee.

Asher watched in disbelief as the wound sealed shut.

Dobbs fired, skimming the side of Eric's neck.

Eric grabbed for Dobbs.

Dobbs jockeyed to the left.

Eric took an awkward step to the side, as if taking his first step with dog-like legs was a surprise. His gangly arms flailed as he managed to balance. He balled his claw-like fists.

"Come on, prissy pants." Dobbs fired again, hitting a kneecap.

It only pissed off Eric more. His torso stretched two more feet.

"Stop shooting him," Asher yelled. He gripped Tes again and started to pull her away.

Thick clouds rolled in, darkening the sky. Lightning pulsed spider veins across the purplish haze. Each pulse increased in volume and intensity. Asher opened his mouth, forcing a yawn to equalize the pressure in his eardrums.

A black ooze pooled under Eric's feet. One slithering tentacle entwined around Tes's leg, yanking her back to Eric's feet. It snaked and twisted up Eric's legs, torso, and arms, pinning them to his sides.

Joni stepped forward, mouthing words he couldn't hear over the pulsing current amping faster and louder above their heads.

A black mass formed on Eric's shoulder, like modeling clay. First it was round, then square with spikes forming on his head. Eyes formed, followed by a nose, and finally a mouth full of jagged teeth. Hot tar-like spit rolled over shard-like teeth, dripping on Tes's leg. It sizzled and burned.

Tes winced and held her head, opening her eyes.

32

W here was she? *What the hell?* Her eyes focused on the roiling black, purple, and greenish-hued clouds above. Lightning lit the darkness from within. Tes had seen this before—the day she was first struck by lightning.

She blinked, turned her head, and looked up at a two-headed demon looming over her. Shock and terror rolled through her and she tried to back away. She tried to roll but realized something was wrapped around her leg. *Oh, hell no.* She kicked at the tether with her other foot.

The ground shifted around her. Was the grass moving? Was she seeing things?

"Tes!" Asher appeared in front of her face, kneeling beside her.

"Asher." Man, was she glad to see him.

"Honey, we're deep up shit creek and could use your powers right now."

"I'm not sure I'm strong enough."

Asher caressed the side of her face. "You're the strongest woman I know."

He said the nicest things.

"Take my energy." He grabbed her hand and put it over his heart.

A black hand breached the soil, grabbing Asher's arm. He dropped her hand and gripped at the fingers, trying to pull them away. Another hand popped up, grabbing his ankle.

Tes gasped. Another hand thrust through the ground and grabbed hold of her head, pinning her in place. Another slimy cold hand gripped her arm.

Gunfire sounded behind Asher. "Fuck! What are these things?" Dobbs fired more rounds.

More shots fired behind her. Zeke jumped on one foot, then the other, trying to avoid the onslaught of hands reaching through the soil.

"Guys," Joni's strained voice cried. "I'm not sure I'm going to be able to hold things still much longer."

Tes took a deep breath. *It was up to her.* She strained against the hands. She splayed her fingers, threading them through the grass, drawing energy from the earth beneath her. She closed her eyes, steadied her nerves, soaking in pulses from magma, stone, and root.

She sent a shockwave through her entire body. The hands that held her yanked away from her and Asher.

The tentacle that held her ankle retreated. She pulled her knees up, rolled over, and came face-to-face with a mini demon. Her long black hair slithered around her face. Tes could see her shocked expression in the demon's black mirror-like eyes. She held up her hand and blasted the demon with lightning. The demon exploded. "So that's how we get rid of them." She blasted her way to Joni. For some reason, they wouldn't go near her.

"These look familiar?" she asked.

Joni cocked her head. "We go way back."

"What the hell is that?" Tes pointed to the two-headed demon.

"That's Eric on the right and the demon I've fought before on the left."

"What does he want with Eric?"

Joni shrugged.

The two demons struggled for footing and power, pushing each other for dominance. Dobbs and Zeke continued to shoot at the smaller demons.

"Tes!" Asher yelled above the din.

One minion had him by the throat, another was about to bite his leg.

Tes zapped them. No sooner had those disappeared than more began a new assault.

Asher whipped one off his shoulders, and drop-kicked it toward Dobbs, who kneed it onto the ground and shot it, shattering its body. He dropped the clip and went to reach for another one, patting his pocket. "I'm out!" He holstered his gun and began kicking away.

Zeke was out of ammo. He grabbed the hose that was near the Ferris wheel and turned on the dial, blasting demons with a hard stream of water.

Not water. Tes glanced at Joni.

Joni clapped and began pulsing a large energy ball between her hands. She hurled her arm back and threw it at the two demons. "Come on, Tes, blast them!"

Tes frowned. That wouldn't work. If she blasted them with electricity, it could make them stronger. Eric had already transformed into his true self. Whatever the black thing was that encompassed his body, it held Eric relatively still, but he'd gotten an arm loose and was strangling the demon.

"You got a better idea?"

Joni widened her stance. "I can open a portal to the other side."

Tes did a double take. "You can what?"

"Put your hand on my shoulder. I need some energy."

Tes did as she asked and gave a slight pulse.

Joni quickly created a ball of light and flung it in front of the demon-duo.

Here goes nothing. Or everything. Tes laced her fingers with Joni's where they held the portal open. "Hang on." She stretched her other hand toward the menacing clouds.

Lightning struck her outstretched hand, flowing through her chest and out through their entwined hands. The portal widened. The minions glanced at Tes. She splayed her fingers. Lightning feathered across the lawn, encapsulating the tiny lifeless souls. Tes whipped her hand, flinging them through the portal.

The spiked demon stared at Joni. Roared. Melted into the ground, leaving Eric vulnerable.

Zeke focused the water on Eric, hitting the lightning stream.

Tes sucked in a breath. The lightning conducted through the water, heading toward the nozzle Zeke held. He dropped the hose in the nick of time and jumped away.

Tes focused the lightning directly on Eric so he couldn't move.

Joni screamed, shoving the portal around Eric. She clenched her hand closed. The blowback of electricity knocked Joni and Tes to the ground.

Asher fell to his knees, gulping air.

Zeke was the first to reach him. "You'll get better at this." Dobbs grabbed his other arm and they lifted him to his feet.

Joni's hair stood on end. Tes felt her hair. It did the same. They both burst out laughing.

The blue sky returned.

Tes looked around. "How are we going to explain all this?"

"We're not." Joni wrapped her hand around her shoulders. "We're leaving."

Tes grimaced at the body parts. "What about Eric's remains? The bullet casings? The carnage?"

"Can we burn them?" She opened her arms and lifted the pieces into the air, forming them into a circular mass, spinning as more pieces pulled from the ground and matted together.

Tes made a ball of energy between her hands and hurled it at the conglomerate floating in the air. It blasted into dust, littering the ground.

Asher wrapped her in a hug. She hugged him back, kissing him all over his face. He smoothed back her hair. "You did it."

"We did it." She grabbed Joni into the group hug. Dobbs and Zeke joined in.

LeBron approached, clicking the keys of his hand-held computer tablet. "I've wiped all the cell phones in the area in case any of them started filming before you froze everything."

Tes touched Joni's tummy. "I hope I didn't hurt your baby."

"You didn't." Joni covered Tes's hand with her own. "Baby's fine. If anything, kicking away like it got a blast of sugar."

Tes's mouth opened in awe, feeling the baby kick against her hand.

Joni squeezed her hand. "One of the demons got away."

Tes whooshed air between her lips. "He lives to fight us another day."

Asher squeezed her hand. "Let's not hang around worrying about that." He paused, smiling. "I believe we have a wedding to get to."

They made their way back to the SUV. As they approached the gate, the whirling of rides returned, hawkers finished their cries, and life returned to normal.

Tes looked at the cloudless sky. One thing she learned was that lightning was her ally, not her enemy. She didn't need to fear the unknown. She and Joni could tackle anything that came their way.

Tes smiled at Asher, wiggling her fingers. "You sure you want to marry me?"

"Wild demons couldn't keep me away."

***

Years from now, Tes was certain she'd laugh at how bedraggled and exhausted they looked in their wedding pictures.

They stood at the altar staring at each other. The long Catholic Mass droned on. Sacred ground would break the curse that had ripped their souls apart for centuries. They exchanged the rings, lit the candle, repeated the prayers, and waited for the songs to be sung by various aunts and close family friends.

Tes didn't hear a word. All she wanted to do was say those special words to Asher.

"Do you, Tesla Curie Brynn, take Asher Milo Hickok."

"Milo?" She laughed. "You never told me your middle name."

He laughed. "I'll never live this down." He turned to his parents. "Mom, Dad, what were you thinking?"

"We're naming the next dog Milo." Tes squeezed his hands.

The church erupted in laughter.

"Yes, I take Asher—" She snickered. "Milo Hickok to be my lawfully wedded husband. To have and to hold from this day forward. In sickness and in health. In times of plenty and times of not-so-plenty. Yeah, I'm going to be with you for the rest of this life and every life to come."

"What say you?"

"I do." Tes could officially say those words, but she would wait until Asher repeated his vows. No way was she jinxing this now.

"Yes, I take Dr. Tesla Curie—cute middle name, by the way—Brynn as my lawfully wedded wife. To have and to hold and love from this day until the end of our days. I'll put up with her whining protests when she's sick and I'll be her pillar of strength when she needs me. We'll always be rich because we have each other and a family who loves and supports us."

"Amen!" Grant yelled from the front row.

"What say you?"

"I do." Asher pulled her hands and kissed her hard, slanting his mouth over hers. She opened her mouth and welcomed his tongue mating with hers.

"I haven't gotten to that part yet." The priest tried to sound gruff.

Everyone burst into laughter.

"I love you," Tes said against his lips.

"I. Love. You." Asher kissed her again.

The church doors burst open, a gust of wind filling the sanctuary. Two doves flew up the aisle, encircled above their heads, and flew back out doors.

"The curse is broken." Tes wrapped him in her arms and kissed him again.

"Thank God. There were some pretty close calls."

The priest stepped forward and looked over Asher's shoulder. "I pronounce you husband and wife. You've already kissed your bride." He addressed the crowd. "I'm proud to introduce Mr. Asher and Dr. Tesla Hickok."

Epilogue

Tes finished her cinnamon roll and tea while waiting for Professor Igmantani to arrive. She and Joni sat in Braewood Manor Coffee and Tea House's private library on the second floor.

Joni had tagged along, but instead of drinking tea, she scanned the leather-bound books on shelves. "Some of these books have to be hundreds of years old. Some aren't even in English." She looked over her shoulder and whispered, "Did you know Carrie's a witch?" Carrington "Carrie" Paige was the establishment's owner.

Tes smiled. "She practices witchcraft. Millions of people do."

"No." Joni lowered her voice more. "She's a high priestess of her coven."

"That would explain why her cinnamon rolls are the best I've ever had. I've got to stop craving them or I'll be fifty sizes too big when the baby comes."

"Is Asher going with you to your doctor's appointment tomorrow?" Joni settled into the chair opposite her and drank some tea.

Tes groaned. "He's so excited about the baby. I'm hoping that store-bought test wasn't a false positive. It'll crush his heart."

Carrie opened the door and Professor Igmantani entered, along with four men carrying a large wooden box. "I'll leave you alone." She crossed the room to a turn-of-the century bell pull. "Pull this if you need anything."

"Thank you, Carrie." Tes stood to greet Professor Igmantani. He'd aged well. A little grayer at the temples and in his goatee. "Professore." She held his hands and kissed each cheek.

"Teslasita." He turned his gaze. "And Joni. Your son found the postcard, correct?"

"It was remarkable how much the card resembled Tes."

The four men unlocked the wood crate and pulled out a large book with a thick wooden cover and put it on the far end of the large library table. They bowed and left the room, closing the door behind them.

A knowing smile framed Igmantani's lips. "It was no accident you found the card." The professor stood in front of the book, measuring about two foot by three foot. Tes stood next to him. "You see, we've been wondering how we could broach the subject and form a new partnership."

"We?" Joni set her cup down, stood, and flanked the professor to look at the book.

"The Vatican." Igmantani pulled out a set of keys from his sleeve and unlocked the tome's three locks. "His Eminence, Our Holy Father."

"The Pope wants to form a partnership with us?" Tes glanced at Joni. "Why?" She frowned.

"Because you are both important in the battle between good and evil."

Joni leaned back. "What battle?"

Tes motioned between them. "We're a couple of housewives and mothers."

Igmantani's laugh held no humor. "You are a resurrection angel, Teslasita. Since you were struck by lightning, we've been following you." He returned the keys to his sleeve. "But first, let me explain how this all began."

He pulled out a pair of white cotton gloves from another pocket and slid them on his hands before opening the book. "The Hall of Miracles was first commissioned during the reign of Pope Gregory the XV. He was best known for imposing conclaves to be conducted by secret ballot. He also issued a constitution against magicians and witches in 1623."

"That was because of superstitions, right?" Joni asked, edging closer to see the book.

Igmantani smiled. "Don't legends and superstitions have a shred of truth?"

The title page was etched in gold leaf and Tes was mesmerized by the letters' intricacies. "Miracula." She pronounced it like Dracula with an M. She glanced at Joni. "Miracles."

"In the deep recesses of the Vatican, there is a hall that holds the paintings in this book. They were painted the last time a Nephilim graced the earth."

Joni cocked her head. "What's a Nephilim?"

"Part angel," the professor answered. "Part human. They are created when male angels breed with earthly women."

Tes stared at Joni, waiting for her to burst out laughing, but she shook her head in disbelief. "That's a thing?"

The professor turned the page. "It's forbidden, but still it happens."

"Wait a minute." Tes thought back. "Weren't they the creatures that were destroyed during the Great Flood? Back when Noah built the ark?"

"Very good." Igmantani bowed his head toward Tes. "You remembered."

"So, are you saying they're back?"

"They never went away. We've kept them sequestered in remote areas so they wouldn't destroy, or influence, humanity again."

Joni giggled. "Are you serious?"

Igmantani didn't crack a smile. "I cannot stress this enough. What you are about to see, few have ever seen. Not every pope has seen these portraits. Not all are worthy to see what is held in the Hall of Miracles."

Tes and Joni exchanged a glance. "We're not going to tell anyone what we see. I want to see the painting of the resurrection angel. That's all."

"Do you know why the church was so frightened of magicians and witches?"

Tes shook her head.

"Because they had powers the church did not understand. A smear campaign to discredit them was one thing, but what they could do was nothing short of the phenomenal feats Jesus performed himself."

Joni smirked. "By women, no less."

"Exactly." Igmantani bowed his head. "Resurrection angels are thought to be among the most powerful angels in the realm. Up there with the Archangels."

"No way." Tes didn't feel *that* powerful. "Wait a minute. They're others like me?"

"We have many records throughout the ages of such people who harnessed the power to bring back the dead." He looked at Joni. "Among other things."

Tes's tongue clung to the top of her mouth. "Like what?"

"Come and see." Igmantani beckoned them to come closer.

That knowing voice intruded into Tes's thoughts. These paintings were censored away from the public's eye because they depicted something the Catholic Church didn't want known. Why didn't they burn them? Why keep them at all?

The first painting was large and wide, taking up both sides of the book. It depicted Jesus and his two crucified companions hanging on crosses on the hill. Some from the crowd bowed their heads in grief, while others gawked. Roman soldiers monitored the masses with hatred, some kicking the new Christian believers. Others threw stones. The Roman citizens stared at the man hanging in the middle. Their expressions held curiosity and hatred, a mixed bag of the tumultuous times.

None of this was shocking. Tes had seen images like these before, but what terrified Tes was the man in the foreground. The menacing gaze in the Roman soldier's eyes terrified her, almost daring the viewer to come and stop what he was determined to do. A slight smile curved his lips. His strong, muscled hand gripped the hilt of his sword. Old scabs and scars branched over his forearm. A crimson cape flapped in the wind, as did his blond hair.

Joni gasped, covering her mouth with her hands.

"What is it?" Tes asked.

"It's my brother. My twin brother, Christian." She pointed to the soldier in the forefront.

Tes leaned over the painting. "Wait a minute. This looks like you." She pointed to a woman near Jesus' feet.

Joni leaned over, the professor stepping back to give them room. "And this is you."

Tes looked at the person Joni pointed to. A Roman woman stood at the forefront of onlookers.

Jesus stared at the woman who looked like her. Chills bit the back of Tes's neck.

"May I?" Igmantani stepped forward and carefully turned the page. "The Resurrection Angel."

"It's more beautiful in person," Joni said. She pointed. "What's not in the postcard is the melted Roman seal and torn vines."

"Nor the dead soldiers." Tes pointed. "Did the angel kill them?"

"Oh my God," Joni gasped, covering her mouth with her hand. "Look."

There was a soldier in the corner. His head tilted at an odd angle toward the viewer. His bottom jaw hung open. His hands dangled from his wrists. It was the soldier from the first painting. The one Joni had called her brother.

Tes stepped back, bumping into Igmantani.

"Teslasita," he whispered in her ear. "This is you."

No way. She shook her head. Yes, she had an uncanny likeness to the angel in the painting, but she hadn't been there personally.

"The Church has claimed for thousands of years that reincarnation isn't possible." Igmantani's stared at Tes. "However, it is. We have living proof of many such cases. There are some souls that come to each age to help mankind in unimaginable ways."

"What good is it to bring someone back from the dead?" Tes's eyes welled with tears. "This is a curse. Not a blessing."

"It is simply what it is, Teslasita." He pointed to the person's signature on the painting. "That emblem is catalogued to a woman. She studied under many great painters, often filling in sketches made by others, like Michelangelo."

Joni squeezed her hand. "What else do you know about her?"

"She could not read, nor write. Never married. Never had children. Some recordings say she was deaf." Igmantani cleared his throat. "Her parents and where she grew up are unknown. Some say she lived in Michelangelo's home as a servant and he'd come upon her in the night, seeing something she had painted and noticing her talent. All speculation."

"What made her paint this?" Tes asked, motioning a hand over the image.

"No one will ever know."

Tes shook her head in disbelief. "Why did the Church keep them? Why not destroy them?"

Igmantani took his time in answering. "There are some who believe in the supernatural. The Church has fought evil, demons, and the wretches of the afterlife since the beginning of time. Some believe we are not meant to know all of God's workings." He clasped his hands behind his back. "All we know is that when they return, they change the world. Not by becoming great politicians, or clerics for that matter. They return balance to the world when it has lost its way."

Joni let go of Tes's hand. "Shift power from evil back to the good?"

"Yes. Defeat evil, in all its manifestations." Igmantani focused on Joni. "You know how to defeat evil."

"I do." Joni glanced away.

Igmantani turned the page. "His Holiness sits and studies this picture at great length."

Joni shook her head and grabbed Tes's hand again.

Tes read the title of the painting aloud. "*Defensorem Mortuus.* Defender of the Dead."

On a grassy knoll, surrounded by trees, a woman stood facing a ghost on one side while a black demon rose out of the ground on the other. Its spiky crown gave it a menacing look. The demon had only one hand. How odd. The woman in the middle was dressed in a long blue gown. A crimson hooded cape hid most of her features. The strange part was that there was an oval light between the woman and the ghost.

"What's that in the middle?" Tes asked.

"Heaven," Joni whispered. "It's what I see when I open the portal to the other side."

"Were you born with this gift?" Igmantani asked.

Tes wrapped an arm around Joni's shoulders and pulled out the nearest chair.

Joni sat. "My brother had left a message for me saying I'd always been able to do things with my mind. Frankly, I don't consider myself gifted. I like helping people connect with their loved ones. That's all."

Igmantani put a hand on Joni's shoulder. "You are blessed among women."

Joni swallowed, her gaze pleading with Tes. "Tes is truly the blessed and gifted one."

Tes came to her rescue. "There's a lot I don't understand about this gift. Any insight you could provide would be greatly appreciated, Professor."

"Who knows what God has in store for us?" Igmantani turned another page. "We need you to find the others."

"What others?" Tes and Joni looked to Igmantani, then each other. *It was a thick book.* How many could there be?

"Each painting features another person here to help mankind or destroy it. We're not a hundred percent sure which." He cleared his throat. "One thing we know from history is that if you two are here in this lifetime, the others are sure to be here as well." He bowed his head. "You were chosen by God to return to us. How we protect you, leverage you, will be beneficial to mankind."

Joni harrumphed. "And to the Church."

Tes wasn't that naïve schoolgirl who'd blindly follow where they led. They'd used her own pride against her. She wanted to see the painting and they took this opportunity to tell her they'd been watching all along.

"We will protect you," Igmantani offered.

What the hell did that mean? Did they need protecting? From whom? From what? Were they going to be indebted to the Church? Guilt seeped in. She'd dragged Joni along for the ride and now she'd been duped into this. "I'm sorry, Joni. I should have known the Church doesn't do anything without having a caveat of what will benefit them."

"Don't feel bad." She pinned the professor with a glare. "Igmantani's got some 'splainin' to do."

Tes stared at the new picture Igmantani revealed. An angel with wing tattoos along her arms, her hair almost white, beautiful features—kind of what most angels looked like that were painted at the time. "Wonder what her secret power is?"

"You both are healers and defenders. Each lifetime, we learn more of your origin and your purpose, but much is still unknown."

Joni asked, "How are we supposed to find the others? You, no doubt, have record of them, like you have on Tes and me."

Igmantani smiled. "Some of them, yes. But this one." He tapped his finger on the tattooed angel. "She's the most important one for you to find."

"Why?"

"Because you need her to help you defeat the demon."

Joni snapped her gaze to Tes, then back to Igmantani. "You know about the demon?"

"We do." Igmantani closed the book, pulled out his keys, and set the locks. He pulled a postcard out of his pocket and handed it to Tes.

It was a miniature of the Nephilim painting. "Be assured, ladies, not all angels are good. Some are demons in angel costumes meant to thwart you. A way to decrease your chances of success."

He clapped his hands. The door opened and the four men who'd opened the box reentered the room, encased the tome, secured the lock, and carried it out. The professor bowed. "I leave you. We will be in touch."

"Lovely. Thank you for coming all this way." Tes bowed her head and waited for him to close the door. Then she placed the card on the table and slid it closer to Joni as she sat in the chair across the table. "We don't have to do what he asked us to do."

Joni brushed a finger along the card. "Don't we?" The side of her mouth tweaked. "We can't defeat the demon." She raised her gaze. "You're not strong enough. I'm not strong enough. Even together, he evaded us." She tapped on the card. "If she's our only hope of kicking its ass, then we need to find her."

When Tes had met Joni at the coffee shop downstairs a couple of months ago, she didn't know she'd become her best friend, ally, partner, and fellow defender against evil. "But first, I'm going to go on my honeymoon, settle two girls into their junior year of high school, and we should have these babies." She sighed. "When are we going to find time to fight evil for mankind?"

Joni stood. "Between diaper changes and date night?"

They both enjoyed a good laugh as Tes picked up the card. "One Nephilim. How hard could she be to find?"

"With facial recognition software?" Joni grinned, snatching the card out of her hand. "Not that hard at all. I'll have LeBron get on it right away. We'll probably have something by the time you're back from Hawaii."

"Sounds like a plan." Tes picked up their empty plates to carry downstairs. Coming to Washington had thrown her life a curveball. No matter how insane and crazy it was bound to become, she knew she wouldn't have it any other way.

THE END

If you enjoyed this book, it would mean the world to me if you could leave a review. http://mybook.to/ULReadyorNot

About the Author

Aedyn Brooks is an award-winning author who recently retired from her data-driven ninja job to write wicked paranormal romances full time. After living most of her life in haunted houses, Aedyn decided to share her terrifying, and sometimes funny, experiences with ghosts by crafting Haunted Romances in her debut Grave Intentions series. One thing she learned from an early age is that the dead can be our greatest ally, especially in our darkest hours.

The Grave Intention series is comprised of full-length paranormal romance novels that are stand-alone books. Characters from previous books make a repeat appearance, living in the fictional small town of Whitman, Washington.

Aedyn calls the Pacific Northwest home. She loves suburbia living with a postage-stamp sized yard, with one of her three grown children, and whatever ghosts happen by. When not writing, you'll find her casting runes, reading tarot, and honing her skills as a psychic medium. She enjoys spending time with family and babysitting her granddaughters. Being a grandmother is the bestest thing ever!

You can also follow Aedyn on FaceBook, Twitter, Instagram @aedynbrooks, or Pinterest (another slight addiction). She shares her personal ghost encounters through her newsletter. To join - sign up here. www.AedynBrooks.com

Other books by Aedyn Brooks

Dead Reckoning, Grave Intentions, Book 1 (Joni & Zeke's Story)

Devil's Due, Grave Intentions, Book 3 (Michaela & Brock's Story)

Devil's Due – Sneak Peek

"Forgive me, Father, for I'm about to sin."

The ancient, dark confessional creaked as Michaela Herald knelt and waited for the priest to relay her next assignment. As an assassin, she found confessionals proved to be an effective way to pass information.

Acrid sulfur stung her nostrils, making her gag. The rotten-egg stench could only mean one thing: Satan himself had arrived.

Beelzebub typically delegated message delivery to a lower demon disguised as a priest.

Today must be special.

"You disappointed me." Satan's deep vibrato rumbled through the oak wall and through her chest. "Again."

Selling her soul to the Devil had been less than a stellar idea, but at the time it was a lifeline.

"Hey, 'Bub. How ya doin'?" She smiled. He hated the nickname.

He exhaled, sending a puff of hot, foul smoke through the fleur-de-lis patterned panel where secrets were whispered and lies were told. "Your orders were clear."

She shrugged. "What are you going to do? Kill me?" Had he finally grown tired of her teasing, failures, and sarcasm? Would he end her life? Would it be painful? She swallowed the fear tightening her throat.

The protective confessional privacy wall disintegrated to ash, like fire devouring paper, revealing Satan in his full glory. His smoke-blackened, red flesh held an odor all its own. Death. Boiled blood. Burnt oil. Michaela held her breath, biting back bile, glad she hadn't eaten breakfast.

Satan uncurled his massive frame. His horns scraped the confessional box's ceiling, forcing him to hunch his head. He loomed over her, intimidating her with his obsidian eyes. His junk hung in front of her face. Uncircumcised. As thick and smelly as the rest of him. Her eyes lowered to his goat-shaped hind quarters that ended in black-hooved feet with ash caked between cloven toes.

Michaela stood. At five-eleven, taller in her Doc Martens, she came to his chest and wasn't as intimidated as if she'd continued to kneel.

Satan curled his tail around his shoulder, and the spear-tipped end came within an inch of her left eye.

She focused her attention on his brass nipple rings. It was easier to look there than into his bottomless, black eyes.

His muscular arms ended with meaty hands tipped in clawed fingers. The scroll she'd signed with her blood seven years ago uncoiled. The yellowed parchment dangled in front of her face. Satan pointed a thick claw at a red glowing phrase. "You agreed to kill the subjects of my choosing."

Her mind jumbled, making it impossible for her to make sense of the fancy curved lines twisting into unrecognizable symbols. The scribbles on the page mocked her dyslexia.

Seeing that contract again only reminded her of how weak she'd been. "I'd be happy to live up to my end of the bargain if you'd give me a copy of my contract to read. Then I could understand what was expected of me."

He huffed, spitting diesel fumes in her face. She coughed. His claw slid down the length of the page where the letters diminished into a size two font. "Clause forty-five. The party of the third part." He dug his pointy nail into her collarbone. "That's you. Shall not demand a copy." *Poke.* "Of said." *Poke.* "Contract."

How convenient. She lifted her head to stare him in the face and wished she hadn't. His deep underbite gave him a menacing look. Thick black fangs protruded from his bottom jaw, curling at the sides of his wide nostrils. Horns wrapped around his head on each side of his ears. They were pointy and sharp, honed white at the tips.

"Without a copy, I'm unable to understand exactly what you need from me. I've told you before. I can't read when you're standing over me demanding I obey."

He gripped her chin, forcing her to look into his eyes. She swore fire burned in their depths. "Do as you're told" —the corner of his lips curled— "and you get to live another day. Simple as that." He let go of her chin and snapped his fingers, chomping his teeth in rapid succession—a habit that annoyed her.

Michaela tried to grab the parchment from his hand. Her fingers swooshed through the air as though it were a dream. She tried again, yielding the same result. The paper reshaped in front of her face.

Satan's laughter echoed around the small chamber. Spittle dribbled from his bottom fangs. He stopped as suddenly as he began. "You failed, Michaela. Because of that, you now owe me four more deaths."

Her heart dropped to her toes. Tears welled in her eyes. She couldn't show weakness. Weakness gave him power. She'd be damned if she'd give him more than he'd already taken. She blinked back her tears, taking in a steadying breath.

He flicked his wrist, coiling and closing the scroll. It disappeared.

"You brought this on yourself. Your contract extends every time you disobey." He paused, leaning closer to her face. "The second you didn't kill Charles Grimly, when you *chose* to disobey, you knew you'd owe me more." He exhaled so hard she closed her eyes. "I believe you rather enjoy working for me."

Michaela waved her hand in front of her face. "Dude. You need a mint." She hid her pain behind insults.

"Why didn't you kill Grimly?"

"If I'd done that, where would the justice be for his victims? I thought of a win-win sol —"

He hissed, growled, and red saliva dribbled as he stomped his hoof.

"You want him dead? Kill him yourself." She smirked and folded her arms. "You have resources in prison. Have one of your cronies shank him."

Satan lowered his voice. "That wasn't our bargain."

He never wanted her to kill the good people—only those that society wanted dead too. Serial killers, pedophiles, and the occasional abusive husband that tortured his wife and children. That perplexed her to no end and made it hard to refuse taking assignments. Why would he want *them* dead? It made no sense. It was like hell was in desperate need of demented souls.

Michaela had lost her blood lust somewhere between Dallas and Phoenix on an assignment where little boys had been kidnapped and left mutilated. It was the first time she'd wanted justice. It was the first case where she'd handed over solid evidence to local authorities. A jury decided their fate. Not her. It was the right thing to do for those who had suffered. In essence, she'd grown a conscience and begged God to have mercy on her soul.

"Be warned. Do not fail me again."

"How many Hail Marys do I have to say? A couple Our Fathers?" She loved goading him. After all, what did she have to lose? She had nothing. *Literally nothing.* A backpack held a set of clean clothes, a few toiletries, flint to build a fire, and a tarp she'd make into a tent when needed. Her prized possessions were an artist's sketchpad and a few charcoal pencils. She had clothes on her back, shoes on her feet, a coat from the lost-and-found, and a beanie she'd scavenged from the side of the road. No computer. No cell phone. Enough money she'd earned from selling her drawings and odd jobs to get the essentials in life, and her trusty switchblades tucked in her pockets. She existed so far off the grid that she was a ghost.

She lived off the land, knowing God would provide for her every need. Perhaps that's what pissed Satan off most. She still believed in God. And she didn't fear the Devil. Much.

The oak wall returned in front of her face. Satan returned to his seat. She knelt and waited for her orders.

"Seems you have a weakness for children."

Boy, did she ever.

"There's a doctor not far from here that's been experimenting on children, and so far, his actions have killed six. You are to kill the doctor."

"What about—"

"*I said, kill the doctor.*" Satan smacked his hand against the wall. "No questions asked." His teeth chattered. "You are not to contact local law enforcement. You are not to save anyone's life. That's an order," he growled. "Kill the doctor. That is your sole objective. Do you understand?"

"Got it, 'Bub."

"Good. If you deviate from my plan, I will kill all the children in White River. Remember that when you're thinking of justice."

***

Michaela didn't want to think about how many ways a doctor could hurt a child. There was more to the story—always was when it came to Satan.

She stepped from the confessional into the quiet sanctuary. Fresh, cool air filled her lungs as she took a deep breath. She might as well start walking and watch for the signs that would lead her in the direction Satan wanted her to go. There were always signs. Arrows where they shouldn't be. Ghosts stepped from shadows, pointing the way. On occasion, she'd been chased by wildlife to skedaddle her along if she wasn't moving fast enough.

Satan had his ways, and he was always watching.

A flash out of the corner of Michaela's eye made her glance into an alcove. St. Michael's statue knelt on one knee, head bowed, leaning on a polished stainless-steel sword. The morning sun poured through the high windows. She dropped her backpack by the entrance inside the alcove, dug in her pocket for change, and slipped it into the offering box. She lifted a wooden reed and lit the end from a burning candle. Another's prayers and burdens, just like her own. Lighting a new candle, she gathered her thoughts.

The flame cast an amber shadow on the marble statue. She glanced at St. Michael's eyes. From this angle, it didn't look like his head was bowed. Instead, it appeared he directly met her gaze.

That wasn't creepy at all. She swallowed.

She dropped to the kneeler and folded her hands in prayer. Closing her eyes, she crossed herself. It'd been a long time since she'd prayed to anyone besides God. "St. Michael, defender in battle." She couldn't remember the words to his dedicated prayer. "I need your help."

Satan's stench filled the alcove. *"What are you doing?"*

Michaela could see his reflection in St. Michael's sword.

"He cannot come in here," the statue whispered. "This alcove is hallowed ground."

Michaela snapped her head in the voice's direction and fell back. She put her hands behind her to brace her fall, then scrambled backward. Her heart lodged in her throat. *What the hell? Statues don't talk.*

The marble statue came to life, standing to his full length. The marble didn't crumble or make a sound. It was as if the stone was St. Michael's flesh and bones. He pointed the sword at Satan as he jumped from the pedestal. He held out his free hand to her.

Satan gnashed his teeth, pacing in front of the alcove's entrance. *"Michaela, I'm warning you."*

What had she done? She'd lit a candle. The outreached hand couldn't be real. This had to be a hallucination. She started to reach out but couldn't believe what she'd witnessed and yanked her hand back.

The living statue smiled. "He can't hurt you in here." St. Michael leaned over, wrapping his warm, lustrous hand around her fingers, and they felt human. Power surged through her palm up her arm, thrumming into her whole being. Visions filled her mind.

Battles fought. Battles won. Battles lost. Blood. Carnage. Hatred. Heathen. Fire. Hell. Damnation—angels being cast from Heaven.

The visions somehow intertwined with her destiny, like she'd lived another lifetime. Except, she didn't believe in reincarnation. That was poppycock, as Sister Agatha used to say.

Deep sadness overwhelmed her while regret ached within her soul.

She stared at the angel pulling her to her feet. Kindness, maybe a bit of love, shown in his expression. "Help me." Didn't he have a reputation for sitting near God's throne?

Could he intercede on her behalf? Would God make an exception for her? "Please."

Satan growled. "You are not to sit in the counsel of those from heaven."

Was that another one of those phrases in the fine print she'd missed? Satan dangled her contract from his clawed fingers, pointing to her latest transgression.

The angel struck out with his sword, piercing the parchment, ripping it from Satan's clutches, and flinging it across the alcove's floor. The metal scroll holders, black and ornate, bounced, clanging against the marble floor.

Could she finally read it? Not when her pulse thumped in her veins and anxiety ruled her heart.

"Michael," Satan's tone softened. His fingers twitched. "Give the scroll back to me...please, old friend."

St. Michael sheathed his sword. "Lucifer, Lucifer, Lucifer." Pity dripped from every word. "When will you learn?" He lifted the scroll, pulled it to its length, and read to himself.

Several minutes ticked by. Michaela stared at the lava dripping from the corners of Satan's mouth. It pooled in a tar-like substance onto the church's pristine floor. His hands gripped the wrought-iron bars to the alcove's entrance, burning red-hot under his hands.

She'd have hell to pay when this was over. "Maybe you should give it back to him."

St. Michael lifted his head and glared at Satan. Disdain curled his lip as he narrowed an eye.

Michaela swallowed. Sweat beaded across her brow and gathered in her armpits. She wiped her clammy hands against her jeans.

When St. Michael finished reading, he stood in front of her. She tried to drop her gaze, but he put his hand under her chin and raised her face to look him in the eye. "My namesake, Michaela, you honored your contract years ago."

What the...? She snapped her gaze to 'Bub.

St. Michael's brow furrowed at his enemy. "How dare you keep her prisoner, asking her to kill for you." He turned back to her. A slight smile eased the tension from his face. "You knew, Michaela. Deep down, you knew. He could never own your soul."

She shook her head. "I signed the contract."

"You're not like other humans, Michaela. You're special. Lucifer hoped he could own you, but he can only manipulate you." The angel looked her up and down. "You are a Nephilim."

"What's that?" She didn't recall hearing that term before, let alone been able to spell it.

"Part angel. Part human." He lowered his voice. "Since making a deal with Satan, part demon as well."

Is that why she struggled with making decisions? Could she be both good and evil? Could she kill and save humanity at the same time? If so, where did that leave her? If she wasn't destined for hell, and she couldn't get to heaven, was she forced to dwell only on Earth?

"Your human side has free will. Your angel side is the one that avenges the victims of your world. The demon side kills those you deem unworthy of life." He ran a finger down the side of her face. "The choice is always yours. A treacherous pinnacle you stand on every moment of every day." He nodded toward Satan. "He knew that. That's why he can't kill you." His gaze drifted to her wrist. "It's why you can't kill yourself."

She pulled her coat's cuffs over her scars.

"Only God can end your life. All creatures exist at God's will."

Creature? "Then why do I exist?"

"You're definitely not what we want roaming the Earth." He paused and poised the scroll over the candle she'd lit earlier, singeing the edge. "Not since the Great Flood." He tilted the scroll as flames licked along the edge. "Sometimes angels fall in love with those they guard."

Satan thrashed against the wrought iron gate. He roared so loud that she covered her ears. Fire ate the dried parchment like wildfire consuming dry grass, leaving smoldering ash in its wake.

"However, God finds your heart to be an advocate for His best interests. Not Lucifer's. Even under his direction, you defied him. This encourages the heavens to believe there is hope for mankind." He bit his lips together. "Hope for your kind."

"There are others like me?"

St. Michael wouldn't look at her but concentrated on the burning parchment. The scroll's last bit of red-tinged ashes floated to the white marble floor.

He smiled as he put the scroll's metal endcaps on the marble pedestal. "I'm afraid I'm not at liberty to say if there are more like you. What I can tell you is that you are free, Michaela. Free of his antics. Free of his lies."

"You are *not* free of me. You will *never* be free of me." Satan rattled the iron bars. "There is no place you can hide that I cannot find you. You are mine. *Mine!*" He thrust his fist inside the alcove. An invisible force seared his flesh. He yanked it back, covering his wounded hand with the other. "I may not be able to kill you, but I can make you suffer. You will complete your mission, or I will kill every child you've ever met."

She looked at St. Michael. "Would God allow him to do that?"

Sorrow tilted his sad eyes. "I cannot say, but it won't stop him from trying."

As the putrid stench of hell faded, she stared at her defender. "Thank you." She stood dumbstruck and lost. What would she do now? Where would she go? She'd spent the last seven years doing what Satan wanted, before that whatever the military wanted, and before that whatever the nuns wanted. She'd never imagined she'd have another chance to have goals of her own. Decide her own fate. Create her own future.

Her knees gave out, and she fell to the marble floor. She clutched her chest, wanting to rewind her life and pull the Deceiver's lies from her tired aching muscles. Her account had been reconciled. She owned Satan nothing. This moment would impact all her tomorrows. Tears dripped down her cheeks.

She was free.

When she opened her eyes, she was back at the kneeler, hands poised in prayer. Had she fallen asleep? Was that a dream? Would God be so cruel as to let her have that moment of freedom, only to rip it from her again?

She looked at the statue of St. Michael bowed in front of her, back on his pedestal, holding his sword. Did she want to be free so badly that she dreamed her contract had been disintegrated?

As disillusionment set in, she spied the metal handles that held the scroll at the statue's base—where St. Michael had placed them.

She grabbed them. They were heavier than expected. Could she risk taking them? What if Satan got hold of them again? She could sell them to a pawn shop. She'd make bank if they were made of a rare metal. Could she risk taking them from hallowed ground?

If she hid them, she could always retrieve them later. A cabinet sat behind the statue's base. She made her way over to it and opened the small door. It held extra candles and votive holders. She slipped the metal handles into the back under boxes of candles. No one would notice them for a while, if ever.

As she left, she glanced back at the statue. "Thank you."

She lifted her backpack, pulling her arms through the straps. How could the alcove be hallowed ground, but the church wasn't? There were a lot of things in life she'd never understand.

Apprehension snaked along her spine as she stepped into the sanctuary. She glanced to the right, then left. Was Satan waiting in the shadows?

Where would she go?

A doctor was torturing children in White River. She couldn't ignore that fact. After all, she had nothing else to do with her life other than finding killers and avenging their victims.

God would provide the rest.

www.ingramcontent.com/pod-product-compliance
Lightning Source LLC
Chambersburg PA
CBHW060314260626
47160CB00007B/2602